Happy trails!

Boomtown
A Novel
By Mark Munger

Cloquet River Press
Publishing Stories from the Lake Superior Basin
www.cloquetriverpress.com

First Edition
Copyright 2016, Mark Munger

ISBN 978-0-9792175-9-3
Library of Congress Control Number 2015912973
Published by: Cloquet River Press
                 5353 Knudsen Road
                 Duluth, Minnesota 55803
                 (218) 721-3213
Edited by Scribendi
Cover photo by Shutterstock. Author photo by Dave Michelson
Visit the Publisher at: www.cloquetriverpress.com
Email the Author at: cloquetriverpress@yahoo.com

ACKNOWLEDGMENTS

I would like to acknowledge the following individuals who served as readers for this project:

The Honorable Dale Harris, The Honorable Theresa Neo, Richard Pemberton, Esq., St. Louis County Attorney Mark Rubin, Jan Larson, *New World Finn* Editor Gerry Henkel, and Ronald McVean.

Without these dedicated folks devoting their time and effort to reading an earlier draft of this work, the content and flow of this finished novel might be vastly different, and—more than likely—vastly inferior.

A bit about the genesis of *Boomtown*. This book is my way of expressing appreciation for the folks who've purchased my work since I began writing for publication. Twenty-five years is a long time to keep at something as daunting as writing, publishing, and marketing fiction. I've never "made it big" or "been discovered" but through countless readings, signings, workshops, and festivals over the intervening years, I've met with and talked to many of you about my stories. Folks who've read a Munger novel (or my short fiction) will recognize some of the characters in this book. That's wholly intentional and my way of thanking you for being interested in what I have to say.

Lastly, a big "thumbs up" to my wife René and my son Jack. Many days and nights have been lost to family while I type away at the keyboard, struggle with revisions, or sleep in my chair because I've been up at five in the morning working on this project. Their patience through the duration of this process is much appreciated.

Mark Munger
2016
Duluth, Minnesota

For the Lord God is bringing you into a good land, a land filled with flowing streams, with springs and underground waters welling up in valleys and hills, a land of wheat and barley, of figs and pomegranates, a land of olive trees and honey, a land whose stones are iron and from whose hills you may mine copper.
Deuteronomy 8:7–10.

In memory of Mike Tierney and Mark Ginder: gifted trial lawyers, good friends, devoted fathers, and loving husbands.

Boomtown

A Novel
By Mark Munger

CHAPTER ONE

Madeline Skurbic sat ten feet above the frozen ground of northeastern Minnesota. Her eyes were closed. Her face was snuggled into the fleece lining of a blaze orange hunting jacket. Her adolescent body was tucked against the cold bark of a yellow birch, and her rump was firmly planted on frosted plywood that served as the seat in her deer stand. Though she was napping, Maddie wasn't in danger of falling out of her perch: descent was thwarted by an aspen railing spiked to three birch trees defining the limits of the crude platform Maddie and her father, Herman "Budd" Skurbic, had built. Crisp November air stirred leafless branches, but the forest's subtle whispers did not wake the girl. Madeline cradled an ancient Winchester 30-30, a rifle that once belonged to her maternal grandfather, Joseph Saari, in her arms. The girl's hands were covered in the same vibrant orange as the rest of her, the synthetic fabric of her hunting gloves buttressed against penetrating chill by Thinsulate inserts. Maddie's feet, warm and toasty in a pair of SmartWool socks inside her fleece-lined Sorels, the brown leather uppers sprayed with silicon to resist water, rested on stout aspen logs forming the platform's floor. Despite the swaying of the trees supporting her deer stand, the girl did not wake. Fragile snowflakes sashayed from an overcast sky and imperceptibly covered the snoring girl in a thin mantle of white.

Before that day, the fifteen-year-old had never carried a rifle in the field. But she was persistent in her pleas to her parents. Maddie had accompanied her dad's only brother, Oscar Skurbic, a wiry wisp of a man who'd worked the Merritt Pit Mine—an open pit taconite mine located across Birch Lake from Maddie's deer stand—as an unarmed apprentice on previous hunts. In her fourteenth year, Maddie completed the state-mandated firearms education course, and under the weight of her petitions, Alice (Maddie's mother) and Budd had given in and

9

allowed their only child to hunt the quarter section of land that defined the Skurbic Farm.

The Farm is a tangle of black alder, overgrown hayfields, second-growth forest, occasional white pines, and modest marshland laced together by Kangas Creek: a trickle of water flowing through the property from Little Lake toward Kangas Lake. Kangas Creek exits its namesake, a eutrophic bowl of black water populated by perch and hammer-handle northern pike, before flowing south into Birch Lake. There is nothing notable about Kangas Creek—no babbling discourse, no falls or rapids, no magnificent drops—just the slow meander of tannin-stained swampy discharge oozing its way through tired land. In reality, the property—known as "The Skurbic Farm" to locals—is actually the ancestral home of Maddie's mother, Alice Saari Skurbic. The old Finnish farmstead had been cleared and built with sweat and blood by Alice's grandfather and Maddie's great grandfather, Juha Saari, during the labor unrest of the early 20th century when many Finns were blacklisted from the iron ore mines and took to subsistence farming to survive.

Throughout the intervening decades defining Ely as a boomtown, Maddie's maternal grandfather, Joe Saari, maintained both the farm and a three-bedroom bungalow in town on East Camp Street, displaying the chest-puffing self-satisfaction of knowing he'd worked the earth as a miner just as his immigrant father had. When he died, Joe's Ely home and the ancestral farm were passed down to Alice, his only child.

This was the personal history that surrounded Madeline Skurbic as she dozed in her deer stand, the hood of her jacket pulled tight against November cold, her inky black hair tied in a ponytail and tucked inside an orange watch cap drawn tight against her scalp, her eyes closed, her breathing soft and measured. As Maddie napped, she dreamed not of family history or the immigrant saga of ancestors, but of Calvin Johnson, a shy seventeen-year-old geek who'd asked her to the hunter's ball. She'd said "yes" despite her girlfriends' decrying Calvin's attributes, his lack of athleticism, his quiet, reserved demeanor. An image of Calvin's gangly arms around her waist, her head resting on his shoulder as they slow danced in the Ely High School gymnasium, their eyes closed, their hearts beating a nervous cadence, occupied Maddie's mind as she dozed.

Boom!

An explosion startled the girl. The ground shuddered. The forest shivered. Madeline's eyes opened. The girl dropped her rifle onto the floor of the deer stand and hugged the trunk of the nearest birch in appreciation that something horrific had occurred.

CHAPTER TWO

The Merritt Pit Deposit runs parallel to the south shore of Birch Lake in the extreme northeast corner of St. Louis County, Minnesota. Birch Lake is over 7,000 acres in size, fed by the Kawishiwi River, a river that flows into the Boundary Waters Canoe Area Wilderness (BWCA) before joining the Rainy River. The Rainy continues north into Canada before merging with other rivers and emptying into Hudson Bay. Of the known copper/nickel ore beds located on Minnesota's Mesabi and Vermillion Iron Ranges, pockets of minerals stretching from the Water-Hen Deposit south of Aurora to the Spruce Lake Deposit on the cusp of the BWCA, the Merritt Pit Deposit is one of the more modest concentrations of copper-bearing ore in the region.

Named the "Merritt Pit Deposit" because the ore body's location was once home to an open pit taconite mine of the same name operated by Denison Mining, the former low-grade iron ore mine was first sold by Denison to Calumet Iron and Copper, and, when Calumet decided to concentrate on richer veins of copper/nickel ore found in the Maturi, Spruce Road, Nokomis, and South Filson Creek deposits, the Merritt Pit site was sold by Calumet to Continental Mining. Prior to acquiring the Merritt Pit property, Continental had never been involved in copper/nickel mining, having been incorporated in Quebec, Canada as the developer and owner of iron ore mines in Canada, Minnesota, Brazil, and Australia. But with copper prices rising, and with the price tag for the Merritt Pit site being reasonable, the powers that be in Quebec City leapt at the chance to become a player in the burgeoning dispute of whether environmentally safe and economically productive copper/nickel mining could be accomplished in northeastern Minnesota: a landscape dotted with swamps, marshes, ponds, and lakes, and crisscrossed by creeks, streams, and rivers.

When Continental Mining of Minnesota, Inc., the American offspring of Continental Mining, International, purchased the Merritt Pit site from Calumet, the property consisted of an abandoned open pit taconite mine, an electrical powerhouse and distribution system, a rail spur, a water treatment plant, several dilapidated buildings, underground fuel oil tanks, and a rusting steel silo once designated for the storage of ANFO, a blasting agent used by the mining industry in lieu of dynamite. Some mixtures of the explosive (which has as its primary component ammonium nitrate prills similar to those used by farmers to fertilize their fields) contain flakes of aluminum to increase brisance: the shattering power of the explosive. ANFO is relatively stable, easy to transport, and inexpensive while packing one-half the explosive punch of military grade C4. The Merritt Pit silo, a cylindrical steel tower standing on four spindly steel legs forty feet above the ground, hadn't been used in years when Continental Mining acquired the Merritt Pit property. There was minimal documentation of the silo's history provided by Denison or Calumet to Continental, though a Phase I environmental assessment had disclosed the silo's prior use. The assessment also noted that underground tanks, vessels used to supply fuel oil to mix with the ammonium nitrate prills to create ANFO, were leaking and that the soil around the tanks, the silo, and adjacent truck scale was contaminated with residual oil and ammonium nitrate. The Phase I report outlined the parameters for safe removal of the underground tanks. Phase II, it was anticipated by the higher ups at Calumet, would detail how to safely remove the silo and the contaminated soil. But Continental bought the Merritt Pit property "as is," before the Phase II study was completed and without regard to environmental issues or safety concerns. It was a gamble for the Canadian company to waive waiting on the final report, one that would detail the extent of the ammonium nitrate and fuel oil contamination of the property, but a gamble the acquisitions and property division of Continental was willing to take given the accelerating demand for copper on the world market.

A year before Madeline Skurbic's first deer hunt, Continental Mining, International organized its Minnesota corporation and lured Ted Huberty—the operations manager at a nearby taconite mine—from a lifelong career with Denison Mining to head up Continental's new Merritt Pit operation. Huberty was provided a generous salary and benefits package as well as great latitude in selecting staff. Huberty's first hire was Neil Yost, a fifty-five year old high school dropout who'd worked for Carson Mines— a copper mining concern headquartered in Butte, Montana—for over thirty years. Yost had climbed the corporate ladder at Carson, advancing from laborer to safety director over the course of his career. Yost's wife, Alana—Ted Huberty's only sibling— longed to return to Minnesota. Alana and Ted had been born and raised in Ely. When Neil Yost got the call from his brother-in-law offering him a job in Minnesota, Yost accepted the position without hesitation. Within three months of Ted Huberty's telephone call, Neil and Alana Yost were settled into a new home on the east shore of Bear Island Lake just off Highway 21 between the Merritt Pit site and Ely.

One of Neil Yost's first tasks as safety director for Continental's Minnesota operation was to inventory the physical assets of the abandoned taconite mine and determine a course of remediation for any environmental or safety concerns he noted. While conducting inspections of the Merritt Pit site, Yost's eyes were consistently drawn to the rusty, precariously perched silo that loomed as a decadent shadow over the property.

"That," Neil Yost said, on more than one occasion, pointing to the ANFO storage tower as he inspected the mine's dilapidated facilities with other employees of Continental's Safety and Compliance Department, "will be the first thing to go."

CHAPTER THREE

Crisp, early morning air stung Diane "Dee Dee" Hernesman's lungs as she skied. There was just enough snow on the ground to glide—in classic style—over the Trezona Trail located a short walk from downtown Ely. Hernesman, a trial lawyer officing in a rickety frame building on East Chapman Street that once housed a pharmacy, skied away from a northwest zephyr. The wind propelled snowflakes into Dee Dee's backside as she moved along the south shore of Miner's Lake. The lawyer knew that once she reached the eastern-most point of the trail she'd be forced to turn into the squall. Her face would then feel the brunt of the weather, but there was nothing to be done about her impending discomfort.

Dee Dee Hernesman was forty-three years old and an avid fitness enthusiast. In the summer, the lawyer ran from her home located on the outskirts of Ely to her law office where, along with her partners Elliot "Skip" Mattila and Julie Somerfeldt, she shared a remodeled storefront that included offices, a sauna, individual lockers for the attorneys and their staff, and bathrooms complete with showers. On summer days when Dee Dee didn't run, she biked to work. Rain or shine, she put in her miles. Hernesman's dogged determination to stay in shape was two-fold.

First, she was between relationships. Dee Dee's long-time companion, Carol Evans, a woman who'd been born and raised in Bismarck, North Dakota, had, after over a decade of living with Dee Dee in Ely, said "enough is enough." Carol left Dee Dee and the below-zero winters and bug-infested summers that define the little town on the threshold of the BWCA. Hernesman was devastated by her partner's desertion. With the arrival of same-sex marriage in Minnesota, there had been serious discussions between the women about making their commitment legal. But despite such dialogue, and despite the fact that Carol and Dee Dee had been together for over twenty years, one day, out of the blue, Carol Evans announced very simply that she was moving to Omaha where a new job, and presumably, a new life, awaited her. There was no invitation extended by Carol to Dee Dee asking Dee Dee to relocate to Nebraska, an act of betrayal that left Hernesman feeling empty and hollow. But the distance of a year, a year during which Dee Dee Hernesman undertook an emotional, spiritual, and physical inventory of herself, provided optimism.

The second facet of Dee Dee's compulsion for fitness was based on Hernesman family history. Both of Dee Dee's parents had died young. Alice Hernesman, Dee Dee's mother, passed away at forty-seven while Dee Dee was attending Tower Soudan High School on Minnesota's Vermillion Iron Range. Alice succumbed to a silent defect in her middle-aged heart just a few years before Dee Dee's father, Henry, passed away in the slowest and most agonizing of ways. Henry died, a victim of Lou Gehrig's disease, while his daughter was attending Concordia College in Moorhead.

Simply put, the early deaths of Dee Dee's parents, coupled with the inexplicable flight of Carol Evans to Nebraska, compelled Hernesman to exercise. She ran and biked during the summer, spring, and fall, and, during the winter, she skied as often as her hectic courtroom schedule allowed.

The lawyer fixed subtle gray eyes on the thin woods surrounding the shallow lake, occasionally diverting her gaze to take in Shagawa's frozen surface in the background. She knew, from her childhood in nearby Tower—and her years as a partner in the law firm of Mattila, Somerfeldt, and Hernesman—Shagawa's history: the near century-long abuse of its waters by the residents of Ely and the surrounding iron mines and commercial concerns. Residents had shown a similar disdain toward the river flowing out of Shagawa. Locals had used the lake and river as an open sewer for more than a century. While attempts had been made to

correct the destruction of Shagawa such that the municipal beach
was now useable and walleye caught in the lake were now
edible, much remained to be done to right humanity's wrongs
against Shagawa. As a conservationist, Hernesman applauded
recent efforts to reclaim the lake but understood that Shagawa
had a long way to go before it could be considered "healthy."
She'd yet to catch and eat a fish from Shagawa while open water
fishing. Despite being an Iron Ranger, Hernesman knew from an
early age that ice fishing wasn't for her. Standing around, arms
wrapped against the cold, warmed by blackberry brandy or
peppermint schnapps, waiting for something to swim by and
snatch a baited hook beneath the ice wasn't her idea of a good
time. But Dee Dee loved casting plugs against the departing dusk
of a warm summer's eve, jigging for walleye and perch over
rock piles, or trolling for lake trout along submerged reefs on
Burntside Lake, a local treasure memorialized by Ely author Sig
Olson in his books.

      As Dee Dee Hernesman turned into the wind, the snow
abated. She moved easily along the north shore of Miner's Lake,
early morning light dawning over the town of Winton to the east.
Wisps of warm breath curled in cold air. It was almost eight
o'clock when Hernesman arrived at the paved lot where she'd
parked her red Ford Escape. An orange sun crested the birch and
aspen and pine trees defining the eastern horizon. Dee Dee
leaned her ski poles against the Escape, pulled off her mittens,
shoved the mittens into the pouch of her pullover, and released
her boots from their bindings. The lawyer was stretching her
calves when distant, artificial thunder interrupted the melancholy
of the morning.

      Boom!

      That's too loud to be blasting, Dee Dee thought as she
looked south, toward the noise.

CHAPTER FOUR

Cook County Sheriff Debra Slater drove her Yukon past city hall. The sun had cleared the tree line east of Ely and was edging toward its winter apex. As Slater's showroom-new porcelain white SUV, "Cook County Sheriff" stenciled in black across its front doors, crested a hill, she saw the reason she was outside her home county assisting St. Louis County Sheriff Brian Nace as a member of the Copper/Nickel Task Force. Two clusters of citizens, one group carrying signs proclaiming their loyalty to the Sierra Club, Friends of the Boundary Waters, and other environmental organizations, and a second group of citizens holding placards boasting slogans such as "We Can Have Clean Water and Mining!" and "Minnesotans for Copper/Nickel" and "Tree Huggers Go Back to St. Paul" stood on opposite sides of Chapman Street, the din of confrontation audible inside Slater's squad.

Every other week, Deb Slater made the long drive down US Highway 61 from Grand Marais—the county seat of Cook County where she was the sheriff—turned right on Minnesota Highway 1 at Ilgen City, and followed the two-lane asphalt highway through the desolation of Lake County until she arrived in Ely, where as the Director of the Copper/Nickel Task Force— a group of local law enforcement officers from Cook, Lake, and St. Louis Counties assembled by Sheriff Nace—Slater spent two days holding briefings, collecting intelligence, and leading investigations into incidents between opposing factions in the debate over non-ferrous mining in northeastern Minnesota. With the opening of the Roosevelt-Taft open-pit copper/nickel mine in nearby Hoyt Lakes and the looming approval of underground mining near Birch Lake, the number of protestors on both sides of the issue was increasing, and the collective rancor of the participants was escalating. Incidents of verbal conflict between opposing ideologues and reports of sit-ins, hints of environmental sabotage, and threats of violence were on the rise.

Deb Slater was on the cusp of fifty and nearing retirement when Sheriff Nace approached her to head up the task force. Brian Nace, the short, burly, thick-chested sheriff of the largest county east of the Mississippi, who, at thirty-seven, was too young to have served with Slater when she was a patrol deputy in the St. Louis County Sheriff's Office, sought out Slater's experience and expertise. Sheriff Nace had cajoled Sheriff Slater into accepting a two-year stint as the director of the task force. Slater would see her commitment through to its culmination and planned to retire at the end of the following year from both her position as Cook County Sheriff and director of the task force.

It's been a good run, Slater mused as she pulled the big rig into her designated parking space next to Ely City Hall. *A shitty two years in terms of my personal life and all, but a solid, well-played career.*

The unspoken reference to Deb Slater's family situation was a not-so-veiled allusion to her husband Rick having recently entered hospice in Duluth in the last stages of mitochondrial disease. It was also an acknowledgement that the couple's only child, Margaret Ann, was a half a continent away—in upstate New York at Cornell—where she was attending college and playing volleyball. It had been difficult on Slater's motherly instincts to insist that Annie accept a full ride at an Ivy League school in the face of Rick's decline, but Deb knew what such a privileged education would mean over the course of her daughter's lifetime. And Slater knew, as a former athlete herself, what playing an NCAA Division I sport would mean for her child's self-esteem.

"But Mom, I can play for UMD *and* be close to Dad," had been Annie's refrain during her senior year at Cook County High School where she not only lettered in four sports but managed to graduate number one in her class, a perfect four-point-oh.

While Deb accepted Annie's loyalty to her father as a given, the sheriff also knew that there was little Annie's physical presence would mean to the unconscious body lying in the hospice bed at Solvay House in Duluth. There was nothing such sacrifice would change. In the end, Deb prevailed, and the only child of the Slater marriage left home with her mother driving the family Suburban—the SUV's cargo hold stacked to the ceiling with Annie's belongings. Mother and daughter drove from Minnesota to New York and, on freshman orientation day, Deb Slater eased the Suburban onto the stately Cornell campus, disgorged Annie and her belongings, helped the girl locate her dormitory and move in, and engaged in an emotional embrace before heading for home.

Sheriff Slater's personal history occupied her thoughts as she sat in the Yukon, the ignition key off, the engine cooling, the tempers of the opposing clusters of protestors rising. Ely police and St. Louis County deputies were stationed near each group, the officers' winter coats buttoned up against the chill, their eyes fixed on the milling citizenry. Apprehension of more violent protest was in the air. An announcement was expected from the Minnesota Pollution Control Agency, the Minnesota DNR, and the United States Army Corps of Engineers approving the necessary permits for the Merritt Pit underground copper/nickel project. It was expected the governor, a conservative Republican, would sign off on the project once the agencies had given the Merritt Pit Mine their collective blessing. Lawsuits brought by conservation groups to stop the mine had been dismissed. Subsequent appeals had failed. Lobbying by environmentalists before the staunchly conservative Minnesota Legislature, the Democrats having been trounced in the last election, fell on deaf ears. Governor Wesley Whitcomb, the state's most conservative leader since Tim Pawlenty, had made reinvigoration of the mining industry in northeastern Minnesota a priority. Whitcomb's campaign promises had helped him wrest control of the state from the liberals. It had been decades since a Republican gubernatorial candidate won the votes of Iron Rangers. Wesley Whitcomb had accomplished that Herculean task and was about to repay that loyalty with well-paying mining jobs.

Winter seeped into the Yukon. Slater remained as still as a statue, her gloved hands grasping the steering wheel, her eyes closed in contemplation of what she had lost and was about to lose. She was deep in self-assessment when the wail of sirens and the crackle of a police band radio disrupted her meditative state.

"Calling all units. There's been an explosion at Continental Mining off the New Tomahawk Road near Birch Lake. Multiple casualties reported. Respond with lights and sirens. Advise when you're en route."

To the untrained ear, the dispatcher's voice seemed calm and collected. But Sheriff Debra Slater noted a catch, a pause, an inflection in the woman's voice that revealed something unexpected and deadly had happened.

I hope to Christ it's not another environmental group trying to send a message, Slater thought as she turned the ignition key, slipped the Yukon into reverse, and backed onto Chapman Street.

CHAPTER FIVE: A MONTH EARLIER

Steven Gruber walked alongside Neil Yost. The men were assessing the work that Hibbing Salvage and Remediation was expected to complete at the Merritt Pit site. The inspection had taken place on a blazing, beautiful autumn afternoon in October. The auriferous leaves of the forest surrounding the old mine fluttered. Sunlight exposed a pockmarked landscape. The day was unseasonably warm. Gruber towered over Yost, Gruber's Germanic face closed to expression, his blond hair disrupted by wind, his bright blue eyes scrutinizing the scene as Yost, the safety director of Continental Mining, described his expectations.

"You'll need to dig up the fuel oil tanks, cut them apart, haul them away, and have the contaminated soil either trucked off site to an earth burner or burn it yourself on-site," Yost had explained as the men stopped next to a fueling station. "That's priority number one. Needs to happen sooner than later. We're about to receive Army Corps, DNR, and MPCA approval for the mine, and we need to be able to show those agencies we're responsible stewards of the land," Yost added.

Gruber pondered the task. "Won't be a problem. I've got two welders who can handle it," he said, thinking aloud. "Feggetti here is as good as they come," Gruber advised, gesturing to a short, black-haired, brown-eyed young man standing behind Gruber and Yost. "Feggetti and Susie Lindahl. Susie's not only great with a torch; she's the best operator around. She can spin a backhoe on a dime with one hand on the controls while drinking coffee and not spill a drop," Gruber added with a grin. "We'll dig around the tanks, loop chains around 'em, and use a rubber-tired crane to lift 'em out of the ground. Once the tanks are removed, we'll wash 'em out, catch the flush in a basin, separate the water and the oil, recycle the oil and treat the water, before cutting the tanks apart with water-cooled saws. That way, we eliminate any chance of fire or explosion. Fuel oil can be nasty stuff if you're not careful, right Feggetti?"

Antonio Feggetti had looked at his boss with cloudy eyes, his twenty-something face unremarkable and expressionless. Feggetti nodded but maintained silence. The young welder stood a foot shorter than his boss but was appreciably thicker, built like a stump, his thighs and biceps hardened by days of wrestling salvaged iron.

"Doesn't say much," Yost observed as the trio began moving away from the fueling station.

"Doesn't have to," Gruber explained. "He says all he needs to say with his torch."

"You're gonna put a girl to work with Mr. No-Talkie here?" Neil Yost continued speaking as the group moved toward an abandoned cement block building and rusty steel silo located at the end of a rail spur. "Don't know that I much like the idea of a girl working salvage, getting her pretty hands dirty."

Gruber frowned. Susie Lindahl was his niece, his sister Judy's only child. When Susie straightened up after repeated bouts of heroin use, coming back to the family with two young daughters conceived from engaging in bad behavior with two different men—men who were nowhere to be found in terms of parental responsibility—Steve had paid Susie's way through the welding program at Mesabi Community College in Virginia, seen to it that the girl had an apprenticeship through the union, and taken her on as his number two burner. Steve Gruber also taught his niece to operate heavy equipment, an aspect of the job Susie took to like a Labrador to cold water. She was only twenty-five, but the girl had lived a hard life and survived the worst of what the world could throw at her. Despite a recent relapse, when she smoked some weed (but declined the heroin a local dirt bag offered her as a pretext to bedding her on a sofa in a room full of people), and lost temporary custody of her girls, Susie was on the right track. She'd get Angel, her youngest, back from Judy and Mark—her parents—and three-year-old Brenda Lee back from Nancy and Tom Devich—Brenda Lee's paternal grandparents—at the end of the child protection case filed by St. Louis County social services and monitored by Judge Aronson in Virginia, Minnesota. Steve Gruber ruminated over his niece's history as he considered how to respond to Yost. But rather than correct the man, Gruber had simply changed the subject.

They were standing next to the block building, a thirty-foot by sixteen-foot structure with a faded green metal roof, broken windows, and a trashed interior. The building was missing its doors. "What was this used for?" Gruber had asked as the men stepped over the building's threshold into shadow.

"That there was the dispatcher's office," Yost said, pointing to one of the three spaces within the structure, each room separated by a block wall, all the trim and flooring and furniture, including the plumbing and fixtures of the solitary restroom, either removed or destroyed or tossed outside. "That was the privy. And this," Yost said, moving through an open doorway into a space warmed by sunlight filtering through a bank of glassless windows, "was the blasting foreman's office."

"Blasting foreman?"

Feggetti's question caught Steve Gruber by surprise. It wasn't often that Feggetti spoke up in the company of strangers. Whatever caused the man to open his mouth was likely significant.

But Neil Yost ignored Feggetti's question as the men exited the building. "What are your plans for the building?" Yost asked. "How will you take 'er down?"

Gruber studied the structure. "Backhoe will make short work of it. There's no value here. You'll pay straight time for demolition and disposal. Doesn't appear to be anything we can salvage so we'll simply tear it down, load the debris in a truck, and place it in the landfill."

Yost nodded and smiled. "Nothin' is free, is it?"

"You never answered Feggetti's question," Gruber noted.

Yost grunted and pointed at the silo.

"Before we bought the place, the prior owners used that to store nitrate: fertilizer. Pulled raw product in here by train, full cars of it, and used that," Yost said, pointing to a screw-type conveyor lying on the ground next to the building, "to fill the silo with prills. Hoses transferred oil from the underground fuel oil tanks into the tower. Sometimes Denison added aluminum flakes as well. Had to do that by hand. Whenever they were getting ready to blast, they'd pull a truck under the silo, open the spout, and load the truck with fertilizer." The safety manager took a deep breath. "Once the truck was full, they'd cover the load with a tarp and use it as needed. When it came time to blast, they'd hand pack the nitrate into plastic sleeves, set the sleeves in blast holes, add detonators, and let 'er rip. Hell of a tidy way to free up taconite!"

Gruber had stared hard at the silo. "We're planning on using acetylene and oxygen torches to cut the legs off the silo, lower it to the ground, and slice it into pieces. We're gonna start at the top and end at that cone on the bottom. Might have to re-think using torches if explosives were stored in that thing."

Yost shook his head. "No need to worry. It's been at least two years since product was run through 'er. What's left behind is inert. Besides, there are open hatches at both ends. Rain has washed 'er clean. She's as empty," the safety manager had said, picking up a piece of rusted re-bar, walking to the silver tower, climbing a steel ladder affixed to the tower's side, and banging silo with the re-bar, "as my billfold before payday."

Bong. Bong. Bong.

The tower had sounded empty.

"You sure torches are okay around this stuff?" Steve Gruber asked dubiously. "You sure whatever's left inside is safe around a flame?"

"Look," Yost explained as he climbed down the ladder, "you encounter anything inside the tower while you're cutting, just scoop it out and put it in that old drum." As he reclaimed the ground, Yost tossed the re-bar aside, and pointed to a rusting oil barrel, the lid of the container askew. "Dispose of any product you find later. Same for the water in the pit below the scale. Just pump it out and haul it away. Ditto for anything you find in that auger," Yost concluded, pointing to a fifty-foot section of rusted steel barely visible in a cluster of dried goldenrod.

"It won't blow? I mean: If it's used to make blasting agent, you'd expect it to react to a flame," Antonio Feggetti had observed.

Yost glowered. "I said it's benign. When it's off spec, when it's been exposed to weather, we burn it in piles to get rid of it. Relax, would you?"

Gruber stared at the safety director. "What about the fumes? Do we need to use respirators?"

Yost shook his head. "You guys worry too much. It's as safe as baking powder. No need to mask up. I told you, it's common nitrogen, fertilizer, like the stuff you put on your tomatoes."

The group had moved out from the shadow of the silo and stood at the edge of the scale pit. An oily sheen floating on top of the water in the pit glimmered under the morning sun.

"How do you suggest I get rid of the contaminated water?"

Neil Yost stared at the greasy slick floating in the pit.

"It's just fertilizer, Steve. Know anyone with a hayfield?"

The inference had been clear to Steve Gruber and Antonio Feggetti. *The contaminated water is also harmless.*

The men moved away from the silo and pit.

"I'll send you a bid," Steve Gruber had said as the men stood around Gruber's fatigued Ford F-250 pickup, the bed of the truck crowded with acetylene and oxygen tanks, cutting tools, hoses, and toolboxes. The rear quarter panels of the truck were rusted through and secured to the truck's frame by wire. The cab of the Ford was littered with paperwork, old McDonald's wrappers, plastic Coca-Cola bottles, and loose tools. "I don't expect it'll be cheap. Two pieces of equipment are needed: a backhoe and a rubber-tired crane. And there's a lot of cutting involved, including cutting up the old rails and that silo," Steve Gruber had added before he opened the driver's door to the truck, the decayed sheet metal of the door threatening to separate from its frame as hinges creaked in protest.

Antonio Feggetti scattered paperwork with his hand and slid onto the truck's dusty bench seat before slamming the door behind him. As Steven Gruber put the Ford in reverse, Feggetti's eyes had fixed on sunlight reflecting off the sheet metal skin of the orphaned silo. There had been something about the tower; something mysterious and inexplicable demanded Antonio Feggetti's attention as the pickup kicked up gravel and left the old mine.

CHAPTER SIX: THREE DAYS BEFORE

Cyrus Oliphant had watched environmental protestors gather outside Ely City Hall with disdain. *Mere pikers,* Oliphant thought. *These imported pack-sackers on a break from sucking at the corporate teat haven't got a clue how to get the attention of Continental Mining.*

Oliphant crossed East Chapman with a letter-sized, stamped envelope in hand. The message Oliphant carried bore no return address. The man's path had been carefully plotted. He walked quickly and with purpose around protestors on the south side of Chapman. *Shows the allegiance of the Ely City Council and the cops,* Oliphant thought as he arrived at a big blue mailbox standing next to the town's only hardware store. *Giving supporters of the new mine the sidewalk closest to city hall, closest to the seat of government, and locating the mine's protesters across the street proves that the local politicians are in cahoots with Whitcomb.*

Oliphant, a reedy man in his sixties, his face scruffy from a three-day beard, his clothes nondescript—blue jeans, an insulated khaki Carhartt jacket, a black knitted stocking hat covering graying blond hair, Red Wing steel-toed work boots, the dark brown polish scuffed and in need of attention—his ruddy face redder still from the exertion of his walk, his hands covered in leather choppers against winter, had stopped in front of the mail box, opened the metal flap, and dropped the envelope into the chasm before joining the protesters. *My work here is in its infancy,* Oliphant thought as he studied his companions, a mixture of aging hippies, middle-aged outdoors enthusiasts, and twenty-something trekkers and kayakers from the Twin Cities. *The letter is only the beginning . . .*

Fresh from a battle in the Chippewa National Forest near Bemidji, where Governor Whitcomb had promoted the exchange of state-owned land dominated by aspen saplings outside the National Forest's northern boundary for a legacy plantation of red pine located inside the Forest, Cyrus Oliphant was an old hand at civil disobedience. The pines he'd spiked, driving foot long nails into the hardscrabble bark of the giant Norways, had been saved from the governor's logging buddies when the Forest Service backed out of the proposed transfer. And the Chippewa Forest protest had not been Oliphant's first exercise in environmental action.

The old man had led a cadre of true believers onto the grounds of an ELF (extremely low frequency) facility in northwestern Wisconsin on more than one occasion in hopes of silencing radio waves emitted by the facility that are relied upon by United States Navy submarines. Oliphant, the son of university professors who'd participated in the battle over civil rights in the 1950s at the University of Florida, was arrested for cutting guide wires to an ELF tower and toppling the structure onto sandy soil, thereby disrupting a naval exercise along Finland's Baltic coast involving British, U.S., and Swedish submarines. The point of the protest was that the British and American boats were loaded to the hilt with atomic missiles aimed at Russia. Cyrus Oliphant had served four years in the federal minimum-security prison in Duluth for the ELF protest but his time at "Camp Walk Away"—as its inmates affectionately dubbed the unfenced facility—had not lessened his desire to right perceived wrongs. He'd used his time in custody to educate himself on environmental and peace issues being debated in Minnesota, the place he chose to call home after his release from prison. One of the issues that resonated with the aging protestor was the copper/nickel debate.

Cyrus Oliphant's interest in the mining controversy compelled the old man to head to Ely where he found work as a handyman at the Burntside Lake Lodge. His job as a "jack of all trades" at the resort was the perfect cover for Oliphant's interest in political action.

29

"Wait until Continental Mining sees what I have in store for them if the governor announces that the mine has been approved," Cyrus had mumbled under his breath as he started to walk away from the babble of the crowd. "Those Canadian assholes are in for one hell of a surprise."

CHAPTER SEVEN: THE DAY BEFORE

Susie Lindahl had pulled the welding shield over her face and ignited her torch. Her partner, Antonio Feggetti, was working on the opposite side of the steel tower cutting a slit from the top of the structure to the welded seam that joined the delivery cone to the silo. Susie was cutting an identical slit on her side of the silo as it rested on snowy ground. Sparks flew as flames cut through 3/8" steel plate. It had been a sunny, warm, November day and Susie had been in a good mood.

Two days from now, Susie thought as she moved flame across steel, *I get the girls back for a trial home visit.* Perspiring under her insulated bib overalls and jacket, sweat forming under her welding shield, Susie stopped, raised the protective glass, and drew a deep breath of clean, brisk, northeastern Minnesota air. She kept the torch burning as she wiped sweat from her eyebrows and youthful cheeks with a red kerchief she kept handy for such duty. *My lawyer says if things go well, I'll get custody of the girls in ninety days. Ninety days. I can do that; keep myself straight, out of the bars, away from drugs, for three months. Hell,* Susie thought, lowering the shield and returning to cutting steel, *I've been clean for over a year. Ninety days more won't be a problem.*

The day before, after the ladder and observation platform had been cut away from the silo, Susie Lindahl, Antonio Feggetti, and Susie's uncle and boss, Steve Gruber, had strung a steel cable from the arm of a rubber-tired crane to the nitrate silo. The cable secured the silo in place while Susie and Antonio cut the tower's legs. Susie began the process by slicing a three-foot section out of one of the silo's rear supports. She and Feggetti then partially cut through the tower's other three legs. The weight of the tower caused it to lean. As the structure listed, Gruber played out the steel cable connecting the silo to the crane by extending the crane's arm. Freed of its legs, the silo settled to the ground, completing a delicate waltz between cable, weight, and gravity. Once the silo came to rest, Gruber climbed down from the cab of the crane, slapped Susie's narrow back in a gesture of appreciation, and inspected the interior of the cylindrical tower by peering through an opening where the screw auger had once entered the top of the structure. Gruber didn't have a flashlight but with the loading hatch rusted open, he thought he as able to visualize most of the silo's interior.

"Looks empty," Gruber said in a gruff, business-like voice. "Rain must have washed 'er clean just like Yost said."

After Gruber's cursory inspection, Susie and Antonio had fired up their torches and made cuts down opposite sides of the silo. They would cut identical, parallel lines from the top of the silo to the tapered cone at the bottom of the structure. Two four-foot by four-foot windows cut by the workers' torches would allow daylight to illumine the silo's interior. After the larger openings were cut, Feggetti would climb inside the silo and remove the steel baffling that divided the interior space into four equal compartments. Gruber's examination had revealed— and he shared this revelation with his crew—that the baffling was the same 3/8" steel as the tower's exterior. With the baffling removed, the only steel holding the structure together would be the top of the silo, the bottom cone, and the last few feet of steel plate at the end of each exterior cut. Susie and Antonio were to burn around the top of the silo, allowing it to fall away. They were to commence a similar burn at the bottom of the hopper, allowing the cone to separate. The welders' final task would be to extend the identical horizontal slits along each side of the tower until the silo was completely separated, which would allow the tower to split in two. Lindahl and Feggetti would then slice the silo into manageable pieces. Susie would load the steel into Gruber's dump truck with the crane, and Feggetti would drive the truck back to the salvage yard where the dismantled

ANFO tower would be unloaded and added to Gruber's inventory of scrap.

Susie and Antonio had cut the windows into the silo and were starting to remove the top of the structure when Steve Gruber drove up in his Ford pickup with Neil Yost in the passenger seat. After the truck came to rest, the men climbed out of the battered blue F-250 and ambled toward the workers. The late afternoon sun had dipped below the top rail of the chain link fence marking the boundary of the old taconite mine. Twilight was imminent. A full moon was rising, bathing the industrial landscape in an unusual hue of blue.

Susie Lindahl stood up, turned off her torch, opened her face shield, and smiled. "Nearly got 'er done," she had said proudly.

Antonio Feggetti continued slicing through steel with his torch, stopping his cut just short of where Susie had ended her burn to leave a four-inch tab securing the top of the silo in place. Antonio shut off his torch, leaned it against the tower's steel skin, opened his face shield, pulled off his gloves, found a Camel straight in a pocket of his battered jacket, lit the cigarette with a butane lighter, and inhaled new smoke.

The tanks supplying the torches with oxygen and acetylene stood 150 feet away, the connecting rubber hoses snaking across the moon shadowed plain like gigantic black cobras. Susie's maroon Dodge 4×4 was parked just beyond the tanks, the pickup's bed filled with extra oxygen and acetylene cylinders as declining night enveloped the Dakota.

"Found this inside the silo," Antonio had said, removing his other glove, reaching inside an open 55 gallon barrel, and retrieving a flaky white lump the size of a softball.

Feggetti handed the crusty chunk to Gruber. Gruber handed it to Yost. "This the fertilizer you were talking about?"

Yost had nodded. "Yup. That's the stuff."

Antonio Feggetti stared at Yost. "The whole damn auger is packed with this shit," he said sternly. "When Susie put her

33

torch to it, it started to smoke. I had to use a fire extinguisher to put it out."

Gruber took the lump from Yost and examined it like a grocery store customer scrutinizing a cantaloupe. He turned the nitrate over and over in his bare hands, his winter gloves forgotten on the driver's seat of the Ford. "You sure this stuff's just fertilizer, that it's not explosive or dangerous?"

Yost nodded. "You could put flame to it for an hour and, at best, it might smoke a little. But it'll never burn."

Susie joined the conversation. "How about explode? The interior looks empty. As Steve said yesterday, looks to be washed clean by the rain. But if there's product stuck in nooks or crannies, will it blow?"

Susie Lindahl had stood eye to eye with Neil Yost, her face shield up, her delicate cheekbones and deep brown eyes in plain view, tufts of auburn hair framing her youthful face.

She's too smart, too good looking, to be doing this kind of work, Steve Gruber had thought, a lament at his niece's troubles, her self-induced under-achievement, behind the consideration. Visions of Susie standing in her cap and gown on stage, of her giving the commencement speech at Hibbing High School when she graduated with honors, a full ride to St. Catherine's College in St. Paul in hand, a nursing career on the horizon, intervened. Steve Gruber wrestled with memory as he listened to his niece and, with great effort, called his attention back to the conversation. "Susie's got a point," Gruber had interjected, tossing the chunk of nitrate back to Feggetti who dropped it into the barrel. "If this shit is confined and a flame is put to it, will it blow?"

Yost's face reddened. It was clear that he was losing patience with folks second-guessing his expertise. "I've told you, in as many ways as I can, that you're dealing with fuckin' fertilizer, if you'd excuse the adjective, ma'am. There's nothing to worry about. You find more of it, like I said, you just scoop it out and put in that barrel. You can spread it on a garden or a

34

hayfield just like store-bought. Same for the water you pump out of the scale pit. That's as plain as I can make it."

Gruber had grimaced but let the curse slide. "Get the top of the silo off and tomorrow we'll finish it up. I'll be by early in the morning to help. Don't try separating 'er until I get here. I don't want anyone getting hurt when that thing splits in two. Got it?"

Susie had considered the full moon climbing to the east of the old mine. The bright globe caused the silo to shadow an empty land. "Understood," she said as she fired up her torch, "Just a few minutes work before we call 'er a day and we'll be ready for tomorrow, Boss. Be here bright and early, ya hear? No sleepin' in," Susie Lindahl teased as she lowered her welding shield and went back to cutting steel.

CHAPTER EIGHT: THREE DAYS AFTER

Katherine "Kat" Carpenter stood in the well of the courtroom. Kat was languidly tall, blond, well proportioned, and bore a striking resemblance to Lauren Bacall. But it wasn't only Kat's beauty that wowed juries (and, on occasion, male and female judges alike); it was her native intellect, her street smarts, her ability to connect that made her the most successful litigator on the Iron Range. At fifty-seven, she'd been around the block, both in terms of the practice of law and personal relationships, having been married and divorced three times, and was not one to shy away from a courtroom brawl. Despite the patriarchal power structure of the Range—the iron ore region of St. Louis County, Minnesota Kat called home—Kat Carpenter had made her mark by being thick-skinned, pragmatic, smart, and, at times, slightly unethical. She'd never crossed the line with the Board of Professional Responsibility, the body that polices attorneys in Minnesota. But every lawyer who dealt with Kat Carpenter sensed she was walking a fine line when it came to ethics. Though some observers predicted Carpenter would topple off the razor-thin moral edge she negotiated, she never did. Her record with the board of discipline was spotless despite her penchant for ethical roulette.

"Your honor," Kat began, starting her pitch for a new trial, "there's an error of law permeating this case. No disrespect, Judge, but allowing the defense to introduce evidence of Ms. Smith's prior DUIs, when there was no evidence that alcohol contributed to *this* accident, was error. Plaintiff objected to that evidence and continues to call the court's attention to Your Honor's mistake as to the law applicable to this case," Kat said, standing as she addressed the court, her client, Jean Smith, a frumpily dressed, pinched-faced, stoop-shouldered woman of advanced middle age seated to Kat's right at counsel table. "This matter was, at its heart, a case of negligence: a rear-end collision where my client was completely stopped at a red light and Mr. Burgess's client, Mr. Cinavich, plowed into the back of Ms. Smith's car. The jury should have heard the facts of this case and the injuries sustained by my client, not some ancient history that poisoned the jurors' judgment and resulted in a finding of no negligence on the part of the defendant."

Judge Delores Peck, who'd once practiced with Kat Carpenter in the largest law firm on the Range—McGovern and Quinn—before assuming the black robe fifteen years before the trial at issue, having been appointed to the position by Republican Governor Tim Pawlenty despite her strong liberal political heritage, scratched her nose as her intellect and decision making were not-so-lightly chastised by her former partner.

"But wasn't your client given a ticket for an open container of alcohol by the officer investigating *this* collision? Wasn't that a sufficient basis under *Spriegl* to allow evidence of her prior conduct involving alcohol before the jury?"

Kat Carpenter shook her head. Her blond hair, cut short so that it barely touched the collar of her suit, bounced emphatically as she objected. Pearl earrings shook from the delicate lobes of her ears as Carpenter attempted to contain her incredulity.

"*Spriegl* applies to *criminal* cases and allows a jury's access to a person's prior or subsequent bad acts. The intent of *Spriegl* is to show motive, plan, or modus operandi; none of which apply in this case, a civil negligence claim in which one driver rear-ended another."

Judge Peck frowned. "Continue, Counsel."

Carpenter cleared her throat, looked at the yellow legal pad on the table in front of her for effect, and soldiered on. But Kat understood from the judge's demeanor that the jury's verdict would not be overturned.

"How'd it go?"

Kat Carpenter was back at her desk in the Tourville Building, an old warehouse located a block off Chestnut, the main drag in Virginia, Minnesota, her nylon-covered feet absent the black pumps she'd worn in court propped up, a cup of coffee steaming the glass protecting the oak surface of her desk, her eyes staring out a bank of windows overlooking Silver Lake, a murky pond covered with thin winter ice located in the heart of the city, when the question was asked.

Kat was not contemplating an appeal. Mrs. Smith had problems far beyond Judge Peck's legal ruling: the woman had a history of neck strains, sprains, and injuries going back a decade. The only medical professional supportive of Mrs. Smith's assertion that she had aggravated a pre-existing neck condition as a result of the accident was Doc Baker, a local chiropractor whose penchant for embellishment was well-known and whose flare for prescribing "alternative" treatments such as magnetic bracelets and copper wrist bands made him, in the eyes of many, including Kat Carpenter, something of a quack. No, once she'd made her pitch to Peck, and known that there was little hope in securing a new trial, the lawyer had let her defeat at the hands of local defense attorney Kyle Burgess, a pup who had, in fairness, played her for a fool, drift into history. *No use in appealing. Even if I'm right on the evidentiary issue, the jury found no damages, no causal link between Smith's claimed neck pain and the accident. Time to move on.*

The question that interrupted Kat's lament was posed by Jimmy Lampi, a Finnish American/Irish American kid who worked at the firm as a paralegal while attending law school on the weekends at Hamline University in St. Paul.

"It sucked," Kat muttered, averting her blue eyes from the wintery landscape and reaching for her coffee cup as she lifted her stockinged feet off the desk. Kat was careful to avoid indelicacy as she shifted to a more professional posture. "Delores made a bad ruling that she's not going to revisit. End of story."

Lampi, the Finn clear in his razor-sharp cheekbones, blond hair, and indigo eyes, nodded. "You worked with the woman for what, ten years? You gotta know how stubborn she can be. I played hockey with her youngest son, Brad. He wanted to quit when he was eight. Judge Peck wouldn't let him. He finally got his way in high school by drinking at a school dance and puking on Principal Dunsten's shoes. That little stunt got him kicked off the team. It was the only way Brad got out of hockey: The judge wouldn't let him quit on his own."

Kat took a long draw of lukewarm coffee and nodded. *Cute kid. Reminds me of my first husband, Luke. Those Finns. Good looking as all get out but talk about introverted! I couldn't get Luke Impola to tell me what was going on in that head of his. It was good while it lasted, until I got tired of being the only one engaged in conversation. Jimmy has the same bluebird blue eyes, the same shy smile. Ah, to be twenty-three again . . .*

The lawyer contained her lust for youth as she considered a reply. "Ya, Peck's as stubborn as all get out. But that was something of an asset when she was defending lawsuits. Insurers would give her a settlement figure, and she'd hold to it like the Steel Curtain on a goal line stand. Insurance adjusters loved her." Kat realized, as soon as she referenced Mean Joe Greene and his teammates that Jimmy Lampi had no clue what she was talking about. "Steelers of the early '70s. Best defense in the history of football," she added for clarity.

Lampi smiled. His gaze fell discretely on the décolletage of his boss's blouse. Kat's bosom, confined in fabric but enhanced by science to a C-cup, drew his attention. *She's old enough to be my mother,* Lampi thought derisively. *Hell, she used to play tennis with my mother before cancer took Mom. Stop staring at Kat's boobs and finish this up before it gets more awkward. Say what you came to say.*

Kat noticed that the kid's eyes were wandering but said nothing. She enjoyed making men, even men as young as Jimmy Lampi, uncomfortable.

"Something on your mind?" the lawyer said plainly, knowing that allowing coyness to infect her speech would simply confuse the kid.

"Remember the mine explosion in the news last week?"

"Over toward Ely?"

"Closer to Babbitt, but ya, that's the one."

"What about it? I heard the task force was looking into eco-terrorism as a possible cause. Damn granola crunchers coming up here, trying to stop progress. That's bad enough. But causing an explosion that kills good, hardworking folks? That's murder, cold-blooded and wrong regardless of the point those pack sackers are trying to make."

Lampi leaned over and braced himself against Kat Carpenter's desk with his hands. He was short, only five-eight or so, but muscular and square. The athlete, the hockey player, was still there despite the fact he'd given up a hockey scholarship at the University of Maine, the home of the storied Black Bears, to attend Concordia-Moorhead where he earned his undergraduate degree in political science. He'd hung up his skates after leading Virginia High School to the state tournament, the only star on a lunch bucket team. The Blue Devils lost the first tournament game to Breck by one goal in overtime, and then, with Lampi out due to the flu, lost to local rival, Hermantown, the team that went on to win the single "A" consolation title, by six goals. As an adult, Jimmy Lampi didn't lace 'em up like so many Ranger "has beens" and "never weres" to play bar league. When he graduated from high school, he gave up the game. But he was still, to Kat's eye, one fine-looking male specimen.

"The task force *is* investigating. But word on the street is it's more likely that something on-site, something under the control of Continental, the mine's owner, caused the explosion,"

Lampi advised. "No one knows for sure. But that's the scuttlebutt."

Kat opened a drawer and removed a tube of ruby lipstick from her desk. Against her better judgment—but true to her predatory nature—she toyed with Lampi as she opened the lipstick and drew the tube slowly over her upper lip then the lower, smoothing the gloss with her tongue before replacing the lipstick in the drawer. The kid stood there, his eyes trying to focus somewhere, anywhere other than on the beautiful older woman sitting across from him. It was a lost cause.

"What's any of this got to do with me?" Kat returned to being the boss. She shrugged, allowing her blouse to settle across narrow shoulders as she stared at Lampi, her own dull, hazel irises enhanced to azure by tinted contacts.

"One of the little girls who lost her mom in the blast is a cousin of mine. I think I can get the little girl's family to hire us."

Lampi's revelation snared Kat Carpenter's attention. Her eyebrows rose. Her spine straightened. Her heart began to race. A wrongful death case against a multinational corporation with unlimited financial resources had that sort of effect on a girl.

CHAPTER NINE

Emergency personnel inundated the Merritt Pit Mine. Within minutes of the 911 call, a call placed by a young woman from a cell phone as she shivered in her deer stand, law enforcement and first responders were on-site in hopes of performing heroic deeds.

Once the aftershock waned, Madeline Skurbic had released her death grip on the birch tree, opened her eyes, and looked south, across the treetops of the pastoral evergreen forest, across the frozen surface of Birch Lake and beyond, toward the source, the direction, from which the terrible sound of earth and snow and buildings and humanity being destroyed had come. She knew, from a lifetime of living on the cusp of taconite mining, that something catastrophic had taken place just south of Birch Lake. She had no idea what had actually happened, but Maddie was sophisticated enough to understand what was ordinary and what was extraordinary when it came to day-to-day mining operations. The distant smoke rising above the snow-covered landscape was unusual even in a place, a realm, where detonations were routine. Maddie knew disaster when she heard it. She could not calculate the extent or the cost of what had transpired. But Madeline Skurbic was keenly aware of the presence of something untoward in the dark pillar ascending above the icy land. It took the teenager but a moment of reflection to regain her composure. The 911 operator kept Madeline on the line while rescuers raced toward the accident scene.

Later that morning, Maddie would talk to Cook County Sheriff Debra Slater and St. Louis County Deputy Kyle Maki about what she'd seen and heard. Maddie would give a recorded statement to the officers, being careful, as her father stressed, to relate only what she actually knew and not embellish, after which the officers would leave their cards, bid Maddie good day, and head toward the explosion site.

As Deb Slater wheeled her Yukon through the open gate of the old taconite mine, dozens of parked squad cars, ambulances, fire trucks, and the personal vehicles of volunteer firefighters—who'd left their jobs and homes to respond to the 911 call—surrounded a gaping crater. As Slater exited the driver's door of the SUV, red and yellow lights dancing over the flat, white plain of the old mine from the light bars of emergency vehicles, she saw the remnants of a pickup truck smoldering in the near distance. Pieces of black rubber hose extended from the demolished vehicle toward the blast site. Railroad tracks that once culminated near the explosion's epicenter ended abruptly, as if severed by a knife. The blast had been no ordinary mining detonation but something gone tragically awry. From the evidence confronting Debra Slater, the sheriff realized that Madeline Skurbic knew what she was talking about.

Something terrible happened here, Slater thought as she took in the scene. The sheriff walked to the crater's edge and joined a cluster of firefighters and cops staring at the smoldering hole.

"What the hell happened?" Deb Slater's question was said to no one in particular.

A uniformed cop, a "City of Ely" patch affixed to his black leather jacket, faced her. The patrolman, a man Slater recognized from her work with the terrorism task force, whose embroidered name—D. Baxter—was prominently displayed against leather, responded in a low voice. "Near as we can figure, something in a silo, a tower that used to stand here, blew when workers used welding torches to cut it up."

"There's nothing left. How the hell do you know there was a silo here?" Slater stared at charred earth. The disruption to the ground was forty feet long, four feet deep, and twenty feet across. That a horrific force had opened up the ground was evident. But there was nothing left behind to suggest that a structure once stood adjacent to the destruction.

"Timmy Mancuso over there, a firefighter from Ely, filled us in," Officer Baxter said, nodding in the direction of a man wearing yellow turnout gear. "He worked here when it was an operating mine. Says there used to be a steel silo—like a water tower on legs—that held blasting agent where the crater is. And that," Baxter added, pointing to a blackened, rectangular concrete pad to the left of where the group stood, "was once a cement block building."

Deb Slater's eyes grew wide. "What the hell happened?

Duane Baxter didn't respond. His attention was focused on the efforts of others. Three firefighters ran to extinguish flames spitting from welding tanks located near the demolished pickup. The firefighters aimed fire extinguishers. Gray smoke drifted skyward from the blast pit and from the firefighters' efforts.

"Baxter!"

The Ely cop had turned toward Slater, a look of uncertainty on his face as he shook his head. "I have no idea."

CHAPTER TEN

Dee Dee Hernesman traversed the icy sidewalk in front of the St. Louis County Courthouse in Virginia, Minnesota. Images of what had been described to her in the living room of the Lindahl home—the utter destruction of the land, the loss of life, the unexpected and catastrophic deaths of two young people trying to make a living against the hardscrabble economic environment of the Iron Range—overwhelmed her as she moved with purpose toward the old courthouse. *This could be the biggest case of my career.*

The brown accordion folder wedged under Hernesman's left arm contained documents regarding the explosion at the Merritt Pit site: a petition for the appointment of a trustee in a wrongful death action, an affidavit signed by her client, a proposed order, a cover letter, and a check covering the filing fee to open a civil file. The folder Dee Dee Hernesman was carrying was modest in comparison to the mountain of documents that would accumulate after Hernesman's initial appearance before Judge Steven Anderson. There was no court hearing set, only an *ex parte* visit by Dee Dee during which the lawyer would present the petition, affidavit, and proposed order to Judge Anderson in the sedate and comfortable surroundings of his chambers—his office. Judge Anderson would scrutinize the documents and, if everything was properly worded, the judge would sign the order appointing Mark Lindahl, Susie's father, trustee in a wrongful death lawsuit. Time was, Dee Dee knew, of the essence.

The Iron Range legal community is a close-knit brotherhood of litigators. *Brotherhood* is an appropriate demarcation since only a handful of women in private practice, including Dee Dee Hernesman and Katherine "Kat" Carpenter, engage in courtroom advocacy. There are female litigators employed by St. Louis County in the Hibbing and Virginia offices of County Attorney

Justin Pappas's operation and in the Sixth District's Public Defender system. Larger employers in the area, the state college system, the state agencies, the mines, the medical facilities, and Allete, the local electrical utility, also employ female lawyers who appear in court. But, by and large, the specialty of personal injury litigation, as practiced on the Mesabi and Vermillion Iron Ranges, is the province, the bailiwick, of men. Men who allow, in most cases, no quarter in the legal skirmishes that take place in front of the judges and juries of northeastern Minnesota. Hernesman and Carpenter are exceptions to this general rule and, as disparate as their personalities and styles might appear, they both, in their own fashion, have been able to navigate the male-dominated world of the practice of civil trial law.

There had been whispers, in the bars and taverns of Ely and Babbitt and Virginia and Hibbing, places where the deaths of the two salvage workers were discussed openly and with passion, that McGovern and Quinn—Kat Carpenter's law firm—had the case locked up. The rumors were just that, inconclusive rumblings with little fact behind them. But as best as Dee Dee Hernesman could unravel the gossip, someone in Carpenter's firm was related to one of the decedents, one of the two workers who died in the explosion. The scuttlebutt was that Carpenter was about to have *her* employee appointed as the trustee in the wrongful death case involving *that* decedent: Susie Lindahl. Hernesman's hurried walk was an attempt at a pre-emptive strike; she had also been retained by Susie Lindahl's family. There was no room for *two* trustees for the next of kin of the unfortunate Miss Lindahl, and Dee Dee Hernesman knew that if there were competing petitions for appointment pending before the court, two things *should* determine which surviving relative was selected to spearhead the lawsuit: How close the blood relationship was between the proposed trustee and the decedent and which proposed trustee was appointed earliest in time. So far as Dee Dee Hernesman knew, the documents she was carrying gave her a leg up on both accounts.

46

Hernesman's relationship with the Lindahl family began with a phone call placed by Susie's father, Mark Lindahl, three days after the explosion.

"Dee Dee Hernesman. How can I help you?"

There had been a pause on the line, an uncomfortable period of silence that Dee Dee later attributed to grief, the plain and simple catching of emotion that locked the despondent father's voice down tight, like a drum, as he thought of how to broach the topic of the death of his only child.

"Hello?"

Dee Dee heard breathing. From the description of the call, information conveyed to her by the firm's receptionist, Candy Dwyer, a pixie of a woman whose age seemed indeterminable and whose demeanor never wavered from perky, the call involved serious business.

The death of a young mother in an explosion at work. Workers' compensation. Personal injury. This might be my first seven-figure case.

"Miss Hernesman?"

The voice had been male.

"Yes, sir, how can I help you?" Dee Dee knew better than to insist on the non-judgmental "Ms." versus "Miss," the term the caller used, a term that presumed her status to be that of an unmarried woman. She left that distinction for another conversation.

"Mark Lindahl. My wife, Judy, and I live over in Hibbing. Our daughter Susie, our only child . . ."

The man's voice had choked up.

"The young woman killed in the accident?"

Another pause. "Yes. Judy and I, well, we wouldn't be doing this if it weren't for the girls. Susie left behind two daughters, Angel, one year, and Brenda Lee, just turned three. I know this might sound bad, calling before we've even laid Susie to rest and all, but damn it, I am pissed off at what happened. I need some answers. Someone needs to be held accountable. You got any kids, Miss Hernesman? If you do, you'll know why I have to make this call. It's not about the money. It's about doing what's right for Angel and Brenda Lee." Mark Lindahl had taken a deep breath. "I have no idea who did this to my daughter. Whether it's her uncle's fault or someone else's. But someone put her and the Feggetti kid in a place of danger and got them killed. We want to know who did that, Miss Hernesman, who made the decision to send Susie to Jesus. Can you help us?"

Dee Dee stood up from her desk, grabbed a notepad from a shelf behind her, and resumed her seat, all the while listening to Mark Lindahl express his outrage and his grief. "I've only heard and read bits and pieces of the story on television, in the *Ely Echo*, and over *WELY*. There's some talk about it being an act of domestic terrorism, somehow related to protests over mining . . ."

"That's all, if you'd pardon the expression, a load of horse shit," Mark Lindahl had interjected. "I've worked at KeeTac for most of my adult life. Ain't no way someone planted ANFO, the explosive we use to loosen up rock to get at the taconite, to protest the new mine. It was in the silo, Miss Hernesman, plain and simple, and they didn't bother to tell my little girl she could lose her life if she put a torch to the stuff. No other explanation. Someone screwed up, and it cost Judy and I our daughter and two little girls their mom."

"The authorities say they have a letter, an anonymous letter mailed from Ely, warning that, if the mining project isn't stopped by the governor, something catastrophic could happen. The Copper/Nickel Task Force is looking into the threat. It's been all over the news."

Again, there was a lengthy pause. "And I'm telling you, with all due respect, ma'am . . ."

Hernesman could hear the man tear up as he tried to regain his composure and make his point.

". . . that someone with the salvage company or the mining company made a big mistake, a mistake that killed Susie and Antonio."

"Mr. Lindahl, I am so damn sorry this happened. I can't understand or appreciate the depths of your sorrow and grief. I can meet with you and your wife . . . Judy was it?"

"Yes."

"I can fit you in today. I'll clear my calendar and come out to your home. You name the time."

Mark Lindahl had covered the phone with his hand while he spoke to another person, likely his wife, before responding. "That would be fine. I'm supposed to work the night shift, but I'm off until next Monday on funeral leave. The medical examiner is supposed to release Susie . . ." Again, the man choked up. ". . . tomorrow. The service will be on Saturday. Burial right after."

Visions of what happened manifested in Dee Dee's head as she tried to fathom what havoc the massive, unexpected detonation of explosives would wreak on human flesh. Try as she might, she couldn't discern the details of what had transpired out on the shores of Birch Lake. The best she had been able to muster, listening to a father's anguish, was an unholy feeling that the last moment of Susie Lindahl's life was not spent in contemplation of God but in trying to comprehend what was happening.

The Lindahl house had been a modest workingman's bungalow on the west side of Hibbing. Inside, with the exception of toys strewn throughout the lower level, the home was as neat as a pin. Dee Dee's meeting with the Lindahls, though tearful and difficult, made all the more poignant by the presence of Angel, newly able to walk on her thick legs, her blond hair stick-straight and filled with static, rolls of baby fat cascading from chin to diaper, had been polite but trying given the emotions of the grieving parents. Judy and Mark had signed retainer agreements

49

for potential workers' compensation and wrongful death claims, and Mark had signed a petition and an affidavit in support of his appointment as the trustee. If the petition was approved by the court, Mark would be named the plaintiff, the party seeking money damages in the civil lawsuit concerning his daughter's death. But, as Dee Dee had diligently explained, there were two things that needed to happen before a lawsuit was started.

First, Dee Dee would need to convince a judge to sign off on Mark's petition. And second, if Mark was appointed trustee, Dee Dee's law firm would need to undertake an exhaustive investigation into the cause of the explosion. To this end, Hernesman had Mark Lindahl sign authorizations to obtain any and all records amassed by the St. Louis County Medical Examiner, the Ely hospital (where Susie Lindahl and Antonio Feggetti's remains were taken after the disaster), the Federal Bureau of Alcohol, Tobacco, and Firearms (the ATF) and the Federal Bureau of Investigation (the FBI), the Minnesota Bureau of Criminal Apprehension (the BCA), the St. Louis County Sheriff's Office, the Copper/Nickel Task Force, the Ely Volunteer Fire Department (the agency that transported the victims to the Ely Hospital), and any and all records of Susie's employment with Hibbing Salvage and Remediation, the firm owned by Judy Lindahl's brother, Steve Gruber.

Throughout the meeting, held at an antique pine table in the dining room of the Lindahls' modest home, Judy and Mark had remained silent, devastating loss apparent on their faces as Hernesman explained the legal process. As she spoke, Dee Dee Hernesman watched Judy's distantly blue eyes well with tears, saw the woman's round and stubby form shake with grief, and marveled at the strength of Mark, whose craggy face was disguised by a thick black beard, no hint of gray in the whiskers despite being on the cusp of fifty, as the father of the dead girl took notes. After listening intently to Hernesman's description of what the grieving parents could expect during the pretrial phase of the case, Mark Lindahl began asking questions. He was hell

50

bent to prove—being instinctively convinced that the explosion was more than a simple workplace accident—that someone had killed his daughter. But with no proof as to the cause of Susie's death, Dee Dee cautioned Mark not to let supposition get ahead of fact. The lawyer's gentle admonition had little impact on the grief-stricken man. Mark Lindahl made it clear, when he finally opened up, that he would dedicate himself to proving that his daughter's untimely death was not the fault of Susie Lindahl or Antonio Feggetti but the result of poor decisions made by someone else.

Near the end of the meeting, little Angel Marie had clambered over to Dee Dee with a plastic brick in hand, smiled cherubically, and offered the toy to her lawyer.

An image of the little girl's sweet disposition, pink skin, and wavy blond curls accompanied Dee Dee Hernesman as she entered the Virginia courthouse for her audience with Judge Anderson.

CHAPTER ELEVEN

Dee Dee Hernesman made her way to the St. Louis County Sheriff's Office in Virginia. The lawyer met with Arson Investigator Harlis Briggs, who, upon receiving an authorization signed by Mark Lindahl, had allowed Dee Dee to review his investigatory file. It was daunting work. Though Hernesman believed she'd steeled herself against emotion in preparation for the task, a task requiring her to read reports, study photographs, and imagine the sudden and unexpected disintegration of a young woman's body, she was in no way ready for the pictures of Susie Lindahl and Antonio Feggetti taken by Investigator Briggs out at the Mesabi Pit site.

There in clear, unadulterated digital clarity were the victims' remains. The welders had been, from what Hernesman could glean from the pictures, in close proximity to the blast's epicenter at the moment of their deaths. According to the narrative reports and diagrams of the scene, Feggetti's body was found more than seventy-five feet from where the silo once stood. Or at least, that's where the unfortunate welder's legless torso, the most intact and heaviest portion of his remains, was found. Feggetti's head had been sheared off. His macabre death mask was located fifty feet further to the north. His left leg was gone. So was his left arm from the shoulder to the hand. Feggetti's right arm was severed at the elbow but, from the right shoulder to the elbow, the limb remained attached to his torso. The forearm and right hand were located a few steps from Feggetti's head. A portion of the right leg remained attached to his torso. But the shin, ankle, and right foot—still encased in the protective brown leather of a steel-toed Red Wing work boot— were found driven into the ground by the force of the explosion twenty feet to the north of the dead man's right hand. Feggetti's left shoulder, arm, and hand were found further north of the unfortunate welder's battered torso.

Susie Lindahl had fared marginally better. Her youthful face was intact, unaffected by the blast, but Susie's body, damaged in a manner that appeared to be consistent with Brigg's theory that the girl had turned away from the detonation, was desecrated. Shrapnel had been propelled through the left half of Susie's trunk: through her work clothes, her long johns, her bra and underwear. In essence, Susie had been impaled by irregular knives propelled by an unimaginable force. The young mother had lost her left arm at the shoulder but her right arm and leg remained intact. Her left leg was severed at the hip. Her left arm was eventually found near Feggetti's head. Her left leg, including her ankle, foot, and black leather work boot, was discovered beneath a fragment of sheet metal that had once been part of the scale house's roof.

"Tough stuff, eh?"

Hernesman reviewed the arson file in a brightly lighted cubicle across the hall from Harlis Briggs's office. The investigator entered the space without making a sound, without disturbing Dee Dee's morbid concentration, and his question, coming as it did out of the blue, startled the lawyer.

Hernesman looked up from the 4"×6" digital photographs arranged on the desk in front of her, pursed her lips and forestalled tears. The lawyer's hands remained clasped to a picture of Susie Lindahl's face, the young woman's eyes blessedly closed, her features unmarred by the hell she'd experienced. "No shit," Dee Dee managed to whisper through her upset. "No shit," she repeated for emphasis.

"Sheriff Nace says we'll copy whatever you want. Standard fees apply. Pity about those two young folks. How the hell they got talked into putting torches to a silo loaded with ANFO is anyone's guess."

Dee Dee shifted her gaze to take in the investigator. Other than the man's eyes, Briggs was an unremarkable specimen. He was of average height, average build, average looks, and average hair (mousy brown with no gray) for a male in his late thirties. But Briggs's eyes, laughing emerald pools, were remarkable.

"I hear the BCA and the Feds think it might be something else, something related to eco-terrorism."

Briggs frowned. "The bomb theory? Related to a letter Whitcomb received? No way in hell an external force disintegrated a steel silo and a concrete building, much less demolished a pickup truck a hundred and fifty feet away from the blast's epicenter."

Hernesman placed Susie Lindahl's picture on top of the other photos. The lawyer folded her hands and looked up at Briggs. "How can you be so sure?"

The investigator retrieved the photographs from the desk and paged through them until he found what he was looking for. The photo Briggs removed depicted a crater defining the fatal work site.

"See that?" Briggs asked.

Hernesman recovered from her shock and managed a weak smile. "Pretty hard to miss."

"Right. Anyway, you see the concrete pad in the lower left?"

Hernesman squinted. "I really can't."

Briggs reached up and rummaged around on a shelf above Hernesman's head before producing a magnifying glass. "Try this."

Dee Dee studied the photograph under magnification. "OK. I see it now."

Briggs chuckled. "What is it, Counselor? What is it that you see, exactly?"

"A piece of concrete, some sort of foundation, partially covered with dirt from the blast."

The investigator removed a laser pointer from his shirt pocket. A red dot appeared on the photo. "Look at the angle of the pad. What does it tell you?"

Dee Dee Hernesman strained to focus on the details of the photo. "I'm sorry. I don't get what you're sayin'."

"The pad's been pushed *downward*, into the ground."

"OK . . ."

"The other theories being tossed around are that, number one, someone planted ANFO external to the silo that blew the tower to smithereens. Or, two, that the ground itself was so saturated with ammonium nitrate that the ground exploded."

"And . . . ?"

"Total bullshit. The blast pattern, including what happened to that concrete pad—located at the end of the rails where the cars would stop and unload—points to the fact that this was an a *confined* detonation. The energy of the blast was limited. Most likely because ignition took place *inside* the silo. If the ground had been saturated and exploded, the pad would've *heaved* upward. If an external bomb had been placed, there's no way the silo would've been destroyed to the extent you see in these pictures. My best guess, one consistent with my written report, is that ANFO was left inside the cone, the last portion of the silo remaining intact when the job site shut down the night before the explosion."

Hernesman set the magnifying glass aside and looked at Briggs. "But both the safety manager for Continental, what's his name . . . ?"

"Yost. Neil Yost."

"Right. Yost. Both Yost and Susie Lindahl's uncle, the owner of the salvage company, Steve Gruber, claim they inspected the silo and found nothing inside. No ammonium nitrate, no ANFO, nothing."

"That's not entirely true."

"How so?"

"According to Gruber, Feggetti found a chunk of ANFO in the silo, removed it, and put it in a barrel. Who's to say that's all there was? I'd love to see blueprints of the tower, to see exactly how the interior was configured, since all we have is

Yost's and Gruber's word that the thing was empty. But from what former employees of the mine remember, the silo was separated into four compartments. That separation continued to the cone where the delivery hatches were located. I seriously doubt that Gruber or Yost could see all the way into the cone. My bet? There was ANFO hung up inside the thing. That's what blew: residual ANFO in the last piece of the silo to be cut apart."

"I sent an authorization to Denison Mining to get a copy of the blueprints," Dee Dee advised.

"I'd love to see them when they come in," Briggs continued. "For my money, this was a preventable industrial accident and not some terrorist act or shortcut gone awry or the explosion of ANFO-saturated ground. The legalities of all that, I'll leave to you."

Hernesman thought a moment. "Any possibility of criminal charges?"

"Outside the wacky witch hunt the feds and the BCA are on? No. No, I can't see criminal responsibility on the part of Continental or Gruber. Certainly not Denison. Denison disclosed what it knew to Continental. How much Continental told Gruber is in dispute. But criminal charges? I doubt there's anything here, as tragic as it is."

"Thanks, Investigator Briggs, for your insights. I'll need copies of everything you've got."

Briggs winked at Hernesman. "It's Harlis."

The lawyer discerned ardor in the deputy's response. *No need to correct the man, being that he's so helpful and all. I'll let him imagine what he needs to imagine.* A quick glance at the investigator's left hand confirmed what Hernesman suspected: Briggs was unmarried, likely, as so many cops, divorced from his high school sweetheart after procreating a child or two. *Police work takes a toll on human relationships,* Dee Dee observed. *I'll let him suppose what he wants to suppose.*

"Thanks for taking the time to go over this with me, Harlis," Hernesman said as sweetly as she could. "You were an immense help."

"Here's my phone number and email," Briggs said, handing the lawyer his business card. "Call or email anytime. I'd love to know how this thing turns out."

"Will do. Just send copies of everything to my office. I gave you my card, right?"

"You did, ma'am," Briggs replied through a seductive smile. "You did indeed."

CHAPTER TWELVE

An Open Letter to Governor Whitcomb:

The Defenders of the Kawishiwi have worked long and hard to protect a delicate and fragile river. We vigorously oppose <u>any</u> copper/nickel mining in the watershed of the Kawishiwi or any creek, stream, or river flowing into the Boundary Waters Canoe Area Wilderness. Ely legend, conservation icon, and writer, Sigurd Olson worked his entire life to protect the BWCA from the sort of man-made havoc and destruction you and your associates seem bound and determined to wreak upon this pristine piece of wilderness owned, not by mining companies or giant international concerns, but by <u>The People</u>. The proposed copper/nickel mine at the former Merritt Pit Taconite Mine is likely but one of many projects that you and your supporters will attempt to force upon Minnesotans in your desire to line corporate pockets at the expense of clean water.

Please be advised that we, the Defenders of the Kawishiwi, may be a small group, but we are determined to stop any and all copper/nickel mining, whether open pit or underground, adjacent to the BWCA. There can be no quarter, no compromise in this debate. To preserve that which cannot be duplicated or replicated, to ensure that future generations can enjoy wilderness, we will take ANY MEASURE NECESSARY to stop planned copper/nickel mining operations.

This is the only warning that the State of Minnesota will receive. What transpires next, whether it includes a peaceful exit from the planned extractive strategy you have been promoting or includes extreme action on our part rests solely in your discretion and authority.

Governor, make the right choice: Make the choice for wilderness.

> *Sincerely,*
> *Defenders of the Kawishiwi*

Despite Garrison Keillor's observations about Minnesotans being "above average," Governor Wesley Whitcomb, the occupant of the governor's mansion on Summit Avenue in St. Paul, didn't make the cut. Intellectually disinterested and routinely ordinary, Whitcomb was a rigid conservative whose "family values" diatribes and anti-union sentiments during the gubernatorial campaign had vaulted him over a crowded Republican primary field and into the highest office in the state. It didn't hurt Whitcomb that the woman nominated by the Democratic Farmer Labor Party to oppose him, State Senator Elise Abernathy, suffered scandal as the campaign entered its final two months. The revelation that Abernathy had been, before her conversion to Lutheranism, a card-carrying witch affiliated with a coven located in New Brighton, did the poor woman in. Why Senator Abernathy's affiliation with witchdom hadn't surfaced ten years earlier when she first ran for public office is a mystery. How Wesley Whitcomb's handlers uncovered the woman's secret wasn't as difficult to understand: Whitcomb's backers were tough, old white guys who owned things, such as banks and multinational grain companies, insurance conglomerates, logging concerns, lumber yards, copper/nickel mines, and steel mills. They had the resources to ensure that their boy trounced his opposition in the Republican primary and stomped Senator Abernathy into the dust in the general election. And that is exactly what Whitcomb did. On the coattails of the governor's easy victory, the Republicans also won significant majorities in the State House and the State Senate, completing a political landslide that swept away more than a decade of liberal control in Minnesota.

Days into Whitcomb's tenure as Minnesota's chief executive, the new governor announced he was turning up the heat on the MPCA, the DNR, and the United States Army Corps of Engineers, the three agencies involved in the copper/nickel permitting process. "Six years of foot-dragging is a travesty," Wesley Whitcomb had announced during his first "State of the

State" address to the legislature. "Merritt Pit needs to be up and running. And it will be," the new governor had promised the faithful. There was little discussion of favoritism or taint from the news media at the governor's pronouncement despite the mountain of cash Continental Mining had funneled into Whitcomb's campaign. The media was simply awed into silence by Whitcomb's rapid ascent to power.

Prior to entering politics, Wesley Whitcomb had enjoyed a lackluster career as CEO of Whitcomb Emulsions, the family-owned chemical company that Wesley manipulated into outsourcing jobs to India until the workforce, once five hundred strong in the Twin Cities, was reduced to less than fifty local employees.

Wesley then changed focus and ran for public office, running for and winning a term as the Mayor of Edina. During his first year as mayor, Whitcomb managed to break the road and sewer worker, clerical worker, and firefighter unions. He left the police union alone, understanding he'd need police support to run for statewide office. But in the process of his anti-union crusade, Whitcomb saved the city of Edina millions and made a name for himself in the Republican Party.

One term as an undistinguished state senator followed, during which Wesley made his mercurial run for governor. At forty-three years old, with an attractive, platinum-headed wife ten years his junior and four little kids in tow, deep roots in the Edina Free Church, a ready supply of Biblical references in support of his moral positions, and a keen interest in Ayn Rand's objectivist philosophy, Wesley Whitcomb was, to the conservatives of Minnesota, the standard bearer they'd been searching for since the retirement of Tim Pawlenty.

Governor Wesley Whitcomb sat in a red leather chair looking out a bank of windows streaming winter light into his office. Whitcomb studied veterans' memorials interrupting frozen ground across the street from the capitol. Like many conservatives, though Wesley had never served—never been in combat or been through the horrors of war as experienced by the Kerrys or McCain or Dole or Bush the Elder—the governor had an abiding, though safely distant, respect for those who'd gone to war. Viewed by the public as tough and unflappable, as the governor stared out newly installed energy-efficient windows and examined snow-covered obelisks to heroes, tears welled in his gray-blue eyes. Removing a handkerchief from the breast pocket of his suit jacket, the Lilliputian man, five-six in his dress shoes but as fit as a fiddle from daily Pilates, dabbed moisture before turning his attention to the letter on his desk.

Zeke Michelson, Superintendent of the BCA, and FBI Special Agent Roberta Shaw witnessed Whitcomb's near meltdown. The officers withheld comment as they sat in chairs across from the broad expanse of the governor's desk, allowing Wesley to deal with his emotions on his own terms, biding their time until they could gain the man's attention.

"We pulled DNA from a hair trapped under the flap of the envelope," Michelson finally said. The BCA Superintendent was a quietly confident man of immense proportions. At six-five, two-fifty, Michelson could be, if necessary during an interview of a suspect, as intimidating as hell. But in the context of speaking to his boss, Zeke Michelson remained respectful. "Agent Shaw here is running what we found through the FBI's data base. We ran the DNA through our lab and came up empty. Should take a week or so to know whether the feds have a match."

Michelson nodded toward Agent Shaw. The woman, no more than thirty years old, her dark African skin glowing under lamps situated around the governor's office, sat ramrod straight, full in the knowledge that she hadn't voted for Whitcomb and knew no persons of color who had. *Still, he's the man in charge,* the woman thought, eyeing Wesley Whitcomb without disclosing her scrutiny, *and we all have a job to do, a puzzle to solve. Two young folks dead from an explosion. The man's politics don't matter. Do your job, Leslie Ann Shaw. Do your job.*

"That right, Miss Shaw?"

Shaw's cheeks flared color. The slight, the governor's lack of decorum was, she surmised, unintentional. *Let it pass.* She couldn't. She'd worked too hard, overcome too much, putting herself through college and law school, the first of her family to attain a degree, to allow the governor's *faux pas* to go unaddressed.

"*Special Agent.*"

"How's that?"

"With all due respect, Governor Whitcomb, the title is 'Special Agent,' not 'Miss.'" Leslie fingered the ring finger of her left hand as she spoke, fully cognizant that the engagement ring, a sign that she was taken, was no longer present. *A whole 'nother story . . .*

Whitcomb beamed. Whether genuine in his apology or not, the governor attempted to make amends. "Sorry. *Special Agent.* It'll take another week to get answers on the DNA, Special Agent Shaw?"

Leslie Shaw nodded. Her dreads shimmered as she moved. The long, waxed ropes of ebony reflected the room's lamplight like the fur of a sea lion reflects the California sun. "With two dead and the letter you received, I got Quantico to put a rush on testing. A week is a pretty quick turnaround for our lab unless it's a case of national security."

Wesley Whitcomb leaned back in his chair. "Seems to me, what with assholes willing to kill folks over trees and trout, that we *are* talking about national security. Without a new source, this country is forced to rely on China and Peru and Chile for copper. We're at the mercy of a supply chain that, at any moment, can be disrupted, shut off like a kitchen faucet. I'd say that this attack, if that's what it is, is all about *national security.*"

The governor changed focus and stared into the dark brown eyes of the young FBI agent. The intensity of the politician's gaze, an attribute he'd perfected during his debates with the unfortunate Senator Abernathy, seemed genuine enough to Shaw. Whitcomb's scrutiny caused the FBI agent to blink. *He's very good at this. No wonder he won: Abernathy underestimated the man. So did I. I'll keep careful watch on this one, yes I will.*

"Well," Michelson said, noting the uncomfortable standoff between the young agent and his boss. "We best get back to work. Leslie is driving up to Ely to meet with Sheriff Slater, the head of the task force. We've got two agents up there right now, but the sheriff thinks that Shaw—with her forensic training and knowledge of explosives—can lend some insight. Right, Leslie?" Michelson put his hand on the woman's left shoulder.

"True enough. If this is a case of environmental terrorism, as that letter seems to hint, then it becomes a federal matter. Besides," Leslie Shaw said through a broad smile, "I think we'd all rather have the federal court system, where the death penalty is on the table, deal with the matter. Minnesota doesn't have capital punishment, right?"

Whitcomb nodded but did not reply. Special Agent Shaw stood up, smoothed her slacks with her left hand, and extended her right hand. The governor reciprocated. The gesture was then repeated between Whitcomb and Michelson.

"Keep me in the loop, Zeke. You figure out who the bastard is who did this, I want to be the first to know," Whitcomb said evenly.

Zeke Michelson followed Special Agent Leslie Shaw toward the door. "I'm on it, Governor," Michelson replied without slowing down, "I'm on it."

CHAPTER THIRTEEN

Dee Dee Hernesman dreaded making the call. She knew that Kat Carpenter would be, despite the logic of any argument in favor of Hernesman's position, intractable. Carpenter had run to Judge Peck, her former law partner, with a competing petition signed by Jimmy Lampi, a second cousin to Susie Lindahl's daughter Brenda Lee through the child's paternal grandparents, Nancy and Tom Devich—Jimmy's cousin Danny Devich having procreated the child only to vanish. Danny was rumored to be somewhere out West and knee-deep in addiction. Carpenter had convinced Judge Peck that Lampi—a paralegal in Carpenter's firm—was the best person to serve as the trustee in the wrongful death case. As a result, there were two competing orders signed by two different judges chambered in the Virginia courthouse.

The one filed by Hernesman listed both of Susie's children—Brenda Lee and Angel—as well as Mark and Judy Lindahl as Susie's next of kin. Dee Dee had made certain that *all* family members were included in her petition to Judge Anderson.

In contrast, the petition filed by Kat Carpenter naming Jimmy Lampi trustee listed only Brenda Lee, the child in the custody of the Deviches, as next of kin. Kat had made no reference to Angel or Susie's parents in her court filing. The reason for the omission was simple: Kat had not been retained by the Lindahls but by the Deviches. This slight grated on Dee Dee Hernesman, made her fume, as she sat in her office on Chapman Street in Ely and telephoned Kat Carpenter.

"Is Ms. Carpenter in?"

Hernesman's call was intercepted by the receptionist for McGovern and Quinn, the law firm headed by Kat Carpenter. The largest law firm on the Iron Range, "M&Q," as the firm is known throughout northeastern Minnesota, consists of ten lawyers whose practices range from probate and real estate law to criminal defense to civil litigation. There are five named partners in the firm—Kat being the firm's managing partner—and five associate attorneys. In addition, M&Q employs four paralegals, including Jimmy Lampi, whose aspirations include finishing his legal education at Hamline and working for the firm as a criminal defense lawyer.

"Whom shall I say is calling?"

Dee Dee realized that she was talking to Kat Carpenter's daughter, Emily Bloom, a twenty-something spitting image of her mother from Kat's second marriage. Emily had her own troubles. DUI arrests, three in less than five years, had left her on the verge of prison. Kat had taken away the keys to the girl's Volkswagen and had used her considerable influence to keep her daughter out of jail. Emily was wearing an ankle bracelet in lieu of doing time thanks to her mom's intervention despite the fact that Minnesota law called for the girl to spend at least three months behind bars. Emily's fall had been swift, but it didn't seem to lessen the haughtiness apparent in the girl's voice, an inflection that Dee Dee attributed to perceived invincibility.

"Dee Dee Hernesman."

"Oh, Hi. Sorry I didn't recognize your voice. I'll see if Mom can take your call."

There was a period of silence before Emily Bloom spoke again.

"Mom's on a conference call. She wants me to take your number. Can I give her a heads up as to what the call's about?"

Hernesman recited her office number, which, given the plethora of files in common between her firm and M&Q, was a redundant exercise. "Tell Kat I'm interested in finding out what the hell she's trying to pull on the explosion case!" Dee Dee blurted out.

There was another pause. "How so?" The girl's voice grew serious.

"Well, it's interesting to me that Kat would list her own paralegal as the trustee in a case where the parents of the deceased girl are both alive and able to function in that role." Dee Dee took a deep breath. *I promised myself I'd keep my cool. That didn't last long enough to pour a cup of coffee.* "Just give her the message and have her call me."

Kat Carpenter never returned Dee Dee Hernesman's calls, not the first one and not the three that followed. In addition, when Dee Dee encountered Jimmy Lampi in the Hibbing courthouse on an unrelated matter, Lampi was sheepish and unable to articulate just what the hell his boss was thinking by having him appointed as trustee. Frustrated by M&Q's stonewalling, Dee Dee decided to put the matter before the court, to have the issue of competing trustees decided once and for all by a judge. Unfortunately, Kat Carpenter outmaneuvered Dee Dee Hernesman. A well-placed "suggestion" to a clerk in the Virginia courthouse saw to it that Hernesman's motion was assigned to Judge Peck rather than Dee Dee's preference, Judge Anderson.

"More bad luck?"

"Bad luck, hell," Dee Dee ranted when she received notice that the hearing to sort out the trustee issue was going to be heard by Judge Peck. Dee Dee was standing in her law firm's reception area as Skip Mattila watched her rip open an envelope from the district court, his question lost in his partner's ire. "That damn witch got to someone. The motion is assigned to Peck. Peck, the woman who was once Kat's partner and, so far as I know, remains one of her best friends. Shit."

Mattila walked across freshly shampooed carpet, reached over Dee Dee's right shoulder, and snatched the notice. "What're you gonna do?" Mattila asked after studying the document.

Minnesota law allows an attorney one free removal of a judge from a case. Mattila's question left the inference unsaid: *You could remove Judge Peck.*

66

Dee Dee stared out grimy windows overlooking Chapman Street. The usual crowd of anti-mining protestors had dwindled to a single pair of pickets. No sane conservationist, in Hernesman's estimation, wanted to be associated with the tragedy that had occurred at the Merritt Pit site. The governor had delayed announcing the approval of Continental's new mine until the criminal investigation into the explosion was completed. Two older women, signs decrying copper/nickel mining held erect in the cold air, stood outside Hernesman's office. Theirs was a quiet, subdued presence compared to the turmoil that had once blocked traffic on the street and the sidewalk in front of Ely City Hall.

Hernesman retrieved the court notice from her partner. "I don't want to waste my strike at this stage of the game," Hernesman said bitterly. "I'd rather use it in Hibbing, where the case will get tried, on the off-chance that Judge Picket, that cranky son-of-a-bitch, gets the case. It's either him or Harriet Smythe. I can live with Harriet. No matter who ends up the trustee, she'll give us a fair shake. But Picket? I'm not so sure we could survive a motion for summary judgment by the defendants if Oscar Picket's the trial judge. Besides," Dee Dee continued, "Jill Bucher, the Duluth attorney representing the family of Antonio Feggetti, has already filed suit in Hibbing and drawn Harriet as the judge. The cases shouldn't be consolidated given the disparate damages—Feggetti leaving behind no kids and Susie leaving two girls under the age of four—but having one judge decide pre-trial rulings on both cases would make a whole lot of sense."

Mattila nodded. "Sounds like you've made up your mind. Who knows? Maybe Judge Peck will be fair."

Hernesman smiled weakly. "Perhaps. But then, you've always had more faith in human nature than me, Skip."

Mattila slapped Dee Dee's back and walked away. "Maybe it's my sunny disposition, Dees, that fuels my eternal optimism regarding the human condition," Skip Mattila added as he retreated to his office.

The hearing was pointless. Despite the fact that Dee Dee Hernesman had both the facts and the law on her side, the obvious choice for the trustee for Susie Lindahl's next of kin being Mark Lindahl, and despite Dee Dee articulating, in her half-hour long argument, all the reasons why Jimmy Lampi could not, under any reading of Minnesota law, be considered a viable option to serve as trustee, in the end Judge Peck ruled that neither Jimmy Lampi or Mark Lindahl would function as the plaintiff in the wrongful death case.

"Here's what's going to happen," Judge Peck said, narrowing her dull blue eyes behind her bifocals, not allowing Kat Carpenter a chance to respond to Dee Dee's speechifying. "Your preferences are out. The two of you are going to pick a neutral third-party—I'd suggest an experienced attorney—to function as trustee and commence the wrongful death lawsuit. The two of you will be co-counsel. You'll both represent all of the next of kin, the two girls, the two grandparents, all four. Together. Got it?"

"But your honor . . ." Hernesman knew that interrupting the judge in midsentence was a mistake. Dee Dee's head told her Peck had made a decision and, rather than look weak in front of other folks in the courtroom, Delores Peck was not about to change her mind. And yet, the fundamental unfairness of the judge's ruling stuck in Hernesman's ethical craw such that the lawyer could not remain silent.

"Sit down, Ms. Hernesman. You don't like my decision? Appeal it. But for now, you two are working together on this case. Got it?"

Dee Dee sat down and focused her eyes on Kat Carpenter's Madonna-like countenance. *That woman is unflappable.* There was no emotion apparent, no objection clear, on the face of the older lawyer.

"Yes ma'am," Dee Dee finally said. "Ms. Carpenter and I will meet after the hearing and talk it over."

"Kat, you on board?" The judge's use of the opposing lawyer's first name was disconcerting to Hernesman but not strident enough to provoke protest.

Kat Carpenter tucked a file folder, pen, and legal pad into a black leather Coach briefcase. "Yes, Judge. I'm completely in agreement with your decision. I'll meet with Ms. Hernesman as soon as we clear the courtroom. We'll have another Petition for Appointment of a Trustee in front of you by tomorrow morning."

Judge Peck smiled pontifically. "See, ladies. That wasn't so hard now, was it? Ms. Evenson," the judge said, looking at the courtroom clerk seated below her, "please call the next case."

CHAPTER FOURTEEN

"I'll only take this on if you two promise me you'll bury the hatchet, play nice in the sandbox, and work together for the benefit of all the next of kin."

Kat Carpenter and Dee Dee Hernesman sat in the conference room of Grand Rapids family law attorney, Kendal "Tubby" Goggleye, their disdain for each other palpable, their upset at Judge Peck's ruling, a ruling that wed them to each other for the duration of the lawsuit, obvious. The corpulent Mr. Goggleye sat across a table from the women, the man's Ojibwe heritage revealed in his ebony eyes and tawny complexion, as he lectured the lawyers.

"I mean it. Kat. Dees. I won't be a party to shenanigans. You two promise me you'll work together to make the real clients in this thing—Brenda Lee and Angel Marie—your priority rather than your own none-too-small egos, and I'll take it on. You can't make that promise? Find another patsy. With Peck limiting my hourly fee to a hundred bucks an hour," the fat little man with the jet black pony tail braided against the back of his neck said with a note of disdain, "I'm considering this a pro bono matter."

Dee Dee eyed Kat Carpenter before speaking. "You're forgetting the other clients in the case."

Goggleye waved his left hand in the air dismissively. "Come on, Dees. We all know that, while yes, the parents of the unfortunate dead girl technically have claims for pecuniary loss—money damages—realistically, it's the welfare of the two little kids that's paramount."

Kat Carpenter adjusted her gym-toned posterior on her chair and looked down her angular nose at Dee Dee. "The sooner that Ms. Hernesman realizes that she's only representing one-half of the fee equation in this case and not two-thirds, the better."

"Girls," Tubby said, a grin creeping across his jowly brown face, "there'll be plenty of time to sort out fees at the end of this thing. Right now, we need to concentrate on finding out what killed young Ms. Lindahl. Where are we with the investigation?"

I've been working my ass off, is where we are. Dee Dee kept the comment to herself as she studied the patrician face of her co-counsel. *No wonder she gets what she wants,* Hernesman thought. *Push comes to shove, beauty triumphs over brains. Shouldn't be that way. But it is.*

"Hugh MacLean from my firm has been working with Ms. Hernesman to gather materials from the ATF, the Task Force, the BCA, the medical examiner, the FBI, the employer, and Continental Mining. We're on top of it," Kat Carpenter said thoughtfully, the pique of her having to share the case with Dee Dee reduced by Tubby Briggs's admonition. "Isn't that right, Ms. Hernesman?"

"*Dee Dee.* If we're going to work together, Ms. Carpenter, we might as well drop the formalities. *Dee Dee* will do just fine."

"Agreed," Kat said through a feigned smile. "*Kat* suits me as well."

Tubby Goggleye beamed. "That's the spirit, ladies! So, you're pulling together the investigative materials. What about serving and filing a complaint?"

Hernesman withdrew the original of the complaint she'd prepared from a Duluth Pack canvas briefcase beneath the table. "Hugh MacLean's approved it. It's ready to go. You just need to sign the Oath and Acceptance of Trustee and I'll file the documents at the Hibbing courthouse later today," Dee Dee explained, pushing the paperwork across the smooth pine surface of the conference room table.

Goggleye is a solo practitioner who shares a secretary with two other family practice lawyers officed in the old Central

71

Square School building in downtown Grand Rapids. The conference room is, like the secretary, a shared resource.

"Why Hibbing? With the mine being on the East Range, shouldn't the case be filed in Virginia?"

Kat Carpenter beat Dee Dee to the punch. "Hibbing is where Continental Mining's headquarters are located. Hibbing is also," Carpenter said through a significant smile, "a hell of a lot better place to draw a jury from: more blue collar and plaintiff-oriented than what we'd pull in Virginia."

Dee Dee nodded. "Kat's right. We're likely to see double the verdict in Hibbing we'd see in Virginia."

The Native American attorney studied the paperwork and then, without any flourish, pulled a gel pen from the pocket of his gray suit coat and signed the Oath of Trustee.

"I'd heard that but not doing jury trial work myself, I always chalked it up to rumor," Goggleye said as he finished his scrawl and placed the pen on the table. "Looks like we're all in this together," Goggleye said as he pushed documents back to Hernesman. "For better or for worse."

Kat Carpenter removed her bifocals, folded them in a leather case, and placed the case in a black leather Coach purse. "For better or for worse. Seems I've heard that phrase before..."

Hernesman couldn't help but smirk as she retrieved the documents from Tubby. "At least, what, three times?"

"Yes. Three times. Pretty sure I'll not hear those words again in this lifetime."

Goggleye chuckled. Kat Carpenter's marital history was well known. "Never say never, Ms. Carpenter."

"*Kat*! If we're going to be working together on this case, Tubby, you've got to get on board.

Goggleye grinned and rose to his feet. "Kat. Dees. It's been a pleasure," he said, showing the women to the door. "Keep me in the loop."

"Always," Kat Carpenter said without conviction as the two women exited the conference room.

CHAPTER FIFTEEN

St. Alban's Catholic cemetery was wind-swept and cold. Susie Lindahl's family, including the Grubers—Judy Lindahl's side of the family—and a small cluster of Susie's friends, stood next to the open grave, a modest chrome and steel casket poised on canvas straps above a concrete burial vault, the last remains of Susie Lindahl inside, expertly stitched together by a mortician from Dougherty's Funeral Home. Father Peter O'Connor, a twenty-something Irish Catholic priest fresh off the plane from Ennistymon, stood coatless and imperious against the gale, his black cassock fluttering in the wind as he recited the Catholic rite of burial in a brogue so thick, Hernesman felt that she was standing on the banks of the Inagh rather than at a graveyard outside Hibbing. The lawyer felt compelled to attend the internment even though she did not personally know the woman being buried. That compulsion was related to Dee Dee's view that her job, her role in the story of Susie Lindahl's demise was, as her mentor and former partner Daniel Aitkins had often counseled her, to seek and find the truth.

"Not justice, Dees," Danny had often reminded her, "but truth, at least, *a* truth, is what you're trying to achieve as a trial lawyer. There may be more than one truth in any given situation. My truth. Your truth. Someone else's truth. You need to find *a* truth that is believable, plausible, and compelling to a jury. Do that," Aitkins had urged, "and you and your client will be satisfied."

Of course, Danny Aitkins had failed miserably in finding *his* truth. Over sixty, twice divorced, chronically dependent on booze, and recently unemployed after being discharged from his last job—that of a law professor at the University of North Dakota—Aitkins's ability to find anything close to personal truth was in serious doubt.

But he knew what he was talking about back then, back before The Fall.

The Fall. The affair that created a child—a daughter with the widow of Danny's best friend—and destroyed a wonderful partnership between Aitkins and his wife, Julie, an author, who went on to raise their three kids without Danny and to remarry, the success of her novels placing her in the upper echelon of Minnesota writers adjacent to Garrison Keillor, Louise Erdrich, William Kent Krueger, Jon Hassler, Sinclair Lewis, and of course, the granddaddy of them all, F. Scott Fitzgerald, in terms of her fame.

A second Fall. Danny's attempt to find love in the arms of a twenty-something teaching assistant, a connection that violated every rule of the university, but which, once Danny and Abigail Hurst married, seemed to make him happy, to tame his wandering eye. Then, inexplicably, another affair. Thankfully, no children with Abigail or the other young student who slept with her contracts law professor. A second divorce, messy and public due to his status at UND. A plunge from sobriety back to the bottle. Missed work. Missed appointments with the dean. Termination of employment and despondency.

Stupid son-of-a-bitch, Dee Dee thought as family and friends gathered around Susie Lindahl's remains to place red roses on the burnished metal lid of the casket. *Danny had the life most men dream of and he messed the whole thing up, including his second act. Still, he was my mentor. Still, I can't help but feel sorry for the man. He taught me how to think like and be a trial lawyer. I wonder what he's up to?*

No hymns were sung at the graveside, though the mourners did join Father O'Connor in reciting the Lord's Prayer. The attendees' words were lost to swirling wind, the northwestern gale too strong for the group's collective voice.

"Thank you for being here," Mark Lindahl said. The father of the dead girl appeared unexpectedly at Hernesman's side as Dee Dee watched Judy Lindahl walk Brenda Lee and carry Angel Marie to a waiting Lincoln Town Car supplied by the funerary. "It's much appreciated."

The lawyer offered her client a weak smile. Tears gathered in the corners of her eyes, evidence that, though she couldn't begin to understand the depths of Mark and Judy Lindahl's sorrow, she recognized her clients' loss. Mark noted Dee Dee's upset and gathered her in with a paternal embrace.

"It'll be OK. We'll be OK."

Hernesman sniffled and wiped tears with a paper napkin she'd brought with from the luncheon after the service at St. Alban's. Judy had invited her to attend the gravesite service after the luncheon. It wasn't expected that the lawyer would accept the invitation. But she had and Dee Dee paid the price for her diligence. The lawyer was, despite never having met Susie Lindahl, upset by the proceedings. *Christ. He's consoling me. The guy who lost a daughter is consoling me! What the hell is wrong with me?*

"Any news?"

The sudden switch of topics momentarily puzzled Hernesman. But after brief reflection, Dee Dee understood, or at least, thought she understood, that Mark Lindahl was trying to change the focus from the negative, the fact his daughter, his only child, was about to be covered with dirt, to the positive, that someone, specifically his lawyer, was trying to find out why Susie Lindahl died. Dee Dee nodded and placed the napkin back in a pocket of her brown wool winter coat.

"I met with Investigator Briggs from the Sheriff's Office. He had lots to say. Mostly, he's convinced that the terrorism and the ground-blowing-up scenarios are bullshit, pardon the expression."

Mark Lindahl's lips formed a subtle grin despite the dour setting. "I'm a big boy, Counselor. An Iron Ranger. I think I've heard just about every curse word at least once."

They walked toward cars waiting to proceed to the Lindahl home.

"So noted. Briggs is sending me everything he has. It's a good start. Photographs, newspaper clippings, statements, the works."

"Sounds like you're on top of things, Ms. Hernesman."

"Dee Dee. Call me Dee Dee. Lots to do but yes, it's coming together."

They stopped next to the Town Car where Judy and the girls waited in the back seat.

"You getting along with Ms. Carpenter?"

"As best I can. She's not really involved in the case. Her associate, Hugh MacLean, is the lawyer from her firm I'm working with. Hugh's nice enough, but he can't pee without asking Kat's permission!"

Mark Lindahl opened the rear passenger door to the limousine and slid onto the black leather seat next to his wife. "Keep your eyes on Ms. Carpenter. I hear she's a real ball buster, someone unafraid to cross lines that shouldn't be crossed if it's in her own best interest to do so."

"Oh, I'll keep her in my sights, all right. I've known Ms. Carpenter—Kat—for more than a decade. I know her well enough to approach with caution."

The father of the dead girl nodded and closed the door. The grin that had graced Mark Lindahl's face disappeared. The light moment Hernesman and her client had shared vanished. The lawyer surmised that the interlude of levity between them ended because Mark Lindahl's attention refocused on the reality that his daughter, the girl who'd given him such joy and pain, such happiness and sorrow during her brief life, would not challenge or bless him again.

CHAPTER SIXTEEN

Deb Slater pulled leather gloves over her bare hands and exited the Yukon. She'd parked the big rig in the parking lot of the Burnside Lodge in front of a winterized cabin occupied by Cyrus Oliphant. As Slater listened to the GMC's engine gurgle, a black Ford Expedition parked next to the Yukon. The sheriff raised her gloved right hand in greeting.

The Feds.

Doors creaked. Three agents exited the Ford and stood in below zero cold. Slater, the law enforcement officer in charge of the search, tucked the warrant she'd obtained from Judge Anderson into a pocket of her winter uniform jacket before exiting the Yukon.

"Sheriff Slater, I presume," an African American woman dressed in a heavy blue wool winter coat, blue wool mittens, matching blue wool hat, black slacks, and just-out-of–the-box Steger Mukluks, said, extending a mittened hand to the sheriff. "Leslie Shaw, FBI."

Slater returned the gesture. "Pleased to meet you, Agent Shaw."

The black woman, who was significantly taller than Debra Slater, smiled. "Leslie will do between colleagues."

"Call me Deb."

A diminutive Asian American man dressed in a puffy red parka, new Iceman boots, and black leather gloves extended his right hand to Slater. "Allen Fong, BCA."

"Nice to meet you, Allen," the sheriff replied, returning his handshake with vigor. "And you must be Byron Muckala, ATF. Am I right?"

"That'd be me," Muckala, a square-built man in a Western-style duster, a coat distinctly out-of-place for the venue and climate, said through a slight smile, extending his bare hand to the sheriff. The two officers shook hands and Muckala retreated behind his colleagues.

"I know the owners. I'll serve the warrant on them. Then we can take a peek and see if Mr. Oliphant has left anything incriminating in his cabin."

The sheriff retrieved the search warrant from her jacket pocket and walked toward the office of the lodge with the legal document in her gloved right hand.

• • •

"I'd love for you to explain, Mr. Oliphant," Leslie Shaw said, her ebony, almond-shaped eyes boring into the suspect, "why we found two sacks of fertilizer in a closet in your cabin. Seems a bit cold outside to be growing vegetables."

Cyrus Oliphant crossed his forearms over the wool fabric of the green Pendleton shirt he was wearing, the shirt's pattern interrupted by brown leather suspenders affixed to the waistband of Wrangler jeans, as he eyeballed the FBI agent. Oliphant's expression gave no quarter. "What if I was to respond with one word, that word being 'lawyer?'"

Deb Slater, who was seated next to Agent Shaw across the table from Oliphant in the interrogation room of the St. Louis County Jail in Virginia, smiled demurely. "That, Cyrus, is certainly your right. But if you've done nothing wrong, have nothing to hide, why would you invoke your right to counsel? Take a few minutes, tell us your side of things and maybe, just maybe, we release you so you can go back to protesting or whatever it is you think you're doing up in Ely."

Muckala and Fong leaned against a cinder block wall, studying Oliphant. Their presence in the room was meant to intimidate. The four law enforcement officers had decided that Slater, who knew Oliphant from her work on the task force, and Shaw, who had the most experience dealing with domestic terrorists and fringe groups, would take the lead. The two male agents were simply window dressing.

Cyrus Oliphant mulled over whether to engage.

"While you're thinking, Mr. Oliphant, let me ask you another question: Did you have anything to do with the explosion out at Birch Lake?"

Slater wasn't so sure that Shaw's direct approach would be productive. The sheriff believed that building rapport with the man, a convicted felon but a dedicated, sincere believer in his cause, would serve their purpose better than confrontation. She was wrong.

Oliphant nodded. "I'll tell you a story, a story involving Mr. Yost. You know who he is, right? The safety director of the proposed mine. Now understand: I wasn't there on the day of the explosion. I was working at the lodge, painting inside a cabin. You can check with the owners. They'll vouch for me. They'll tell you I was working the day those young folks got killed. So what I'm about to tell you isn't firsthand. I didn't hear it from Yost. But the talk around town is that Yost showed up the night after the explosion at Tommy's, his usual watering hole, already lit up pretty good. He got weepy after too much Johnny Walker Black. Word is, he kept saying, over and over, 'It happened again. I can't believe it happened again.' He might have tossed in an expletive or two. Don't know and don't care. I don't know the man. Never met him. But if I was interested in what killed two kids doing their jobs, well, I'd pay Mr. Yost a visit and ask *him* some questions."

Leslie Shaw pushed herself away from the table, as if she was ready to leave the room. Slater placed a hand on the agent's shoulder as if to say, *Wait, let's hear what the man has to say.*

"Go on."

"This idea that Continental can safely tunnel under Birch Lake, extract rock, remove little bits of copper and nickel from tons upon tons of waste, stockpile the overburden, let the rains leach over that poison and not destroy the BWCA: That, ladies, if you pardon the expression, is a goddamned fairy tale. Am I upset that Governor-shit-for-brains is pushing the project forward? Absolutely. Everyone in favor of this thing, from the mayor of Ely to Whitcomb, to the steelworkers' union, to the construction workers, to the local chambers of commerce, all point to the success of the Roosevelt-Taft Mine near Aurora as proof that copper mining can be managed through technology, that the disasters of the past, disasters that destroyed pristine waters in Montana and other Western states and Canadian provinces, won't happen here." Oliphant paused and clasped his hands as he gathered his thoughts.

The environmentalist wanted to point out that Roosevelt-Taft Mine, which was up and running and producing copper and nickel concentrate, was an open pit operation far removed from the BWCA and that the history of that mine was of short duration, that the results of the project in terms of its long-term impact on the St. Louis River watershed—where the Roosevelt-Taft Mine is located—were unknown. But the man realized he was wandering off track and that the patience of the officers was wearing thin.

Slater frowned. She was sorry she'd encouraged Oliphant's tangent. She sensed that Shaw was about to object to the man's speechifying when he started in again.

"I know, I know. Stay on topic. Here's the thing. Yes, I've done time in prison. I've damaged federal property to make a point. And yes, maybe I was thinking about liberating a small amount of fertilizer, three sacks from the twenty I bought at Pamida for the resort, for my own personal use. I'm just spit balling here, but maybe I was thinking I could sabotage a dozer or two once construction began. Send a message to those who'd destroy our last bit of Midwestern wilderness. But endanger two innocent kids? Take their lives? No way in hell. I'm telling you: Ask Yost some questions. See what falls out of *that* tree. You'll get no answers from me as to how and why two young people were killed doing their jobs."

Allen Fong, his Asian facial features blurred by the English/Welsh/Irish blood bestowed upon him by his mother, smirked. "And of course, that's why we found a strand of your hair—as established through the DNA sample you gave when you were convicted for the Clam Lake incident—embedded in the glue of the envelope holding the letter you sent to the governor. You've got a lot of answers, Oliphant, but none for that little tidbit of truth, I'll wager."

"It was a warning, is all. Like I said, there's a *remote possibility* this protest I'm involved in *might* result in some *minor* property damage. *Might*, as in 'I haven't made up my mind.' The letter doesn't change the fact I had nothing to do with what happened on Birch Lake."

Muckala joined the inquiry. "We're supposed to take the word of a convicted felon, with evidence of the intent to make a bomb hidden away in his closet, and his DNA connected to a letter threatening violence, as gospel? And what, drag an executive of a local mining company in for questioning on the off chance that his drunk talk might lead us in the right direction? That's just plain bullshit, Oliphant. Bullshit."

The ATF agent's diatribe didn't deter the old protestor.

"Ask around, Agent Muckala. Ask folks who were at the bar the night those kids met their maker. Ask them if Mr. Yost didn't lament in his cups about something that took place a long while back. I can't tell you how that gossip relates to what happened out at Birch Lake. But I can tell you this: I want my lawyer and I want him now."

CHAPTER SEVENTEEN

Andrew "Hoot" Holt sat at on a stool at the bar in Tommy's, a glass of Budweiser reflecting fluorescent light. The private investigator let cold beer slide down his parched throat. Sixty-seven years old, tall, and large paunched, the retired deputy considered the slender crowd in the place and mulled over what he'd already learned.

Sherri, a forty-something, slender-hipped, flat-chested, redhead tending bar was the person in the place most interested in Hoot Holt. Hoot couldn't quite discern the basis for the woman's attention. Sure, he was a bit of a local celebrity, having made Junior College All-American as a defensive tackle on the Vermillion football team, an honor that Hoot turned into a two-year ride to the University of Michigan where he started at left defensive end his senior year. Coach Bo had taken Hoot's raw talent for hurting folks and developed it to the point where the Lions and the Vikings were interested in Hoot until bum shoulders made Hoot give up thoughts of playing professionally. The big man joined the St. Louis County Sheriff's Office in 1973 at a time when an intimidating demeanor meant everything and formal law enforcement training was in its infancy.

Though in physical decline, Hoot Holt remained a six-six, two-hundred-and-sixty-pound presence of humanity. But more importantly, Holt was also an astute student of human behavior, an attribute that served the ex-cop far better than his size. Even so, Hoot was unable to determine whether Sherry was coming on to him based upon his backstory or because she found him attractive.

Doesn't really matter. She gave me what I needed.

Sherri LaPointe, the half-Ojibwe, half-Finn bartender at Tommy's, had been on duty the night of the explosion. Sherri explained, over a diet Coke while making moony eyes at Hoot, that Yost wasn't the only one who sought refuge after the tragedy out on New Tomahawk Road. Locals—from as far away as Babbitt and Embarrass—had crowded into the bar that night upon hearing the news. However, Neil Yost was, according to Sherri, the most despondent, the most upset, and the most emotional of the patrons in the bar.

"Said he wasn't driving home, to keep the Blacks coming. I poured quite a few and the booze loosened him up. At first," the bartender revealed, "all the guy did was cry. Not little man tears but big sobs. Uncontrollable, I think you'd say."

"And then . . . ?"

"Like most drunks, he started to talk. Not about the two kids, which I thought he might, but about something that happened years ago. Didn't give details, or, if he did, his speech was so fucked up, I couldn't understand what he was trying to say."

Hoot had drained his second beer.

"Wannanother?"

The PI had nodded. "And . . . ?"

"Hold your horses, Hoot."

Sherri picked up the PI's glass and walked to the tap where she proceeded to refill Holt's glass with Bud. "Here," she said upon returning, sliding the glass into the investigator's oversized left hand. "Where were we?"

The PI sipped foam. "You were telling me about some yarn Yost was spinning."

"Right. I got the impression something happened to him in another place, another time, on another job. I got that it involved mining. Copper mining, I think," Sherri said and flipped a strand of dyed red hair away from her mouth. "Can't tell you much more other than, when I quizzed him about details, he grew quiet and the tears started up again."

"Thanks."

"Don't mention it. And it's been what, like six months since you've been in? A girl gets lonesome, ya know. Don't be a stranger."

The PI had nodded. "I need one more and the tab."

After the refill, Sherri swung her hips suggestively toward the register and rang up Hoot's bill. She'd walked in similar fashion back to where the old football player was seated on the cracked vinyl of a bar stool, his eyes riveted on a Minnesota Wild game on the flat screen behind the bar. No words were spoken as the bartender slid a register slip toward the PI, her phone number written under a scrawled signature and a smiley face.

I'm single. She's fairly attractive. A bit used by life. A little skimpy in the tits. But nice legs, hips, thighs. Big brown eyes and a wry smile. Wry. Where the hell did that come from? Anyway, I could do worse. She gave me her number for a reason. She's hot to trot: Ready to try the old horizontal bop with the Hootster.

Andrew Holt was a methodical man, a man not given to acting on impulse. He was due in Hernesman's office in the morning to report what he'd learned about Neil Yost. From what he could surmise, the story the bartender told Hoot had not been shared with anyone else.

A leg up. Hernesman needs that, dealing with the likes of the defense attorneys in this case.

The PI raised the beer mug to his lips and drained the last of the Bud. The effort caused Hoot's face to grimace from arthritic pain in his left shoulder.

Goddamn old age. Goddamn football the ex-deputy thought as he slid off the barstool and headed toward the door.

CHAPTER EIGHTEEN

Snow swirled over the Yukon's hood. The white SUV was
nearly invisible as it negotiated Highway 61. Though engineers
had lessened the worst of the hairpin turns that once graced the
two-lane—the only road connecting Duluth with Thunder Bay,
Ontario—by tunneling through impressive cliffs of eons-old
basalt, winter driving on 61 remains a challenge. Cook County
Sheriff Deb Slater had driven this stretch of asphalt hundreds,
perhaps thousands, of times in her career such that Slater knew
every bump, twist, or surprise ahead. But the combination of the
cascade of white disrupting visibility, coupled with the
emotional weight of Slater's errand, slowed the Yukon to a
crawl.

"I wish this damn snow had waited an hour," Slater
muttered as the SUV's defroster purred.

Margaret Ann "Annie" Slater, the only child of Rick and
Deb Slater, sat in the front passenger's seat, her butternut eyes
scanning the plain of lake ice out the side window, her mouth
held in a pronouncement of pain; the effect of her father's
passing so close and personal that she hadn't really come to grips
with the finality of the task that she and her mother were
engaged in.

Deb felt the angst welling inside her daughter and
recognized that everything about her own life—personal,
professional, and familial—had changed.

*I'm Rick Slater's widow. A widow. A woman in
mourning. A single mother. Where the hell do I go from here?*
The sheriff stopped her line of thinking to consider the selfish
nature of her reflection. She corrected her inquiry to include
Annie's loss. *Where do <u>we</u> go from here?*

Rick's remains had been waiting for Deb and Annie at Cavallin's
Funeral Home in Grand Marais. There had been so little left of
the physical Rick by the time he breathed his last at the Solvay
Hospice House in Duluth that even if Rick *had* chosen burial
over cremation, an adult-sized casket would have been overkill.
Mitochondrial disease had reduced Deb Slater's once strapping
husband to a skeleton on life support. *An awful end to a once*

hopeful story. Stem cell therapy, expensive and experimental, at the University of Wisconsin Hospital in Madison had bought them time. But in the end, medical wizardry had been no match for the unstoppable progress of nature. In the end, there had been tubes and machines and IVs and monitors and the loss of dignity and poise and personality and intellect. In the end, there was a church service at Bethlehem Lutheran, ELCA. Though Bethlehem wasn't the Slaters' home congregation, a large crowd of mourners and well-wishers was expected for the memorial service, which necessitated using the larger church in town instead of the little ELCA chapel on Devil Track Lake. At the service, there were shared memories, tears, nice words by the pastor, massive quantities of hotdishes, and the holding tight to a daughter too inexperienced in life to appreciate the finality of loss.

"He loved this place," Annie said as they stood next to a gurgling tendril of open water, the roughhouse plummet of the Cascade River exposed to settling snow, the flakes as big as a quarter, Duke, the family's aging black Labrador who'd been Rick Slater's companion on countless trout fishing and grouse hunting expeditions up and down the woods, ridges, and streams of the North Shore, nosed ahead of the women.

They'd hiked in, snowshoes strapped to their Sorels in an effort to avoid sinking in the thigh-high drifts of January lake-effect snow. Snow originating from the open water of Lake Superior and empowered by Canadian winds into squalls along the North Shore had accumulated in depth, making hiking, even in snowshoes, problematic. Duke didn't appear challenged by the snow. With puppy-like glee, the ten-year-old Labrador, fattened by love and too much kibble, bounded ahead of the sheriff and her daughter, Rick's remains portaged in an urn stowed in a Frost River knapsack strapped to Annie's narrow back.

"He did indeed," Deb agreed. She'd been to the quick flowing rapids that emptied the Bachelor's Pool, a deep hole in the Cascade that had been Rick's "go to" spot for catching speckled trout, many times with her husband. Sometimes Deb joined Rick in tossing handmade flies beneath cedars at the end of her custom-made, nine-foot graphite fly rod in hopes of enticing fat brookies. On other visits to the river the sheriff simply sat on the bank with a good book, content to allow her man some time on the water. Annie had also made trips to the Bachelor's Pool with Rick, though she'd never caught the infectious compulsion necessary to become an ardent fly angler. "This was the place he wanted his ashes spread," Deb whispered, wiping tears from her eyes with the back of her gloved right hand, "and I can see why."

Without warning, Annie doubled over. Nausea descended in waves, causing Annie's slender form to buck and pitch as she sought to empty her stomach, though only a small trickle of noxious spittle emerged.

"Stomach upset?"

The girl wiped her mouth on the sleeve of her winter parka and nodded.

"Sick?"

Annie shook her head. "Too much emotion. I'll be fine."

Deb studied her daughter but said nothing more as she turned toward the stream. Duke snuffled toward Annie.

"Git," Annie said, kicking at the Lab to discourage investigation. The dog looked at the girl, wagged its tail, and left the vomit alone.

Powdery snow settled over the valley. There was no wind. The woods were silent save for the gurgling of black water where river escaped pool. Duke, as if on cue, as if he understood the sacredness of the moment, stopped cavorting and sat on thick haunches, waiting expectantly for someone to act. Without ceremony, Deb removed her gloves, undid the leather straps of the knapsack on her daughter's back, and removed an unmarked steel canister. The sheriff twisted the lid of the urn. Annie studied the river. Deb Slater observed, for the first time since her daughter was back from college, that Annie's face revealed new weight. The change in her profile was slight but noticeable, something that Deb would normally have raised in discussion. But Deb and Annie were at the Cascade to memorialize a husband and father, not to address the risks of all-you-can-eat college buffets.

"Rest, my beloved, rest," Deb Slater whispered, pouring half the urn's contents—gray and white specks of ash and bone—into the river. The sheriff handed the container to her daughter.

"I love you, Dad. I'll never forget you."

Annie spilled the last remnants of Rick Slater's earthly existence into the Cascade. The young woman's eyes filled with tears as she handed the canister back to her mother. Deb replaced the urn in the backpack and secured the straps. The pair was silent as they hiked out of the valley, their snowshoes compressing snow as they climbed toward the Yukon.

Emotionally spent, mother and daughter remained silent as the SUV rumbled over gravel roads. Duke snoozed on the Yukon's rear bench seat, his snoring the only noise inside the vehicle. Concerned with Annie's well-being, Deb glanced at the young woman during the drive home.

I'll have to talk to her about dorm food, the sheriff thought. *She's gonna have a tough time playing varsity next year if she keeps eating everything they put in front of her!*

The GMC stopped in front of the Slaters' garage. Deb sat behind the steering wheel while she pondered how to reach her daughter. Annie remained stoic and imperious, the bout of emotion and nausea that had gripped her at the Cascade concealed by steely determination. But there was something, an urgency, a need to dialogue, apparent on the girl's face despite the girl's bravado that compelled Deb Slater to engage.

"Somethin' you want to say, Margaret Ann?"

Annie looked out the passenger's window. Her eyes followed the hectic flight of a blue jay from a snow-covered spruce to a bird feeder.

"Annie?"

The only child of Rick and Deb Slater tried to fend off more tears, more emotion, as she faced her mother. It was a hopeless exercise.

"I'm pregnant."

CHAPTER NINETEEN

Peder Johansson, former President of the Minnesota Bar
Association and a courtroom legend from Duluth Dee Dee
Hernesman had locked horns with in prior lawsuits, was hired by
the primary liability insurance carrier to defend the legal actions
brought against Continental Mining on behalf of the dead
welders. Johansson, a tall, lanky marathon runner boasting
prescient green eyes and wavy, silver hair, the chairman of
Johansson, Edwards, and Masterson (the largest law firm in
northeastern Minnesota) had been in the game of defending
multinational corporations for nearly four decades. There was
nothing subtle or cautious about the Silver Wolf: what you saw
with respect to Peder Johansson was what you got. He was a
straight shooter—which meant if you were opposing counsel,
you had best be ready for a knock-down-drag-out-fight but one
founded on fairness and principle.

In contrast, Bruce Cutler, the lawyer assigned by
Continental's excess liability insurance carrier to backstop
Johansson, was an entirely different breed of legal cat. Saturnia
Insurance's "pot of gold" was only available to the surviving
next of kin if and when Hibbing juries awarded damages that
exceeded the primary insurance coverage—the million-dollar
policy issued by Mercury Mutual Assurance Group and defended
by Peder Johansson. The Silver Wolf had the dual obligation of
representing Continental *and* Mercury Mutual. Bruce Cutler had
a similar dual loyalty to Continental *and* Saturnia. But whereas
Johansson recognized the inherent conflicts in such a role,
standing at the ethical crossroads between two clients with
disparate interests, Cutler's view of the legal landscape was not
so refined.

Bruce Cutler was known as a "slash and burn" litigator,
a fierce and slightly unethical legal pugilist who routinely
sauntered near the precipice of violating the Minnesota Rules of
Professional Responsibility but never actually crossed ethical
lines. Cutler's risky behaviors, displayed for the benefit of the
insurer at the expense of the actual client, made the Minneapolis
attorney the male equivalent of Kat Carpenter. Cutler and
Carpenter were well matched in terms of their ability to creep up

to an ethical line only to pull back at the last possible moment to avoid reprimand or suspension or disbarment at the hands of the lawyers' board.

Rotund, balding, and burdened with poor eyesight requiring trifocals, Bruce Westin Cutler's physical presence wasn't as regal as Peder Johansson's. In an attempt to camouflage his physique, Cutler adorned his billowy countenance in thousand-dollar suits, custom-tailored shirts, designer neckties, and nine-hundred-dollar GJ Cleverly shoes. But behind Bruce Cutler's dour deportment and over-the-top wardrobe beat the heart of a competitor and the brain of a world-class poker player. Though Cutler would not take an active role in the case—his role in the lawsuit being subservient to that of the Silver Wolf—when numbers were crunched during settlement discussions, Bruce Cutler would be there to assert his protectionist vision. Any settlement that exceeded one million dollars and invaded Bruce Cutler's purse would be hard fought and difficult given Cutler's view that the insurance coverage under his control was *his* personal treasure to be parceled out with great care.

Upon learning that Judge Oscar Picket had been randomly assigned to the lawsuit, Dee Dee Hernesman filed her paperwork—her one "bite of the apple"—to remove the doddering crank from the case. Hernesman and Hugh MacLean, the M&Q associate assigned by Kat Carpenter to keep tabs on Hernesman, were surprised when Peder Johansson didn't remove Picket's replacement, Judge Harriet Smythe. Johansson had the same right to remove a judge without cause but chose, for whatever reason, not to resort to that gambit. The defense icon's refusal to strike Smythe puzzled Hernesman until Dee Dee learned through the courthouse grapevine that Judge Parker Farris, a Duluth judge and a former ambulance chaser appointed to the bench by Minnesota's last Democratic governor, was next up to handle the case. Somehow Peder Johansson had discerned that Farris would be assigned if Smythe was removed and the Silver Wolf declined to replace a neutral magistrate (Smythe) with one whose views were clearly adverse to the interests of Johansson's clients (Farris).

A week after Harriet Smythe drew the cases—Jill Bucher, the attorney representing the Feggetti family having previously exercised her right to remove Picket and *that* case also having been assigned to Judge Smythe—Harriet Smythe held a scheduling conference with the attorneys in both matters: Dee Dee Hernesman and Kat Carpenter appearing for the Lindahls, Jill Bucher for the Feggettis, Peder Johansson for Continental and Mercury Assurance, David Van Clive for Calumet (named as a third-party defendant in the case by Continental for failing to disclose the dangers of the ANFO silo), and Cicely Thompson for Hibbing Salvage and Remediation and Steve Gruber, personally (brought into the case by Johansson in a similar fashion to Calumet based upon a third-party complaint on behalf of Continental).

Allegations of negligence against Steve Gruber and his company were claims, given the exclusive nature of Minnesota worker's compensation, which Hernesman and Bucher could not bring absent a showing of willful or gross negligence on the part of Gruber. No such evidence existed. Dee Dee was convinced that the smarter play, the better play, was to work with Cicely Thompson, Gruber's attorney, to point *Gruber's* finger at Neil Yost, who, in the assessment of the plaintiffs, was the culprit, the cause of the explosion that killed two innocent welders. Hoot Holt was working on an angle, retrieved from a bartender at Tommy's, which would cast Yost in an even more sinister and despicable light. The ex-football star had a theory based upon whispers of a shadowy past. Hoot did not have in his possession—as yet—facts upon which Hernesman and Bucher could act. But even without juicier accusations of wrongdoing, Hernesman believed that Neil Yost was the real villain in the case. Given that the families couldn't sue Gruber, there was little point in alienating the man. *Better*, in Dee Dee's assessment of the case, *to cultivate Gruber's assistance, to form an alliance with Gruber through his attorney in hopes of pinning Neil Yost and Continental to the mat.*

A murder—as in a gathering of crows—of legal talent congregated in Judge Smythe's courtroom, one of two courtrooms available in the St. Louis County Courthouse in Hibbing, a modern building that is noteworthy for its bland architecture and a large plaque displaying the Ten Commandments on the wall leading to the courtrooms. Hernesman paused as she climbed the stairs leading to Judge Smythe's courtroom, Kat Carpenter a few steps ahead, to marvel at the religious text.

There's never been one peep from the locals about displaying God's Word in their courthouse, the lawyer thought. *The West Range is indeed its own kind of place.*

The attorneys claimed seats in the spacious courtroom. The judge was not yet on the bench. Hernesman, Carpenter, and Bucher—a short, fairly complected, woman of fifty-five who had no children but who'd been widowed twice, her head topped by stark white hair shorn to her scalp—sat at a table furthest to the right facing the bench. Cicely Thompson, David Van Clive, and Peder Johansson joined the plaintiffs' attorneys at the counsel tables. The defense lawyers were arranged—from right to left as the judge looked at her courtroom—based upon their perceived loyalty to Neil Yost; from Thompson, seated next to plaintiffs' counsel, to Van Clive, to Johansson on the far right.

Bruce Cutler was not with the other lawyers. He sat in the last pew at the back of the courtroom. During the proceedings, Cutler would scribble on a yellow legal pad resting in his ample lap, an expensive Parker pen in hand but, given his ancillary role in the case, Bruce Cutler would remain mute unless called upon by Judge Smythe.

Dee Dee Hernesman and Hugh MacLean had cobbled together a Summons and Complaint, the charging document in civil cases, with assistance from Jill Bucher. Bucher, representing Antonio Feggetti's next of kin—Antonio's parents—had fired the first salvo by serving a Summons and Complaint on Continental Mining of Minnesota, Inc. and Neil Yost a month before Hernesman and Carpenter became co-counsel. Hernesman and MacLean borrowed legal theories from Jill Bucher's Complaint—negligence, strict liability, and absolute liability—and grafted them onto the Complaint naming Continental and Yost as defendants in the Lindahl case. The Lindahl Complaint was served upon Continental and Yost and filed with the clerk of court, commencing a second lawsuit arising out of the explosion.

The first theory of recovery advanced in both cases—negligence—was based upon a simple premise: Yost, as the employee of and agent for Continental, had been careless. The negligence count was based upon the allegation that Yost had failed to exercise due care by concealing the dangers of ANFO from Steve Gruber and that Yost's carelessness caused the deaths of the two welders. The burden of proof at trial under this theory would be simple: Did Neil Yost act as a reasonable person would act in the same or similar circumstances? If the jury found Yost acted unreasonably, the plaintiffs, the trustees in the two cases, would recover damages so long as the damages were caused by Yost's negligence. Negligence is a legal theory that allows both sides an equal playing field: Whichever side tips the scale of justice in its favor wins the day. It is a theory based upon a computation of fault: prove that the defendant is more at fault than the plaintiff, and additionally prove causation and damages, and the plaintiff wins. Absent proof of fault and causation, no matter how horrendous the result, no matter how egregious the loss, no matter how high the jury's damage award, a plaintiff is sent home with empty pockets.

The second cause of action advanced in the Complaints was based upon the doctrine of strict liability, a legal precept that does not require fault. However, strict liability is a theory of limited applicability; its relevance is confined to activities that are inherently dangerous. In the cases involving the explosion at the Merritt Pit site, all that the plaintiffs had to prove was that ANFO residue existed on the site and that the residue caused the deaths of Susie Lindahl and Antonio Feggetti. The plaintiffs would not have to prove fault—only that a condition on the site caused the tragedy and that the defendants knew, or should have known, of the condition. However, the defendants would be able to argue that the workers assumed risks inherent in dismantling the silo. If the jury found that such risks had been explained to Feggetti and Lindahl and that the dead welders assumed such risks, the dead workers, not the defendants, would be held responsible for the accident.

Finally, the plaintiffs had also alleged the unique theory of absolute liability. Hernesman, MacLean, and Bucher argued that the owner of the facility had been engaged in an activity "ultrahazardous" to human life and safety. If Judge Smythe allowed this final theory of liability to proceed, the plaintiffs would be required to establish that there was an ultrahazardous enterprise being conducted on the property owned by Continental and that the explosion and resulting deaths were caused by that enterprise. The defendants would not be able to hide behind the comparative fault of the two dead welders (as would be allowed under a negligence theory) or allege assumption of the risk (as applicable under strict liability) if absolute liability was allowed as a theory of recovery. If the jury found that the defendants were engaged in an ultrahazardous activity, and that Susie and Antonio died as a direct result of that activity, the plaintiffs would prevail.

Harriet Smythe was a sprite of a woman nearing mandatory retirement. Despite her waif-like stature and a countenance reminiscent of a prairie schoolmarm, when Judge Smythe entered the courtroom, echoes of "All Rise, the Honorable Harriet B. Smythe presiding" reverberating off the blond wood walls and acoustic ceiling tiles of her courtroom, the attorneys and the curiosity seekers in the gallery stood and acknowledged Judge Smythe's authority. It was, in Hernesman's estimation, a display of respect that was well deserved.

No fairer jurist in northeastern Minnesota, Hernesman thought as she reclaimed her seat and studied the older woman who was, by circumstance, now in control of legal rulings and decisions that would dictate the course of two lawsuits.

"We're here on the matters of Feggetti versus Continental, et al., and Lindahl versus Continental, et al. Counsel, please note your appearances for the record."

As the lawyers stood and stated their names, their respective law firms, and the identities of the parties they represented, Delphinium Molick, the judge's court reporter, a woman with nearly forty years' courtroom experience, tapped the keys of her stenography machine to create a verbatim record of the proceedings. When the lawyers were finished with their introductions, Judge Smythe noted Bruce Cutler's presence in the back of the courtroom.

"Mr. Cutler, nice to see you," Smythe said evenly. "Are you affiliated with these cases?"

Cutler placed his legal pad on the pew and struggled to his feet. "Yes, your honor, I am. I represent Defendants Continental and Yost through the excess liability insurer, Saturnia Liability. But I am here merely to observe, not to participate. I'll leave any argument from our side of the aisle to Mr. Johansson, who represents the primary insurer and the named defendants."

To Dee Dee Hernesman's eye, Judge Smythe, despite her reputation for innate fairness, seemed, for a brief moment, to disclose favor toward the portly attorney from the Twin Cities.

I'm likely being paranoid, Hernesman thought, *still a bit shell shocked after being steamrolled by Judge Peck into a co-counsel relationship with Miss Beauty Queen here.*

"So," Judge Smythe said, turning her attention to the attorneys at the counsel table, "is there any interest in consolidating these cases for trial, at least in terms of liability?"

Hernesman knew what the judge was hinting at: bifurcation, the splitting apart of fault or liability from the damages to be proven in the two cases. Defense lawyers leap at the suggestion to bifurcate because, until their client is found legally responsible for an accident or occurrence, the jurors in a bifurcated proceeding learn very little about the victims. A bifurcated proceeding, in Hernesman's view, would dehumanize the pageantry of the trial and diminish the contest to an analytical exercise applying law in a vacuum, on a stage absent human feeling and emotion.

Kat Carpenter nudged Dee Dee's elbow.

"No way in hell do we agree to consolidation or bifurcation. We want to tell Brenda Lee's story, the *whole of it*, to the jury and not be tied to what Bucher does or doesn't do," the older attorney hissed.

Dee Dee nodded, ignored the fact that Carpenter centered her argument on the child Carpenter originally represented to the exclusion of Angel Lindahl and Susie's parents, and rose to her feet.

"With all due respect, Your Honor, though it's premature because the defense has not moved to consolidate these cases, we'd oppose such a motion. Both matters involve highly complex facts that are unique to each case, beginning with the exact location of each decedent at the time of the silo's explosion, the work they were undertaking at that crucial moment, and whether or not that particular decedent was acting with due care. There are just too many moving parts for us to consent to consolidation." Hernesman paused before continuing. "We'd also oppose any suggestion that the trial be bifurcated. Telling the story of what happened out at Merritt Pit site on the day of the explosion is the telling of what happened to Susie Lindahl. To isolate fault from damages in this matter would be, in a word, a travesty of justice."

Hernesman returned to her seat and listened to Jill Bucher echo Hernesman's arguments. Van Clive and Thompson took no position on the judge's suggestion. The Silver Wolf predictably sided with Smythe's inclination.

"Good day, Your Honor. Though I have yet to file the motions outlined by the Court, I concur with your observation that the two matters, arising as they do out of a singular incident, should be consolidated, at least for purposes of the liability phase of the proceedings. This process, of course, would require bifurcation, reserving the issue of damages for a second phase of proceedings when and if the plaintiffs have established their right to recover in the fault or liability phase of trial." Peder Johansson paused but did not look down at his iPad, the device he'd been using to take notes, before continuing. "I would also suggest that you join these matters for purposes of discovery deadlines, pretrial, and trial to encourage judicial economy and efficiency."

Johansson reclaimed a hard oak chair behind the counsel table as Hernesman stood to reply.

"There are no motions to consolidate or bifurcate before the Court," Hernesman countered. "I'd request, as I am certain Ms. Bucher will, that the two cases be scheduled independently, starting with the Feggetti matter since it was served and filed first in time."

As Hernesman reclaimed her chair, Jill Bucher rose. "I concur. We'd ask that the Feggetti case be tried first as it was indeed served and filed first in time."

The judge looked out over the courtroom, sucked in her cheeks, blinked her thin, cinnamon eyes, pondered the issues, and nodded.

"Plaintiffs are correct. There are no motions pending. For now, we'll schedule each case independently, beginning with the Feggetti matter. Counsel, when do you think discovery can be completed?"

What followed was a lively discussion of dates and scheduling across multiple calendars, all of which Judge Smythe orchestrated. The Feggetti case would be tried the week after Thanksgiving with the Lindahl matter to begin the following February. Unspoken, by any of the attorneys in attendance or the judge, was the reality that if the Feggetti case went to trial and a verdict favorable to the heirs of Antonio Feggetti was obtained, the jury's decision would likely compel Johansson and Cutler to dig deep into the pocketbooks of the insurers to settle *both* cases. But if the jury in the Feggetti case returned a verdict in favor of the defendants, or awarded only modest damages to the Feggetti family, then the Lindahl case would be approached by everyone, including the judge, in a vastly different light. A Hibbing jury in the Feggetti case would have assessed the value of human life and that assessment, as unfair as it might appear, would impact the next of kin of Susie Lindahl.

CHAPTER TWENTY

Deb Slater sat in a cramped office in the Ely post office building on South 2nd Avenue and Chapman, which served as the command center for the Copper/Nickel Task Force. The sheriff was considering evidence assembled through the efforts of the ATF, the FBI, St. Louis County Arson Investigator Harlis Briggs, the Task Force, the Ely Police Department, and the Minnesota BCA. It was late February. The criminal investigation had stalled. The questioning of Cyrus Oliphant had hit a dead end. There was nothing, other than suspicion and supposition, linking the eco-terrorist to the explosion at the Merritt Pit site. Given that the man was off federal parole, Oliphant's post-prison supervisory period having expired before two bags of purloined ammonium nitrate were found in his possession, and given that his alibi—that he was working at the resort at the time of the explosion—had been verified with the resort's owners, Slater had concluded that, while the man harbored bad intentions, he'd done nothing illegal. Oliphant was, given the status of the evidence, no longer a person of interest.

"I'm missing something," Slater mused as she read and re-read reports, statements, and eyewitness accounts and as she studied photographs, maps, diagrams, and blueprints of the ANFO silo obtained over the course of her four-month inquiry. "What am I not seeing?" Fingers turned pages. A familiar name caused Deb Slater to pause.

> *Duane Baxter. The Ely cop I spoke to at the scene. He said something, something about a firefighter, Manchester? Mannerheim? A guy from Ely who had a conversation with Neil Yost at the scene. Did Baxter follow up? Did he take a statement from the firefighter?*

The sheriff scrutinized the paperwork.

> *Ah. Not Mannerheim. Mancuso. Timothy Mancuso. Here it is.*

The sheriff studied the narrative Baxter had prepared from an interview with the firefighter. The cop's report made Slater straighten up in the padded office chair behind the institutional gray, government surplus desk she'd been allocated by the St. Louis County Sheriff as a workstation. Slater's eyes diverted to a nearby window. She took in the empty scene outside her office. It was thirty below zero and no one was out and about in Ely. The protestors who'd once gathered in numbers in support of—or in opposition to—the Merritt Pit Mine were gone, dispersed by tragedy and inhospitable cold.

Had a hell of a time getting the Yukon to turn over this morning. I let it idle a good ten minutes. Damn tires were nearly frozen to the blacktop. Cold as hell inside the Super 8 too! But what do you expect? You're on the state's dime. It'll all be over soon—my work with the task force. My career. Retirement sounds good. I'll have more time to spend with Annie. Poor, pregnant, confused Annie. Still hanging on at Cornell. Volleyball coach says she sees no reason why Annie can't medically red shirt and come back as the starting setter. Baby will have to spend time in the college's daycare. Lots of time in college daycare! Due date is September 1ˢᵗ. I never put it together! New Year's. Annie got knocked up on New Year's! Likely drunk—unprepared and unprotected. What's that line from It's a Wonderful Life, *where Annie, the Bailey housekeeper urges George and Harry to exercise caution? "Boys and girls and music. Why do they need gin?" That's it. That's the line. Annie the maid had it right about Annie my daughter. Likely fell into bed with that basketball player, Thomas Jones, after too many vodka and grapefruit juices.*

The sheriff paused to consider webs of frost spreading across window glass.

Not that I was perfect when I was Annie's age. No, not at all. But that was another life, another time, before middle age, before gravity had its way with me.

Deb Slater touched the edges of her jaw, her face rounded from weight she'd gained since entering menopause, more weight added to her hips and thighs and stomach and bottom as she lamented Rick's demise. *Food is no substitute for love. Tough to blame the kid. Desire. I know what that's like. I had plenty of hormonal urges in my day. Plenty. Mostly, though not exclusively, for Rick, the one man I truly loved. Love. Present sense. I still love him.*

A tear descended Deb Slater's downy cheek. She made no attempt to wipe away the moisture as she thought about other boys and men that had piqued her interest over the course of her life. *Never acted on such impulses once Rick and I were together. But I understand how it could happen, how Annie could make a snap decision to lay down with someone like Thomas. I'm not happy about it—not in the least. But I understand.*

Slater reached across the borrowed desk, retrieved a Kleenex, and dabbed the corner of her right eye with the tissue.

She said it wasn't love, said they weren't in a relationship when I asked, "What comes next?" "Just a mistake," she said. Really? "One hell of a mistake" is what I wanted to say. But I didn't. Wouldn't change what happened. What irks me is that I preached protection from the time Annie had her first period at age eleven. She was pretty smart about such things until she went off to Cornell. Now, she'll need to adapt. Not just to a new baby and the changes an infant brings but to negotiating Thomas's family, his culture. There's little I know, or Annie knows, about African Americans. Well, that's not true. She knows <u>something</u> about one African American basketball player, that's for sure! But beyond that personal connection, we're both clueless. We'll need to work hard to understand. Thomas says he wants a relationship with the child. That's good. I wondered about an abortion, but that's not Annie's style. It's not about religion. It's about personal integrity. She just wouldn't go there. If she had, she would've made <u>that</u> decision before telling me she was pregnant. Would've gone that route if she wanted privacy, to avoid "the" conversation with me. Didn't choose that option. I'm happy— despite what she'll face up the road—she didn't go down that path. Her choice. Her right. But I'm happy she's keeping the baby.

Deb watched through a single-pane window as a woman rushed across the street with an infant wrapped snuggly in a blanket, the baby clutched to the mother's mustard yellow wool coat, wind whipping the woman's hatless brown hair into a snarl and swirling vagrant snow into cyclones around the woman's boots. The sheriff averted her gaze and refocused her attention on her newly acquired status.

"Widow." How I hate that label. It sounds so sad and pathetic and needy. But there it is. It's what others say I am. I feel the loss—the emptiness in my bed and in my life—routinely

assigned to women burdened by that label. I can't deny the reality of unanticipated singleness. But God how I hate the term "widow." The Widow's Club: It's not a club I ever thought I'd join. Damn it, Rick. Why did you have to go and get sick?

Slater placed the wet tissue on the desk next to the paperwork. Her eyes closed as she fought despair and returned her focus to Annie's predicament.

Rick would have lamented Annie's mistake. And then, true to his nature, he would've embraced the situation. Rick would've made the perfect grandfather. Wouldn't matter if the baby were a girl or a boy. Rick would've adapted, as his daughter and his widow (there's that word again!) will have to. But the transition for Rick, even with the added factor of the child being of mixed race, would've been seamless. No glitches. Can't say the same for me. Not that Thomas Jones's ethnicity is an issue. Hell no. My closest friend in law enforcement, Herb Whitefeather, long retired to Florida with his pretty wife and his Chris Craft sedan cruiser, is full-blooded Lakota. We got along famously. Interesting word choice: "famously." Shit, I better stop ruminating and get back to work.

Sheriff Slater refocused her attention on Duane Baxter's report.

To: Lindahl/Feggetti Investigative File
From: D. Baxter
ICR: 111214EPD23
Date: 11/12/2014
Re: Interview with T. Mancuso

I, D. Baxter, met this date with Timothy Mancuso (218-555-1346) at the Merritt Pit site where two individuals employed by Hibbing Salvage (Owner: Steven Gruber) were killed in an industrial accident. (See reports of D. Slater and others for details.) Mancuso responded to the location as a firefighter with the Ely Fire Department and was posted by Assistant Chief Fred Michels at the mine's front gate to discourage sightseers. One of the first individuals inside the mine's perimeter after Mancuso was deployed was Neil Yost (218-555-4433), safety manager for the mine's owner, Continental Mining. Mancuso indicated during our interview that he had a brief interaction with Yost, the gist of which was that Yost was upset and that Yost said "Not again, not again," and "I can't believe this happened again" more than once. I asked Mancuso if he questioned Yost as to what Yost meant by those statements but Mancuso indicated that, due to Yost's demeanor, he (Mancuso) did not pursue the issue.

When I located Yost on premises, he was inspecting a demolished Dodge Dakota pickup (titled in the name of victim S. Lindahl) approx. 150 feet from the crater deemed by SLC Arson Investigator Briggs to be the epicenter of the blast. When asked about statements made to Mancuso, Yost didn't respond. Given Yost's upset, I didn't pursue the matter further that day. Subsequent attempts to interview Yost about his statements have been refused by his lawyers.

D.A.B.

"Why haven't we followed up on this?" Deb Slater asked in a whisper. "What the hell was Yost trying to tell Mancuso? That he'd been involved in a similar incident in the past? That he'd been responsible for another fatal accident?"

The sheriff glanced out the window. The woman and the baby were gone. The Ely streets were silent, cold, and empty as Sheriff Deb Slater returned to the stack of documents on her desk.

CHAPTER TWENTY-ONE

"What is this friggin' case gonna set us back?"

It was the second week in March. Dee Dee Hernesman and her partners, Skip Mattila and Julie Somerfeldt, were cloistered in their conference room, black binders of pleadings, discovery documents, photographs, diagrams, and expert reports stacked in front of Hernesman like the Great Wall of China, an unconscious attempt by Dee Dee to protect herself from the barrage of questions launched her way by her partners.

"Skip has a valid point, Dees," said Somerfeldt, a tall, thin, bookish-looking woman with alabaster skin and artificially black hair, her forty-something face pulled tight by surgical magic. Julie's twenty-year-old marriage to Bob Somerfeldt, a local wilderness guide and outfitter, was on the rocks due to Julie having discovered Bob in the Somerfeldt marital bed with his Levi 501s and his red boxers clumped around his ankles, his face buried between the youthful thighs of son David's sixth grade teacher, Miss Hannity. "We're putting nearly all of our operating funds into this case," Somerfeldt observed. Julie Somerfeldt was the firm's transactional, estate planning, and real estate attorney. She generally left the drama of litigation to her partners, though, for a time after her husband's indiscretion, Julie's usually calm demeanor had boiled over, and she'd been more disagreeable than a leg-trapped she-wolf. But with time the woman's upset had waned and her rancor had lessened until she was left only vaguely sad and occasionally quarrelsome.

Hernesman detected a new aspect of flightiness in Somerfeldt's persona: A fidgety nature that Dee Dee had not seen in Julie before Bob was sent packing, reduced to couch surfing with friends while Julie considered a course of action. Three kids under the age of thirteen made leaving the guy dicey, though Julie had made it clear to Hernesman and Mattila that leaving Bob was an option she was contemplating. Dee Dee swept Somerfeldt's private turmoil out of her mind, looked over the protective barrier of paperwork, and tried to maintain a calm, even manner as she explained the status of the Lindahl case. "We're halfway through putting it together. I've received a final report from Oliver Neilsson, the expert we hired to look into industrial safety. He's on board with Yost and Gruber being at fault, but he places the lion's share of blame on Yost. We walked the site last month and Neilsson took measurements and photographs to support his opinions."

"I'm a little confused," Mattila said, the heavy jowls of the thick-limbed criminal defense lawyer at odds with his high-pitched voice.

"Yes?"

"Where the hell is the Task Force on this thing? I mean, two kids were blown to bits through no fault of their own. I get that there are *civil* wrongful death actions here. But what about *criminal* repercussions? Shouldn't the county attorney be considering bringing charges against the yahoos who killed Lindahl and Feggetti?"

Hernesman nodded.

"Agreed. But so far, the best that can be said is that both Continental Mining and Hibbing Salvage were cited for OSHA infractions and paid fines for violating safety standards."

Somerfeldt sat down across from Hernesman. She was tall enough to peer over the wall of binders. "I've never been a prosecutor or a criminal defense lawyer, but what happened sure seems like murder."

"Hit the nail right on the head," Skip Mattila agreed as he claimed a chair. "But let's get back to the money issue. How much, Dees? How much more is this case gonna cost us?"

Hernesman looked at her hands. "Best guess, with M&Q and Bucher contributing equal shares, is sixty to seventy thousand. Each. We still have to pay Dr. Thor Erickson, the ANFO expert from the South Dakota School of Mines. He's submitted a preliminary report, based upon soil samples and testing done by Dr. Stephens, the defense expert from Michigan Tech. But Erickson has a lot left to do to tie up loose ends and refute the alternative theories that Peder Johansson and his minions are arguing in the case. Some of the theories are serious, such as the hypothesis that the silo was empty of ANFO—based upon the depositions we took of Gruber and Yost—and that the ground was so saturated with ANFO that it was the ground, not the silo, that blew."

Mattila looked skeptical. "Really? The ground blew up? That's the defense?"

"Let her finish," Somerfeldt urged.

"I know," Dee Dee added. "Doesn't make much sense but Erickson doesn't discount it quite so cavalierly. He's not on board with it, is convinced that residual ANFO, perhaps up to 800 pounds of the stuff, was trapped in the cone of the silo, and that's what blew when a torch finally came in contact with the residue. Remember, the access doors at the bottom of the tower were rusted shut, which means that neither Yost nor Gruber can establish with certainty that the bottom cone was free of ANFO. Plus, there's the chunk of ANFO Feggetti removed from the silo the day before the explosion. That chunk confirms the silo wasn't empty." Hernesman sipped warm coffee from a mug bearing the logo of a local eatery, The Chocolate Moose, before gathering her thoughts. "But the 'ground did it' proposition isn't the most ridiculous theory being advanced by the defense."

"What's that? I'm all ears after the 'we didn't do it, the ground did' fairy tale."

Hernesman smiled at Mattila. "The very learned and credentialed Dr. Stephens has postulated the idea that either Susie Lindahl, or Antonio Feggetti, or both, with or without the knowledge and/or permission of their boss, Steven Gruber, tried to cut corners.

"How so?" Somerfeldt's query was tinged with curiosity.

Dee Dee Hernesman paused and took another sip of coffee.

"Come on, Dees, spill the beans," Skip urged, interest palpable in his voice. "What crock of shit is the guy from Houghton, the asshole of Michigan, going to try to sell eight smart men and women on a Hibbing jury?"

"Dr. Stephens seems determined to say, unless Judge Smythe can be convinced to block such testimony as lacking in foundation, that either Susie Lindahl or Antonio Feggetti or both, brought additional nitrate onto the work site the day they were killed. His theory is that one or both of them tried to speed up the dismantling of the silo by blowing it up."

There was absolute silence in the conference room as Hernesman's partners considered the outlandish, unkind, and untoward alternative reality being postulated by the defense. A wall clock ticked loudly. The attorneys sat in silence, each considering the preposterous nature of the allegation, how it cut to the core of who the two dead workers were: diligent, careful, loyal blue color folks who had nary a blemish on their respective work records.

"Really?" Somerfeldt asked.

Dee Dee folded her hands and nodded. "God's honest truth. Stephens claims he discovered prills, with a chemical makeup different from the microscopic footprint of the ANFO stored in the silo, left behind in the blast crater."

"You believe him?" Mattila asked.

"God no. It's pure bullshit. But he's an expert and we need to parade our own expert in front of the jury to refute his fairy tale."

Skip Mattila stood up and slammed his right fist on the table. "Fuck Johansson. Fuck Cutler. Fuck Stephens. Spend whatever you have to, Dees. Bury the assholes. Their clients killed two innocent kids, and now they want to tarnish the victims' reputations? Bullshit. I'll put up my house, like the guys in *A Civil Action* did, if that's what it takes to finance this case."

"We're not there yet, Skip, though I appreciate the offer," Hernesman said through a tenuous smile. "But I do hope this case turns out a hell of a lot better than Jan Schlichtmann's crusade. I'm not interested in starting over as an ambulance chaser in the Twin Cities. I'm an Iron Range girl. I love the Range, love you guys too much, to have to declare bankruptcy, leave Ely, and start over in some Bloomington strip mall."

Julie Somerfeldt smirked as she stood up from the table. "Just don't spend everything in the checking account, Dees. I may need a little cash to hire a PI and find out who else that no-good-son-of-a-bitch husband of mine has been screwing while I've been raising three kids and working my ass off."

"Jules," Mattila said incredulously, "such language. I didn't think you knew how to curse!"

Julie Somerfeldt didn't crack a smile as she ignored Mattila's jibe. "Dees, I'm all in with you and Skip on the Lindahl case. Just don't make me a pauper."

Skip Mattila and Julie Somerfeldt left the conference room. Once the door was closed, Dee Dee Hernesman reached into her purse and retrieved her Samsung Galaxy.

Time to call Hoot Holt and see what he's learned about the ghosts in Neil Yost's past.

CHAPTER TWENTY-TWO

Thor Erickson, doctor of chemistry and chemical engineering and the Department Chair of Chemical and Biological Engineering at the South Dakota School of Mines, stood on the tarmac of the Duluth International Airport, a balmy spring wind tousling his hair, his flimsy overcoat flapping in the breeze, as he waited to walk from a commuter jet, the emblem of a regional affiliate of Delta affixed to the Bombardier's tail. The professor was one of seven passengers on the airplane who had flown from Rapid City to Duluth by way of Minneapolis. The jetway was on the fritz, forcing Dr. Erickson and other passengers to cluster on the asphalt and wait for the "all clear" sign that would allow them to move toward the warmth of the new terminal. A hand rose. The group surged forward. Inside the building, Dee Dee Hernesman and Hugh MacLean waited for their expert witness, a span of synthetic fabric separating spectators from arriving passengers.

"Dr. Erickson," Hernesman shouted as she recognized the tall, angular, and distinguished-looking Norwegian immigrant, his sandy blond-turning-to-white hair covered with an alpine fedora complete with blue feather. "Over here!"

The professor ambled his way through the gate carrying a heavy black briefcase in his ungloved left hand. Hernesman removed the black leather glove from her right hand and extended it to the older man.

"Dee Dee Hernesman. Nice to meet you, sir. Good of you to come on such short notice," the lawyer said with enthusiasm as they shook hands. "This is Hugh MacLean, another lawyer who'll be working with us."

Erickson nodded and extended his right hand.

"A pleasure to meet you, sir," MacLean said, repeating the professor's gesture with exaggerated emphasis. "Ms. Hernesman filled me in on your qualifications."

"Likely gave me too much credit, I'd imagine," the old man replied. "Lawyers always seem to give me too much credit. I'm just a chemist who also knows something about explosives."

The group moved toward the baggage queue and waited for Erickson's luggage.

"It's a two-hour drive to Ely," Hernesman said in an off-the-cuff manner. "I thought we'd get you settled in at the Grand Ely Lodge, order a bite to eat, and talk about tomorrow's visit to the mine."

Erickson nodded, reached toward a small valise moving on the turnstile in front of them, and lifted the suitcase free of the conveyor. "That's all I have," the professor said quietly. "I tend to travel light."

• • •

"What the hell?"

Dee Dee Hernesman stood ankle deep in mud and surveyed a scene that had been vastly altered since her last visit to the epicenter of the fatal explosion with Oliver Neilsson, former safety director for Anaconda Copper's Montana mining operations and the plaintiff's expert witness regarding industrial safety. When Hernesman, MacLean, and Neilsson had inspected the Merritt Pit site a month prior to Dr. Erickson's arrival, accompanied by Bruce Cutler, Peder Johansson, Dr. Stephens, Neil Yost, a gaggle of legal assistants and investigators, Jill Bucher, Steven Gruber, and Gruber's and Calumet's attorneys, the scene of the disaster, including the charred ruins of Susie Lindahl's Dakota, the blast crater, the punctured acetylene and oxygen tanks, the ruptured hoses, the debris field, and the scale pit were all in the same condition they had been immediately after the accident. But on the day of Erickson's visit, that evidence no longer existed.

Peder Johansson moved over the mucky residue of winter and stood next to Hernesman. "I had nothing to do with this," Johansson said, the Silver Wolf's eyes locking on Bruce Cutler. Cutler, his custom-tailored coat buttoned snugly over his ample girth, didn't respond immediately to Johansson's scrutiny.

The fat man's face flushed slightly before regaining its natural skin tone. "I authorized it," Cutler finally said with feigned confidence. "Plaintiffs had completed their court-ordered inspection with Mr. Neilsson. Continental is on a timetable. The permitting process is nearly complete. My client needs to operate a copper/nickel mine—not maintain a museum."

Dee Dee stared at the newly leveled terrain, all evidence of the crater, the explosion, and the tragedy wiped clean by bulldozers. Hernesman angrily confronted the Silver Wolf. "You knew we weren't done with our analysis, Peder. I sent you an email requesting that nothing happen out here until Dr. Erickson inspected the site."

Bruce Cutler wedged his ample body between Hernesman and Johansson. "I received no such email. And even if I had, you have no authority, short of an order from Judge Smythe, to preclude my client from operating its business."

"Cutler. A word," Peder Johansson said, motioning with his right index finger. The rotund attorney followed the taller man out of earshot.

Hernesman turned to Jill Bucher and Hugh MacLean. "I can't believe it!"

MacLean's ruddy face frowned. "They've really screwed the pooch."

Bucher nodded. "Judge Smythe isn't gonna like this. I think we've got the perfect scenario for an adverse inference instruction."

"Spoliation," Hernesman whispered, referencing a sanction that, if granted by the trial judge, would allow the jury to draw negative inferences against the defendants due to Continental's obliteration of evidence.

"Exactly."

Dr. Erickson looked at the landscape, the flat, altered plain of the old mine site barren of any clues of evidentiary value. "What do we do now, Ms. Hernesman?"

Dee Dee's eyes fixed on a Nikon digital camera hanging from the Norwegian's neck by a lanyard. "Take a boatload of pictures, Doc. We need to document what Continental did here."

Erickson nodded and began shooting the scene. In the near distance, the sounds of an animated discussion between Peder Johansson and Bruce Cutler disturbed an otherwise quiet morning on the south shore of Birch Lake.

CHAPTER TWENTY-THREE

Deb Slater sat at a table in Tommy's Bar. She was alone, whisky and sour in a half-empty glass sitting on the weary pine top of a round table, an empty chair across from her, as she listened to live music. Amy Maddox, a slightly busted, pony-tailed, diminutive woman a few years older than the sheriff, sat on a stool on a makeshift stage finger picking a battered Martin twelve string. Gabriella Pierce, raven haired, brownly hued, tall, lithe, and years younger than Maddox, stood in front of a microphone singing the last strains of a song Slater recognized to be Maddox's one and only certified hit. A LaPlant mandolin hung by a leather strap from Pierce's left shoulder. Gabriella Pierce appeared to be Indian or Pakistani, though, having never met the woman, Slater couldn't pinpoint the roots of the young singer's exoticism. Pierce's bronze skin gleamed beneath diminished lighting as she sang the last verse and chorus of the song.

They hanged him good
from that trembling tree
they left him dead
part of a mystery.

His name was Olli Kinkkonen
a Finn wouldn't dance
a man who wanted to go home
but never got the chance.
His name was Olli Kinkkonen . . .

The crowd was packed tightly around the stage. Illuminated signs backlit the performers and announced the tavern's restrooms. Patrons whistled and cheered as the music ended.

"We'll take a short break and be back with another set," Amy Maddox said, her voice barely audible over the din. "We'll play requests," she continued, her fawn-colored eyes dancing as she grinned, "but only if we know them."

The women placed their instruments in metal stands, stepped off the stage, and waded through the crowd.

"Amy!" Slater yelled, thrusting a hand into the room's muggy air.

The musician changed course. "Small world," Amy Maddox said through a wide smile as she arrived at Slater's table. "You're a long ways from Grand Marais, Sheriff." The musician nodded to an empty seat at an adjacent table and addressed a couple engaged in deep conversation. "That seat taken?"

"It's yours," a thirty-something, bear of a man dressed in rumpled work clothes and mud-caked leather work boots replied. "I enjoyed your set," he added lifting a brimming glass of beer toward Maddox. An extremely drunk woman sitting next to the man also raised her glass, sloshing red wine on her companion in the process.

Maddox nodded. "Thanks," she replied, pulling the chair to Slater's table, and motioning for her partner to take a seat. "Gabriella Pierce, meet the Sheriff of Cook County, Debra Slater."

The women shook hands. Pierce sat lightly on black vinyl. Sherri LaPointe emerged from the crowd.

"What'll you girls have?"

"The usual," Maddox said quietly.

"Two Sprites with lemon it is." LaPointe turned to Slater. "Refill, Sheriff?"

"No thanks. Two's the limit. I'll take one of those Sprite and lemon concoctions."

The bartender-turned-waitress smiled widely, exposing tobacco-affected teeth. "Three Maddox Specials coming up," LaPointe said as she retreated to the bar.

"So how are things on the Copper/Nickel Task Force?"

Amy Maddox knew, as most of Slater's constituents did, that the sheriff had been asked to serve as the head of the special law enforcement unit. The voters of Cook County knew about Slater's role with the task force because the Cook County Board of Commissioners had approved the sheriff's assignment to that unit.

"The investigation into the explosion is essentially over," Slater said, "and the protests have died down. Things are pretty damn quiet."

Gabriella Pierce studied the older woman across the table. "Horrible the way those kids died."

Slater nodded but given that St. Louis County Attorney Justin Pappas was still considering whether to level criminal charges against Continental, Neil Yost, Hibbing Salvage, and Steve Gruber, the sheriff didn't respond.

"I guess you can't really talk about it," Amy observed, moving her arms off the table top as LaPointe placed three glasses of Sprite, lemon wedges riding on the edges of the tumblers, in front of the women. "There are probably civil lawsuits involved. A multinational company, an accident, and two dead kids adds up to a seven-figure payday for some lucky lawyer."

Slater smiled weakly and changed the topic. "So how are Bill and the twins faring while you're out trying to become the next Shawn Colvin?"

Maddox sipped soda and thought a moment before answering. "Bill's great. Retirement suits him. But at thirteen, the girls are a handful."

Slater laughed. "Don't I know it! Annie went through that phase when Rick was really, really sick. It was tough enough dealing with his illness, much less the hormonal surges of a teenager!"

"Sorry I missed Rick's funeral," the singer said softly. "We were in Austin doing a workshop."

"The donation you made to the library in Rick's memory was too kind," Deb replied, fighting emotion. "Rick loved borrowing his murder mysteries instead of buying them . . ."

A squarely built, thick-hipped woman in fitted black Levis, black leather hiking boots, and a black cardigan pushed her way through the crowd and stood next to the women's table.

"Sheriff?"

The woman's eyes, vaguely hazel and bearing no malice, fixed on Slater.

"Yes?"

"We've got something in common. The explosion case." The woman extended a thick hand, the nails expertly trimmed

113

and painted silver, the color closely matching her eyes. "Dee Dee Hernesman."

"Ah."

Hernesman's gaze diverted. Her attention was drawn to the young woman seated across from the sheriff.

Gorgeous.

There was no way, in that instant glance, that Hernesman could ascertain the woman's orientation. And yet, there was something, some remote clue that told her, that announced Gabriella Pierce was attracted to other women. After a moment of subtle consideration, Hernesman redirected her attention.

"I'm not here to talk shop. I'll leave you folks to your privacy. I just thought," Dee Dee said, continuing to offer her hand to the sheriff, "that I should introduce myself, leave my card, and extend an invitation to compare notes on the case whenever you have time."

Slater accepted Hernesman's hand and shook it in a wary, perfunctory way.

"Here's my card. Anytime, Sheriff—call me anytime. I'd love to sit down and go over information uncovered by our investigator, Andrew Holt. Might pique your interest, send the criminal investigation in another direction."

"Another direction?"

Dee Dee Hernesman didn't respond. Her focus had returned to the lanky young woman. Gabriella Pierce sipped Sprite, her eyes seemingly open to suggestion, yet distant in the same glance. She cocked her head and studied Hernesman's wide face. A Cheshire grin spread across the musician's cheeks.

"Gabriella," she said evenly. "Gabriella Pierce."

Hernesman was caught off guard and remained mute.

Amy Maddox smiled.

"Counselor, I think my partner is trying to tell you something."

"And I'm trying to understand what it is you're telling *me* . . ." Debra Slater added with insistence.

"Ah. Sorry," Hernesman said. "As I was saying, our investigator . . ."

"Hoot Holt. Know him. Used to work with him. We were both deputies in St. Louis County back in the stone age."

114

"Yes. Hoot," Dee Dee stammered, her eyes unable to keep from scrutinizing Gabriella Pierce's face. "He's dug up some dirt on Continental's boy, Neil Yost. Followed up a lead he found on the Internet. Looks like Yost was involved in something similar back in Montana. Anyway, like I said, this isn't the time or the place. Call me. We can talk over a cup of coffee."

Slater eyes widened. "You've aroused my interest, Counselor. Expect a call in the next day or so."

Hernesman pulled a pen out of her purse, scrawled her cell phone number across another business card, handed the card to Gabriella, and retreated into the crowd.

"She's like what, twice your age?" Amy Maddox asked. "You are so friggin' shameless."

Gabriella's eyes batted. "I like her smile. Her dimpled cheeks. And the fact that, even though she's obviously been around, she's vulnerable, unsure. Plus I'll take smart and experienced over drop-dead gorgeous. Any day. Any time."

Slater tilted her head and studied the young singer.

"I agree with Amy. She seems a bit old for you, Gabriella. And not all that good looking."

Gabriella Pierce guffawed so hard that Sprite erupted from her nose.

"Damn it, Sheriff, that shit burns!"

"Sorry. Wasn't trying to be funny."

"But you are. Hilarious, that is. A straight woman giving a gay woman dating advice? That's rich! Thing is, I've been with a few women since coming out. I was eighteen, just starting UMD when it dawned on me. I figured out what had been perplexing my relationships. I figured out that I liked men well enough as friends but that I had no physical reciprocity for the male gender. Hit me all of a sudden. Not a gradual unveiling," Gabriella said quietly, humor dissipated by her recollection of the moment of realization that had changed her life. "Caught my whole family unawares when I made the announcement at my college graduation. Some—like my little sister Katie—had already figured it out. But Mom and Dad were shocked. Same sex attraction is frowned upon in Mom's culture. Dad, being English and all, well, it didn't hit him the same way. I didn't mean for it to come out just then but it did. I think, in hindsight, it had to. I'd held it too close for too long."

"Time to get back to work," Amy Maddox said, pointing to the stage. "Confession time is over."

"Just about done educating the sheriff on the nuances of being a lesbian woman in modern America," Gabriella said with a wink. "Anyways, I like that lawyer lady. You're right: she's a bit old for me and a bit of a Plain Jane. But after all," the singer returned to playing the coquette, switching her voice to a soft, feminine purr that bore just a hint of her mother's Mumbai upbringing, "older women are infinitely more interesting, aren't they, Sheriff Slater?"

Maddox pulled Pierce out of her chair by an arm. "Stop flirting with the sheriff. It's time to earn your keep," Maddox grumbled good-naturedly.

"Nice to meet you, Deb. Ms. Maddox says it's time to go to work."

"Sing well, Gabriella," Slater said, through a grin. "Sing well."

Outside Tommy's, vaporous fingers of green and blue danced across the black vault of the night sky. Sheriff Deb Slater stood on the sidewalk watching solar flares waltz as she contemplated love. Impossible, forbidden, difficult, trying, treacherously simple, bar-the-doors romantic love between two people. There had been a time when Slater had compromised her political views and Christian values by accepting civil unions between same-sex couples. That same value set had fueled an objection to same-sex marriage. But as she nurtured friendships with gay men and gay women, Slater's rigidity softened. She'd come to accept marriage as a natural extension of the love folks in committed partnerships feel for each other regardless of orientation.

Love, the sheriff thought as she studied the sky, *is love. You can't control it, can't contain it. It just is.*

As quickly as the aurora appeared over Shagawa, it was gone. Deb Slater shoved bare hands into the pockets of her wool coat and moved east on Central toward the dismal confines of her home away from home. As she walked, the sheriff considered the love that might be possible between two women of disparate ages, the love experienced by a fair-skinned college volleyball player and an African American point guard, and the love that remains after a partner is taken bit by agonizing bit by an illness that no loving God could countenance.

CHAPTER TWENTY-FOUR

Katherine Carpenter stood in Judge Harriet Smythe's courtroom. The lawyer's blond hair was razor cut in a style that was all the rage in Minneapolis. She was dressed in a five-hundred-dollar suit—the jacket and pleated skirt impeccably pressed. Her white blouse was open to the second button and displayed a hint of cleavage. A string of luminescent natural pearls highlighted Kat's swan-like neck as she considered a notepad containing the outline of her argument.

"Your Honor. The motion before you is a motion to compel Defendants Continental and Yost to produce any and all records in their possession regarding Mr. Yost's employment, to include his job application and references: in sum, anything and everything that Continental may have been privy to before hiring Mr. Yost."

"How are those documents relevant?"

The judge didn't look up from the computer screen crowding the top of her bench as she asked the question. Judge Smythe was one of four judges in the 6th Judicial District, the district encompassing St. Louis, Carlton, Cook, and Lake Counties in northeastern Minnesota, whose courtroom and hearings had gone "paperless." Despite being the most senior judge in the district, Harriet Smythe was computer literate and, as the judicial system moved toward electronic filing, Smythe was ahead of the curve.

Dee Dee Hernesman sat next to Kat, content to listen to the tall, poised woman argue the motion. Up to that point in time, Kat Carpenter had relied upon Hugh McLean to keep tabs on M&Q's financial investment in the lawsuit. When Dee Dee proposed, based upon Hoot Holt's investigation of Yost's history in the mining industry and his retrieval of shocking bits and pieces concerning Yost's past from the Internet, that there was more to Neil Yost's background than met the eye, Hugh McLean had taken the suggestion of a motion to compel back to his boss. The idea of putting the defense on the defensive brought a smile to Kat Carpenter's inscrutable face. Kat initiated a telephone call to her co-counsel and convinced Dee Dee that Carpenter, not Hernesman, should make the pitch. But, as had been the norm since the lawsuit began, Dee Dee Hernesman was the workhorse: She prepared the legal brief supporting Kat Carpenter's argument. Kat's only contribution was her stylish manner and staidly clear diction—attributes that Dee Dee had to admit, as she watched and listened to Carpenter—were perfectly suited to the task at hand.

"Judge: Remember that discovery is not limited to what is relevant. The rules of procedure allow us to delve into matters that *may lead to the discovery of relevant, admissible evidence.* This isn't, as Mr. Johansson has argued in his paperwork, a case where the plaintiffs are on a fishing expedition, attempting to harass the defendants with discovery requests that cannot lead to useable evidence. The affidavit of Mr. Holt, a decorated deputy, honorably retired from the St. Louis County Sheriff's Office, makes it clear that there is something in Mr. Yost's past that needs exploring and that it is likely Continental either has documentation of that situation or failed to investigate it. Either way, the information is relevant. If Mr. Yost was involved in another incident where co-workers were injured due to his mishandling of explosives and that information was not provided to Continental by Mr. Yost, or Continental simply declined to investigate the man's past—then there may well be a claim here for negligent hiring based upon a failure to inquire." Kat took a deep breath and scanned notes on the yellow legal pad in front of her. "If, on the other hand, Continental did its due diligence and determined that something untoward had happened during Mr. Yost's employment with another mining concern, something akin to what we're claiming here, but decided to hire Mr. Yost despite his past, those facts may support a claim of negligent hiring. But we can't determine whether either contention is valid if Continental and Mr. Yost refuse to divulge pertinent information. There's no legal basis for objecting to the production of the documents we are seeking and without the documents, we have been unable to complete the deposition of Mr. Yost. We need his entire employment file so that when we re-convene his deposition, we can inquire as to what Continental knew, or should have known, before it hired Mr. Yost. If it's not relevant, that will become obvious after disclosure. But if there is, as we strongly suspect, a grain of truth to the rumors and the Internet article uncovered by Mr. Holt, well then: This case takes on an entirely new complexion in terms of Continental's legal responsibility."

Kat Carpenter paused, reconsidered her notes, and nodded. "I'd welcome any questions you might have in this regard," the attorney said, before adding "Your Honor," hastily, as if an afterthought.

"No, I think I understand plaintiffs' position. Mr. Johansson?"

"With all due respect, Judge, a fishing expedition based upon alcohol-induced rumor, or fostered by innuendo posted on the World Wide Web, is all that is being presented to you for your consideration," the Silver Wolf argued as he rose to his feet in reply. "The plaintiffs have absolutely no foundation, no facts, no documents, no basis upon which to pursue a claim of negligent hiring against Continental Mining. The best that can be said is plaintiffs *wish* there was some basis that such a claim could be brought. But even then, there remains the issue of causation. Even if there is some grain of truth to Mr. Holt's supposition that something in Defendant Yost's past mirrors the plaintiffs' claims in this case, our expert, Dr. Stephens, has postulated that it was the negligence of the *decedents*, Ms. Lindahl and Mr. Feggetti, who we allege attempted to ease their task by intentionally detonating explosives *they* brought to the work site, or, alternatively, that it was the completely unforeseen detonation of the ground, saturated as it was with ANFO—a hidden condition of the premises that no one involved in this tragedy could possibly have anticipated—that caused the explosion. In either scenario, there is nothing to be gained by investigating Mr. Yost's employment history. It is, simply put, a red herring."

"I see that, in addition to refusing to answer questions at his deposition, questions linked to his past employment, Mr. Yost has not signed authorizations to retrieve his employment records at Continental and at his prior employer, Carson Mining. What harm is there in having Mr. Yost sign the authorizations, allow plaintiffs to review those records, and then proceed with arguments as to whether or not plaintiffs have a right to amend their complaint and assert a claim for negligent hiring?" the judge asked. "Especially based upon the article that Deputy Holt retrieved from the Internet."

The snippet that Hoot discovered isn't much, Dee Dee Hernesman thought, *but it's salacious enough to gain the judge's attention.* Hernesman found herself opening a manila folder to a 2003 article from *The Montana Standard.* Hoot Holt had copied and printed the piece from the Internet and provided it to the plaintiffs' attorneys. *Not much detail in here about Yost's part regarding what happened in Montana. But I think Harriet gets it. The defendants are stonewalling with respect to Yost's past. There must be something about the 2003 incident that's damning, worth concealing. She won't let that happen, not in a case as important as this.*

Dee Dee Hernesman shifted her gaze from Judge Smythe's thin, haggard face, to the artificially bronzed countenance of Peder Johansson. If the judge's inquiry, and the tipping of her hand ever so slightly toward the plaintiffs affected The Silver Wolf, it didn't show.

"Your Honor, I would strongly disagree. The article is of no consequence, with all due respect, to the events that transpired on the shores of Birch Lake. This case is complex enough, with the divergent expert views as to liability and causation, without unduly complicating matters by allowing plaintiffs to pursue dead ends. I think our brief adequately describes our position and the case law supporting it. The Court should deny plaintiffs' motion and allow the parties to get back to discovery that is calculated, to steal Ms. Carpenter's phrase, to lead to relevant, admissible evidence."

"Ms. Bucher, I noted that you simply submitted a letter agreeing with Ms. Carpenter. Do you have anything to add?"

Jill Bucher, the Duluth litigator representing the next of kin of Antonio Feggetti, her white hair aglow beneath the courtroom's harsh lighting, struggled to stand. Before Bucher could respond, Peder Johansson reclaimed his feet and addressed the court.

"Your honor, I am happy to advise the court that the matter involving Ms. Bucher's client has settled. The parties entered into a full, final, and complete resolution of all claims pending between the Feggettis and defendants Continental and Yost, leaving any cross-claims between my clients and the third-party defendants for trial."

Peder Johansson's announcement shocked Dee Dee Hernesman, Hugh McLean, and Kat Carpenter. None of the lawyers representing the next of kin of Susie Lindahl had an inkling that a deal was in the works between Johansson, Bruce Cutler, and Bucher. The three lawyers representing the family of Susie Lindahl—Carpenter and Hernesman seated to the left of Jill Bucher at counsel table and McLean in the public gallery— were gape mouthed and stunned, unable to articulate surprise, betrayal, or any other emotion appropriate to the news.

"Is this true?" Judge Harriet Smythe asked, looking up from her computer screen, her eyes riveted on Bucher.

Jill Bucher nodded. The Duluth lawyer refused to look at her former associates as she addressed the judge. "Yes, Your Honor. Mr. Johansson and Mr. Cutler and I have come to an accord. It is a full, final, and complete settlement, confidential as to its terms and the amount, and once the appropriate documents are executed and a check is cut, I will be filing a Stipulation of Dismissal with Prejudice, signed by all relevant parties, ending my involvement in this case."

Smythe scrutinized the lawyer. "Since there are no minors involved, you won't need a hearing to approve the settlement. However, if the parents aren't in agreement as to distribution . . ."

"Sorry to interrupt, Judge Smythe, but they've agreed that, after fees and costs, they will each receive one-half of the net settlement amount," Bucher interjected.

"Then the only role the court will have is to sign the Stipulation for Dismissal when presented, correct?"

Bruce Cutler—who was sitting in the rear of the courtroom—and Peder Johansson and Jill Bucher all nodded in unison.

"Very well. I assume that, given this new development, Ms. Bucher, you take no position on the pending motion?"

"That's true, judge. My involvement in the matter is over."

"What just happened?" Dee Dee asked Kat as the two lawyers stood at the bottom of the stairs leading out of Judge Smythe's courtroom, the Ten Commandments boldly affixed to the wall behind them.

"Cutler. That bastard. He's a master of the 'divide and conquer' strategy," Carpenter replied. "He convinced Johansson to settle the Feggetti case. I'd wager it cost Mercury Mutual no more than a quarter mil. All Johansson's money. Cutler's client, Saturnia, didn't contribute a dime. And they preserved Continental and Yost's cross-claims against Gruber, Gruber's salvage company, and Calumet for another day. Smart. Leaving us to consider broaching settlement while we wait to see whether Harriet will let us dig into Yost's past or not. Meanwhile, we keep writing checks to our experts. The defense took out Bucher and we lost one-third of our funding for the case. They hit us where it hurts—in the pocketbook. Smart play, I'll give the bastards that."

"The Lindahls' claim is worth a hell of a lot more than a quarter mil," Hugh McLean observed.

First time that milquetoast has opened his mouth in front of his boss, Hernesman thought.

"True enough, Hugh." Kat agreed. "But it doesn't matter. Bucher got what she wanted and is no longer a factor. We're on our own. I hope to God your experts, Hernesman, are as good as you think they are."

"We've still got the spoliation argument up our sleeve as well as a potential claim for punitive damages," Hernesman countered. "If Harriet rules in our favor on the discovery motion, and if we find some dirt that supports the article Hoot found, we can push for punies. That would put both Johansson and Cutler in a corner that'll be hard to come out of."

The lawyers began walking. "Agreed. But punitive damages are a rare bird," Carpenter continued. "It's not often a judge will allow a plaintiff to seek to punish a defendant in a civil lawsuit. And we have nothing other than a rumor shared by an Ely bartender, an off-the-cuff statement by a grieving Mr. Yost at the disaster site, and an article from a Montana newspaper buried on the Internet to support opening up Yost's past to inquiry," Kat added. "I don't like our chances on the motion, and I like our chances of convincing Judge Harriet Smythe that this is a punitive damages case even less."

Dee Dee Hernesman matched the taller woman stride for stride. After exiting the courthouse, the three attorneys stopped in front of Hernesman's Escape.

"I guess all we can do is wait for Judge Smythe to make a decision," Kat Carpenter conceded.

Hernesman nodded but did not reply. *We wait,* the lawyer thought as she opened the driver's door to her Escape, slid behind the wheel, closed the door, and started the SUV, *for Judge Smythe to do the right thing.*

CHAPTER TWENTY-FIVE

Sheriff Deb Slater sat in the office of the St. Louis County Attorney, her khaki uniform blouse and dark brown uniform slacks impeccably pressed, her auburn-turning-to-gray hair tied off her shoulders in a ponytail, the seat of the antique oak side chair she was occupying crowded by her sidearm, Taser, handcuffs, and assorted pouches affixed to her utility belt. She'd been called to a meeting with *the* St. Louis County Attorney. The fact that Justin Pappas had personally summoned Slater to his office on the fifth floor of the county courthouse in Duluth troubled the female officer.

> *I am in deep . . .*

Her speculation as to *why* she might be in trouble wasn't multifaceted. She understood the exact issue that had compelled Pappas to summon her.

> *Yost's employment records. Hernesman shares the Internet article with me. Based on the article, I ask an assistant county attorney in Virginia to pull a subpoena for Continental's records, including any employment applications and references that Yost submitted before being hired by Continental. The next thing I know, Pappas is on the phone, demanding a sit-down. Dee Dee Hernesman is right. There's something to Yost's past. The article Hoot Holt copied from the web makes that clear. But a newspaper article isn't evidence. I need Yost's employment records to pursue Hoot's lead. But the county attorney's office isn't interested in continuing the investigation in that direction.*

After the chance meeting with Dee Dee Hernesman in Tommy's, Slater had nearly forgotten the lawyer's offer to discuss the explosion case. It had taken persistent emails and telephone calls from Hernesman to awaken Slater's curiosity. The subsequent conversation between Slater and Hernesman was accomplished over slices of homemade apple pie and cups of aromatic black coffee at A Taste of Ely, a local downtown Ely eatery frequented by Hernesman. In the end, the lawyer's passion and dedication to uncovering whatever truth lay behind the rumors of Yost's proclivity for disaster, along with a snippet of old news copied from a Montana-based website, convinced Deb Slater to call Jennifer Berg, the Assistant County Attorney in Justin Pappas's Virginia office assigned to assessing criminal charges regarding the deaths of Antonia Feggetti and Susie Lindahl.

It seemed, upon reflection by Slater as she awaited an audience with Justin Pappas, her eyes downcast to avoid the innately nosey receptionist across the lobby, to be such an innocuous request: *Pull a subpoena so we can look at Neil Yost's employment file.* And then, out of the blue, before a low-level court clerk could sign off on the subpoena, before Slater could start digging, Pappas had called.

The receptionist's phone jangled.

"He'll see you now. Do you know how to get to his office?"

The woman's eyes darted like ball bearings in a pinball machine as she addressed the Sheriff of Cook County.

"I do."

Deb Slater rose carefully to avoid catching her holstered .40 M&P automatic on the arm of the chair. As she stood, Slater smoothed the creases of her slacks before heading down the hallway to Pappas's inner sanctum.

The door to the county attorney's office was open. Deb Slater stepped into the room with feigned confidence and noted that her interview with the chief prosecutor of St. Louis County would not be a private affair. A very pregnant Jennifer Berg and a very nervous looking Brian Nace sat in upholstered mahogany chairs in front of Pappas's oversized desk. A picture window spanned the office's west wall and revealed Duluth's hillside, the Bong Bridge, and the St. Louis River. The sun shone brightly. The leafing of oaks and maples and birches and aspen greened

126

the crowded bowl occupied by the city. In the near distance, a Burlington Northern and Santa Fe locomotive pulled a string of tank cars filled with crude from the Bakken through a rail yard. Puffs of diesel smoke roiled from the engine as it strained to break the tanker cars free of gravity. Slater found herself momentarily lost in the industrial waltz occurring outside Pappas's window.

"Have a seat," Justin Pappas said quietly—no hint of emotion apparent in the request—as he motioned for Slater to claim the chair between Nace and Berg.

Slater did as requested. "What's this about?"

"Direct. I like that," Justin Pappas replied, his eyes fixed on his blue-veined hands.

The county attorney was, at sixty-seven years old, a man of modest proportions, thinning hair, and nondescript eyes. Justin Pappas was a veteran prosecutor who'd served as an assistant in the office for three decades before a heart attack claimed his boss and mentor, John Ferguson, a legend in the local legal community who'd been elected to the office of St. Louis County Attorney three years out of law school and served in that role for generations. Severe juvenile acne had left Pappas's face a mass of craters, creating an embattled appearance. His office voice was nearly inaudible and in stark contrast to the oratory thunder Pappas summoned during cross-examination and closing argument.

He's tried some of the most notorious murder, rape, incest, and other high-profile cases to come across the desk of the county attorney, Slater thought. *He doesn't look so powerful, what with the ravages of time creeping into his bones and skin, reducing him measure by measure to the earth. But his mind. Ah, that, I must assume, is as sharp as ever. I need to be cautious in dealing with Justin Pappas. He's adept at negotiating with the disparate egos of the St. Louis County Board and has managed to survive two or three high-octane electoral challenges over his career. The list of favors owed to the man is legendary. I best listen before I speak.*

"I'll get right to the point," Pappas said in the same, firm yet steady tone. "The investigation into the history of Mr. Yost's hiring by Continental Mining, your request for a subpoena to retrieve Yost's personnel file, ends here, on my desk," the attorney said, picking up the subpoena that Jennifer Berg had requested from the courts in Virginia, holding the legal document in front of his slight frame and ripping it slowly, deliberately, in half. "We're done with this witch hunt. Understood? There's nothing left to uncover in this case. Yost made some mistakes. He miscalculated how much ANFO was either on the ground or in the silo. That's fairly obvious and the heirs will likely either settle their claim or prevail in front of a Hibbing jury on that account." Pappas stopped to sip from a delicate china cup on his desk. Steam from hot herbal tea wafted toward the ceiling as the old man swallowed. "But there's no point in your making any more noise regarding Mr. Yost. Are we clear?"

Debra Slater's face reddened. She was unaccustomed to being chastised like a schoolgirl by anyone, much less an attorney who, in reality, had no real authority over her work as the Director of the Copper/Nickel Task Force. Her direct supervisor was Sheriff Nace, who was noticeably quiet during the conversation, with the ultimate accountability for her work in St. Louis County being under the auspices of Governor Whitcomb, the man who'd appointed her to lead the task force.

Slater turned toward Nace. "What's going on here, Brian?"

The Sheriff of St. Louis County shook his head. "Don't go there, Deb. Pappas says it's over, it's over. He's the boss when it comes to prosecuting cases in this county—task force or no task force. Best to forget about it and move on. Cyrus Oliphant is still out there. I'd focus my attention on Oliphant and his kind if I were you. Whitcomb is only days away from

128

approving the permits for Continental's new mine at the Merritt Pit site and it's likely you'll be dealing with more protests, more confrontations between the factions, and, likely as all hell, more arrests."

Slater leaned back in her chair, folded her arms across her chest, and stared hard at the county attorney.

No way Brian Nace backs down from investigating a crime simply because Pappas tells him to. There's something more going on here. Pappas has leverage on Nace, a card he's decided to play, a chip he's cashing in. What is it? What information or secret is the county attorney privy to concerning the sheriff that compels Nace to side with the old man? Whatever it is, it's considerable.

Slater wanted to ask Nace why he was bowing to Pappas's pressure. Instead, she chose to redirect her question to the source of the conflict.

"What's really going on here, Justin?"

Justin Pappas swiveled in his chair to deposit the shredded subpoena in a garbage can. "Nothing, Sheriff Slater," Pappas said tersely. "There's only this: I am suggesting that you stop investigating the unfortunate and accidental deaths of Antonio Feggetti and Susie Lindahl. Persist in this line of inquiry, and I'll have no choice but to give the governor a call and have you removed from the task force. And that," the county attorney said evenly, leaning back in his chair to match Slater's posture, "would be most unfortunate seeing as how you've only a few months to go before retirement. That wouldn't be a very prudent move for a woman of your reputation, someone known for making wise decisions. Think about your legacy, Sheriff Slater. How folks will remember you. If you buck me on this, people won't remember the decades of fair and even-handed service you gave to the residents of St. Louis, Lake, and Cook Counties. They'll remember that you got the boot from the governor. Is that how you want your career to end?"

Slater shook her head. "You still haven't answered the question. Why, with information out there waiting to be explored that *might*, and I emphasize the word *might*, link Yost and his bosses to crimes, perhaps manslaughter, perhaps murder, are you making this call? Tell me that and I'll back off. I'll turn around and drive back to Grand Marais and leave Continental Mining and Neil Yost the hell alone. Just explain the 'why' behind your position and I'll be the compliant, perfunctory lackey you want me to be."

Justin Pappas's fists tightened. His face flushed crimson. He was, to Slater's observation, on the brink of exploding.

"I do not have to justify myself to you. I have my reasons, reasons that do not require explanation or illumination. That's it. That's all you need to know. Cease and desist or I will go to the governor and have you removed. This is not a debate. It is an order. Ignore my request and you'll face the consequences. But understand this: you'll receive no assistance of any kind from my staff or the staff of any office of St. Louis County if you choose to continue on this path. Correct, Sheriff Nace?"

Brian Nace tried to disappear into the oxblood fabric of his chair. Nace's long, lean form folded as he sought to make himself nonexistent, as he sought to avoid participating in the conversation. "Deb, understand. I've got to go along with Pappas on this one. You keep kicking the beehive; you'll get us all stung. Simple as that. Leave it alone. Go back to Ely and keep the peace. That's what you were hired to do."

Slater stood up and stared hard at Brian Nace. She was about to raise her voice, to protest the cowardice of her fellow officer but instead, Deb Slater looked past Nace's humbled form, nodded toward the picture window, and focused her attention on an onslaught of unseasonable weather. "It's snowing outside. It's May and it's friggin' snowing outside," the sheriff muttered as she edged her away from her chair, opened the door, and left the meeting.

CHAPTER TWENTY-SIX

There was nothing of substance in the employment records of Continental Mining of Minnesota, Inc. beyond a brief rendition of Neil Yost's work history with Carson Mines in Butte. The documents revealed no references to any sort of discipline or difficulty regarding Yost's employment in Montana. Dee Dee Hernesman and Hugh McLean found nothing of evidentiary value in the thin stack of documents produced by Continental pursuant to Judge Smythe's order.

"I thought we'd find something," McLean said as the two lawyers sat at a conference table in the offices of Mattila, Somerfeldt, and Hernesman, dusk softly falling outside the windows, dim light filtering in from East Chapman Street and bathing the room in gold. McLean's pinched face was highlighted by a shaft of departing sun. "I really thought Hoot had brought us a lead that would bear fruit," McLean added as his nondescript eyes shifted from side to side.

Dee Dee Hernesman's notorious attention to detail was diverted—not by the other lawyer's patter—but by thoughts of Gabriella Pierce. The younger woman had called. They'd arranged to meet. When Hernesman balked at the singer driving clear over from Grand Marais "just" for a cup of coffee, Gabriella Pierce had sniggered.

"Missy, I'm the one driving to see *you*," Gabriella had purred, "let *me* decide whether the effort is worth it or not."

Hernesman reflected on the woman's use of an archaic endearment as she stared into space.

"Did you hear anything I said?" McLean asked, arranging the papers in a short stack of inconsequence.

Dee Dee nodded reflexively, her thoughts engaged in recalling, in great and excruciating detail, the line of the younger woman's chin, the curvature of her jaw and neck, the feline quality of Gabriella Pierce's eyes.

"So, whenever we find *Richard Nixon's* report card from eighth grade in this mess, we'll have hit the jackpot. Am I right?"

"Right."

It was McLean's standard ploy when someone wasn't paying attention to what he was saying. The insertion of the name of the most disgraced president in American history into the conversation was a technique he'd developed to determine how closely someone was listening. It was clear, given Hernesman's response, that she hadn't heard a word McLean had said.

"You aren't paying attention. You're off in la-la land, thinking about god-knows-what. I was pointing out that . . ."

McLean stopped abruptly. The resulting silence called Dee Dee Hernesman away from the shapely contours of Ms. Pierce's youthful body and back into the conference room.

"You were saying something about the article Hoot pulled off the Internet. I have it right here," Hernesman said, digging through Hoot Holt's investigative file. "Says here, in this clipping from *The Montana Standard,* June 28th, 2003, that Carson Mines was fined by the State of Montana for violations relating to an accident in April of 2003 at Carson's Charlie Russell Pit. The article names Neil Yost as the Safety Director responsible for an accident where three workers apparently died. But there aren't any details about what actually happened and Hoot's efforts to dig deeper, to uncover specifics, hit a dead end. The paper doesn't maintain electronic copies of articles written before 2005. Hoot got lucky, finding this one. It was maintained on an industrial safety blog, not archived on the *Standard's* website."

Hugh McLean put up his left hand as his right hand pawed through documents demarcating Neil Yost's career at Carson Mines. "I remember seeing something, something out of place. I think we're being played, Dees. I think pieces of Yost's past are being deliberately withheld."

Hernesman leaned back. "You're kidding, right? Peder Johansson is as straight as they come."

McLean's inspection came to a sudden halt. He removed a document from the stack of papers produced by Continental. "Here. Tell me what you see," he said, handing a letter typed on Carson Mines stationary to Hernesman.

"Well," Dee Dee said, examining the document closely, holding it a fair distance from her face to allow her no-line contacts to focus. "It's a cover letter from Carson indicating that Yost's personnel file is being forwarded to Continental. It's dated around the time Yost was applying for work in Minnesota. The Bates stamp number on the lower right corner is consistent with the other documents we've been provided. The Personnel Manager of Continental Mining of Minnesota, Inc., and I can't read the signature, has signed the bottom of the letter, indicating Continental received Yost's file from Carson. What's your point?"

Hugh McLean leaned back in his chair, a smug look on his face.

"What?"

"Read paragraph two again."

"*We are enclosing, per the signed authorization of Mr. Yost, his complete employment file with Carson Mines, including 46 pages of records . . .*"

McLean's smile broadened. "Still don't see it, do you? Took me a while too."

Dee Dee Hernesman dropped the letter on the table. "We don't have all day, McLean. Spill the beans."

"Actually, Ms. Hernesman, we *do* have all day and, I might add, we would have had this discussion a few minutes ago if you hadn't been daydreaming."

Hernesman's face reddened. The images of Gabriella Pierce that had compelled her to drift off still resonated, still manifested in her mind at the slightest suggestion. *Lust is a powerful thing,* Dee Dee mused. *Can't call it love at this point.*

What I'm experiencing is simple physical and emotional attraction. It's been a while since I've felt this way. I haven't lusted since Carol dumped me and moved on. It's been over a year. That's too long to be alone. I need a partner—someone to share life with. Gabriella? She's awfully young, maybe too young for an old woman like me. Wait. I'm not that old. I'm in good shape. My mind is still sharp, though, apparently, as McLean's pointing out, not as focused as I thought!

"Would you please pay attention?" Hugh McLean's voice rose to a near shout. "I'm trying to make a point here, a point that may prove invaluable in our battle with Johansson and Cutler."

The tone of McLean's voice startled Hernesman, dispersed the images of Gabriella Pierce, and garnered Hernesman's attention. "Yes?"

"Well," McLean said, paging through the stack of documents, "there are only thirty-two pages here. The letter from Carson Mines indicates that *forty-six pages* were provided to Continental. We're missing fourteen pages of Mr. Yost's personnel file from Carson Mines!"

Dee Dee Hernesman's mouth opened, but the lawyer had no clever retort or ready response to Hugh McLean's discovery.

CHAPTER TWENTY-SEVEN

"Pappas closed down the investigation." Deb Slater sat in quiet repose, her eyes fixed on a mug of hot cocoa in front of her on a table at the Chocolate Moose. The sheriff was in plain clothes, in the process of driving back to Grand Marais to resume her duties as sheriff of Cook County.

"Why'd he do that?" Dee Dee Hernesman asked, her voice edgy but restrained so that the other patrons in the eatery couldn't overhear the conversation. "We're on the cusp of finding out something, something about Neil Yost and Continental Mining that may change the outcome of the civil case. That information might also prove useful to the county attorney in bringing criminal charges." The lawyer stopped talking, raised a fork, and bit off a corner of a cheese and mushroom omelet. Her hazel eyes were bright and alert as she waited for the sheriff to respond, to reveal more.

Slate sipped hot chocolate and considered the point. "That may be true. And there are still the property damage claims to consider; something everyone seems to have forgotten. Over a hundred home and business owners within a ten-mile radius of the blast site have filed claims for broken windows, cracked foundations, disrupted wells, and the like as a result of the explosion . . ."

"Detonation," Hernesman interrupted.

"Pardon me?"

"Dr. Thor Erickson, our mining and explosives expert from SDSU, caught me making the same mistake. Corrected me on the spot. *Explosions* are the result of detonations, the setting off of bombs or other explosive devices." Dee Dee paused. "A *detonation*, on the other hand, is the sudden initiation of the combustion of a substance causing an explosion and a resultant shock wave. According to Dr. Erickson, the terms, in the parlance of the mining and explosives world, have two very different meanings."

"What's that got to do with this case?"

Hernesman raised a tumbler of orange juice, the edges of the glass beveled, before continuing. "Everything. Dr. Erickson and Oliver Nelson—former safety director at a number of industrial sites including a copper mine owned by Anaconda—have analyzed Continental's contention that other scenarios caused the detonation and resulting explosion: namely, that the ground detonated due to the soil being saturated with ANFO or that the two victims planted ANFO on-site in an attempt to make their work easier." The lawyer's head turned to observe patrons wandering in and out of the restaurant.

"Yes?"

"Sorry. Lost my train of thought."

"You were talking about alternative theories . . ."

Hernesman smiled. "Ah, yes."

The attorney didn't reveal to the sheriff that, in addition to considering folks in the Chocolate Moose, her thoughts, ever so briefly, had returned to Gabriella Pierce. The women had managed to find some time alone, taking in *Germinal*, an English-subtitled French film of Emil Zola's 19th century novel, one of Dee Dee's favorite books, at Zinema in Duluth. Over a light dinner and a bottle of Chablis at the Zeitgeist Café before the movie, Pierce detailed her life story, a story of gender confusion, failed relationships, parental disapproval, and a driving desire to write and sing folk music in opposition to her mother's insistence that she attend medical school. Dee Dee was amazed at how freely, how without constraint or limitation, Gabriella Pierce said what she said over fresh Lake Superior whitefish, mashed potatoes, and asparagus to someone she had just been introduced to. But, despite the conflicts and the pain and the angst clearly interwoven into the young woman's story, Gabriella shed no tears, uttered no words of lament, and sought

136

no pity as she unburdened herself. Hernesman was stunned by the candor displayed by Pierce. She wanted, as the pair sipped hot tea in the café after the movie, to reveal her own path to that moment. But Dee Dee Hernesman had been raised in a conservative Missouri Synod Lutheran family in Tower, Minnesota. She did not have the flare or the innate acumen of her companion for displaying such truths. And so, the women had left Zeitgeist holding hands, a light kiss on Gabriella's cheek in the dimness of the gaming casino parking ramp across Superior Street the only revelation exposed by Dee Dee Hernesman that evening.

"We don't have all morning, you know."

Hernesman smiled sheepishly at Slater's insistence. The smell of Gabriella's perfume, the velvety touch of the woman's skin against Dee Dee's lips, vanished as the lawyer sought to regain her composure.

"Our experts are convinced that the defense scenarios are hogwash," Dee Dee said confidently. "Computing the rainfall since the silo was last used by Calumet, there's no way that the ground, as Mr. Johansson and Mr. Cutler would have us believe, 'blew up.' Impossible, really." Hernesman took a deep breath and looked confidently at the sheriff. "And the second scenario, that two welders went out and bought fertilizer, added fuel oil to create their own ANFO, and then packed the homemade explosive into the silo, well, that's just plain meant to stir up my dander. Erickson is at a bit of a disadvantage here because he wasn't able to take soil samples to confirm or deny the defense expert's premise that *two* distinct chemical combinations of nitrate prill were found on-site. Lost that ability when that asshole Cutler gave the go-ahead to Continental to clean up the property. But, even without that bit of sleuthing, Erickson is convinced the defense scenario is hogwash. Plus, given Cutler's breach of the civil discovery rules, there's a pretty good chance Judge Smythe will never let that the jury hear about the supposed 'mystery' ANFO prills. We'll be asking Smythe to exclude that theory due to the defendants' conduct."

Debra Slater moistened a napkin in her water glass and dabbed the corners of her mouth. Her wide-set blue eyes studied the other woman as she tidied up the residue of a banana/nut muffin. "Understood. But what does all of this have to do with the fact that Justin Pappas pulled the plug on the criminal investigation? You can proceed to trial, if that's what it takes, to seek a civil judgment for the Lindahls." Slater paused to collect her thoughts and take a final sip of cocoa. "But that doesn't change the fact I've been told to keep my nose out of it."

Hernesman's mind finally focused on the conversation. She had managed, with great difficulty, to force the image of Gabriella Pierce, as the young singer sat behind the steering wheel of her battered silver Honda Accord, an enigmatic smile beaming at the lawyer through the driver's window, into memory. "We think we're on to something else, something that will change the way that Pappas looks at this case despite whatever pressure Whitcomb and the Ely Chamber of Commerce might be putting on the county attorney."

Slater stood up from the table. She locked eyes with the lawyer. "What is it? What have you uncovered about Continental and Neil Yost that could possibly alter the course of the criminal case?"

Dee Dee Hernesman followed the sheriff's lead and stood up from the table. She reached into her purse and withdrew a crisp twenty, the sort of unsullied bill dispensed by ATMs. "I've got breakfast," she said, placing the money on the varnished pine table.

"And?"

The two women walked toward the exit. Slater held the door as Hernesman stepped into spring drizzle.

"We think Yost caused a similar accident while working for Carson Mining in Montana." Hernesman paused to focus on the sheriff. Mist embroiled the two women as they scrutinized

138

each other. The tearful sky was close, so close the rooflines of the buildings lining Central disappeared as one looked up the street toward the old movie house, long dormant but rumored to be part of the town's renaissance now that copper/nickel mining money was beginning to flow.

"And?" Slater repeated.

"We think Continental knew about Yost's past and hired him anyway. The details of what happened in Butte and what Carson told Continental, well, we're still ferreting that out. But there are pages missing from Yost's employment records, records sent by Carson to Continental and produced by Continental as part of discovery. I'm pretty sure what we'll find, once we obtain the original employment records from Carson, an effort and expense that'll take sending Hoot Holt out to Butte to secure them by subpoena, is knowledge, Sheriff Slater: knowledge that Mr. Yost is a careless and dangerous man who killed folks in Montana. I want those documents before I reconvene his deposition. I want them in hand before I confront Neil Yost with the truth." Dee Dee took a deep breath. "And you'll likely want them as well, to pin homicide charges on Mr. Yost for the deaths of Antonio Feggetti and Susie Lindahl."

Deb Slater placed her right hand on the shorter woman's shoulder. "You find me something like that, Ms. Hernesman, and to hell with Justin Pappas. I'll contact Sarah Westin—the Minnesota Attorney General—about prosecuting Yost and Continental." The intensity of the rain increased. Slater's face turned thoughtful as she withdrew her hand and nodded, her resolve clear despite the sheets of rainwater pummeling the women. "I've got a high school classmate, Dave Posten, who works in the criminal division of the AG's office. You get me something that ties Yost to prior accidents where folks died due to the unintended *detonation* of ANFO," Slater added, her emphasis on the word deliberate, "and I'll bring the whole mess to Posten and see if he can't nail the sonofabitches who did this to the cross."

CHAPTER TWENTY-EIGHT

"Three hundred and fifty," Hugh McLean whispered to Dee Dee Hernesman as the two lawyers sat at a long, rectangular, walnut table in the conference room of the law firm of Johansson, Edwards, and Masterson.

Windows behind the plaintiff's lawyers and Kendal "Tubby" Goggleye—the trustee appointed to represent Susie Lindahl's survivors—bathed the room in early summer light. The sky outside the conference room was devoid of clouds, displaying a sapphire hue conjured from Matisse's palette. McLean leaned toward Hernesman. The lawyers were dressed in their best "goin' to court" suits and sitting in Peder Johansson's elegant offices on the top floor of the Unity Bank Building on the east side of Superior Street in downtown Duluth. Hernesman and McLean were waiting for Edwin Mooseberger, the court-appointed mediator, to shuffle back to the conference room with an offer of settlement from the defendants.

"How's that?" Hernesman asked.

McLean nodded toward the door. "Bucher got three-fifty. Three-fifty is what the Feggetti family settled for."

The fact that Jill Bucher, who was not noted for taking matters to trial, had settled the Feggetti case didn't shock Dee Dee Hernesman. But the manner in which the Feggetti claim had been trundled up and closed—completely in secret and while the attorneys for the grieving families were deep in pre-trial discovery—had taken Dee Dee aback. She'd expected that Bucher, who she'd known for over a decade and considered a friend, would give her a heads up if Cutler or Johansson broached settlement.

Divide and conquer. Carpenter warned me that Cutler is a master at the oldest gambit in the lawyering playbook.

When Peder Johansson announced in open court that the Feggetti case had been resolved, that revelation had sent a shiver through Dee Dee Hernesman. But, as an advocate of considerable experience, Dee Dee Hernesman had calmed her nerves and allowed Kat Carpenter to make their pitch without interruption.

Hernesman's efforts to corner Bucher, to find out what the other attorney had settled for and why Bucher had pulled the plug just when the case was gaining traction, were met with recalcitrance.

"Any hint that I spilled the beans," Jill Bucher had said during a heated conversation between Bucher, Carpenter, Hernesman, and McLean outside the Hibbing courthouse following the motion hearing, "and the deal is off. I can't risk it. I'm a one-woman office. This case has drained every dime of my savings. My clients wanted to settle. I called Cutler. He put pressure on Johansson. That's all there is to it."

Subsequent attempts by Dee Dee Hernesman to ease Bucher into disclosure had failed. So it was a surprise to Dee Dee that, sitting in the quiet confines of Peder Johansson's suite, the conference room door closed against the hustle and bustle of a thirty-lawyer firm at work, Hugh McLean was privy to the magic number.

"How'd you find out?"

Hernesman mussed her dyed black hair; the bangs cut short and touching the shoulders of her charcoal gray suit, as she asked the question. She glanced toward the door, hopeful that the mediator remained in discussion with defense counsel across the hall.

"I can't tell you the hows and the whys. All I can say is that I have it on solid authority that Bucher settled the case for three-fifty. There's nothing in writing, at least not that you can access. Everything was sealed by Judge Smythe. But that's the number. You can take it to the bank."

"It would've been helpful for me to know this little secret *before* we walked into mediation," Hernesman said with pique and loud enough for Tubby Goggleye to overhear.

"Agreed," Goggleye said with a nod. "If I'm supposed to make a recommendation to the judge about settlement, it would be nice to know what the Feggetti family, a family devoid of surviving children as next of kin, accepted to resolve the case."

"Well," Mclean said through a crooked smile, a grimace really, that reminded Dee Dee of his boss, Kat Carpenter, a likeness that was unnerving, "now you know."

"So, in essence, our demand, as it sits, at three-point-five, is exactly ten times what Bucher settled for?" Dee Dee asked.

Hernesman watched through glass as Edwin Mooseberger exited an office across the hallway.

"There's no harm in shooting for the moon and accepting something less," Hugh McLean said as the elderly mediator opened the door and entered the room.

"That was freakin' useless," Hernesman moaned as the three lawyers—Hernesman, McLean, and Goggleye—sat in a booth in Carmody's Irish Pub on East Superior Street sipping Guinness and lamenting the mediation session that had left them with little hope. "One-fifty for the family? A hundred and fifty thousand dollars for the death of a mother and daughter? When the very same assholes paid over twice that for the death of an unmarried guy? What gives?"

McLean sucked foam from a pint glass. The bartender, a young lass of no more than twenty-five, had poured the stout expertly, as if born to the task, stopping appropriately during the pour to ensure the correct amount of froth. McLean had tipped the bartender generously for the effort and had, as he carried three pints to the booth from the bar, left his card atop a twenty in the off chance that a young lady ten years his junior might be interested in a twice-divorced litigator with thinning hair, thickening belly, and, due to child support payments for four kids, an impoverished wallet. "You said it before, Dees," McLean replied, his voice no longer carrying a Kat-Carpenterish-edge, "divide and conquer. By taking out Bucher, the defense eliminated one-third of our funding. And, just to remind you of where we are, we're still nowhere closer to proving that Yost has skeletons, relevant skeletons, in his past. Johansson and Cutler are like sharks smelling blood in the water. The defendants aren't gonna go down easy, at least, not without something more on Yost."

Hernesman took a significant pull on her Guinness. She was deep in contemplation when Tubby Goggleye spoke.

"Seems to me, anything over a million is in the ballpark," the trustee observed, fingering the base of his glass, its contents untouched. "They offer anything in seven figures and I'm duty bound to consider the risks of trial. And given those risks, I'd be hard pressed not to recommend accepting a seven-figure offer."

"The parents have claims too," Hernesman asserted quietly. "And a million is about a third of what this case is worth."

McLean shook his head. "Pie in the sky, Hernesman. Look at the verdict research I pulled together for the mediation. Death cases are based on the decedent's income. Yes, having minor children as survivors, as next of kin, increases the value of the case. No question. The pecuniary loss: the loss of advice, comfort, aid, and society tied to surviving kids trumps any loss an adult parent or sibling can claim. But," McLean stopped in mid-thought, drained his pint, and raised his right hand to gain the bartender's attention, "none of the Minnesota cases in the past five years I found involving slightly-above-minimum wage-workers like Susie Lindahl approach the sort of numbers we put out as a demand. Kat's right," McLean added as another pint appeared and a fiver was whisked away by the pretty coed who delivered the stout, "you're too emotionally involved to think straight. Our number is too damn high. I should've talked you down, to say two mil, as a starting point. Then maybe we'd be celebrating settlement of the case instead of trying to figure out what went wrong."

Dee Dee bit the inside of her left cheek to control herself. "I doubt that would've made a difference. I think Cutler is driving this bus. He's hell-bent-for-leather to keep us from dipping into his pot of gold. If Cutler can get Johansson to settle for a million or less, his five million isn't in play and he's a hero. Reducing our demand at this point won't do much to move the needle, I'm afraid."

McLean sipped Guinness and pondered the woman's statement. "Maybe. But Kat . . ."

"Screw Kat," Hernesman spit the name like a child spewing Brussels sprouts into a napkin. "She's done absolutely nothing on this case. You and I have done all the heavy lifting. She's been a backbencher from day one, with the exception of agreeing to let Tubby join the ride and making one argument in court. Beyond that, she's done precious little to advance our cause."

"So where do we go from here?" queried Tubby Goggleye, his milk chocolate Ojibwe skin highlighted by a light suspended over the trio's booth. "What's our next move?" he asked, bent on smoothing over the discord between his companions.

McLean looked out a bank of dirty, steam-clouded windows, a cold front having swept into Duluth from Manitoba, bringing with it, despite the fact it was the first week of June, the possibility of snow. "We keep after the employment records. The news clipping that Hoot Holt found proves there's something missing, something important and damning that Continental thinks is too incendiary to give up without a fight."

The tension between the lawyers eased.

"This case does that, doesn't it?" Hernesman smiled weakly and fingered the rim of her nearly empty pint.

"What?"

"Makes one prone to bad puns. *Incendiary.* Christ, what a cluster of saps we are, drinking stout and making jokes over the corpse of poor Susie Lindahl."

McLean lifted his Guinness. "Here's to Susie."

"To Susie," Hernesman and Goggleye said as the lawyers drained their glasses.

Hugh McLean wiped foam from his lips with the sleeve of his sport coat. "I was serious, Dees. Where do we go with the Yost thing?"

"I was thinking of sending Hoot Holt out to Montana to pick up a subpoena at the Silver Bow County courthouse in Butte and have him serve it on Carson Mining. That way, we'd be able to recover the missing pages of Neil Yost's employment file directly from Carson."

Tubby Goggleye fixed his jet black eyes on the woman. "'But' . . . I sense there's a 'but' here."

"Hoot had a heart attack. Ended up with stents. He's out of commission," Hernesman said softly.

"Shit. He's the best investigator around," McLean said with respect.

"I was thinking of going myself," Dee Dee said, her eyes drifting toward three young musicians preparing to perform. Two men carried guitars into the bar and a woman, a girl barely out of her teens, placed a fiddle in a music stand as the group set up microphones. Posters around Carmody's proclaimed that the three were collectively known as "Clan O'Molly" and that the trio played tunes from Ireland, Scotland, and Cape Breton. "Or sending you, Hugh. But we've got the depositions of our clients coming up. We need to prep for that." Hernesman took a breath before continuing. "I was also gonna have Hoot look into why our county attorney, Justin Pappas, is so hell-bent-for-leather to close the criminal case. He's 'persuading' Slater to end her investigation. Has the St. Louis County Sheriff, Brian Nace, backing his play. Nace is generally a bulldog. It's odd he'd go

145

along with pulling the plug on a potential murder case. But, according to Slater, Nace is on board with Pappas." Dee Dee looked at her companions to ensure they were following her line of thinking. Both men appeared fully attentive. "I was gonna have Hoot poke around Yost's past *and* also try to uncover whatever leverage Pappas has over Nace. But my investigator got sick before he could get started. That's when I came up with this crazy idea . . ."

"I don't think Kat has any intention of flying to Butte. It's not ski season," McLean offered through a weak smile.

Hernesman grinned. "Oh, I wouldn't dare ask the queen of the Iron Range Bar to dirty her hands in such tawdry and common a fashion," Dee Dee retorted. "No, I've got something far more novel in mind. My old partner, Danny Aitkins, is available. Needs something to do. I thought I'd run it by him."

McLean's eyes rose in skepticism. "Doesn't he have a booze problem?"

"That he does. But he's available, cheap, and a quick study," Hernesman said as she tucked a wayward bit of blouse into the waistband of her skirt.

"Really? We're gonna send a drunk, a guy who no longer holds a license to practice, out to Montana in hopes he comes back with what could turn out to be the most crucial evidence in our case? And then, we're gonna ask that same drunk to check out our county attorney and our county sheriff to see if there's some skullduggery afoot?"

Tubby Goggleye rose from the bench. "Why not? Everyone deserves a chance at redemption. Hell, the first part of the equation is just a simple errand. Fly out, go to the county courthouse, file Judge Smythe's order, get a subpoena, serve it on Carson, get the papers, and fly back." The Ojibwe lawyer stopped to catch his breath. "The second task? More difficult, I'll grant but one that needs exploring and one that the two of you don't want to leave fingerprints on. From what I hear, Pappas can be a vindictive sonofabitch. Who better to take a peek under

146

his desk than a disgraced lawyer? I say, give it a whirl. Nothin'
to lose at this point."

Hugh McLean joined the Ojibwe lawyer standing next to
the table. "This better not turn into a shit storm, Hernesman. Kat
will definitely not be happy if Mr. Aitkins's little trip goes
sideways."

Dee Dee stood up and smoothed the pleats of her skirt.
"Oh, I'm sure it'll work out just fine, Hugh. Remember: I'm all
about keeping Ms. Katherine O'Donnell Carpenter pleased.
That's my intention, my life goal, my singular task in life:
keeping Kat Carpenter happy."

CHAPTER TWENTY-NINE

"So, Mrs. Lindahl, you were Susan Lindahl's mother?"

Peder Johansson asked the question of Judy Lindahl in the conference room of his Duluth office, the same room where Dee Hernesman and Hugh McLean and Tubby Goggleye had met unsuccessfully with mediator Edwin Mooseberger. The Silver Wolf was respectful in his interrogation. Johansson was no fool. He knew that in litigation, as in life, you catch more flies with honey than vinegar.

"I *am* Susan Adeline Lindahl's mother."

Johansson nodded. "Sorry if my use of the past tense was inconsiderate. You *are* Susie's mother?"

"Yes."

"You understand that I am here to ask you some questions related to Susie, her work, her children, her family? If at any time I ask a question you don't understand, please, just stop me and I will restate or rephrase the question. Agreed"

The woman's blond hair, dyed, long, and tied in a bun, shimmered as she nodded in reply.

"I'd also ask, so that Mr. Bystedt here, who is taking down everything you say," the lawyer paused and gestured with pen in hand toward a dignified, sixty-something, thinly built gentleman in a business suit seated behind a stenography machine, "that you refrain from nods or shakes of the head, or uh huhs, or the like."

Judy Lindahl nodded and then quickly added:

"I understand."

The court reporter's stern demeanor cracked ever so slightly as he transcribed the woman's words.

"So. Let's start with Susie's upbringing. She was an only child?"

"Yes."

"And she was born and raised in Hibbing?"

"Born in Virginia while my husband was going to community college. I was working in the Virginia hospital as an LPN. Mark was in the drafting program at Mesabi."

"When did you folks move to Hibbing?"

"Mark finished school and got a job with KeeTac. Susie was two. So that would be about 1992. She was born in '90."

"Her date of birth?"

"November 12, 1990."

Johansson paused and looked carefully at his notes through a pair of drugstore cheaters, the cheap eyeglasses distinctly at odds with his expensive pinstriped baby blue, summer weight, business suit and two hundred dollar haircut. A lump formed in the lawyer's throat.

"She died on her birthday?"

Judy Lindahl looked at her hands. A tear formed and began its descent. "Her twenty-fifth," the woman whispered.

"I am so sorry for your loss."

Mrs. Lindahl nodded but Peder Johansson thought better of correcting the gesture. Dee Dee Hernesman, seated to Judy's left, reached across the conference table, plucked a tissue from a cardboard carton, and handed it to her client. The grieving mother dabbed her eyes with the Kleenex.

"Do you need some time?"

"I'll be fine. Let's get this over with."

Johansson nodded and began anew.

The day passed slowly. Hernesman raised objections to Johansson's questions of Judy and Mark Lindahl, Mark's deposition being taken after Judy's was completed and after the attorneys recessed to use the john and telephone their offices. The room was stuffy and hot, the smell of sweat and perfume and deodorant and men's aftershave permeated the thick air, as first Judy, then Mark, underwent interrogations into their daughter's life, educational history, romantic partners, criminal background, drug and alcohol abuse, and children. Similar questions were asked of Nancy and Tom Devich, the paternal grandparents of Brenda Lee Devich, Susie's eldest daughter who had been three years old at the time of Susie's tragic death. When the Deviches were questioned, Kat Carpenter took the seat to the left of the witnesses, the seat formerly occupied by Dee Dee Hernesman, and raised objections to Johansson's queries when necessary. Neither Hernesman nor Carpenter forbade their clients to answer questions; the plaintiffs' attorneys simply preserved their objections regarding foundation, relevancy, hearsay, and the like for the record—for later decision by Judge Smythe. The clock had inched past 4:00 p.m. by the time Johansson completed his questioning. The other defense lawyers in the room—David Van Clive, a nondescript middle-aged white guy representing Calumet Mining, Defendant Continental's predecessor in ownership of the Merritt Pit site; Cicely Thompson, a large-busted, dreadlock-headed, black woman representing Steve Gruber, Susie Lindahl's employer and maternal uncle; and the portly Mr. Bruce Cutler, protector of excess insurer Saturnia's fortune—were present, but only Van Clive asked a few perfunctory questions, questions advanced merely to establish that he was in attendance.

"That was brutal," Mark Lindahl said as he and Nancy sat across the table from their attorney eating pasta at Valentini's, an Italian eatery located on Duluth's east side.

Hernesman smiled wearily as she sipped Merlot from a large wine glass. "You did fine. Better than fine, actually. You painted an accurate picture of Susie. Smart. Hard working. In recovery. Battling through addiction and relapse. On the road to being a good mom and a loving daughter. Not a perfect child, by any means. But someone, I think, Hibbing jurors will recognize as the girl next door or their daughter or their granddaughter."

"That was the hardest thing, next to laying her in the ground, I've ever had to do," Judy said quietly, her eyes downcast, a fork full of rigatoni poised over her plate. "I hope, in the end, it was worth it."

Mark leaned back in his chair. "The kids. Brenda Lee and Angel. We're doing this for them. Hell, I could care less if we get a goddamn dime when all is said and done. It's about making sure the girls are taken care of."

Judy frowned at the curse but held her tongue.

Dee Dee took another sip of wine. "Don't discount your loss and the fact that Neil Yost stole your daughter from you."

Mark stroked his beard. "Oh, I am fully aware of what we lost, Ms. Hernesman."

"'Dee Dee.' How many times have I told you to call me 'Dee Dee?'"

"OK. *Dee Dee*. Thing is, no amount of money can make up for not having Susie there for the girls' birthdays, for summer weekends at the cabin, for Thanksgivings and Christmases. No amount of money can replace her smile, her laugh, her goofy puns and silly jokes." The father took a breath, placed his fork on his empty plate, and fought tears. "I was looking forward to someday, when my little girl got her head together, walking her down the aisle of St. Alban's and handing her off to a guy who deserved to spend his life with Susie." Mark Lindahl stared hard at his lawyer. "So please, *Dee Dee*, don't try to lecture me as to what we've lost."

The lawyer raised her wineglass but kept her eyes focused on the white linen tablecloth as she gulped Merlot. "I don't," Hernesman said, placing the empty glass on the linen tablecloth, "pretend to know the depths of your loss, Mark. Or yours, Judy. I'm an attorney. Trying to do my job is all, trying to make the best, for you, for the kids, of a bad situation. I didn't mean to infer . . ."

Judy Lindahl placed the palm of her thick, pasty hand on Hernesman's wrist. "I know you didn't mean nothin' by it. It's just that, after what that asshole put us through today, well, I think everyone's nerves are a bit on edge."

Mark Lindahl grinned weakly. "You've never been one to swear, dear."

Judy raised a tumbler of ice water and drank greedily before replying. "I've spent my whole life surrounded by miners and loggers and railroaders. You don't think I know the same words you know?"

Mark Lindahl kissed his wife's cheek before returning his attention to the lawyer. "So, Dee Dee, what's going on with that bastard Yost's Montana records?"

Judy raised her eyes. "Just because a person *knows* a word, doesn't mean a person has to *use* a word."

"I suppose I could call him an *asshole*, the word you used to describe Johansson. But that would be a compliment, I think, when talking about Yost."

An unintentional laugh escaped Hernesman. "Sorry. It's just that . . ."

"Laughter can't hurt after the day we've had," Judy Lindahl interjected. "What's going on with Mr. Yost's employment file?"

Dee Dee wiped red sauce from her lips and placed the stained white, cloth napkin on her plate. "My former partner, Danny Aitkins, is flying out to Butte, to Carson Mining's headquarters, to obtain Yost's employment file. I would've used my normal investigator but unfortunately, he's out of commission."

Mark Lindahl frowned. "Sending a lawyer on an errand . . .isn't that overkill?"

Hernesman shook her head. "Former lawyer. He was a professor at the UND Law School for the better part of a decade, he's . . ."—and here is where Dee Dee shaded the truth so as not to reveal the real reasons for Aitkins's ability to assist her, the fact he'd been fired for alcohol addiction and sexual indiscretion—". . . retired."

"What do you hope Mr. Aitkins finds in Montana that you can't find here?"

A tall, gangly boy, a high schooler likely on the cusp of graduation, brought Hernesman the bill. She reached beneath her chair, retrieved and opened her purse, located her wallet, and removed a Visa card. The boy accepted the credit card and retreated to run it through Valentini's register.

"Evidence," the lawyer said when the waiter was out of earshot. "Evidence that Neil Yost is, as Mrs. Lindahl would say, an asshole."

CHAPTER THIRTY

Debra Slater sat in the stern of a sixteen-foot side console Lund, the fishing boat drifting across Devil Track Lake, an open-faced bait casting reel with six-pound test and a seven-foot, medium-action walleye rod in her left hand as she sipped Grain Belt Nordeast from a can, the tip of the rod twitching slightly from the action of a spinner and minnow tempting fish ten feet below the choppy surface of the lake.

"How ya feelin'?"

The sheriff asked the question of Annie, who, being seven month's pregnant, had slowed down in pace and personality. The girl was sitting on a pedestal seat in the bow of the Lund, a spin cast outfit in her hands, her once thin, post-adolescent form covered head to toe in a Big Red Cornell Volleyball warm-up, her lightly tinted brown eyes riveted on the point where fishing line merged with lake. Deb's daughter had completed her first year at the prestigious Ivy League university poised, before her misstep with Thomas Jones, to be the starting setter on the varsity volleyball team.

"Like a stuffed green pepper."

Deb smiled and took another swig of lager. "I remember that feeling. Had it with you. You start out with a queasy stomach, nausea, constantly running to the toilet. Then things settle down and you simply feel like you're gaining weight. Until . . ."

". . . the little guy or gal crowding your insides starts thumping on your stomach and lungs and kidneys with his her feet and hands," Annie interrupted, never lifting her eyes from the rolling surface of the lake. "Right now, he or she is kicking the crap out of my right side. I swear I can feel toenails digging into my appendix."

There was so much Deb wanted to say, so many words she wanted to impose on her daughter. But none of them would change reality. None of them would unwind or undo the New Year's Eve entanglement of white girl and brown boy in a dorm room bed on the Cornell campus learning love, but, unfortunately, at least to Deb Slater's way of looking at it, making a child. *What's done is done. There's no good to be gained by chastisement or reproach. She's gonna be a mom at nineteen. I'll be a grandma before my fiftieth birthday. Not the way either of us envisioned the future, I'll wager. But there it is.*

"Say it, Mom. Say whatever it is you need to say." Annie's voice, harshly edged and louder by a few decibels than it had been, interrupted Deb's digression. "I know there's some big lecture, an 'I thought I explained where babies come from' or 'why weren't you on birth control' or 'why didn't you make Thomas wear a condom' speech you feel you need to give. Go ahead. I deserve it. Unload whatever it is you need to unload."

Deb placed her beer can in a cup holder on the gunwale of the boat and looked across gray water, back toward the family cottage on the eastern shore of the lake. "That isn't where I was going, Margaret Ann. There's not much use in trying to reinvent history."

Annie swiveled her seat in her mother's direction and nodded. Tears descended the downy skin of the young woman's face. "If you say, 'what's done is done,' I swear . . ."

Deb smiled weakly. A fish tapped her bait down in the crystalline depths of Devil Track Lake. She let the fish inhale the chub before setting the hook. The rod tip bent. "Fish on."

Their dinner of pan-seared walleye, fried potatoes spiced with green pepper and onions, and boiled corn on the cob smothered in butter had been a quiet affair. When the dishes were done, Deb washing, Annie rinsing and drying, mother and daughter had retired to a screen gazebo in the backyard. Early summer chill emerged as the sun disappeared. A loon called. Another answered. Newly hatched mosquitoes buzzed the metal screen of the gazebo, attracted by human breath and the yellow glow of a

Coleman lantern providing light as the mother and daughter played cribbage, their cards, the board, drinks, and a bowl of freshly popped popcorn crowding the surface of a round cedar picnic table inside the screen house. Stars leaked through ebbing twilight. A quarter moon rose. A male mallard quacked. There was no response to the drake's lonesome lament.

"So next year . . ."

"Fifteen-two, fifteen-four, and a pair is six," Annie said evenly, ignoring her mother's attempt at serious talk.

"I've got sixteen, plus four in the crib for twenty. I'm out," Deb said as she pegged to victory. "About next year . . ."

Annie picked up a plastic tumbler containing virgin piña colada and sipped the coconut-flavored drink, sans alcohol, through a plastic straw. "I think it's time you started dating again," the girl said quietly, her eyes locked on her mother's timeworn face. "Dad would want you to be happy and God knows, Mother, you won't be happy until you have someone to share this place with."

A lump rose in Deb's throat. Raw emotion: angst or fear or longing or dread—Debra Slater couldn't discern which emotion screamed for attention—overwhelmed the woman. Her rugged hands, hands that had skillfully filleted four walleye, hands that had once clasped her husband's paper-thin, decaying skin as he fought to breathe in the hospice bed in Duluth on the very last day of his existence, IVs and plastic tubes and mechanical devices omnipresent in the room, evidence of an end, of a decline, that she had hoped would be forestalled for years, grasped a glass half-filled with brandy, 7up, and ice. Deb's fingernails were unpolished and chewed to the nub. She shook her head. "It's too soon, Annie. Too soon. I'm not ready."

Annie frowned. A lock of thin, brown hair fell across her nose, causing the young woman to place the deck of cards she was shuffling in her left hand while she repositioned the strand with her right. Before the girl could reply, Annie Slater grimaced in pain. "Ouch!"

"Something wrong?"

"This kid," the expectant mother said, trying to regain her breath, "just kicked the crap outta me."

Debra smiled. "Active little guy or gal, eh?"

"Don't try to change the subject."

"Let's leave your mother's love life out of the conversation, shall we? I'll let you know if and when I am ready to find someone to spend time with. For now, I'm content to spend time with my lovely daughter and . . ."

"Your grandson or granddaughter," Annie added. The girl resumed shuffling the cards. A wolf howled in the dark. Another answered from a few miles distant. Fireflies emerged on the lawn. "I love those bugs. Used to catch them and keep them in jars."

Deb nodded. "Me too. Lots more of them where I grew up, in farm country."

The young mother became introspective as she dealt the cards. "I have a name picked out."

"Really. Does Thomas approve?" Deb asked, cutting the cards and handing the deck to her daughter.

Annie smiled as she turned up the top card. "Jack of spades. One."

"Does he?"

"He does."

"Six."

"Nine for fifteen two."

"Another nine for twenty-four and two."

They played on, their conversation held in abeyance as they concentrated on their cards.

"Well, are ya gonna share?" Deb asked as they counted.
"Huh?"

"The name, silly. What's the name you picked out?"

"Riki, with a 'k' and an 'i' if it's a girl. Ricky with a 'ck' and a 'y' if it's a boy."

The sheriff smiled. "'Richard' or 'Ricarda' would be a bit much. 'Riki.' I like it. Your dad would too!"

The girl finished her drink. "And he'd like it if you got on with your life and found a nice man to be my stepfather."

"I'll give you one thing, Margaret Ann Slater."

"What's that?"

"You're persistent," Deb said as she counted the crib and pegged out.

The girl chuckled. "I wonder where I get it?" Annie put the cards back in the box, put the pegs in the base of the cribbage board, and stood up. "It's been a long day. Riki with a 'k' and an 'i' needs to get to bed."

"Sure that it's a girl, are you? Don't be disappointed when a little curly haired, baby boy pops his head out, you hear me?"

"Not sure of the gender. But I'm sure of one thing: This kid will be born with a ball of some sort in his or her hands. Goodnight, Mom," Annie said, leaning over and kissing her mother as she opened the door, stepped outside with speed to avoid letting mosquitoes in, and closed the gazebo's screen door behind her.

"Goodnight," the sheriff said, staring into her drink glass, ice slowing melting into brandy. The girl didn't reply. A gentle breeze stirred, the premonition of a front coming in from Ontario. Debra Slater reached across the table, poured another shot of brandy, this time, without 7up, and stared at the quarter moon standing boldly above the shifting surface of Devil Track Lake.

"It *is* too soon," she whispered, raising her glass to the moon, "much too soon."

CHAPTER THIRTY-ONE

The man trundled across asphalt, dawn creeping over mountains to the east, sunlight touching the two-day stubble covering his jowls, a battered leather brief case in his right hand as he moved toward the terminal of the Bert Mooney Airport. Despite the week of swelter that had stalled over Butte, the city nestled in a modest valley created by tectonic disruption and sculpted over time by Silver Bow Creek, the morning was cool, requiring the man to pull the edges of his jacket across his ample gut and zip up against the chill.

What the hell am I doing in the middle of goddamn Montana in July?

When Danny Aitkins finally got around to calling his former partner, Dee Dee Hernesman having left three messages on Aitkins's answering machine in the hovel of an apartment that he'd been reduced—through debauchery, chronic alcoholism, and consistent failure—to occupying above Hansen's Variety Store in downtown Grand Forks, their conversation had been polite and to the point. Hernesman offered Aitkins a shot at redemption, modest as it was, by enlisting him to run a couple of legal errands. Danny had listened intently and then, because he was down to the last hundred dollars in his checking account, his severance pay from the University of North Dakota Law School, from which he'd been unceremoniously fired after bedding a leggy second-year student, nearly exhausted and with no job prospects in sight, he swallowed his pride and accepted Hernesman's charity. Aitkins hated doing it, hated taking anything from anyone. And yet, he needed money. Dee Dee didn't offer salvation; her recruitment of the downtrodden wasn't a permanent solution to Danny's demise. But the offer of work, readily accepted by the disgraced lawyer, would allow him to pay his rent and hang on to his paltry existence for another month.

After that, who knows?

So Danny Aitkins, his license to practice law in North Dakota and Minnesota suspended, had met Hernesman at a little eatery on the main street of Park Rapids, a slender slip of a tourist town in northwestern Minnesota, where Hernesman had filled Aitkins in on what it was he was expected to find and retrieve in Butte, Montana, and whatever nooks and crannies he was expected to explore regarding the dirt St. Louis County Attorney Justin Pappas was privy to on St. Louis County Sheriff Brian Nace.

Aitkins's investigation into the connection between Pappas and Nace, with input from a recovering Hoot Holt over a couple of warm cups of bad coffee at Hoot's cabin on the shores of White Iron Lake outside Ely, hadn't been time consuming. In fact, Aitkins found the smoking gun, the leverage that Pappas had against Nace, without much effort. A few twenties slipped to folks working in places Nace and his wife frequented, a few discrete inquiries, and the truth came bursting forth. Seems that Jennifer Nace, the sheriff's wife, had a gambling problem, an addiction to Indian gaming casinos—one that caused her to pilfer cash as the treasurer of the Proctor Amateur Hockey Association (PAHA). The numbers weren't easily discerned from casual conversation, but Aitkins came away from encounters with locals at the Powerhouse Bar in Proctor, encounters where the defrocked lawyer sipped Coke over ice and refrained from the clutches of booze with steadfast clarity, understanding that Jennifer Nace's indiscretions totaled tens of thousands of dollars, illegalities sufficient to charge the unfortunate Mrs. Nace with felony theft. Remarkably, no charges were ever brought against Jennifer Nace. The stolen money was repaid, rumored to have been ponied up by Sheriff Nace, the result of a loan taken against his pension, and the matter forgotten.

"Makes sense," Dee Dee had said after Aitkins revealed what he'd learned by time spent in the dank recesses of the Proctor watering hole. "If it got out that the lovely and demure Mrs. Nace, darling daughter of Proctor, former class salutarian and head cheerleader, had stolen from PAHA, the sheriff of St. Louis County would be toast come next election."

Aitkins had provided his former partner with the information regarding Pappas's leverage over Nace during lunch at Beaner's Coffee Shop in West Duluth.

"Nicely done, Danny. Now, if only you can come back from Montana with similarly useful news . . ."

The former law professor had nodded. "That'll take a bit more doing than plying a few barflies in a railroad town with free booze."

"Likely a wild goose chase," Aitkins mumbled as he opened a door into the air-conditioned expanse of the airport terminal, his purposeful shuffle carrying him away from people, from the baggage carousels, from scrutiny, and toward the Hertz desk where he'd reserved a Corolla. "What the hell does Hernesman expect me to find out here in the boondocks anyway? Fourteen missing pages aren't gonna make her case. This," Danny Aitkins said to himself as he stood at the counter, the lone attendant busy handling a disgruntled customer on the phone, "is a waste of my time and her money. But, what the hell? It's not like I've got folks pounding on my door, seeking to pay me for my wisdom. A thousand bucks plus expenses for two days' work is pretty good for a guy with no license and no prospects," the lawyer continued beneath his breath, his jabbering attracting the attention of the young Native American woman, perhaps Crow, perhaps Blackfoot, trying to dislodge herself from the telephone. The native woman smiled weakly and shrugged. Aitkins could hear the screaming and the profanity and the anger of the caller over the phone's earpiece. "You don't get paid enough to deal with assholes, ma'am," he whispered.

The woman hung up on the irate customer and smiled at Danny. "How can I help you?"

Aitkins had already scrutinized the three credit cards in his wallet. His only option was American Express. His Visa and his Discover cards would be rejected; both were maxed out, and, like the cardholder, beyond redemption. *Bankruptcy might be the only way out*, the fallen lawyer thought, masking his discomfort with the same false smile, keeping his poverty and his disgrace sealed behind a façade. His eyes fell on his cowboy boots, Tony Lama's that his first wife, Julie, the writer and the mother of three of his four children—all of them grown up, distant, and removed from his life—had bought him one Christmas. The toes of the boots were paper-thin. The Lamas had been without polish for so long, the leather had dried and cracked, much like the skin of Aitkins's hands. The symbolism of his aging boots was not lost on the aging attorney.

How did I fall this low? How did I screw so many things up over such a long period of time? Two marriages. A sweet-ass job as a law professor. Shit, I've fallen so far, my own kids want nothing to do with me.

Despite his inner turmoil, Danny Aitkins maintained a poker face as he filled out the rental car agreement and paid the woman with the one credit card that he knew wouldn't trigger rejection. "Thanks," Aitkins said, accepting the keys from the woman in his right hand, the briefcase, as battered and shopworn as his boots, shifted to his left, as he started toward the exit.

"A subpoena, you say?"

Danny Aitkins sat in a modest office deep within the sprawling headquarters building of Carson Mines, the single-story edifice spread out over two acres of land near the Charlie Russell Pit, the last vestige of Carson's copper mining presence in Montana. Hundreds of acres of mined-out land had been remediated across the flat plain of the creek valley north of Butte, the result of increased regulatory and environmental scrutiny by the state and the federal governments. The Russell complex was the end of the line for Carson's mineral rights in the state.

"Yes. For production of the complete personnel file of one of your former employees, Neil Yost. He's a defendant in a lawsuit in Hibbing, Minnesota." Aitkins, nervous because he'd been removed from the litigation game for over a decade, felt his heart gripping, felt his blood racing, felt his temples pounding as he addressed a thirty-something corporate lawyer. The young man—dressed casually in a short-sleeved shirt, no tie, Levis, and freshly polished black ostrich skin cowboy boots—was seated behind a small maple desk in a claustrophobic office of the mine's legal department.

"Everything seems in order. I'll email HR and have them pull the electronic file. I'd access it from here, but our servers are a mess. Upgrading, you know."

Aitkins felt the tension dissipate. The young lawyer's demeanor—business-like, but infused with decency—affected the old man in a positive way. *But better keep up my guard,* Aitkins thought. *Never can tell when the worm may turn.* "Thanks. I'd appreciate that."

"It'll just take a moment or two." The young lawyer scrutinized the Dell in front of him, tapped keys, and hit "return." "Done. HR should forward the file in a few minutes. Coffee?"

Danny nodded.

The young lawyer, who, as he unfolded his frame and stood, stretched out to over six-five but weighed less than two hundred pounds, asked: "You take anything in it?"

"No. Just black. Scandinavian influence, you know."

"Hershel Ghent." The lawyer extended a narrow right hand.

"Danny Aitkins," the older man replied, accepting the gesture.

"Lawyer?"

"Used to be." A lump formed in Aitkins's throat. "Retired."

"You seem too young to be retired. I'll get that coffee. Hang tight; the file should be here shortly."

Danny was thankful Hershel didn't follow up with more questions. Aitkins was content to let the subterfuge hang out there, dangling in the wind. He was unwilling to expound upon his deception.

Ghent returned with two cups of coffee, "Carson Mines" and the company's corporate logo affixed to identical ceramic mugs. The young lawyer extended a mug to Aitkins. "Sorry: cinnamon flavored. I'm not a fan, but it's all that's ready."

Aitkins smiled, accepted the cup, but didn't reply.

The tall man reclaimed his seat, placed his coffee on his desk, and stared at the computer. "HR is having trouble finding the file. It's apparently archived in an older server. Shouldn't take but another few minutes." Ghent let the message sink in. "So, about this lawsuit . . ."

"They're having trouble finding Yost's employment file," Danny said into his cell phone as he waited in the lobby of the Carson Mining legal department, Mr. Hershel Ghent having profusely apologized and explained that he was walking over to HR to locate the documents. "Their master copy seems to be missing."

"Shit."

"Dees, that's *exactly* what *I* said when young Mr. Ghent made that revelation to *me*."

"You think they're hiding something?"

"Seems so. I mean, why are there fourteen pages missing from the middle of the man's file you received? You have the Bates stamped copies, showing that the missing documents aren't from the beginning or the end of the sequence, but from smack dab in the middle of Yost's personnel record. That is, at the very least, a bit odd, wouldn't you say?"

There was only silence from the Minnesota end of the conversation.

"Dees?"

"I was just thinking. If you can't get the complete file, I don't know what my next play is gonna be."

Aitkins thought for a moment. "Well, you could get an order from Judge Smythe, an Order to Show Cause, requiring Carson to show up in Minnesota in front of her to explain the missing file. But Smythe's jurisdiction ends at the Minnesota border."

"Shit."

Aitkins smiled. "You already said that." He watched visitors to Carson's legal department come and go from the comfort of an armchair. For the first time since his termination from the university, the disgraced attorney reached into his mental storehouse of legal knowledge to solve a lawyerly problem. "Maybe there's a way to put some teeth behind an Order to Show Cause."

"How so?"

"You'll need to dig into the connections between Continental and Carson. There's something odd about the way I'm being stonewalled and how Continental didn't give you the entire file. I'd check into the corporate ownership of Carson. See if there's some relationship between the two companies. Find that connection and then, if you've got the goods on them, get Smythe to issue an Order to Show Cause. Hire a Montana lawyer to have it served on Carson for a hearing here in Butte, in front of a Montana state court judge. I'd do it if I had a license to practice in Montana but hell, Dees, I don't even have a license to practice in Minnesota!"

"I'll get on it. I'll dig into the ties between Continental and Carson, and if I can prove they're related, I'll get Smythe to issue an order compelling Carson to appear in Montana state court. What's the county Butte is in?"

"Silver Bow."

• • •

"It is indeed an unfortunate circumstance that Ms. Hernesman in Minnesota was unable to retrieve the complete personnel file of Mr. Neil Yost, former safety manager of Carson Mines' Charlie Russell Pit, without the involvement of *two* very busy trial court judges: Judge Smythe in Hibbing, Minnesota and you, Judge Grange, here in Montana. There's really no reason why we are here other than corporate subterfuge," pronounced a dignified, small-boned woman in her early sixties, long, luxuriantly white hair pulled into a ponytail, a blue business suit hanging from her slender form as she stood behind counsel table and argued the plaintiff's cause in a Silver Bow County courtroom.

Judge Eddie Grange, thirty-five years old, newly appointed to the District Court trial bench from his position as Assistant Silver Bow County Attorney, once mired in the prosecution of traffic tickets and petty crimes but now empowered to hear all major civil and criminal matters, adjusted his eyeglasses, smoothed his neatly trimmed black beard, and listened intently to Liz Tyner, the lawyer hired by Dee Dee Hernesman to enforce Judge Smythe's Order to Show Cause in Montana.

"Agreed," Judge Grange, known throughout western Montana as a no-nonsense prosecutor who carried his disdain for delay and obfuscation from his law practice to the bench, said before turning his attention to Hershel Ghent, the lanky lawyer curled into the fetal position behind the overly large screen of an open laptop at the far end of the counsel table. "Seems cut and dried, Mr. Ghent. The Minnesota lawyers have established, by supplying copies of corporate documentation from Continental Mining International, that the Canadian company recently acquired fifty-one percent of the stock in Carson. There's a connection between the two entities that apparently has led Carson to do the bidding of its Canadian master. This tie has compelled Carson Mines to conceal evidence of its employee's

166

past. This cannot be allowed, Mr. Ghent. Where, pray tell, is Mr. Yost's personnel file?"

"Your Honor. We've conducted an exhaustive search of the computer servers in our HR department and we been unable to locate Mr. Yost's file. I really don't know what else to say. We have made every effort to comply with the Minnesota subpoena, but we can't produce what doesn't exist . . ."

Judge Grange glowered. "Really? That's the best Carson can come up with? 'We can't produce what we don't have?'"

Ghent's Adam's apple worked as the lawyer sought to address the judge's skepticism. "What can I say, Judge? It's the truth. We simply can't find the man's personnel file. Anywhere."

Eddie Grange leaned back in his chair. "What would you have me do, Ms. Tyner? Young Mr. Ghent here says the papers your Minnesota associates seek are no longer available. Are you suggesting I start locking up Carson's corporate officers until someone at the company produces the missing file?"

Liz Tyner smiled, confident the judge was on her side of the argument. "Not at all, Your Honor. Not at all. My suggestion would be for the Court to retain a Special Master, an outside computer forensics investigator—an expert in these sorts of things—to examine Carson's computer servers to see if Mr. Yost's file can be located. At the very least, such an expert will be able to determine when, and by whom, the file was removed or deleted."

The judge frowned. "Sounds expensive. Sounds like a fishing expedition."

Ms. Tyner brightened. "There's a simple solution, Your Honor. Yes, in my experience these sorts of forensic reviews *are* expensive, likely upwards of ten thousand dollars. But as Carson is the party that misplaced the documents, documents that Judge Smythe in Minnesota believes are critical to the plaintiff's case, a case I might add, that involves the deaths of two innocent salvage workers, and as Carson is the corporate stepchild of Continental Mining Incorporated of Minnesota, a firm owned by

Continental International, I'd suggest that Carson foot the bill for the Special Master. That way, you're indirectly requiring the responsible party in the Minnesota case to fund the forensic inquiry. Order Carson to deposit twenty thousand dollars in the Court's escrow account. That should cover the cost."

"Your Honor . . ." Hershel Ghent rose to his feet and looked appealingly at the judge, ". . . to require Carson to pay for, what, as you have already stated, is in essence a fishing expedition, a wild goose chase, is unfair. We didn't kill anybody. We're not a party to the Minnesota lawsuit. We've done nothing . . ."

"I get the point, Mr. Ghent. Carson is blameless. Well then, your company shouldn't have an issue with my ordering a Special Master to have a look-see into your computer servers. I like Ms. Tyner's approach. It's sensible and efficient. Yes, that's exactly what I'm going to order in this case."

Within two hours of executives at Carson Mining receiving, scrutinizing, and debating Judge Grange's curt, one-page order, a packet of documents—Neil Yost's *complete* personnel file—was delivered by courier to Ms. Elizabeth Tyner's law office in the Equity Building on West Granite Street. Liz Tyner called Danny Aitkins's cell phone and within minutes, Danny pulled his rental Corolla into the parking lot next to the Equity Building.

In the quietude of Tyner's conference room, the office closed because it was after 5:00 p.m., Liz Tyner and Danny Aitkins pieced together the history of Neil Yost's tenure at Carson Mining. What the lawyers discovered in the newly produced documents compelled Danny Aitkins to lean against the back of his hard, wooden chair, stare at the room's antique tin ceiling, and sigh.

"That sonofabitch," Aitkins said in a subdued voice, "that murdering, stupid-ass sonofabitch."

CHAPTER THIRTY-TWO

The bedroom warmed. Daylight invaded the space through a picture window overlooking the Ely municipal golf course and bathed Dee Dee Hernesman's bed—a queen-sized frame and box spring complete with a pillow-top mattress, antique black walnut head and footboards, the wood gnarled, well grained, and polished to a high sheen—in gilded brilliance. Natural light illumined the pale skin of Dee Dee's exposed back—the knobby joints of her spine apparent despite the thickness of her torso— and the curves of her small breasts pressed into crisp linen. Morning moved incrementally across rumpled white sheets and a folded quilt to reveal the dark skin of a younger woman, the woman's neck supported by pillows, her hands clasped behind her head exposing hairless armpits. The woman's neatly shorn pubic hair, angular hips, extruded navel, elongated breasts and cocoa-hued areola and nipples were exposed as she lay, eyes wide, staring out the window. Hernesman's companion watched a doe and twin fawns, the newborn deer nibbling tender July grass on the golf course's fifth green as the pin flag rustled. The doe stood sentinel, her head up, her ears erect, alert for wolves and coyotes and dogs and black bear on the prowl.

"Pretty."

Dee Dee Hernesman's eyes jetted open. "Yes you are," Dee Dee said, modestly covering herself with a crisp white sheet as she flipped over to face her partner, her black hair tangled, her gray eyes clear and vibrant despite just having awoken from slumber.

Gabriella Pierce remained uncovered, fully confident in her body, as she corrected Dee Dee. "I meant the deer," Gabriella said in the same whispered tone, as if the animals could hear her despite two panes of glass and significant distance between the women and the deer.

"Oh."

It had been their first time. Admittedly, Dee Dee was out of practice. It had been over a year since Carol up and left for Nebraska, hijacking Hernesman's desire in the process. Despite the fact that Dee Dee Hernesman was more than a decade older than Gabriella Pierce, the younger woman took the lead. Once their evening together turned from two friends watching *Avengers: Age of Ultron* in the newly refurbished State Theater to sipping cabernet in the Ely Steakhouse, once their eyes met in that ancient and knowing way of anticipated love, Gabriella drove them to Dee Dee's house. Between shifts of the Accord's manual transmission, Gabriella had placed her thin, brown hand on the soft white flesh of Dee Dee's thick wrist, transmitting intention without uttering a word. And despite the long—overly so, to Dee Dee's way of thinking—interlude between Carol and Gabriella, things had worked out. Patience and tenderness and gentle exploration had led to finality, to satisfaction, and to humble and blissful repose.

"I better get going," Gabriella finally said, moving with fluid grace from the bed. The woman's curves, her lean runner's form, were backlit by the sun as she reached for a blaze orange Big Bang T-shirt, black underwear and bra and brown cotton mini-skirt bunched on an end table. Strands of ebony swayed in rhythm to Gabriella's gait as she walked toward the bathroom. "I'll just take a quick shower and be on my way," the younger woman said as an afterthought, sliding into the bathroom and closing the door behind her.

"No breakfast? I could make some eggs and bacon and toast," Dee Dee called out as she sat upright in the bed, her back planted against the walnut headboard. "It's only six. You have time."

"We start summer inventory today. I have to be at the store by six-thirty. Those books won't count themselves," Gabriella added, a touch of her mother's Hindu heritage infecting her words. The woman's reference to her employment highlighted the fact that Gabriella had moved from Grand Marais to Ely. The woman no longer sang exclusively with Amy Maddox. She was also trying her hand as a solo performer. After the move, a move Pierce made with no promise of a job, a move true to her "I work without a net" philosophy, she'd been hired as the assistant manager of Piragis's Bookstore. The salary was modest but allowed Gabriella to afford a small apartment, pay her bills, and maintain a slender existence in the old mining town.

Dee Dee listened as water splatted and sprayed. She allowed her imagination to recreate Gabriella standing naked in the shower. But uncertain of her role, of her ability to initiate love, the lawyer did not act on her fantasy. She shifted beneath the sheets. The picture window came into view. The deer were gone. Dee Dee Hernesman closed her eyes and fell back asleep.

• • •

"It's exactly what we needed," Dee Dee had exclaimed as she spoke with Danny Aitkins over the telephone. The parcel containing Yost's employment file had been more closely scrutinized by the disgraced attorney in the quiet confines of his motel room in Butte before placing the call. Danny had re-opened the envelope he'd received from Liz Tyner, re-inventoried its contents, and had not been disappointed by the information supplied by Carson Mining. As required by the Order to Show Cause, the documents chronicled Yost's troubled employment with Carson Mines. Of particular interest to Danny, and, subsequently, to Dee Dee Hernesman and Kat Carpenter when Daniel scanned the paperwork into a computer located in the lobby of his motel and forwarded the file to the Minnesota lawyers, was a series of articles clipped from Butte's daily paper, *The Montana Standard,* and archived in Carson's records.

Mining Explosion Kills Three
(04/23/2003)
By Anna Gerling, Local Reporter

Silver Bow County Deputy Sheriff Dennis O'Hara, lead investigator in the Butte office, advised that the explosion at Carson Mine's Charlie Russell Pit at approximately 4:00 p.m. yesterday was the result of an accident. According to the prepared statement read by O'Hara, three workers at the mine were killed when off-spec ANFO (ammonium nitrate, fuel oil, and aluminum: the same mixture used to destroy the federal building in Oklahoma City and a commonly used blasting agent in the mining industry) was unintentionally detonated during an attempt to dispose of off-specification product.

"We have few details right now as to the exact cause, who was involved, or the reasons behind the explosion. We are also not releasing the names of the victims until the next of kin have been notified. Further details will be provided by Sheriff Hobbs as they become available," Deputy O'Hara said during a press conference.

The three deaths are the first in several years at the Carson Mines operation in Butte. The last known fatality at the Russell Pit was in 1999 and occurred when Wendell Larson, an independent mining engineer, fell from a pit shovel while inspecting a defective cable. Larson's safety harness failed, leading to his death. Civil litigation was commenced by the Larson family that resulted in a settlement of the claim by Carson Mines and its insurer. Fines were also levied against Carson by the United States Department of Labor's Mine Safety and Health Administration (MSHA) and paid without contest. No criminal charges were brought in that case and, according to Deputy O'Hara, it is too soon to determine whether or not criminal charges will be forthcoming in the most recent tragedy.

Though Danny Aitkins wasn't an expert on the Minnesota lawsuit, Hernesman had given him the basics—a paint-by-numbers version of the case. From the cursory information supplied by his former partner, Aitkins understood that the second news article in the packet was a bombshell.

Safety Manager at Carson Mines Accused of Gross Negligence:
Names of Mining Disaster Victims Revealed
(04/25/2003)
By Anna Gerling, Local Reporter

Preliminary investigation into the deaths of three miners working at the Charlie Russell Pit north of Butte who died in an explosion last week is, according to unnamed sources linked to the federal MHSA investigation of the matter, centered on the actions of Butte resident and Carson Mines Safety Director, Neil Yost. The same confidential source indicates that Mr. Yost is being investigated for both criminal and federal safety violations. A decision on whether to charge Yost with violations of Montana criminal statutes is expected once the initial investigation of the accident has been completed. Speculation is that Yost either required or suggested the method used by the three workers attempting to dispose of off-specification (off-spec) ANFO (a blasting agent). The unusable ANFO was required to be removed from the premises or destroyed on-site by the Montana Department of Environmental Quality (DEQ). Details as to how the explosion occurred have not been revealed but experts contacted by The Standard *regarding the disposal of off-spec ANFO have confirmed that controlled burning of the product, with close supervision and appropriate permitting, is an approved method of disposal. Those experts were unwilling, without knowing the specifics of the cause of the blast at the Russell Pit, to speculate as to whether or not the method allegedly recommended by Yost and used by Carson Mining in this instance was safe, within environmental standards, and approved by MSHA or other regulatory authorities.*

Investigator and spokesman for the Spring Bow County Sheriff's Office, Deputy Sheriff Dennis O'Hara, also revealed the names of the workers killed in the accident to be: John Simmonds, age twenty-seven, a single man from Anaconda; Benjamin Hicks, age forty-eight, married and father of six from Walkerville; and Jason Williams, age thirty-two, single, father of three, from Butte. An ecumenical funeral service will be held for the workers and their families at Holy Spirit Catholic Church in Butte. Details as to the service are listed in the obituary section of today's Butte Standard.

"You're kidding me, right?"

"'Fraid not, Dees. That asshole Yost, he killed *three* men back in 2003, in Montana, sent them to their deaths, just like he did Susie Lindahl and . . . what was the other kid's name?"

"Antonio Feggetti."

"Ya. Feggetti. The articles confirm, as do the MSHA and sheriff's reports in the Carson Mining file, that Yost was the Safety Director who orchestrated the disaster in '03. He gave the three men their marching orders, told Hicks, the dozer operator, to push pallets of off-spec ANFO into a burning fire, with Williams and Simmonds standing by with fire extinguishers. Can you imagine, Dees? Goddamned fire extinguishers! There were nearly four tons of degraded, off-spec ANFO on pallets, bags of the stuff stacked as high as a man, some of the bags broken open, spilling product on the ground. And Yost has two guys standing a few feet away with fire extinguishers. The fire, I might add, was started illegally by burning old railroad ties, a big no-no according to the DEQ."

"DEQ?"

"Montana Department of Environmental Quality. Yost took out a burning permit through the local office. There's a copy of it somewhere in the stuff I sent you. He told the DEQ he was burning 'brush.' Nothing about railroad ties. Lied. The bastard lied on the permit application!"

"Go on," Hernesman said, sitting at her desk, the excitement in her former partner's voice causing her own pulse to race.

A dry cough from a third participant to the telephone conference interrupted conversation.

"Sorry. Need some water," another woman's voice said. Sounds of swallowing could be heard. Kat Carpenter was listening in from her office. But, true to form, unwilling to disclose her insight, her thoughts, Kat Carpenter refrained from volunteering her views. "Continue," Kat said with authority, as if *she* was orchestrating the conversation.

"In the end, Carson paid financial penalties: sixty-five thousand for MSHA violations and an additional ten thousand in environmental fines. But that was pretty much the end of the matter."

Dee Dee sat upright. "No civil lawsuit? No criminal charges?"

Danny Aitkins sipped chilled Coke from a can. He had the urge, the need, to find a local bar, a place in Butte where he could tie one on and try to forget his failures, his disappointments, his losses. Like a lecher drawn to porn, Aitkins had an unmitigated desire to lose himself in risky behavior. And yet, Coke can in hand, he resisted the pull of personal demons.

"The families tried to circumvent the exclusive remedy of workers' compensation. They tried to argue that Yost, as the supervisor, committed an intentional tort—fraud in fact, based upon his lie on the burning permit application—but while that argument worked with the trial court, the Montana Supreme Court thought otherwise and reversed the trial court's decision. The families were left with workers' compensation as their sole remedy and Montana benefits in that respect are none too generous."

"Bad decision, that," Kat Carpenter said quietly. "Yost's fraud should have gotten them around the exclusive remedy of workers' compensation."

Hernesman found herself surprised by Carpenter's compassion. It was indeed, out of character for the hard-edged litigator. "Agreed. A shortsighted decision. And the local authorities? No criminal charges were brought against Yost?"

"None. Not against Yost and not against his superiors at Carson. The families were left with workers' compensation and the company paid the fines and that, unfortunately, was the end of that."

"And Carson didn't fire the sonofabitch?"

Dee Dee was taken aback by the curse. It was unexpected, coming as it did from the reserved Katherine Carpenter, a denizen of the Mesabi Country Club and Daughter's of the American Revolution set. "Good point, Kat. Yost kept his job?"

"He did. For whatever reason. I have no idea why," Danny added, "Based upon his job performance evals, up until 2003, he did his job competently. But after 2003, his marks weren't so good. I would have canned the man for idiocy. But that's not what happened. He stayed on, kept his position as *Unsafety* Manager," Aitkins paused to let the joke sink in. No one laughed. "Until he was hired by Continental. But before he was hired, all of what you now know was in the hands of Continental. They knew, when they hired the man, what happened in Montana and they hired Yost anyway. Go figure."

"Good work, Danny. When you heading back?"

Dee Dee stood up, her attention drawn to noise in the hallway of her law office. The door to Hernesman's office was closed but she could hear Gabriella Pierce talking in the lobby.

"Tomorrow. Couldn't get a plane out of Butte until morning."

"I'll let you two catch up," Kat interrupted, "we'll talk about bringing a motion to add punies and negligent hiring tomorrow."

Which means, Hugh and I will be putting the documents together, Your Highness.

"Sounds good. Actually, Dan," Dee Dee had said quietly, her attention drawn to the beautiful young folksinger/bookseller standing outside her office, smiling profusely, a loaf of French bread tucked under her left arm. "I have to run. Have a safe flight. See you soon."

The summer sun stood high above Butte when Danny Aitkins emerged from his motel room, took a deep breath of warm, moist mountain air, and began walking toward the nearest saloon.

CHAPTER THIRTY-THREE

"You look like shit," Dee Dee Hernesman observed, buttermilk
pancakes, hash browns, and sausage links crowding her plate.
Hernesman's comment was directed at Danny Aitkins, a
disheveled, hung-over, decrepit manifestation of humanity
slumped in a chair across the table from Hernesman in the trendy
301 Restaurant of the Duluth Sheraton. A manila envelope, the
trove Aitkins had retrieved from Butte, occupied the table
between them. "What the hell were you thinking?"

Danny Aitkins struggled to remain upright, his head
pounding, his eyes barely open. He'd not only tied one on at the
Last Stand Saloon in downtown Butte, but after a brief nap on
the flight from Montana to Minnesota, followed by a bouncing
shuttle ride in a twelve-passenger van from the Cities to Duluth,
he'd wandered across the street from his room at the Sheraton to
spend the evening in conversation with locals at the bar of the
Zeitgeist Café. The disgraced lawyer picked up a coffee cup, his
right hand trembling to the point where he needed both hands to
steady the cup, and sipped. The question Dee Dee posed was one
she'd asked him years ago, back when they were working on a
case in Winnipeg, and she discerned that he'd slept with a
paralegal working for opposing counsel, a woman who also
happened to be the widow of Danny's best friend, out of which
emerged Aitkins's fourth child, a daughter, and Danny's first
divorce. He didn't have an answer to Hernesman's question then,
and he didn't have one as they contemplated breakfast in the
Sheraton.

"I fucked up."

"Really? Six months of sobriety flushed down the toilet.
And for what? A goddamned hangover? I'll never understand
you, Daniel Aitkins. Never."

Aitkins looked at Hernesman with pleading eyes.
"Didn't expect you to. I tried, Dees. I tried keeping it together.

But with my addictive DNA, the one gift my dearly departed mother left me, I just can't beat it. You gave me a chance to feel useful. For that, I'm grateful. But there's nothing you can say or do or try that I haven't already heard, done, or tried on my own. I'm just too weak to beat the curse my momma left me as my inheritance."

Hernesman nodded. "I know. I get it. But if you keep at it, you're not gonna see sixty-five."

Aitkins looked at the cheese omelet on the white ceramic plate in front of him. "I don't think I can eat."

"You need food," Dee Dee whispered, carefully scanning the room to see if other diners in the restaurant were listening. "At least try a few bites."

Aitkins placed his cup on its saucer, picked up a fork, sliced off a bit of egg and cheese, and raised the food with a tremulous hand. The lawyer gagged when he smelled egg. "Can't do it. Gonna heave." Danny rose from his chair and moved with uncanny speed toward the men's room.

"I have no idea what to do," Dee Dee said to herself, watching her former mentor dash through the hotel lobby. "He's about the biggest mess of a human being I've ever come across."

• • •

"Your Honor, Mr. Goggleye, as the Trustee for the Next of Kin of Susie Lindahl, has brought two motions for the Court's consideration," Kat Carpenter announced in a steady voice, in a tone evincing complete command and control of the Hibbing courtroom. "The first motion for the Court's consideration is a Motion to Amend the Complaint to add a claim of Negligent Hiring. Essentially we are saying that, after uncovering what Continental Mining knew about Defendant Neil Yost at the time he was hired, including all the information we retrieved at great expense and effort with this Court's kind assistance from Carson Mines, information which Defendant Continental had in its

179

possession before it decided to hire Mr. Yost, there is no way a responsible employer should have or would have hired Mr. Yost as Safety Director."

Judge Harriet Smythe studied the case file on the computer monitor in front of her on the bench. She used the mouse—rather than the touch screen capabilities of the Dell—to flip pages. "Let's stick with that motion, shall we? We can turn to your second motion, the Motion to Add a Claim for Punitive Damages, after we've heard from Mr. Johansson. But before Mr. Johansson says his piece regarding the hiring of Mr. Yost, I have a question for him."

Kat Carpenter sat down. She knew, from years of courtroom work, from thousands of hearings and countless trials, from hours of interaction with Judge Harriet Smythe, what was about to happen.

The Silver Wolf stood. The other defense attorneys, David Van Clive for Calumet, and Cicely Thompson for Hibbing Salvage and Remediation and Steve Gruber, sat stoically between Dee Hernesman and Johansson at counsel table. The other defense lawyers had no dog in the fight. Whatever Judge Smythe ruled in the pending matter would not alter or change their trial strategies: They would continue to point their collective fingers at Neil Yost and Continental as the parties responsible for the death of Susie Lindahl and stay as far away from antagonizing Kat Carpenter as was humanly possible. Johansson scanned his paper file, raised his eyes, cleared his throat, and nodded.

"You have a question, Your Honor?"

Judge Smythe leaned away from the computer monitor. A significant squeak emitted from the judge's high-backed, black leather chair. "I do."

"Yes, Your Honor?"

"Why in hell did it take a court order from me and the involvement of a trial court judge in Montana to obtain for these people what was rightfully due them?" The jurist's face flashed

180

red. Judge Smythe, not known for outbursts or displays of temper, was clearly pissed off.

Shit. I really don't have an answer for that question other than, "Because my client lied to me, told me it didn't have any of the missing documents, much less the newspaper, MHSA, and sheriff's records that Aitkins brought back from Butte." But that's not gonna go over so well with Judge Smythe, now is it? Ah, hell. Continental and Yost and Carson did this to me. It's on them that I'm in this mess. Screw it. "I'm as puzzled by my client's lack of candor as you are, Judge."

A loud cough echoed from the gallery. Bruce Cutler, the portly attorney representing the excess insurer in the case, the moneyman to Hernesman's way of thinking, the person who controlled whether the case settled or went to trial, was also present. Before Judge Smythe could acknowledge Cutler's interruption, the man stood up, picked up his briefcase, waddled to the exit, opened the courtroom door, and disappeared.

"Seems Mr. Cutler didn't appreciate your candor, Mr. Johansson. But the Court does. And, without wasting everyone's time here, after having read the briefs, it's clear to me that plaintiff prevails as to adding claims for both negligent hiring and punitive damages. With all due respect, Counsel, when an international company hires a loose cannon like Neil Yost, a man who knows full well what happens when you mix ANFO and fire, as its Safety Director, whatever damage flows from Mr. Yost, here, the death of an innocent young woman, is owned not only by Mr. Yost but by his employer." The judge took a breath to regain her composure. "Yost was grossly, undeniably negligent if plaintiff's expert affidavits and the newly discovered materials are to be believed, giving rise to the necessity to punish both Yost and Continental beyond mere compensatory damages. And it seems pretty clear," Judge Smythe added for drama, "that the reason the information sought by Ms. Carpenter and Ms. Hernesman regarding Yost's hiring by Continental was not provided to them is tied to the fact, as alleged by the plaintiffs and verified by my law clerk, that Continental owns a majority interest in Carson Mines."

Kat Carpenter couldn't suppress her delight. She shifted her gaze from Johansson to Dee Dee Hernesman and winked. Hernesman grinned in reply.

"We'll let a jury figure out whether punishment, in the form of punitive damages," the judge concluded, "is warranted in this case."

"But your honor . . ."

The Silver Wolf attempted to argue his clients' cause, but Judge Smythe was done listening.

"Stop, Mr. Johansson," the judge said, raising her right hand like a traffic cop. "There's no point in continuing. In addition to Yost's alleged conduct regarding Miss Lindahl's death, Continental hid vital, relevant information from the plaintiffs. If Ms. Bucher had been apprised of what Ms. Carpenter, Ms. Hernesman, and Mr. McLean now know, I seriously doubt that the Feggetti family would have settled so cheaply. But there's nothing I can do about that now. I can," the jurist said, reaching with an unsteady right hand for a glass of water, sipping from the crystal tumbler before placing it back on a marble coaster, "and I will do something about *this* case. First, by granting the motions. Second, by advising both parties that I am considering giving the jury an adverse inference instruction regarding the cause of the explosion. Plaintiff filed a motion in limine regarding spoliation long ago, after the mining company altered the accident scene and obliterated evidence," the judge took a deep breath, "before plaintiff's expert had a chance to view the site and collect soil samples in response to Defendants' allegations that the ground, not the silo, exploded, or that rogue ANFO had been introduced into the salvage operation by the two dead workers. I told you when *that* motion was brought that I would defer deciding *that* issue until sometime in the future. Well," and at this point the judge turned her attention and focused her gaze on Dee Dee Hernesman, the author of the

182

motion for an adverse inference instruction, "the future is now. Ms. Hernesman, you will, if this matter proceeds to jury trial, receive the benefit of an adverse inference instruction based upon spoliation of evidence as you requested."

"But your honor . . ."

"Enough, Mr. Johansson! You know me well enough to sit down and shut up when I tell you to do so. I am telling you to do so now. Continental Mining and Mr. Yost have screwed this thing up so badly . . . please excuse the curse, but I can't think of any more polite way of describing your clients' collective ineptitude in this case, from the hiring of Mr. Yost, to the improvident alteration of the accident scene, to the concealment of vital documents." The judge paused in an effort to calm her racing heart. She was visibly upset, and she knew she was letting the conduct of the defendants get to her. She closed her eyes and collected her thoughts. "The other thing that I'll be doing," and at this, Judge Smythe opened her eyes and focused her attention on Kat Carpenter, the attorney arguing the motions, "is entertaining sanctions against Continental Mining and any officer of the company who signed discovery responses, whether answers to interrogatories, or requests for admissions, or requests for the production of documents, where those answers or responses concealed the information retrieved from Montana. I do not announce my intentions lightly; it is a rare thing for me to apply the power of a monetary penalty against a party in a case. But the conduct of the corporate defendant in this matter has been so over the top, it may well be warranted."

"If I may, Judge."

The Silver Wolf was back on his feet. Peder Johansson's tone was quiet, subdued, and deferential as he sought an audience with the court.

"No arguments as to the merits, Mr. Johansson."

"Understood. I would ask, that, given the Court's strong personal dislike, really, disdain, for Defendant Continental in this case, that this Court recuse itself from any further consideration of this matter. In short, with all due respect to you, Judge Smythe, your comments here today make it impossible, in my humble view, for you to continue on as the judge in this case."

Judge Smythe removed her bifocals and grinned quixotically. "That might be a valid argument, sir, if your clients hadn't acted in a fashion that would provoke a nun. Motion to remove denied. Motions to amend the complaint and for an adverse inference instruction at trial are granted. I'll reserve any discussion of monetary sanctions against Defendant Continental for after the trial."

Judge Smythe, who rarely, if ever, used her gavel, slammed wood against wood. The jurist stood, stepped away from the bench, and exited the courtroom, leaving behind a stunned and silent audience.

CHAPTER THIRTY-FOUR

It was dark as the old green Chevrolet pickup truck bucked and pitched. The yellow glow of the C-10's headlamps, the light seemingly as old and worn out as the truck, illumined aspen and balsam, second-growth trees that sprouted—after the forest had been clear-cut of its native red pine, white pine, and black spruce—alongside a single-lane gravel track leading to a back entrance to the Merritt Pit site. It was early Sunday morning. Construction workers were asleep in trailers erected just outside the fenced perimeter of the work site. Four unarmed security officers patrolled two miles of steel mesh fencing defining the project. Four unarmed guards riding Polaris ATVs carrying flashlights and portable radios were all that stood between the work being done and folks who weren't keen on allowing sulfide mining on the cusp of wilderness.

The pickup truck, the sheet metal of its box pockmarked with rust, the beams of its headlamps undulating with each bump and dip in the road, veered to the right. The driver didn't need a map to tell him that the rugged trail his Chevrolet was purring along in the cool northeastern Minnesota summer night, mosquitoes subdued by air as crisp as an October morning, would lead him to an abandoned test pit used by Continental's engineers to confirm the wealth hidden beneath the land's scrubby surface.

"Quiet and cool tonight," the driver said as he sipped a can of Venture. "Damn that's good," he said just before the Chevy hit a significant pothole and forced beer up his nose. "But it's hard to drink and drive on this goat trail!"

This wasn't Texas, where drinking and driving is legal, but northeastern Minnesota, where such behavior is frowned upon. The fact that the driver was breaking the law had little effect on him as he downed the last of the lager, reached across the dusty vinyl bench seat for a second can, cracked the tab, and took a draw of slightly chilled beer.

"Ah. Here we are."

The truck slowed to a stop in a bowl-shaped depression lined with pin cherry and aspen trees. An old John Deere utility tractor and loader sat to one side of the test pit, the tractor's right rear tire flat, the bucket of the loader half-full of earth growing weeds. The intruder stepped from the Chevy, chugged the last of his beer, and tossed the can into the truck's bed. Shivering from the cold, the old man unlatched the Chev's tailgate and lowered it until rusted levers came to rest. He lifted two five gallon plastic jugs of pancake syrup, an item he'd added to the grocery list he'd filled out at his new job as fry cook at Frank's Café in Tower, free of the bed.

The old man had ensured his tracks were covered, that he had an ironclad alibi. He'd commenced a relationship with a needy and loyal Native woman who would, if interviewed by the authorities regarding his whereabouts, lie through her teeth to protect him.

"Shit that's heavy," the old man mumbled as he placed the jugs on the ground and turned on a headlamp. "Damned arthritis is acting up again. But what's protest without sacrifice. Am I right?"

The old man reclaimed the jugs and followed a narrow trail. The path came to an end at a chain link fence. The fence was too high to climb. A nearby gate was padlocked. The man placed the syrup on the ground, retrieved a Diamond Tool wire cutter from a leather pouch on his belt, and snipped the fencing. The old man extinguished the headlamp, grabbed the jugs, ducked through the hole in the fence, and entered the Merritt Pit Mine.

Two months earlier, Governor Wesley Whitcomb had announced that the environmental permitting for the new Merritt Pit Copper/Nickel Mine had been completed. Continental Mining of

186

Minnesota, Inc. had been ready, at a moment's notice, to begin construction of the mine's infrastructure. Within a day of the governor's announcement, Nolan Excavating of Deer River, the largest earth moving company in northeastern Minnesota, moved on-site with dozers and scrapers and dump trucks and backhoes and excavators. By the time Cyrus Oliphant trespassed, initial preparation of the site had been completed. Dozens of pieces of heavy equipment remained in place, ready to begin the actual construction of the mine and attendant sorting, washing, and finishing plants that would process bits of copper, nickel, gold, silver, and platinum. Oliphant had selected Nolan's equipment as his target of protest. And while the man was smart enough to know his civil disobedience—the disabling of a few pieces of machinery by pouring maple-flavored pancake syrup and plastic beads into their fuel tanks—was nothing more than a child's prank, it was the best plan Cyrus Oliphant had been able to come up with.

"There's a likely candidate," Oliphant said, slipping between two dump trucks to stand next to a large bulldozer. "A little syrup and plastic in that big fella's tank should screw things up royally once the operator fires 'er up, lets 'er idle, and tries to move 'er."

Oliphant slid latex gloves over his hands, opened the dozer's fuel tank hatch, unscrewed the fuel cap, and poured syrup. He reached into a jacket pocket and removed a small bag of plastic BBs of the type sold as ammunition for toy guns. Oliphant removed the glove on his right hand, tore the plastic sack open, and dumped beads. After shoving his bare hand back into latex, Oliphant replaced the fuel cap, closed the metal fuel door, and repeated the sequence on seven other pieces of equipment until the syrup and the beads were gone. The sabotage was over in less than ten minutes. Oliphant's covert operation was completed without detection.

Oliphant retraced his steps, stopped at the breach in the fence, looked back at the mine, and smiled. Distant stars blinked overhead. Canada geese argued on Birch Lake. Cyrus Oliphant took in the sights and sounds of the night before slipping through the hole in the fence—empty bottles of syrup in hand, crumpled packaging that once held plastic beads stuffed into a jacket pocket—to emerge on the footpath leading to the test pit. After tossing the syrup jugs into the pickup's bed, the old man opened the driver's door, slid behind the steering wheel, put the key in the ignition, and fired up the 350. Cyrus Oliphant kept the Chevy's headlights off as he drove away from the Merritt Pit Mine, contemplating the soft sheets and pillows of his rented bed back in Tower.

CHAPTER THIRTY-FIVE

Native American drummers, singers, and dancers stood beneath a sweltering sun in front of Ely City Hall, a dozen or so performers surrounded by several hundred spectators. Some of the Ojibwe held signs proclaiming support for the actions of the mysterious saboteur or saboteurs who had stalled the Merritt Pit project. The culprit or culprits who'd slipped onto the mining company's property in the dead of night and protested copper/nickel mining by engaging in felony-level property damage had not been caught, but the Bois Forte band members assembled in town were deifying whoever accomplished the task. The seminal issue that prompted the Native Americans to support such civil disobedience was their concern over sulfide contamination and its impact on wild rice.

The industrial process that would soon be in place at the Merritt Pit Mine was essentially the same process that had been used in Montana, Colorado, Arizona, Alberta, and British Columbia to ill effect on creeks, streams, and rivers. Copper mining in those far-distant places had left legacies of environmental degradation that various governments were forced to remediate when the offending mining concerns pulled out and invariably filed for bankruptcy to avoid responsibility for the environmental damage they caused.

A collateral consequence of copper/nickel mining is that the resultant mine waste, placed in overburden after flecks of copper and nickel and other precious minerals are removed, is high in sulfide. When rain falls or snow washes the overburden and the resulting runoff follows gravity, adjacent waterways become contaminated as water combines with the mining waste to form sulfuric acid. If the resulting runoff enters northeastern Minnesota creeks, streams, and rivers, acid contamination will ultimately impact Hudson Bay (for rivers flowing north) or Lake

Superior (for rivers flowing south). The accumulation of acid in the water kills fish, harms wildlife, and, most important to the Ojibwe, has the potential to destroy the sacred food provided to them by the Great Creator: *Manoomin.* Wild rice.

Save Our Manoomin

Sheriff Debra Slater stood in the crowd listening to Clarence Bighead, a respected elder of the Bois Forte Band of the Minnesota Chippewa Tribe—Bois Forte being located along the shores of Nett Lake and Lake Vermillion west of Ely—as the elder recited poetry written in his ancestral tongue. Slater couldn't follow the words spoken by the old Indian, but she was fairly certain that the verses praised wild rice, family, and a culture painstakingly preserved by tribal leaders.

As Sheriff of Cook County, Deb Slater had experience with the Ojibwe. Grand Portage, another band of the Minnesota Chippewa Tribe, occupied a reservation in her jurisdiction. Slater had an excellent rapport with the Grand Portage Tribal Council, the band's governing body. When vandalism, sexual assault, and domestic violence escalated on the reservation, the band, with limited casino revenues and significant issues of poverty and substance abuse straining its resources, asked Slater to assign a full-time deputy to the reservation. An agreement was reached between the two governments: Cook County supplied a deputy and the band paid the costs of a new squad car and the deputy's salary and benefits, thereby saving the band from creating a tribal police force, a solution that would have been prohibitively expensive. Deb hired a new deputy, Sarah Hanson, a rookie just out of Fond du Lac Community College's two-year law enforcement program who had, despite her blond hair and blue eyes, Ojibwe heritage on her mother's side, to be the law enforcement presence in Grand Portage. Other Cook County officers, including Slater, spelled Hanson when she was off duty or on vacation. The arrangement worked well, and Sheriff Slater was in discussions with Grand Portage regarding the possibility of hiring a second deputy to patrol the reservation.

Though Deb Slater was ignorant as to the exact meaning of the words being recited by the elder, she understood the gist of Clarence Bighead's message: *We Ojibwe oppose copper/nickel mining on or near our traditional lands because we believe sulfide mining will taint the water and kill our beloved* Manoomin.

"Fuckin' Indians." Someone behind Slater muttered the curse. "Tryin' to stop progress. They don't want progress? Maybe they should close their casinos and hand in their car keys and their outboards and go back to paddlin' canoes and living in teepees."

The sheriff turned her head. A middle-aged white man, a man she'd not seen or encountered at past rallies and protests, his beer gut protruding over his belt, his Wranglers smeared with grease, oil, and dirt—the look of a mechanic or a plumber about him—was making the statements even though he was clearly outnumbered by the Native Americans in the crowd. Sensing trouble, Slater slid between two Ojibwe women, one short and fat wearing a Minnesota Vikings sweatshirt, the other tall and thin dressed in a traditional native dance dress complete with beads and bells, to confront the angry man.

"Sir," Slater said politely, "I understand you might not like what the gentleman has to say. It's absolutely your right to disagree. But do you really think this is the time and place?"

The white man stood a full head taller than Slater. His eyes were clear and defiant. A wad of chew caused his left cheek to bulge as he raised his right hand.

Shit. Not here. Not in this crowd. I don't even have enough room to deploy my Taser.

But the man was merely reaching to adjust his Twins cap. A curious calm came over the stranger's angry face.

"I get it, Sheriff. Message understood. Next time, I'll bring my own fuckin' sign, something like 'Columbus Had it

Right' or 'Go Back to the Rez,'" the logger said quietly. "I got a right to do that, don't I? I mean, I served my country in the First Gulf War. Honorably discharged from the United States Marine Corps. Two tours. Ain't I earned the right to say my piece?"

Slater nodded and stepped back. "Indeed you do. I'm just asking that you tone it down a bit. We don't want trouble. Let these folks have their say. That's all I'm asking."

"I can do that," the man agreed. "Don't understand a lick of what the chief there is sayin'. But I know he's not happy. Too damn bad. This town is dying. The tourists dribble in for a few days, spend a few dollars, and then go back to Minneapolis. Or Duluth. Or Chicago. The money they leave behind is just a temporary fix, a brief shot in the arm. We need real jobs. Good-payin' jobs. The copper/nickel mines will do that. Put folks back to work. This here debate is wrongheaded. We can have clean water and jobs is all I am sayin'. You agree with that, don't you, Sheriff?"

The Native dancer placed a finger to her mouth to shush the white man. "Have some respect. An elder is speaking."

Crimson flashed across the stranger's face, but he held his temper. "Sorry. Anyway, I'll behave myself, Sheriff. Next time, I'll bring my own fuckin' sign."

The older woman, her right hand clenched around the hand of a child, likely her granddaughter, took exception to the curse. "Watch your language, sir. There are children present."

Another cloud crossed over the man's brow but passed without emerging as anger. "I apologize, ma'am. Didn't see the child."

"We're good, Mister . . ."

"Roberts. Ed Roberts. You don't remember me, Sheriff Slater, but you gave me a DUI, back in my drinking days, when you was a patrol deputy out of Duluth."

Slater studied the man. His face wasn't the least bit familiar, but, given she'd handed out over a thousand DUI tickets during her career, that wasn't surprising. "Sorry. Name doesn't ring a bell. Anyway, thanks for being understanding. And," Slater said as she turned back toward the speaker, "thank you for your service."

Ed Roberts nodded but didn't reply. Polite applause erupted as Clarence Bighead ended his recitation. Another speaker, Joyce Running Bear, a noted Indian activist, closed the program. Drummers, singers, and dancers returned to the front of the crowd and performed a final song. Slater made her way toward Bighead. The old man was four to five inches shorter than the sheriff, and, truth be told, no more than a hundred pounds soaking wet. The slender, wizened Indian nodded as Deb Slater approached.

"Sheriff, nice of you to come out and support our cause," Bighead teased, knowing full well that Slater's politics tended to be conservative, knowing that she was present due to official duties and not to hear his poetry or support the band's protest.

"Clarence, you know better. Let's not waste time debating politics. I need some information," Deb Slater said quietly, gesturing for them to move away from Bighead's family and friends in order to hold a private conversation.

"What's up?"

The officer studied the weathered face of the little old man, his eyes as black as a starless night, his hair white, thick, and braided into a long rope descending from the back of the man's narrow head to his trim waist. "You know anything about the troubles out at the mine?"

Bighead smiled. Dental implants had replaced the old man's natural teeth. Bighead's new smile was brilliant, even, and took years off the man's age. "You're asking if I know who decided to 'sweeten' the fuel tanks of a few pieces of construction equipment?"

Deb Slater nodded. "That would be the question."

Bighead bit his lip. "We've known each other a long time, Debra. Ever since you worked patrol in northern St. Louis County, what, twenty years ago?"

"Twenty-five."

"Time passes, doesn't it? Can it really be a quarter-century since you responded to calls at Boise Forte?"

Slater nodded.

"So you think I might know who did the deed, eh? Well, sorry to say, as much as I admire whoever stepped up to the plate to make his or her point, I have no idea who pulled off the caper. Not a clue."

Slater tried to keep skepticism from showing but was unsuccessful.

"Truly. Of course, if I *did* know who trashed those dozers and trucks, I wouldn't be at liberty to share the name or names. But I don't have to resort to deception. Sheriff, I really don't know who the hell put that gunk in the fuel tanks. I can tell you this: I've had my ear to the ground around Nett Lake and at the casino and I'm pretty sure that the prank wasn't done by an Indian. Rumor has it, it was one guy. One white guy, likely a Sierra Club type. But that's about all I know."

Debra Slater stared hard at the old man. She locked her gaze with Bighead's inky, serious eyes long enough to know the old man was telling the truth. "If you hear anything . . ."

Clarence smiled. "I'll be sure to keep it to myself, Sheriff. Like I said, I admire the guy's work. I wish I would've thought of the stunt. Maple syrup! That's rich. Seems like something an Indian would dream up. I'll hand it to the guy: It's one original way to send a message," the elder observed. "Gotta run. Grandkids are waiting for me to take them to Dairy Queen."

The sheriff watched the elder collect a gaggle of children ranging from toddlers to teenagers—a full dozen or so kids—and walk east, toward Ely's DQ.

Slater returned her attention to the crowd. Across the street, a lone white man stood near the curb sipping soda or beer or ice tea from a can. The man's face was familiar. But before Slater could question Cyrus Oliphant about where he had been the night construction equipment was disabled by maple syrup and plastic beads, the tall man was gone.

CHAPTER THIRTY-SIX

Annie Slater carried dirty plates and saucers and cups and silverware into the kitchen of the Blue Water Café. Stan Olson, a skinny kid with average looks and a cheerful disposition working as a dishwasher at the café during the summer between his junior and senior years at Cook County High School, rinsed debris into the sink before loading dishes and utensils into a steel rack, inserting the rack into the dishwasher, and hitting the power button. Annie, her stomach extended to the limit of her skin, the baby filling every nook and cranny of Annie's belly at thirty-one weeks, moved gingerly to avoid slipping on the wet floor. It was Annie's last week of work before taking time off to prepare for motherhood. The girl was tired. Dog tired. All of her attention was focused on staying upright. Given the unnatural center of gravity created by the baby, maintaining balance was no easy task even for a Division I athlete.

"Hey," Stan said as Annie shoved a rack of dirty dishes across a stainless steel counter toward the dishwasher.

"Hey yourself."

"You're getting pretty damn big. How's the kiddo?"

Annie stood up and massaged her belly with both hands through the cotton pregnancy smock she wore over her expanded panel Levi's.

I must look really, really fat right now. God, how did I let this happen? Stretch marks and a kid before my 20th birthday. I am one ignorant girl. And don't get me started about the sore boobs, the acne, the screwed up plumbing, the shortness of breath. Maybe for some women pregnancy is a glorious experience. That ain't me.

"She's stopped kicking, stopped moving at all, really. I think Riki's run out of room."

Stan had been a sophomore when Margaret Ann Slater graduated from Cook County High. The boy had grown some and now stood eye-to-eye with Annie as they talked. Cook County High School is small and, despite the difference in their ages, Annie knew Stan Hanson because his brother Matt, the captain of the football team, was Annie's classmate. But despite that connection, with Annie being a senior and Stan being a sophomore, their interaction had been limited to a perfunctory "hey" in the hallways, a relationship not dissimilar to their current one at work.

Hanson slid the rack of dishes toward the sink. He grabbed a flexible nozzle, turned the hot water spigot, picked up a dirty plate, and flushed food down the garbage disposal. "You sure it's a girl?"

"Positive."

"You had an ultrasound, to see if it has a third leg?"

The boy's inability to say the word "penis" made Annie grin.

"No. I just know she's a girl."

"How's that?"

"Intuition."

"Ah."

The boy turned his attention back to his work but continued talking. "How's the sheriff?" Haven't seen her around town much this summer."

Annie moved toward the cook's station—intent on picking up orders to be delivered to hungry customers—but stopped and faced the dishwasher. "She spends a lot of time in Ely with the task force. Some idiot poured maple syrup and plastic beads into equipment at the new mine. Screwed things up royally. She's trying to catch whoever did it."

Stan smiled as he shoved the rack of dirty dishes into the dishwasher. "I hope they never catch him. The guy's like Robin Hood."

The young woman shook her head. "What makes you so sure it's a guy? Could be a girl. And he or she isn't a hero, Stan. He or she is a criminal. Plain and simple. And," Annie added,

197

flipping a strand of hair off her forehead, "that mine's gonna get built whether Robin Hood or Jesus Christ tries to stop it."

"Maybe. But it's gonna bring in what, two, three hundred jobs? We'd risk destroying the BWCA with sulfide pollution, wreck one of the only wilderness areas we have left, for a couple hundred jobs? I don't see the point."

Annie waved a hand in the air and moved toward steaming plates of food. "Your brother Matt would never say something that stupid. He'd agree with me on this one. A few hundred jobs are better, by large measure, than no jobs, which is what we have now." Annie picked up a tray filled with sandwiches, soup, and drinks from the cook's station. "And both the state and the feds have signed off on the mine, say that there's no risk to the watershed. You tree huggers," she clucked derisively, straining to straighten up under the weight of the tray, "you are . . ."

Annie Slater didn't complete the sentence. Without warning, the young mother-to-be dropped the tray and dishes and food, grabbed her belly, and collapsed to the floor.

CHAPTER THIRTY-SEVEN

Hugh McLean and Dee Dee Hernesman sat quietly in the fifth floor conference room of the law offices of Mooseberger and Patton waiting for the court-appointed mediator, Edwin Mooseberger, to return from meeting with Peder Johansson and Bruce Cutler across the hallway. Tubby Goggleye stood at the far end of the long, narrow room. Windows displayed the panorama of the Mississippi as the river wove its way through downtown St. Paul. Goggleye's attention was captured by a two-engined prop plane doing touch and goes at the municipal airport located in the river's floodplain. "Must be practicing," the Ojibwe lawyer said to no one in particular. "What the hell is taking Mooseberger?" Goggleye asked, changing the subject as he turned toward the other attorneys.

"Dunno," Hernesman said quietly. Dee Dee was wearing her best "going to court" navy blue pants suit—her bow to Hillary Clinton—a conservative white blouse, a necklace boasting a single natural pearl on a delicate gold chain, and matching pearl ear studs—gifts from Gabriella Pierce. "We told him three million was as low, given Judge Smythe's ruling on the punitive damages, spoliation, and negligent hiring issues, as we'd go short of trial. Johansson, and Cutler—that stingy old sonofabitch, haven't offered seven figures yet. Six-fifty. What the hell is that? It's not even double what they paid the Feggetti family and Antonio Feggetti died without leaving behind children. What the hell do you think is taking so long, Hugh?"

Hugh McLean shook his head.

Goggleye looked at McLean with scrutiny. "*Kat* got your tongue?"

The Indian's attempt at levity, by invoking a shopworn play on Katherine Carpenter's nickname, didn't prompt a response from Hugh MacLean.

"Hugh, you must have some idea of the game Cutler and Johansson are playing here," Hernesman said, looking directly into the man's milky gray eyes. "Surely you and Kat talked strategy. You gotta have some insight into where this thing is headed. Last email I sent her, Kat was fine with three million as our 'drop dead' figure. Has something changed?"

McLean cleared his throat. "You and Kat are driving this bus, Dees. I'm just an observer. Kat would have been here herself but she's in depositions on another case in Minneapolis, a nasty medical malpractice suit venued in Bemidji that she's defending."

Hernesman leaned back in her chair and studied the younger man. "Didn't know your firm was handling med mal defense."

McLean nodded. "We have a contract, or I should say, Kat has a contract, to provide coverage for the northern half of the state."

Goggleye resumed watching the airplane. "I don't know how she does it."

McLean looked at the Indian quizzically. "How's that?"

Tubby turned his attention to McLean. "Adjusts her loyalty to plaintiffs or defendants—like turning a water spigot on and off. I should think that's tough to do, philosophically, I mean."

Hernesman laughed. "Katherine's only philosophy is to cherish the color green. If there's a payday behind it, Kat will take the case, plain and simple."

McLean frowned. "That's a bit harsh, Dee Dee. Kat's as ethical as they come . . ."

"And I'm Mother Theresa," Hernesman quipped. "Pure of heart and dedicated to God."

McLean smiled weakly. "Maybe. Maybe not. I leave it to a higher power to be the judge. But our firm has been comfortable doing both plaintiff and defense work for a long,

long time. Taking on med mal defense cases isn't that big a deal for Kat."

The door to the conference room opened. Edwin Mooseberger, a dapperly dressed octogenarian whose face had been surgically altered but whose sagging neck betrayed age, stepped into the room and closed the door. Mooseberger claimed a chair across from McLean and Hernesman. Tubby Goggleye resumed sitting at the head of the table.

"Well, I'm afraid we're at a bit of an impasse," the mediator said quietly, his hands folded in front of his finely tailored summer weight, gray business suit.

"How so?" Hernesman asked.

"I think I could move the other side a bit. At least, that's the impression I got from speaking with Johansson with Cutler out of the room. Cutler took a walk. He's talking to his people— the money folks at Saturnia. He'll be back in an hour or so."

"Hasn't the man heard of those new gizmos called 'cell phones?'" Hernesman asked, the ire in her voice clear.

Mooseberger smiled weakly. "What can I say? Old men and technology . . ."

"I sense there's a 'but' to your observation about being able to move defense counsel after Cutler returns," Tubby interjected.

Hernesman glanced at Hugh McLean and noted that the man was sweating profusely. She found McLean's reluctance to join the discussion, on the heels of his refusal to engage in private conversation with her and Tubby about numbers, odd behavior from someone she'd worked so closely with over the course of eight months. *Something's up. Don't know what. But something is up with Hugh McLean that I can't put my finger on.*

"Cutler is fairly insistent that Saturnia will offer nothing toward settlement. Given that Continental's primary carrier, Mercury Mutual, has only a million in coverage, anything more than that and you're into Saturnia's pocket, a pocket controlled by Bruce Cutler," the older attorney said. "I thought it best to at least give Mr. Cutler some time to see if he can't convince Saturnia that its position is, shall we say, a bit wrongheaded given Judge Smythe's recent rulings."

"Doesn't sound promising," Hernesman observed.

Mooseberger smiled more broadly.

Hernesman suspected that the older lawyer had more to say. "And?"

"Johansson will go to one million; the Mercury Insurance policy limit under his control. That's what's on the table right now."

Tubby Goggleye bit his lip. "That's a lot of money, Dees."

"It's not half what this case is worth."

Edwin Mooseberger looked hard at Hernesman. "Is that a counter proposal? Because if it is, maybe I can put a bit of pressure on Mr. Cutler when he returns. Maybe convince him to open up Saturnia's billfold."

Dee Dee shook her head. "No. Kat and I agreed that three was our Waterloo. Three million dollars, full, final, and complete, or we let a jury decide this case. I hope," the female attorney continued, "that you've pointed out the reality of a jury awarding punitive damages against Continental and Mr. Yost to both Mr. Johansson and Mr. Cutler."

"I have."

"And the fact that they are, by failing to bargain in good faith here, likely putting their *actual* clients, the ones the Board of Professional Responsibility will care about—Continental and Yost, not Mercury and Saturnia—in a position where corporate and personal assets will have to be surrendered if we prove our punitive damages case? Punies aren't covered by insurance, which means Continental and Yost are exposed above and beyond the limits of coverage. Do Johansson and Cutler appreciate the conflict of interest Judge Smythe's ruling on punitive damages creates for them?"

"They do."

Tubby stood up. "And Cutler still won't come to the table?"

"He hasn't as of yet. And I am pretty certain he will never move the needle to three million. Maybe to two. But at three, he's as closed up as a clam in cold water."

Hugh McLean cleared his throat. "Maybe I should call Kat, get her on the line."

Dee Dee Hernesman shook her head with such vigor, her short black hair danced across her square face. "No! Kat and I are of one mind on this thing. Three million is our drop-dead number. We came down to three-point-seven-five and they've come up only a few hundred thousand. After Judge Smythe gave us everything we asked for? Hell, the spoliation instruction alone will cause the jury to look right through any so-called defense Johansson thinks he can muster. No, we don't need to call Katherine. We're good to go."

There was a sigh, the sound of resignation from Edwin Mooseberger as he reclaimed his feet. "I understand. I'll tell Mr. Johansson we're at an impasse."

"'Tell Mr. Johansson.' What about 'tell Mr. Cutler?'" Dee Dee asked.

The old man stood at the door, his hand on the knob, as he turned to respond. "As I said, he's ducked out for an hour or so. Do you want to wait for his return?"

Dee Dee Hernesman shook her head. "Screw Bruce Cutler. This isn't going anywhere. We might as well get back in the car and head north."

Mooseberger feigned a smile. "Your choice, Ms. Hernesman, your choice. Gentleman," the mediator said, nodding to McLean and Goggleye, "have a safe trip home. I'll send a letter to Judge Smythe advising her that the parties were unable to come to an accord. Good luck with the trial," Mooseberger added as he closed the door.

CHAPTER THIRTY-EIGHT

Deb Slater sat in the office of St. Louis County Attorney Justin Pappas on the fifth floor of the Duluth courthouse. She wanted Pappas to understand what she was saying, for the man to fully comprehend what she, with the assistance of Dee Dee Hernesman, had uncovered with respect to Continental Mining's culpability in the deaths of Antonio Feggetti and Susie Lindahl. From the expression on Pappas's face the man didn't seem interested in what Slater had to say.

"Are you listening to me?"

Pappas, his bald head shining under the LED lighting of the room, his lean, runner's build angled defensively behind the big desk, his eyes fixed on the sheriff, nodded.

"To every word, Sheriff. Every word."

"You understand that officials within Continental knew Neil Yost's history, knew he'd killed three innocent men in Butte when he was the Safety Director at Carson Mines' Charlie Russell operation?"

"I heard you say that."

"And you understand that, in response to both the civil wrongful death case and our criminal investigation, Continental knowingly withheld a portion of Yost's employment file?"

"I heard that too."

Slater's ire rose.

"And you heard me when I told you that it was only after Ms. Hernesman's investigator, Mr. Aitkins, traveled personally to Butte with subpoena in hand and retrieved copies of Yost's personnel file from Carson Mines that we learned the truth about Yost's past?"

"I understand that to be the case," Pappas replied matter-of-factly as he reached for a porcelain cup.

"So why in hell won't you take a look, or have Jennifer take a stab, at bringing charges against Yost and Continental?

Hell, if you think there's iffy PC here, Jennifer can empanel a grand jury and see whether there's enough to charge someone at Continental, maybe Yost, maybe whoever hired the guy, maybe both, with negligent homicide."

Left unsaid was the information Dee Hernesman had supplied to Deb Slater, the motivation behind Sheriff Nace's reluctance to back her play. *Revealing what I know about Pappas's leverage on Brian Nace isn't going to move Pappas; he's nearly unflappable. Best save that information for a discussion with Dave Posten of the AG's office if and when I need to bring Dave on board.*

"Ms. Baxter is otherwise occupied. She's on maternity leave," Justin Pappas replied.

The reference to Jennifer Baxter, the Assistant St. Louis County Attorney originally assigned to the explosion investigation, caused Slater pause. The sheriff's attention shifted to a vision of her daughter, Annie's belly round as a beach ball, working as a waitress at the Blue Water in Grand Marais during her summer off from Cornell. *I need to call Annie. We haven't talked today.*

"Sheriff?"

"Sorry. Thinking about my daughter."

Pappas smiled. The gesture seemed genuine but, with politicians, especially ones as polished as Justin Pappas, Slater knew not to accept things at face value. "I heard. Sorry, I guess. Unexpected, right? Away at college, Cornell, isn't it?"

Damn he's good. Knows way too much about my personal business. Best stay on topic and get to the point.

"Something like that. Anyway, about a grand jury . . ."

"Grand juries are cumbersome, expensive, and time consuming. Plus, you're going after a rare bird here, the legal equivalent of a California condor. I've never charged a corporation—or a corporate officer—with homicide in all my decades of prosecuting cases. Never heard of it happening, either."

"Ms. Hernesman found a case on point."

"Oh, is that a fact?" Pappas leaned forward, animus flashing in his eyes. "And since when did I deputize that ambulance chaser as an *assistant county attorney*?"

Slater discerned Pappas was losing his cool.

If I respond in kind, he won't reconsider and put another assistant county attorney on the case and convene a grand jury. Best ignore his pique.

"The case is entitled *State v. Arkell*. In *Arkell*, the Minnesota Court of Appeals determined that a corporate officer can be held *criminally* responsible for building code violations."

"Building code violations?" Pappas asked incredulously. "Violations of the building code aren't implicated in this case!"

Slater maintained calm. "You're right, Justin, they aren't. But there are violations of OSHA. And the theory of criminal liability is the same. OSHA tagged Continental for Yost's failure to provide the salvage operator, Steve Gruber, with accurate information regarding the silo's contents."

"Okay."

"Continental was also cited for failing to provide proper training to Yost."

"So?"

"The actions or inactions of Continental and Yost add up to negligence. Under *Arkell* and the manslaughter statute— Section 609.205, causing death by creating an 'unreasonable risk'—someone at Continental, perhaps Yost, perhaps his bosses, perhaps all of the above, is criminally responsible for what happened."

"Okay."

"Just failing to provide Yost's complete employment file to OSHA is enough to support misdemeanor or gross misdemeanor charges under our OSHA reporting statute, Section 182.667."

"Really? I had no idea," the county attorney said through a disingenuous smile.

Debra Slater shifted her rump on the hard oak chair. Slater's cell phone buzzed just as she was about to resume the discussion. She'd turned off the ringer but left the phone on to accept calls since she was officially "on the clock." "I've got a call coming in. Mind if I take it?"

Justin Pappas lifted his cup and sipped tepid coffee. "Sure. No problem."

The caller was a registered nurse in the emergency room of the Cook County Hospital. The RN informed Sheriff Debra Slater that Annie was headed to the St. Mary's/Duluth Clinic (SMDC) medical center in Duluth for an emergency delivery. The sheriff thanked the woman and hung up the phone.

"Sorry, Justin. I have to go."

"Something wrong?"

"My daughter."

"The one who's pregnant?"

His intelligence isn't perfect or he'd know that I only have the one.

"Yes, Annie. Seems she's headed toward Duluth in an ambulance."

Pappas's expression flashed concern. Slater couldn't discern if the man's empathy was genuine or part of his act.

Doesn't matter. I need to be at the ER when they bring Annie in.

"Sorry to hear that. Let me know if there's anything I can do."

Deb Slater stood up and adjusted her utility belt. "Thanks. About putting another lawyer on the explosion case . . ."

"Go, Sheriff. Now is not the time."

Slater nodded and moved toward the oak door leading from the office. She stopped and turned to face the county attorney before opening the door and exiting the room. "You'll look into it? Charges or, at the very least, convening a grand jury?"

Justin Pappas maintained a poker face. "Go, Sheriff. Go and be with your daughter."

CHAPTER THIRTY-NINE

When the man woke up in a motel in Ely, Minnesota, the thousand dollar retainer gone, his head pounding from a massive hangover, vodka bottles and beer cans and cardboard pizza boxes from Sir G's littering the room he'd paid for with the last of his cash, it was Monday. He'd crashed and burned after closing down Tommy's, having started the evening with a big rib eye at the Ely Steakhouse courtesy of his former partner and her statuesque girlfriend, tossed back a couple of doubles with the girls before embarrassing Dee Dee and Gabriella by suggesting, half in jest, a threesome. Up to that point, the trio had gotten along famously, but Danny Aitkins knew where he was headed. As the booze poured into his bloodstream despite Dee Dee's protestations that he was ruining his life, as his inhibitions collapsed like trees felled by a logger with a chainsaw, as his libido ignited, the months—years really—of loneliness forced him to act like a brash, stupid, drunken asshole.

"Christ."

The television blinked the name of the local cable provider. Aitkins had finished the evening watching an R-rated flick, *Chloe*, a movie that featured Amanda Seyfried and Julianna Moore making love. His intention, replicating desire and achieving release while watching soft porn in the dirty, cluttered confines of his room at the Ely Super 8, was foiled when, inexplicably, he couldn't perform. He had poured so much beer and Finlandia into his bloodstream that scenes of two attractive women grinding away against each other on the flat screen across the room provided a focus for his curiosity but nothing more. He'd passed out long before he achieved anything close to success. His comment, his taking the Lord's name in vain, wasn't only due to his pounding head, parched mouth, and aching limbs: Danny Aitkins, former trial lawyer, devoted husband and father, and beloved law school professor, had pissed himself.

Aitkins threw off the bed covers, swiveled his hips, lowered his feet to the tread-worn carpeting, and stood up.

"Goddamn it to hell!"

Danny Aitkins rolled his Lee's down his thighs, his once-proud physicality bloated into the puffy, overweight, water-retaining body of an old man—an alcoholic old man. Danny shook his head. Tears slid down his cheeks. He felt so helpless, so hopeless against alcohol's power. There was, in the former lawyer's mind, only one way out.

But I tried that before, up in Winnipeg, in a rented cottage on Winnipeg Beach. Couldn't pull off a Hemingway because I am, in the end, a coward. Couldn't do it then and I can't do it now. Christ.

Time in the shower was palliative, not curative. Streams of hot water cascaded over Danny's naked back and buttocks, reddening skin, bringing clarity to his thinking. But a few minutes under a showerhead were no answer for the depths of Danny Atkins's addiction, his self-loathing, his loss of ambition and drive.

I thought that, after succeeding in the little errand Dees sent me on, things would be different, that something inside me would change. It almost worked. For what—a few hours? Once I stepped into that saloon in Butte, my vision of the future, so crisp and clear: reunification with the kids, a new start as a paralegal or working as a farmhand somewhere in the Red River Valley, and maybe, just maybe, love, was shattered like a window hit by a baseball. That first beer, Danny lamented as he shut off the water, opened the glass shower stall door, grabbed a towel from a nearby rack, and stepped onto vinyl flooring, *was all it took.*

Aitkins stopped at the bathroom mirror and studied his face. His eyes were bloodshot. His eyelids drooped. His jaw and jowls sagged. His once thick, sandy hair was thin, silver, and lifeless. His gut hung over the towel wrapped around his waist and jiggled like Jell-O when he reached up to touch a nasty cut on his temple. Blood had crusted over the wound, which, had he been a sober man with common sense, he would've had stitched at the Ely hospital. He winced in pain as he touched the cut. Danny opened a Duluth Pack ditty bag and removed a plastic bottle. The former lawyer popped five Advil, bent at the waist toward the faucet, turned on the cold-water tap, made a bowl with his shaking hands, and drank.

"Shit."

In the main room, Aitkins sorted through his overnight bag until he found clean boxers, a clean T-shirt—a souvenir from a performance of Tom Petty at the Red Rocks Amphitheater in Colorado he'd attended with his first wife, Julie, when their first born, Adam, was still in utero—and a pair of khaki cargo shorts. Fighting a hangover, Danny slipped on the underwear and shorts before stepping into a pair of well-worn leather sandals.

"Check-out day. I better get some of this shit cleaned up before I head back to Grand Forks."

Aitkins moved about the room picking up Finlandia bottles and crushed Miller Lite cans, amused that he had, in his quest for quantity, bought beer he disdained. He was a lover of locally crafted brands and despised mass-produced swill. And yet, when the rubber hit the road, he'd bought two cases of Miller and downed every last can along with two fifths of Finlandia over the course of two days and nights hunkered down in the motel.

If I were trying to drink myself to death, Danny mused, *I could've at least shown a little class!*

After tossing his piss-soaked underwear and jeans, flattened beer cans, and booze bottles into the room's tiny garbage can, Aitkins picked up empty pizza boxes, food wrappers, and pages from the *Ely Echo* scattered across the floor. As Danny bent to retrieve the last piece of trash, a half-empty plastic Evian bottle, there was a knock at the door.

Who the hell could that be? Aitkins thought as he glanced across the room. Green numerals on a plastic alarm clock glowed: *6:30 a.m.*

Danny dropped the Evian bottle in the trash and shuffled toward persistent knocking.

"Hold your horses."

Danny unlatched the safety chain and opened the door. Fresh air infiltrated the stale, musty confines of the rented room. Sunlight warmed Danny's face. Dee Dee Hernesman, Danny's ex-wife Julie, and all four of his children, including the three he'd been blessed with during his marriage to Julie—Adam, Amanda, and Michael, now all grown and living on their own—stood outside Danny Aitkins's motel room. But most surprising of all was the fact that Ruthie, the product of Danny's illicit affair with a friend's wife, also stood outside his door. Ruthie was newly graduated from Fergus Falls High School, Fergus Falls being the northwestern Minnesota town Ruthie's mother, stepfather, and two half-siblings called home. Seeing Ruthie for the first time in more than a year, after having missed both her eighteenth birthday and her graduation, was a shock to the old man.

"What the hell?"

Of Aitkins's significant family, only Danny's father, Emery Aitkins, was missing. Emery was still alive. But Lewy Body Dementia, a form of mental decline that is unfailingly quick in its destruction, had forced the elder Aitkins into a memory care unit in Detroit Lakes, Danny's hometown. The son had not seen the father in months. Their last visit had been so disheartening that Danny could not return. With the exception of his father, everyone who mattered to Daniel Aitkins was assembled outside the motel room, and Danny had a pretty good idea of why they were there.

CHAPTER FORTY

Kat Carpenter sat at a table in Keys Café on the main floor of
the Foshay Tower in downtown Minneapolis, her fork poised
over the restaurant's signature chicken salad smothered in honey
mustard dressing, a glass of Cabernet perched next to the
brimming plate of food as she smiled at her the man seated
across the table.

The woman's portly companion had arrived late. He had,
as he claimed his chair, apologized, explaining in dead-pan
fashion that his tardiness was because "that damned
Mooseberger is like a pit bull holding on to a burglar's pants
leg," in that the mediator had delayed the lawyer's exit from the
negotiating session at the offices of Mooseberger and Patton just
a few blocks from the restaurant.

"What looks good?"

The waitress, a pert, middle-aged Vietnamese woman,
arrived with a menu just as the man asked Carpenter for
suggestions.

"This salad is nicely done," Kat said before moving her
right hand to the stem of the wine glass, lifting the glass to her
lips, and sipping, "and this Cabernet is delightful," the female
attorney added after swallowing, her voice far more feminine
and subdued than the tone she invoked during courtroom
appearances.

"I'll try the tuna melt," the man said to the waitress as he
closed the menu. "No fries. Just a cup of your soup of the day.
And a glass of the same wine Ms. Carpenter is having, if you
would."

"Yes sir. I'll be right back with the Cabernet."

Kat placed her fork on the tablecloth. "Soooo . . ." The
woman extended the word like a cheerleader coming on to the
captain of the boys high school soccer team, ". . . what are we
going to do to settle this case, Mr. Cutler?" she continued,

careful to show bare thigh as she crossed her legs, the hem of her short business skirt purposefully hiked to reveal skin.

The waitress returned and placed a glass of wine in front of Cutler with efficiency.

"Three is too much, Kat. You know that."

Katherine Carpenter nodded. "Okay. But I'm not negotiating against myself, Bruce."

As she said his name, Kat's left shoe gently touched Cutler's calf. The toe of her spiked heel nudged the inside of Cutler's leg. The move was deliberate but done in such a way as to convey an accidental connection.

Cutler took a swig of wine but did not address the distraction. The man cleared his throat.

"Johansson is all in at one million. I can add two-fifty. Cost of defense. That's a pretty damn good payday for your firm, Kat. That's what, a fee of four hundred thousand?"

Kat Carpenter removed her shoe from the inside of Bruce Cutler's thigh, smiled demurely, and took another bite of chicken salad before shaking her head.

"You're forgetting that I have to split the fee with Hernesman."

"Ah, yes. It is indeed unfortunate that you've been put in a position where you are, shall we say, inadequately compensated. But I can't be concerned with your misfortune. I have to do what's best for my clients, not what's best for you."

The woman nodded. "Understood. But one-point-two-five is still light."

"As you said, Kat, I'm not going to negotiate with myself. And, if we strike a bargain here today over this excellent wine and palatable food, can you guarantee me that you can sell our deal to Mr. Goggleye? I don't give a rat's ass about Dee Dee Hernesman. It's the trustee and the judge who are going to control whether this case gets settled or not."

"I can sell it to Goggleye. He's nervous as hell at one million. Doesn't want Hernesman trying this thing and having the jury come back with less than your offer. Egg on his face and all that," Kat whispered, moving her hand across the table until her long, elegant fingers rested on the bare wrist of her companion. Her touch landed where the cuff of Cutler's laundered white shirt gave way to folded, pale flesh. "And I'm in complete agreement as to Hernesman: she's a royal pain in the ass, standing on her high horse, lecturing me about principle and fidelity to the Lindahls. I could care less about the adult survivors. It's the little girls who lost their mother that I need to watch out for . . ."

"And," Cutler said discreetly, removing Kat's hand as the waitress arrived with his tuna melt, "you also need to look out for Katherine Carpenter. Am I right? If we don't look out for ourselves, who will?"

Anger flashed across Kat's patrician face. "I am not settling this case to line my pocket! I am doing what I am doing, ducking the mediation and meeting privately with you, because I am representing the Deviches, decent folks who lost the mother of their grandchild. That's the bottom line."

"Understood."

Carpenter's rancor dissipated. She reached for her wine glass and drained it. "The real issue here is resolving the case so that the girls are protected, not so some grand notion of justice can be demonstrated. Yes, Neil Yost is a stupid sonofabitch. And Continental was stupid to hire the guy. But my role, and yours, is to end this dispute and not worry about guilt or innocence or justice. Damages—money—is all we have to talk about. That's where Hernesman goes off the rail. She's so blinded by what happened, by the stupidity of what Yost did, she can't see that, in the end, it's about money, not justice."

"Agreed," Bruce Cutler said as he picked up a triangle of bread, cheese, tuna, and mayo and bit into the sandwich. "And so . . . ?"

"Two. I can get Goggleye to settle for two million."

215

Cutler put down his food, grabbed a white linen napkin, and touched the edge of the napkin to a corner of his lower lip. "Too much. I can do one-point-five."

Kat Carpenter shook her head. "You're light, Bruce. You need to play ball. Two is fair. At that price, Saturnia would be paying the same amount as Mercury and getting out from beneath a great big headache. If the jury comes back with a number higher than two million for compensatory and then hits Continental and Yost with punies, well, I won't be sitting back, making deals. At that point, I'll let Hernesman off her leash to chase your clients, the *real* clients; Continental and Yost. Period. End of discussion. Two million, Bruce, that's the number."

Cutler pushed his belly away from the edge of the table. Patrons walking between tables were forced to move to accommodate the repositioning. "Can't do it. Saturnia's number, quite frankly, to settle this case and wrap it up right here and now, before we both order our second glass of wine, is one-point-seven-five."

"You're offering $1,750,000.00 to settle this case?"

Bruce Cutler smiled. "Today and today only. You reject the offer, all bets are off. We will, unfortunately, spend a great deal of cross-examination time asking tough questions of Mr. and Mrs. Lindahl as well as Mr. and Mrs. Devich, questions about young Susie's promiscuity and IV drug use. We'll also delve into the removal of those precious girls from Miss Lindahl's care due to neglect. I won't relish Johannson doing this, of course, being that I am a family man and have raised a defiant child or two in my day. But rest assured, Kat, we will do whatever it takes—in front of a jury—to limit our clients' exposure."

Katherine Carpenter sat back in her chair to take in the man. "Like removing evidence before our experts could conduct testing? Like hiding employment records? Like lying to the BCA, the ATF, the police, and the task force about Yost's past?"

"Wasn't me who made those decisions, Kat, I can assure you of that. But you're playing in the big leagues: Brush back pitches are part of the game."

Kat smiled, exposing luminously white, capped teeth. She turned thoughtful before nodding. "One million, eight hundred thousand dollars," she whispered, her blue contact lenses reflecting the afternoon sun streaming in through newly cleaned windows.

Cutler winced. "You'd sabotage . . ."

"Interesting word choice given the recent news coming out of your client's construction project . . ."

Cutler smiled. "Okay. I concede. You are quicker than a . . ."

"Kat?"

A huge laugh erupted from the portly lawyer. "Yes, exactly: than a Kat." The older lawyer extended his right hand across his food and the table. "$1,800,000.00, agreed?"

"You have a deal, Mr. Cutler, provided you buy me another glass of wine and pick up the tab for lunch," Kat Carpenter said, shaking the portly lawyer's hand to settle the case.

CHAPTER FORTY-ONE

Debra Slater sat next to a hospital bed in an uncomfortable chair, head tucked against chest, drool dangling from her mouth and wetting the fabric of her wrinkled, tan uniform blouse, the sound of a blood pressure cuff intermittently activating across the room. A monitor screen displayed vital signs in orange numerals. Annie slept soundly, her ordeal in the operating room over, the massive exit of uterine blood having been stemmed by Dr. Jill Trachel, an emergency room OB/GYN at SMDC.

The sound of shoes against vinyl startled Deb.

It was Slater's third day at the hospital. She was desperately behind on sleep from having to juggle her duties as Cook County Sheriff, head of the Copper/Nickel Task Force, and motherhood. She was commuting from Grand Marais to her daughter's bedside. She'd been absent from the task force office in Ely since Annie's complications, the sheriff's attempts to stir Justin Pappas to action rebuffed, her investigation into the sabotage of Nolan Excavation's equipment at the Merritt Pit site stalled. The primary suspect in the property damage crime, Cyrus Oliphant, his presence at the test pit confirmed by DNA pulled from a plastic wrapper, a wrapper identified by the BCA as once containing plastic beads—the same plastic beads removed from the fuel tanks of dozers, trucks, and backhoes—had vanished. Slater had obtained a search warrant for Oliphant's apartment in Tower, but there was a leak. The sheriff suspected a cousin of Clarence Bighead, Lizzie She-Who-Rides-Horses, a somewhat shy clerk in the district court office in Hibbing, a girl rumored to have briefly dated Oliphant, of getting word to the eco-terrorist that the noose was closing, that Judge Peck had issued a search warrant for Oliphant's Chevy, apartment, and personal property. But the sheriff had only rumor and innuendo behind her suspicion. She had no evidence, no hard facts, upon which to bring in the Ojibwe girl for questioning. It seemed that, as to both the original investigation regarding criminal charges against Continental and Neil Yost, as well as any potential consequences for Cyrus Oliphant, Debra Slater had hit a wall.

At the sound of footsteps, the sheriff wiped spittle from the corner of her mouth with the back of her hand, sat up in her chair, and opened her eyes. As her mind cleared and her eyes focused, Deb noted that a tall, young African American man was standing next to her daughter's bed.

"Thomas? Thomas Jones?"

The newcomer's face broke into a wide smile. "Yes, ma'am."

"Well," the sheriff said, standing up and moving with agility toward Jones. "It's a pleasure to meet you, sir." Slater extended her right hand. Thomas Jones reciprocated. "Hey, that's some grip you have there, Mr. Jones."

"Thomas. Call me Thomas. I got here as fast as I could. I was playing summer ball in Chapel Hill."

Debra Slater motioned for Thomas to take the seat she'd just vacated. The young man sat down next to Annie and placed his hand on the wrist of the slumbering patient, the contrast in the dark of his forearm and Annie's Nordic skin not lost upon the sheriff.

"How's she doing?"

"She's fine. Just tired. She lost a lot of blood before they got her stabilized in Grand Marais."

Jones smiled weakly. "Annie loves that town. It's all she talks about," the young man said. "To tell you the truth, it's a little annoying."

Slater smiled. "It's hard to explain the connection we folks have to the Big Lake, the forest, the lifestyle. We're living," the sheriff continued, "in a modern age but trying to hold onto the past. I get that maybe someone who's from the big city—Chicago, right?—might not understand the draw of the North Shore."

"South Chicago, the projects. Same complex where Kirby Puckett grew up," Jones replied.

"My favorite Twin. My husband," Deb stopped short, the memory of Rick's slow, agonizing demise still vivid in her mind, before finishing the thought, "was always a Tony 'O' fan."

Thomas stood, leaned over the sleeping girl, and kissed her on the forehead. "You sure she's all right?"

"Positive. She's on morphine but she'll wake up soon enough. Then you two can talk. I'm juggling being here and trying to solve some things . . ." Again, Slater's thoughts intruded. Visions of the earth being rendered apart and Susie Lindahl's demolished Dodge Dakota smoldering caused her to pause. "I'll be heading out, getting back to it. That'll give you both some time to figure things out."

Jones nodded. The young man's face had lost its joy, had turned serious and adult. "We never meant for this to happen."

Slater bit her lip. "No one ever does. God has a way of reminding us of the consequences of our actions."

The young man's demeanor turned somber. His eyes grew misty. "I have no idea how we're gonna sort this all out."

Slater's mouth opened, ready to chastise, ready to tell Thomas Jones that he had little choice but to own up to his part in it all and accept responsibility. But instead of recrimination, Slater chose kindness. "I think, Thomas, it's time you met your daughter."

CHAPTER FORTY-TWO

Dee Dee Hernesman sat in the bow of Skip Mattila's fishing boat, her left foot on a pedal controlling a Minkota trolling motor, her St. Croix rod bent under the weight of a Rapala and a lead torpedo attached to a downrigger that sent the lure to the depths of Burntside Lake. It was a cool, late summer morning. Fog lingered across flat, calm water as the sun attempted an appearance. Skip sat on a pedestal seat in front of a seventy-five-horse Honda four-stroke in the aft of the boat. Gabriella Pierce, her form concealed beneath layers of Thinsulate long underwear, fleece pants, a matching fleece sweatshirt, and a St. Johns Bay windbreaker, sat in the middle of the boat holding a fishing rod in her right hand as she dragged fingers through the warm surface water of the lake.

"Got one!" Hernesman shouted as the weight of an angry trout released the downrigger clip. "Skip, get the net. I think it's a beauty."

Mattila reeled in his lure, grabbed the landing net, and stood next to Dee Dee as she played the fish. "Don't horse it in, Dees. Be patient. Work it until it tires," Mattila urged.

Hernesman scowled. "How many fish do you think I've landed?"

Mattila spat a wad of brown chew toward the lake.

"Could you not do that?" Gabriella asked, lifting her hand out of the water to avoid contact with the floating mess. "It's disgusting."

"Stop bickering. I've got a fish to land."

"My mom agrees with you, Gabby," Mattila said. "She calls chew a 'filthy habit.'"

"Get the net ready," Dee Dee said sternly. "I've almost got it in."

"Your mother is right," Gabriella said, her own lure trailing behind the boat as the electric trolling motor purred. The Indian woman shook her head in mock upset. "Men. What the hell good are they?"

A flash of silver appeared next to the boat's black hull. "Holy shit. That," Mattila exclaimed, "is a hog!" The man leaned over the gunwale, slid the net under the fish, and lifted trout free of lake. "Nice one, Dees. Must go at least twelve, thirteen pounds."

"I've got one too!" Gabriella shouted, the excitement of a near double covering her disdain for Skip Mattila's tobacco addiction. "I think I'll need some help."

Mattila hoisted Hernesman's prize free of mesh, desposited the flopping trout on the floor of the boat, and moved, net in hand, toward Gabriella. Though she had never been fishing before that day, Gabriella Pierce was a natural. She played the trout until the fish was exhausted and cruising next to the Lund. Mattila reached out with the net, captured the tired fish, and swung a four-pound lake trout, its pewter sides reflecting the meager sun that had just, at that moment, chosen to emerge from dissipating fog, into the boat.

"Nicely done, ladies."

Mattila removed the treble hook of a Red Eye spoon from the smaller fish's mouth. Gabriella beamed as Skip lifted her catch. Dee Dee dug into the pocket of her vest and removed her Galaxy. "Gabs, move in so I can get both of you in the picture," Dee Dee said, pride in her girlfriend obvious on her face as she snapped the photo.

"Here," Mattila said, putting the smaller trout in the Lund's live well and closing the lid. "I'll take a picture of the two of you with the Loch Ness Monster."

Hernesman extended her phone toward Mattila. Sounds of Clapton's "You Are Wonderful Tonight" began playing softly from the phone. "It's Julie," Dee Dee said as she retracted the phone, hit "accept," and held the Galaxy to her left ear. "Hello?"

"Dees."

"Hi, Jules."

"Where the hell are you?"

"On Burntside with Skip and Gabby. We just had a double. Mine," she said, glancing back to Gabriella and smiling, "is *much* bigger, of course."

"Reception's shitty. I can barely hear you. But you and Skip need to get to the office right away."

Julie Somerfeldt's voice expressed a note of urgency that Hernesman knew meant something was brewing.

"It's Saturday, Jules. Can't it wait until Monday?"

The big trout flipped and flopped on the boat deck. Skip Mattila bent over, retrieved the heavy fish, and dropped it into the live well. "Why the hell is she calling on the weekend?" he asked.

Hernesman turned away from the warming, southerly wind to hear. "Skip is pissed that you're interrupting our fishing trip. He's behind, needs time to catch up."

Silence.

"Jules?"

"It's the Lindahl case."

"What about it? I'll be ready for trial. I've got plenty of time to prepare. Even though Judge Smythe moved us into the November trial slot because the Feggetti case settled, that's no big deal. I'll be in tomorrow after church to work on the case. You can catch me in the office then if you need to."

Another pause.

"Jules, this silent treatment thing is so unbecoming. I said I'll be ready for trial and I mean it. I WILL BE READY FOR TRIAL!"

"That's just it. I was doing the books when today's mail came. You got a big envelope from Kat Carpenter. I opened it and according to the cover letter and the documents inside, the Lindahl case is settled. There won't be any damn trial, Dees. That's what I'm trying to tell you!"

CHAPTER FORTY-THREE

"How could this happen?" Judy Lindahl asked—her hazel eyes flashing anger, her short, rotund form shaking with upset—as she sat next to her husband in the jury deliberation room adjacent to Judge Harriet Smythe's chambers.

Dee Dee Hernesman and Skip Mattila—Mattila tagging along to ensure that Hernesman didn't physically assault Kat Carpenter—sat across a long, maple conference table from the Lindahls. The Deviches, Brenda Lee's paternal grandparents, were across the hall in the jury deliberation room of Judge Picket along with their attorneys, Kat Carpenter, and Hugh McLean. Tubby Goggleye was in Judge Smythe's chambers in private audience with Her Honor.

The lawyers and their clients had assembled to try and solve a singular question: whether the explosion case had in fact been settled. The defense attorneys were nowhere to be found as they had no stake in the outcome of the discussions. Bruce Cutler and the Silver Wolf had collectively ponied up $1.8 million and were more than willing to sign off on the agreement reached between Cutler and Carpenter over Cabernet and lunch.

Dee Dee Hernesman shook her head. "I never should have trusted that witch."

Mark Lindahl held his wife's hand. His beard, which, at the beginning of the case had been completely black, was flecked with gray.

"Sorry to say, Ms. Hernesman, but you are too nice, too ethical, to play in the sandbox with Ms. Carpenter. She screwed us from the outset when she had that little pipsqueak, Jimmy Lampi, appointed as trustee," Mark Lindahl replied. The man extricated his hand from his wife's, reached across the table, poured himself a glass of water, and drank ravenously before continuing. "It doesn't surprise me that she went behind your back. I've dealt with folks like her my whole life. Self-centered, egocentric Rangers exist, Ms. Hernesman, I can attest to that. To be sure, such folks are in the minority. Most of us who call the Iron Range home are hardworking and honest. We look out for our family and our friends and try to give something back to our community. But I recognize Kat Carpenter as someone I've come across before. Her lack of morals isn't surprising to me in the least."

Skip Mattila nodded. "Judge Smythe has our motion to set aside the 'agreement' under advisement. We've argued that anything less than . . ."

Judy Lindahl interrupted. ". . . two million is not reasonable. I know what you said. But how likely is the judge to undo what's been done? I mean, one-point-eight million is a lot of money. And isn't the trustee in support of the settlement?"

Dee Dee stood up and walked to the far wall where a coffee maker warmed coffee. "He is," Hernesman agreed, pouring steaming coffee into a paper cup from a stainless steel pot. "I tried to convince Tubby otherwise, but he's nervous and uneasy despite the fact that a jury might give us more than two million in compensatory damages and then award something more in the form of punitive damages to punish the defendants. To be fair to Mr. Goggleye, there's no guarantee a jury will see it our way. In the end," Hernesman concluded, sipping hot coffee after taking her seat, "I can't fault the man."

Mark Lindahl wore a defeated expression. "So what are the chances that Judge Smythe goes along with the other part of Ms. Carpenter's motion?"

The reference was not lost on Dee Dee Hernesman: her client was talking about the language in M&Q's motion where Kat Carpenter urged the court to deny awarding any portion of the settlement to Judy and Mark Lindahl. M&Q argued in their motion and legal brief that only the minor children should be compensated. But Katherine Carpenter hadn't stopped at merely insulting Susie Lindahl's grieving parents. Carpenter was also arguing that, instead of the 50–50 split of fees between the two law firms, there should be a different allocation of attorneys' fees in the case. Kat claimed that the settlement was only in place due to her expertise. In Kat Carpenter's view of reality, Dee Dee Hernesman had nearly botched the case by holding fast to an unattainable settlement demand. The first point, disenfranchising the parents, was simply mean-spirited. The second, Kat's motion to award seventy-five percent of the fees to M&Q, leaving a paltry twenty-five percent to Hernesman, evinced Kat's no-holds-barred greed.

"I don't think her requests will get very far."

Hernesman's response was flat, evincing a damaged faith. Kat Carpenter's motion, coming as it did on the heels of the Motion to Approve a Minor's Settlement she'd sent to Hernesman's firm without notice or warning, had been a shock. It had taken much counseling by Skip Mattila and Julie Somerfeldt to reign in Dee Dee's upset and get her focused on representing the interests of the Lindahls and the interests of the firm rather than entering into an out-and-out legal brawl with Kat Carpenter.

"Why do you say that?" Mark Lindahl asked.

"Because Mr. Goggleye won't allow it," Mattila responded. "He's on our side in every way except for the amount of the settlement. On that score, you're right. Carpenter has won. I don't see Judge Smythe overruling Tubby's inclination to accept one-point-eight. The risks to the kids, that a jury will do something less, are, as Dees has said, too high. But," Skip leaned back and folded his hands behind his neck, his eyes wide and clear as he looked at Mark and Judy Lindahl, "Tubby knows who worked this case to the point where that bastard, excuse my French, ma'am, Cutler felt the need to open up Saturnia's wallet. Tubby knows that Dees here is the reason, despite whether or not we were played from beginning to end by Kat Carpenter, that the defendants are nervous about this case. Tubby won't sell us short and he'll insist, I'm certain, that the settlement proceeds be distributed fairly, with one-third of the net going to you and Mark as Susie's parents."

Judy Lindahl's eyes teared. She was distraught at her daughter's death being reduced to an argument over money. Mark reached for a tissue box, retrieved a Kleenex, and handed it to his wife. The woman dabbed at the moisture, but her tears did not abate.

There was a knock. Hernesman stood up, walked across thick carpeting, and opened the jury room door. Tom Devich stood in muted light, his eyes downcast, his hands shoved deep in the back pockets of his Lees. "Can I come in?"

Hernesman moved aside. Devich entered the room.

"I'm not sure we should be talking, Mr. Devich. You're represented by M&Q."

Tom Devich, a tall, broad-shouldered man in his early fifties, his stomach lean and flat from his work as a logger, nodded. "Then let me talk. You don't have to say a word."

Hernesman motioned for the man to take a seat. Devich shook his head.

"Been sitting all morning. If it's all right with you, ma'am, I'd rather stand."

Hernesman reclaimed her chair.

"Anyway," Devich began, his voice filled with emotion, "me and Nance, well, we're just sick over what Miss Carpenter has done. Not the settlement. We're okay with that. We think it's fair and all given the risks of trial, the uncertainties of life. But," the man stopped to gather his thoughts, "we're not comfortable with her trying to cut you out of this thing," the man added quietly, looking at the Lindahls. "Not comfortable at all. Susie was your little girl. If it was us, even knowing that money means nothing after a loss like this, we'd want the defendants to know that we, not just the grandkids, lost something when our child was killed."

Judy's tears increased. Mark handed his wife a second tissue.

"Go on," Mark said quietly.

"Danny, our boy, Brenda Lee's father, he's gone. Disappeared. Last we heard he's in Vegas. Sometimes, as a parent, you try to do your best, and it just doesn't work out. Our two girls, fine upstanding, hardworking, smart kids, are married, doing fine. Danny? He was a mess when he met your Susie and never got any better. I don't," Tom Devich added, a catch in his throat as he spoke, "even know if he's aware of the accident. We haven't heard from him in over two years."

Mark Lindahl shook his head. "Shouldn't be that way."

"But it is. Anyway, I came here to say my piece and this is what Nance and I think should happen. We'd be happy to go to the judge and tell her that we support you folks receiving a *minimum* of twenty-five percent. If the judge goes to one-third, you'll hear no objection from us. But if we can get this damn thing over and done with at twenty-five, we're behind you and we'll say that to Judge Smythe."

Judy Lindahl stood up and hugged Tom Devich. "Thank you, Tom. Thank you."

"I think what my wife means to say, Tom, is that we accept your offer. We can live with twenty-five percent. The girls can share the other seventy-five."

Tom Devich slipped out of Judy Lindahl's embrace. "Then that's what Nance and me will tell the judge. There's just one more thing . . ."

Hernesman braced for the "but" that she thought was coming. She was certain that, with Kat Carpenter working the Deviches, they were likely seeking to have Hernesman and her partners accept something less than a 50–50 split of fees. "I'm not sure . . ."

Skip Mattila raised a hand to stifle his partner's protest. "Let the man talk, Dees. You might like what he has to say."

"It's just, well, the thing is, Nance and I are not happy, not happy at all with the representation Miss Carpenter and Mr. McLean have given us, eh? Hell, Miss Hernesman, you did ninety percent of the work and then Miss Carpenter slips in, like a relief pitcher in a no-hitter, and takes credit for the victory? It's not right that your firm is willing to split the fee equally with Miss Carpenter's firm. That's not fair."

"Thank you for saying that."

Tom Devich folded powerful arms across his broad chest. "So what we'd like to do, Miss Hernesman, is fire Kat Carpenter and have the judge give you the entire fee."

Dee Dee was stunned. Flattered, to be sure, but stunned. She looked at Tom Devich, his eyes reflecting the lights of the jury deliberation room. "I'm afraid, Tom, that can't be done. It's too late. Kat is entitled, whether I think she and Hugh earned it or not, to half the fee. That's what I agreed to, and that's what I'll ask Judge Smythe to award."

Devich shook his head. "Isn't fair. Not a bit. But if I can't talk you into fighting for your fair share of the fee, can I ask you a question? A legal question?"

Dee Dee Hernesman shrugged. Their discourse had gone so far beyond ethical propriety that it seemed foolhardy to constrain the man.

"Sure."

"Well, the way I understand it, Kat didn't talk to you about the offers she was receiving from Mr. Cutler."

"You're right; I wasn't privy to those conversations."

"And she certainly didn't tell Nance and me about any offers."

"OK."

"And, as I understand it, the first time Mr. Goggleye knew a settlement had been reached was after the fact, in a phone call from Miss Carpenter to his office."

Dee Dee nodded. "That's what Tubby told me."

"So my question, Counselor, is this: Isn't a lawyer obliged to pass along all offers of settlement to his or her client and let *the client* make the decision to settle the case or not?"

Hernesman's mouth broke into a tired smile. "That's our ethical duty: We can give advice, but the final decision rests with the client."

Tom Devich grimaced, as if hit by a sucker punch. "Well then, I'd say Miss Carpenter is in a spot of trouble since she never consulted with me, my wife, or Mr. Goggleye about the offers she received. Am I right?"

Dee Dee shook her head. "I really can't give you legal advice, Mr. Devich. You're represented by the very attorney you're talking about."

"Understood." The big man paused before casting a pleading look at Dee Dee Hernesman. "But I need some non-legal assistance. Nance and I want to report Miss Carpenter for her conduct. Do you happen to have the phone number for the lawyers' ethics board?"

CHAPTER FORTY-FOUR

Governor Wesley Whitcomb arrived in Ely for the groundbreaking of the first building being constructed at the Merritt Pit site—a power generation system that would turn biomass into steam to produce electricity for the new mine.

The governor's Cirrus Vision SF50, a new-age jet designed and manufactured in Duluth, an expense that Whitcomb justified as being "necessary" in that the airplane allowed him to remain attuned to the needs and desires of voters across Minnesota, landed on a new runway at the Ely airport. The Vision taxied down fresh asphalt, carrying the governor, the governor's chief of staff, the governor's administrative assistant, and Gail Henry—a thirty-two-year-old, evangelical, blond-bombshell-former-state-senator—playing the part of Lieutenant Governor. Two Minnesota State Troopers piloted the jet and were tasked with providing security for the governor's visit.

"That was smooth, Captain Stebenvold."

Whitcomb's observation regarding the plane's landing was both a compliment to the State Trooper's abilities as a pilot and to the design of the new jet. "Damn good thing I stepped in and helped Cirrus stay in Duluth."

Cirrus had been an economic experiment, a crapshoot in corporate development, when the Klapmeier brothers rolled into town with an idea to reinvigorate the moribund world of personal aircraft. Despite experiencing setbacks during the Great Recession, Cirrus had, through innovative engineering and marketing—and an influx of cash from the company's new financer, the People's Republic of China—created small, piston and propeller airplanes that are fuel efficient, safe, and easy to operate. The gamble that the City of Duluth and the State of Minnesota took in backing the firm's beginnings is one of the rare success stories regarding governmental incubation of industry. The piston models of Cirrus aircraft gave rise to the development of the SF50, a jet the likes of which had never been produced. Whitcomb arrived in Ely in one of the first SF50s assembled by the company after years of design, development, and testing. The governor was proud of what Cirrus had accomplished despite having played no role in the company's success. In truth, Governor Wesley Whitcomb had voted against every bill supporting the company introduced in the Minnesota Legislature during his brief stint as a state senator. It was only after Whitcomb announced his candidacy for governor and began campaign swings to a part of the state he'd never visited—the cold, frozen counties north of Hinckley—that Candidate Whitcomb started paying attention to the upstart company making news in Duluth.

Captain Tom Stebenvold knew his boss's expression was a reinvention of history. But, true to his nature as a "close to the vest" cop, the trooper kept his opinion to himself. Stebenvold also did not point out that the airplane they were taxing in, while accurately and proudly displaying a "Made in America" label, could not have taken flight but for the backing of a communist regime. Pointing out the incongruity of Whitcomb's praise for Cirrus, coming as it did from a dyed-in-the-wool Ayn Rand capitalist seemed, in Stebenvold's mind, to be without purpose given that the governor would not appreciate the irony.

"Agreed. It's a sweet little plane and a good thing it's made in Minnesota."

Whitcomb had unbuckled his seat belt despite a cautionary light urging the contrary and was crouched between the pilot and co-pilot in the cockpit as they conversed. "Not just Cirrus, Captain, but all the spinoff businesses: the suppliers, the designers, the maintenance firms. All of them are contributing to the rebirth of aviation in Duluth. Think of it, Stebenvold: all because the State of Minnesota was willing to back two men's vision of a new era of flight."

Stebenvold knew better than to insert facts into the conversation. He smiled and eased the plane to a stop next to the terminal. "We're here, folks," the pilot advised over the intercom. "Lieutenant Marx will open the doors, lower the stairs, and see that you exit safely."

Several hundred people were assembled at the Merritt Pit Copper/Nickel Mine. Euclid trucks, Caterpillar bulldozers, Mack dump trucks, International scrapers—and a host of other heavy equipment—stood shiny and polished beneath an autumnal sun.

It was September. Construction of the mine was not yet at hand. The governor and his entourage were present at the Merritt Pit site not to cut a ribbon memorializing that notorious event— notorious in the sense that tunneling beneath a pristine walleye fishery didn't sit well with local fishing guides, canoe outfitters, environmentalists, or the Ojibwe—but to memorialize the groundbreaking for the biomass plant designed to supply electricity to the mine.

Two black Escalades approached the mine on a gravel entrance road. The Caddies passed a guard shack and gate that had been installed to regulate access to the site, passed throngs of eager Rangers of all ages on hand to witness history—the spectators pressed together and constrained by rope strung between pylons—and skidded to a collective stop next to a brand new Komatsu shovel. Captain Stebenvold and Lieutenant Marx exited the SUVs. A wasted land greeted the visitors. The old taconite mine was a never-ending scene of scarring, a place where trees and brush had disappeared beneath the steady work of machinery. Hundreds of acres of what had once been forestland had been denuded to form a hubbub of activity in the midst of wilderness. Isolated clouds—thin, white, and without threat of rain—drifted over the distressed landscape intermittently blocking the sun.

"Governor Whitcomb, welcome!"

A distinguished-looking man moved with confidence toward the governor. The man, who appeared to be in his early sixties, dressed in an expensive Brooks Brothers black business suit, white long-sleeved dress shirt, black tie, and keenly polished black dress shoes, extended a hand.

"It's good to be here, Lawrence," Whitcomb replied, engaging Continental Mining International CEO Lawrence St. George with a handshake. "It's about damn time, wouldn't you say?"

St. George, whose primary language was French but who spoke English without accent and who stood a full head taller than the governor, smiled. "Agreed," St. George said. "And of course, you know Roberta Frazier, CEO of our Minnesota affiliate," the Canadian added. St. George moved aside to allow a forty-something woman with neatly trimmed blond hair, her square, muscular form confined in a tight yet smartly tailored navy business skirt, matching jacket, and white blouse, to shake the governor's hand. Whitcomb, who was known to have an eye for the ladies, scrutinized Frazier despite the fact that they'd met many, many times.

"Nice to see you again, Roberta."

Roberta smiled and accepted the governor's hand. "Likewise, Governor. It's been too long . . ." she added coquettishly through a smile that told Whitcomb she'd caught him inventorying her. "Shall we deal with the press first, do a photo-op, and get to the heart of why you're here: to give a speech thanking everyone for supporting this economic boon to northeastern Minnesota?"

Wesley Whitcomb patted the left side of his suit jacket with a delicate, pink hand. "Got my notes right here. I think you will be very happy with what I have to say."

I seriously doubt you wrote a single word of it, Frazier thought to herself, knowing full well, from myriad meetings with Whitcomb, that he was articulate, forceful, and immoveable but intellectually disinterested: the perfect ally for her company's interests in Minnesota.

"Lawrence, Roberta, let's make some history, shall we? The first underground mine in Minnesota in what, sixty years?" the governor said, waving to the crowd as the entourage made its way to a line of No. 2 shovels stuck in the ground.

Ten individuals—including the two executives from Continental, the governor, the lieutenant governor, the Mayors of Babbitt and Ely, and other dignitaries—lined up behind the shovels. On cue, the dignitaries dug into hard ground and lifted clods of dirt. The crowd cheered. A flock of pigeons rose from behind the stage as if on cue. The guests of honor jammed their shovels into the soil and climbed rough sawn pine stairs onto a plywood stage. The mayors warmed up the crowd. The mining executives thanked the politicians and the common people of northeastern Minnesota for their support. And the governor, despite Ms. Frazier's reservations, delivered the speech of his career.

"Nicely done, Wesley," Lawrence St. George said, walking toward the waiting Escalades as rusted pickup trucks, battered SUVs, sedans, and vehicles of every year, make, and model exited the gravel parking lot. "That's about as good a speech as I've heard you give."

"Thanks."

As they made their way over rugged terrain, a man exited a blue Dodge Durango and strode toward the dignitaries with purpose.

"Hold up a minute." Tom Stebenvold commanded, raising his right hand to halt the entourage. "Ed, get up here, will you? Looks like we have company," the trooper added into his shoulder mic.

Lieutenant Ed Marx, short, burly, and like Stebenvold, unaffected by the unexpected, joined Stebenvold at the head of the column. "What's up?"

Stebenvold placed his left hand on a Taser holstered in his utility belt and cocked his head. "Hold up, sir."

The stranger, an evenly demeanored man dressed in a navy business suit, red necktie, white long-sleeved dress shirt, and dust covered black loafers, stopped.

"What's this about?" Governor Whitcomb asked. "Who the hell are you?"

The man offered a weak smile. "We've met before, Governor. Back when you were on the campaign trail. In Perham. You were in the Labor Day parade. I introduced myself. Hell, I voted for you," the stranger added. "Had to. Didn't see there was any other choice."

"Who are you, sir? Do you have business with Governor Whitcomb?" Stebenvold asked with authority, moving so as to cut off the man's access to Whitcomb.

The stranger, Asian by appearance, though it was difficult for Stebenvold to determine the man's exact ancestry, stood a head shorter than the state trooper and extended his right hand. "Allen Fong, BCA."

Stebenvold remained vigilant but returned the gesture. "Why is a BCA agent seeking an audience with the governor?"

Fong retrieved a document from the inside pocket of his coat. "I'm not here to speak to Governor Whitcomb," the BCA agent said politely. "I'm here on other business. Is Ms. Roberta Frazier part of this group?"

Stebenvold nodded. "She is. Why?"

Fong shifted his weight. "I have a legal document to serve on Ms. Frazier."

Roberta Frazier stepped out from behind the governor. "What sort of document?" Frazier asked.

Fong handed the paperwork to Roberta Frazier. "A subpoena ma'am. For your appearance at a grand jury. In Hibbing."

The woman reviewed the subpoena. "The civil cases were settled. The money's been paid. What the hell is this about?"

"Doesn't involve the wrongful death cases, ma'am. The state is looking to bring criminal charges against your company and Mr. Yost for the deaths of Antonio Feggetti and Susie Lindahl."

Wesley Whitcomb lunged out from behind the troopers. "What the hell are you talking about?" the governor asked, grabbing the subpoena. "Justin Pappas isn't about to launch a witch-hunt against Continental," he added, stopping himself before including the incriminating truth, *because Pappas promised me he wouldn't bring charges, that the Task Force's investigation into Continental's criminal conduct had been ended before it could be leaked to the press. Such a leak,* Whitcomb thought as he glanced through the legal documents, *would be devastating to my re-election campaign given that Continental is one of my biggest contributors. Pappas gave me his word. What the hell is going on?*

Fong scratched his chin with his right hand. "Mr. Pappas has nothing to do with this," the BCA agent said quietly.

"Then who's forcing Ms. Frazier to testify? Pappas is the only one empowered to convene a grand jury," Whitcomb said forcefully.

Fong shook his head. "Consider yourself served, ma'am." The BCA agent withdrew a second subpoena from his coat and scrutinized the dignitaries. "Ah," Fong said, stepping up to a blond man, "Mr. Theodore Huberty, I presume?"

Ted Huberty, operations manager of Merritt Pit Copper/Nickel Mine, Neil Yost's brother-in-law and the man who'd hired Yost, nodded. "That would be me."

Fong handed Huberty the document. "You heard me talking to Ms. Frazier?"

Huberty nodded again. "I did. I know the drill. My lawyer will deal with this," he said, accepting the paperwork.

Fong retreated. "Folks, the dates and times for your testimony are noted in the subpoenas. To answer the Governor's question, you're being summoned to provide testimony by the one person, other than Mr. Pappas, who can compel your appearance in a criminal proceeding."

Captain Stebenvold took the subpoena out of the governor's hand and reviewed the document. "He's right."

"What the hell are you talking about, Stebenvold. If the county attorney isn't bringing this to court, who the hell is?" Whitcomb asked.

Fong turned away and walked toward the Durango. The BCA agent had a long drive back to St. Paul. Upon his arrival, he would report to Minnesota Attorney General Sarah Westin, the only Democrat holding statewide office, a woman who'd inexplicably claimed her first term as AG in the same election that brought Wesley Whitcomb to power. Fong would advise the Attorney General that Neil Yost—who'd been served at his home on Bear Island Lake, where he'd retreated after being fired by Continental Mining—Ted Huberty, Merritt Pit Operations Manager, and Ms. Roberta Frazier, the company's CEO, were on notice that the Minnesota Attorney General was interested in learning what Yost, Huberty, and Frazier knew about the deaths of Susie Lindahl and Antonio Feggetti.

CHAPTER FORTY-FIVE: TWO WEEKS BEFORE

The aroma of cinnamon had permeated the thick, warm air of the kitchen. Gabriella Pierce stood at the stove, stirring steel-cut oats in a boiling pot of skim milk, Gabby's body suggested by sunlight embracing her silk robe. Coffee perked, the odor of freshly ground vanilla-flavored beans rising into the close air of the warm room to merge with the scent of cinnamon. The Indian woman heard footfalls against the granite tile of the hallway leading to the kitchen, smiled at Dee Dee Hernesman, and returned to stirring bubbling oats.

"Smells wonderful," Dee Dee had said, stopping at the threshold of the kitchen and leaning against plaster. "It's like, what, six-thirty? What time did you get up, anyway?"

Gabriella smiled. "Six. I have the day off from the bookstore, but I have a gig at Silver Rapids tonight with Amy. I need to practice if we're not going to suck. It's been months since we played together and Amy won't be in town until just before we go on," Gabriella said quietly, turning off the gas burner and placing a lid on the steel pot. "Oatmeal's ready. Rolls will be done in five. Grab a cup of coffee and I'll join you in the nook."

Hernesman reached into a kitchen cabinet, retrieved a mug bearing the Duluth Huskies team logo and poured coffee. "I didn't know you and Amy were playing together again."

Gabby repeated the actions of her partner. The women claimed benches opposite each other in the breakfast nook. "We're booked for three weekends at Silver Rapids. I thought I told you that."

Dee Dee shook her head. "No, I'd remember if you did. But it's not a big deal. Later today, I'm wrapping up loose ends on the explosion case. I met with Sheriff Slater a few days ago, and she filled me in on an angle she's working regarding the criminal investigation. She was a bit cagey when we first got together, but I think she's come to appreciate that we're essentially on the same side."

The younger woman sipped coffee and studied her partner. *I have no idea why I fell for Dees. She's not that much to look at. Oh, I'll give you that she's pretty in a solid, pedestrian sort of way. But her eyes make her face. Though they're not remarkable, there's a sparkle to them that is, well, captivating. And she is so patient and tender and honest and . . .*

"Are you listening to me at all, Miss Pierce?"

. . . loving. That's it. Dee Dee Hernesman is, in the end, a loving woman. That's it. That's why this thing seems to work. Whatever, this "thing" is.

"Sorry." Gabriella hadn't revealed her thoughts as she took another draw of vanilla-flavored coffee and smiled. "You were saying?"

• • •

The conference with the sheriff had been an eye-opener for Dee Dee Hernesman. They met at the task force office in Ely. Slater had talked. Hernesman had listened.

"I think I've found a way to get Justin Pappas to move," the sheriff had said, shuffling papers in front of her as she sat rigidly behind the desk in the tiny office. "It won't be, shall we say, 'conventional.' Not in the least. But I think I've found a chink in that old boy's armor that will give the Lindahls and the Deviches a shot at real justice."

Hernesman was dressed casually, in a gray summer blouse, blue shorts, white ankle socks, Nikes, and a black Piragis baseball cap—courtesy of Gabby. She leaned toward Deb Slater, unable to keep the smile off her face, unable to let the moment unfold without emotion. "No shit? You really think you've found a way to knock that old bastard off dead center, get him to do the right thing?"

Slater nodded. "I have a friend, a high school classmate. Dave Posten. Works in the attorney general's office. When Pappas kept stonewalling me, telling me to back off, that the deaths were unfortunate but that there was nothing criminal about what Yost or Continental did, it got me to thinking about the OSHA violations and the *Arkell* case you found and copied for me. It also got me to thinking about the past, about the details of Yost's work in Montana and the three men he killed there and the fact that Continental knew full well that the man was, in a word, a loose cannon."

Dee Dee had nodded. "And?"

"I share your clients' upset that the case never went to trial, that the truth may never come out because Continental bought your clients' and the Deviches' silence, bought it pretty cheaply under the circumstances I might add."

Hernesman frowned.

Slater raised her right hand, palm toward the lawyer. "Understand: I don't blame you for settling. You gave me the lowdown on the shit Kat Carpenter pulled. I get that Carpenter put the trustee in an impossible position. You didn't reveal what Continental paid, but scuttlebutt being what it is up here on the Range; I have a pretty good idea we're looking at just south of two mil. That," Slater continued, returning her right hand to the desk, "is too much money to roll the dice on. Not your fault, counselor. You were in bed, through no fault of your own, with a snake."

Hernesman cleared her throat. "Actually, it was my fault. I didn't remove Judge Peck from the case when I had the chance. I suspected she'd side with Kat on the trustee issue and still, I hoped she'd do the right thing. So yes, the fact that I ended up partnered with a cobra was my fault," Dee Dee said quietly. "But enough about ancient history. What's your idea?"

• • •

"These rolls are to die for," Dee Dee had said with affection as she bit into a cinnamon confection created by Gabriella. The sun, large and yellow, sat just above the green grass of the golf course outside the bungalow's kitchen window. Rain clouds gathered, low, dark, and threatening in the west. Robins bounced along a newly mown fairway probing for worms. A raven sat in a birch across the fairway and cawed in protest. "Where did you learn to cook?"

Gabby smiled. "My dad. My mom's a terrible cook. She's great when it comes to laundry, house cleaning, and organizing, but Dad has always been the cook."

Laughter erupted from Dee Dee despite the fact she was still chewing the roll.

"What's so funny?"

"Well, given that just about every piece of clothing you own is strewn about our bedroom, I'd say it's a damn good thing

239

you take after your dad in the kitchen!"

Gabriella considered the slight. "I guess," she finally admitted, the evidence of her sloth too entrenched to refute. "But what about the sheriff and the explosion case? You were saying something, before we got sidetracked, about there being a way to bring the folks who caused the accident back into court."

"Sheriff Slater has a contact, a friend, in the attorney general's office. Justin Pappas, our county attorney, has told her to cease and desist, that his office won't prosecute Neil Yost or Continental Mining or any of the company's higher ups. But Slater, and you have to keep this in the strictest of confidence, thinks she's found a way around Pappas. She'll need his assistance, which will be tough to obtain without a bit of arm-twisting. If Pappas won't pursue criminal charges on his own—most likely because he's beholden to Continental for campaign contributions *and* because his constituency on the Iron Range is salivating over the prospect of new mines and new jobs—the AG's office can, under certain circumstances, take over the case."

The Indian woman had stood up, moved across the kitchen, lifted the tin pot from the stove, and poured herself a second cup of coffee. "How so?" Gabby asked, reclaiming her seat.

"Pappas can *request* that Sarah Westin, the AG, take the case due to a conflict of interest or inadequate county resources to prosecute . . ."

Pierce interrupted her partner. "That, given Pappas's statements to Sheriff Slater, doesn't seem too likely."

". . . or the *governor* can sign an order requesting that the AG prosecute."

Gabriella sniggered and spewed coffee. "Now that is even more implausible, given what you've told me about the ties between Whitcomb and Continental Mining. And isn't the AG, Sarah Westin, a Democrat? Won't Westin's chasing after a supporter of our Republican governor seem politically motivated?"

Hernesman reached across the table, touched her lover's wrist, and smiled. "You're such a smart whippersnapper."

Pierce frowned but did not remove Hernesman's hand. "We can make nice after you finish your story. Get to the part

240

where Slater's friend in the AG's office rides in on his white horse and saves the day."

"Funny, hadn't thought of it that way. But you're right: If David Posten can make this happen, he is indeed my Sir Lancelot!"

"I didn't think, at your level of life experience, Ms. Hernesman, that you believed in fairy tales," Gabriella said demurely, her fingers stroking the back of Dee Dee's hand.

"Camelot isn't a fairy tale, Miss Pierce. It's a legend."

The younger woman grinned. "I stand corrected. I didn't think you put much stock in *legends*."

Dee Dee Hernesman stood up and pulled Gabriella Pierce to her feet. The two women stared into each other's eyes, dirty dishes, half-empty coffee cups, and soiled utensils littering the table. "I don't. But I do believe in happy endings," the lawyer had said as she led her partner toward the bedroom.

CHAPTER FORTY-SIX

Sheriff Debra Slater drove the white Yukon west on Forest Road 11 out of Silver Bay, a North Shore community that is the headquarters for North Shore Mining. Nearly everyone in Silver Bay either works at or is affiliated with the taconite processing plant located just outside of town. Slater was taking the back roads to Hibbing. Her high school classmate, Assistant Attorney General David Posten, had subpoenaed her to appear and testify before the grand jury. The State of Minnesota was alleging that Neil Yost, individually, and Continental Mining of Minnesota, by and through its employees and officers, had caused the deaths of Susie Lindahl and Antonio Feggetti. Slater enjoyed the October scenery, the maples ablaze in red, the isolated oaks retaining dark brown, the aspens and birches displaying brilliant yellow, with the tamaracks—their seasonal needles still green—ready to erupt in gold. Slater watched a line of snow geese take flight from a pothole behind the vivid curtain of forest, the birds forming their instinctual "v," their honking audible inside the SUV, as she thought about her life and the changes in store for her and her daughter. "Nothin' easy about it," the sheriff lamented, a weak smile forming. "Nothin' remotely easy about it."

• • •

Annie had come through Riki's birthing like the athlete she was. A little over a month before Sheriff Deb Slater's daughter was to return to Cornell, her sophomore varsity volleyball season on hold—the coach allowing the girl to medically redshirt, nurse her baby, enroll in classes, and maintain her scholarship—Annie had brought the infant into the world, early to be sure, but healthy and intact. Thomas Jones had advanced the crazy notion that he and Annie should marry, an idea he suggested at Annie's bedside in St. Mary's Hospital. But the levelheaded girl had turned Thomas's spur-of-the-moment offer down. Flat.

"Thomas, you sentimental dweeb. I am not," Annie had said emphatically, "allowing you to propose to me out of some sense of obligation or guilt while I'm still sore from having your baby."

"But . . ."

The young woman wagged her right index finger at Thomas Jones, adjusted Riki on her left breast, and shook her head. "Ain't no 'buts' about it. I'm in no position to get married to you or anyone else. I've got three years of varsity volleyball, three years of college coursework, and *many* years of living as a single woman ahead of me before I settle down! No, I'll not accept a bedside proposal from you, sweet as it is. We're too young, too unsure of what it is we want in life. You can be a good, loving father. You can pay child support, send Riki birthday and Christmas cards, and be there for her when she needs her daddy. That's what you can promise me, Mr. Jones. Not your love and your fidelity, which, quite frankly, we both know you're not all of that certain of."

Thomas had accepted Annie's rejection with relief. He'd said the right things, stepped up to the plate out of a sense of moral duty, and the sheriff admired the kid for it. But Annie was spot on: She and Thomas weren't ready for marriage or any sort of commitment to each other. A commitment by the father toward his child? *Now that's doable. That's reasonable. That makes sense. But marriage? Or moving off campus, living together, trying to play house? Not a likely recipe for success. God bless Margaret Ann. God bless my smart, clear-thinking daughter.*

As she had for Annie's freshman orientation, Debra Slater drove Annie and Riki back to Ithaca, the family Suburban a year older, a year rustier, and a year more tired, crammed to the ceiling with baby clothes, a highchair, a crib (unassembled and still in its packing carton), and boxes of toys as well as Annie's

243

things, and left her daughter and granddaughter on campus, situated not in the dorms—where Annie had spent her first year at Cornell sharing a single room with a teammate, Ashley Hurd from Williston, North Dakota—but in a two-bedroom apartment a stone's throw away from the gym. The cost for the extra living space was steep. Debra had been forced, over the vociferous declinations of her daughter, to take out a home equity loan against the family cottage on Devil Track Lake to make it happen.

"I can go to UMD," Annie had pleaded, though from the inflection in the young woman's voice, Deb knew her daughter's concession was half-hearted. "I can play volleyball for the Bulldogs just as well as I can for the Big Red."

"Not on your life, missy. You'd trade a free ride to an Ivy League school, an education worth hundreds of thousands of dollars, for a state school education? No way, Margaret Ann Slater, am I gonna let you make that choice. Your father would smite me dead from heaven if I fell for that. You know it. I know it. No, you'll stay at Cornell and play for the Big Red, and I'll dip into my savings to make a second mortgage payment to ensure that you do!"

They'd had the conversation after Thomas's proposal of marriage was rejected and, to Slater's eye, the young man had literally skipped out of Annie's hospital room, little Riki fast asleep in an acrylic crib occupying the space between the women.

"What's done is done. You can stay in school and play for Cornell just like you planned. I'm not sayin' it'll be easy, being twelve hundred miles away from home, on your own, relying on the kindness of strangers. But you've got your daddy's strength about you. This is not the time to cash in your chips. Buck up, Annie. You'll do just fine."

The girl's face had clouded and tears had fallen. "I am so stupid . . ."

Deb had reached over the slumbering baby and stroked her daughter's youthful face. "There, there, child. Is that what Rick Slater would do? Cry over the past, over things that can't be changed? No way. Remember how tough your father was, how he stood up to that god-awful disease, how he fought so hard for so long? You're a chip off the old block, Annie. You are your father's daughter. Act like it."

The sheriff's voice had been emphatic but compassionate. Annie Slater nodded, reached for her baby, and nuzzled her nose against the sweet-smelling, pliant skin of Riki's cheek. Silence ensued. After a while, the daughter looked at the mother and spoke. "So. That asshole governor took you off the task force?"

Deb had smiled. "That he did. After the subpoenas were served on Continental, Huberty, and Yost, Whitcomb put two and two together, likely with some help from Justin Pappas."

Annie tilted her head and looked at her mother with intensity. "I thought Pappas was the one who asked the attorney general to step in, citing a conflict of interest in his office, saying that Continental had given his campaign money during his last election, which meant his office couldn't ethically evaluate the criminal case."

"True. But that didn't stop Pappas from seeking some measure of revenge," Deb said with a slight laugh. "Doesn't matter. I would have been done in December anyway. Now I can concentrate on transition planning. Retirement is just around the corner, and I'm still unsure as to who should be the interim sheriff. It's between Ed Neuman and Cindy Salo."

Annie frowned. "Neuman was the school liaison officer when I was in high school. He's a turd. Cindy, I like."

Slater had laughed again. "You're still pissed that Ed caught you skipping class and turned you in? Last time you did that, so I guess he did his job. He's a good man, Annie. Solid. But you're right: Salo is a tad bit better. Same work ethic but has a softer edge and is more politically astute. I think she'd work well with the county board and that, even in an interim appointment, is something worth considering."

"Whitcomb's an asshole," Annie observed, changing the subject.

"Give it up. Nothin' you or I can do about it. I voted for the man. And, unless someone stands up and makes me take notice, given he's my party's standard bearer, I'll likely grit my teeth, curse under my breath, and vote for him again."

Annie shook her head. "I will not waste a vote on that jerk. He's like Walker in Wisconsin. Leave him in long enough, he'll ruin the state. Plus, like I've said before, I'll take smart over stupid any day."

Deb had stood up, leaned over, and kissed her daughter and the baby in turn. "So, like the last election, when you cast the first vote of your life in the Republican primary for that Tea Party wacko from Palo running for the House and I voted for the more sensible, conservative incumbent, our votes will forever cancel each other out?"

Annie had sniggered. "Exactly. And Travis Nevonen isn't a wacko. He's a Libertarian, like Rand Paul."

Deb Slater had smiled. "I'm not so sure there's a difference . . ."

• • •

The sheriff's time in front of the eighteen men and women in Judge Smythe's courtroom in Hibbing went smoothly. She was the second witness, taking the stand behind Neil Yost whose history in Montana, his deception of Steve Gruber, and the resulting explosion at the Merritt Pit site were agonizingly extracted from him by Assistant Attorney General Posten. Yost's attorney, Gordon Ames, a flashy criminal defense lawyer from Minneapolis, wasn't allowed to interject or object or question witnesses during the proceedings. The grand jury process is a substitute means of determining whether probable cause to charge a person, or, in the case of Continental, a legal entity, with a crime exists. It's not a process for establishing guilt: only a process for determining whether a threshold of evidence supports criminal charges. Deb Slater spent four hours answering Dave Posten's questions and then, she was back in the Yukon, headed for home. Ted Huberty, Roberta Frazier, and other witnesses followed Slater to the stand. Over the course of a week, Posten brought in everyone who had anything to say about the deaths of Susie Lindahl and Antonio Feggetti. The grand jury deliberated less than two hours. The people of northern St. Louis County, having lived their lives in the shadow of economic uncertainty and turmoil, but steeped in faith and well-read and educated no matter their station in life, found little difficulty in indicting Neil Yost and Continental Mining of Minnesota, by and through Safety Manager Yost, Operations Manager Huberty, and CEO Frazier, for criminal violations of Minnesota's OSHA laws under section 182.667 of the state statutes. But those charges, being at best only gross misdemeanor-level wrongs, were only the beginning of Mr. Yost's and Continental's woes.

When the bill of indictment was returned by the grand jury and opened by Judge Smythe, it also included a finding that there was probable cause to believe that Neil Yost and Continental Mining had committed homicide: Manslaughter in the Second Degree, a felony punishable by up to ten years in prison. For the first time in Minnesota legal history, a corporation had been indicted for murder.

CHAPTER FORTY-SEVEN

He awoke to the sound of corn rattling. The stench of hog manure hung over him like a nasty shroud. Pungent air filled the claustrophobic room Danny Aitkins occupied on the third floor of the men's dormitory of the New Beginnings Treatment Center in Panora, Iowa. The disgraced lawyer opened his eyes and stared at the plaster ceiling, his head clear of cobwebs but his soul filled with anguish for a life trashed, ruined, and discarded between bouts of sobriety and decadence over the course of thirty years. "What the hell?" Aitkins asked aloud, though the other patients in the treatment center were already at breakfast. "Dees gave me a shot. And what did I do? I drank myself comatose in Montana and didn't stop drinking until family and friends dragged me kicking and screaming from the Ely Super 8."

Aitkins sat up. Bedsprings creaked. His girth had expanded due to alcohol abuse and now, as a patient at New Beginnings, from the three squares he was wolfing down. Though the male dormitory at New Beginnings was air conditioned, the artificially cooled air did nothing to lessen the smell of pigs surrounding Lake Panorama, a reservoir located a few hundred yards from the treatment center. The presence of hogs was all encompassing as Aitkins stood up, scratched his head, and stared at a photograph on the wall.

Danny had noticed the picture when Maggie Prescott, the social worker and therapist assigned to exorcise his demons, had guided him to his new digs.

"Who's that?" he'd asked, his face flushed from the effort of lugging a suitcase up three flights of narrow, wooden treads, Aitkins's right index finger pointing at a color photo of a young, attractive African American woman, her hair in dreads, her lips curved in a sedate smile.

"Esther DuMont. Now Esther Erickson. She was a patient here when we only took in female clients—before we bought and remodeled this wreck of a house into a treatment center for men. She was an RN before coming here. Got straightened out, went back for her Master's, became a nurse practitioner. Works in Duluth at an inner-city clinic. Hell of a woman. Married a local—Mason Erickson—an Iowa farm boy."

Danny Aitkins had noted, on first meeting Maggie Prescott that the amply girthed, plain-faced woman liked to gab. During a lull in their banter, he'd opened his suitcase, removed the Aitkins family Bible, and placed the book on a nightstand next to his rented bed. "This place in the habit of memorializing every patient who comes through its doors?" he finally asked with evident sarcasm.

"No. Esther's special. She saved the life of another patient, turned her own life around, and—here's the real reason why her picture is on that wall—she and Mason and their two girls, beautiful kids, a year apart, who remind me of Esther and her twin sister, Lilly—endowed a scholarship fund for folks who need help getting straight but can't afford it."

"Sounds like a saint. Saint Esther," Danny had muttered as he looked away from the portrait and stared across the back lawn of the treatment center past a line of mature oaks to fix his gaze on a cornfield, rows of corn flowing to the horizon in an endless, rippling sea of precision.

The insult hadn't upset Maggie Prescott. She simply sighed. "Well, she's no saint, I can tell you that. But, after listening to what I and Dr. Hodges—our clinical director—had to say, after accepting the help this place offers, she not only saved her life; she changed it. You get yourself comfortable, Mr. Aitkins. Dinner is at six," the woman had said, leaving the drunk with a memory of cheap perfume and an energetic smile after she exited the bedroom.

He was in his fourth week at New Beginnings and, uncharacteristically for Danny Aitkins when thrown into treatment, things were starting to click. After a quick shower, he pulled on running shorts, a pair of New Balance cross-trainers, and a Winnipeg Blue Bombers T-shirt. In his youth and middle age, Danny Aitkins would have been gearing up for a long-distance run. For decades, Danny's cure for a hangover was to jog until the mental fog and headache and aching limbs of too much booze subsided. But he was an old man. He hadn't, given his steady decline into mediocre health, bad knees, and a sore low back, run anything more than a city block in over a decade. *A walk works just as well,* the lawyer thought, lacing his shoes. *It was all I could do, two weeks in, to walk a half-mile without collapsing. Now I'm doing three miles at a pretty good clip. Feels good. Praise God,* the man thought, his eyes diverting to the Bible on the nightstand. *I've worked my way into the New Testament. Not much of interest in the legends and myths and fables of the Old Testament. But John's Gospel? Now there's theology that piques my interest! Who is this Jesus character and what sort of love can he offer me?*

The lawyer stood up, made the bed, closed the door to his rented room, and clambered down the stairs. A telephone—the treatment center's landline—rang. Aitkins heard other residents in discourse over breakfast as he arrived on the main floor.

"Mr. Aitkins," Emmy Wilks, the receptionist manning the front desk, called out in a lilting, post-adolescent voice, "you have a call."

Danny stopped in front of the girl. Emily smiled, exposing two large dimples, as she handed Aitkins the phone. *She'll make a lovely bride,* the old man thought, noting with a tinge of sorrow that his boys were either married or in steady relationships and thus unavailable. "Hello?"

"Danny – Dees."

"Hey."

"How's it goin'?"

"It's goin'. Can't believe that you and Julie pulled this on me." Aitkins began to tear up as he remembered the intervention in the trashed, dirty, soiled motel room that sent him packing to Iowa. Dee Dee and Gabriella Pierce had driven Danny to New Beginnings. There had been no time to wash laundry or go back to his little rented flat in downtown Grand Forks or stop for anything more than gas, meals, and essential toiletries purchased on the run as the women drove Aitkins to his rendezvous with Ms. Prescott and Dr. Hodges. Beyond a few days' clothes, a razor and blades, a toothbrush and toothpaste, a can of Old Spice deodorant, and the family Bible, which, despite his decay, Danny never traveled without, the man was deposited by Hernesman and Pierce in front of Miss Wilks with a near-empty suitcase.

But Danny had survived and, given his progress in the program, as he unraveled the depths of his addiction, a family curse passed on to him by his mother—a mess of a woman who ultimately curbed her desire for booze by committing suicide—Danny Aitkins was, after a month in farm country, beginning to believe he too might, like Esther DuMont, turn his life around. "But I've gotta thank you and Gabriella and Julie and the kids for doing what you did. I was . . ." the man struggled to find the words, ". . . at the end. There was no way I was gonna come out of the dark place I'd fallen into on my own. You are one great friend, Diane Emily Hernesman. I can never repay you for your kindness."

Dee Dee wept. She held her cell phone to her right ear as she stood outside her Ely home and watched scarlet maple leaves tumble against an overcast sky. "I did what any person who loves another person, Danny, *must* do."

Silence ensued. The pause wasn't awkward but necessary, essential so that they could gather their thoughts and press on. "So how's that girlfriend of yours? She's a fox!"

Hernesman laughed. "You are such a pig. But yes, she is one gorgeous woman. Smart and talented too. You haven't heard her sing, have you?"

"No. Isn't she part of a folk duo?"

"At times. She also performs on her own. Either way, she's got a great alto voice. She's also a damn fine songwriter. Some of the stuff she's written is Mary Chapin Carpenter quality."

Aitkins looked toward the New Beginnings' dining room. Other patients were filtering out. The clock above the reception desk indicated the time stood at ten minutes to eight. The kitchen closed at eight. "Gotta go, Dees. I'll miss breakfast if I don't get moving . . ."

"Stay strong, Danny. Like Red Green says, 'Keep your stick on the ice: We're all in this together.'"

Aitkins smiled. "You couldn't come up with an American to quote? You gotta resort to quoting a Canadian dressed in a flannel shirt and suspenders to make your point?"

"Go eat breakfast, my friend. I love you."

"I love you too."

The lawyer was just about to say goodbye when an emergent, lingering question caused Aitkins to keep Hernesman on the line. "Wait. Whatever happened with that case, the explosion case? I know you settled the civil part of it. Weren't too happy with the outcome, as I recall. But did anything ever happen on the criminal side of things?"

Dee Dee Hernesman gathered her thoughts as she watched a grey squirrel scamper across the leaf-littered fairway behind her house. "Yup. There's much to tell about what happened once the attorney general got hold of the bastards running Continental Mining. Much. But you need to get to breakfast, and I need to drive Gabriella to church."

"A bit early for services isn't it?"

Dee Dee giggled. "We're not going to church to pray, Mr. Aitkins, though I know a few folks, including a former

252

lawyer, who could likely use me praying for them. We have a meeting with Pastor Holm at Grace Lutheran. Andrea Holm. Nice lady."

"A meeting with a Lutheran pastor? I thought *you* were Catholic . . ."

From the tone of the man's voice, Hernesman knew Aitkins had guessed the reason behind her early morning visit to Grace Lutheran. Rather than string him along, Dee Dee was happy to confirm her mentor's suspicions. "Yes, Danny, Gabriella and I are getting married. She's Hindu but insists on something sacred. And yes, I'm Catholic but my church hasn't quite caught up to society with respect to the same-sex marriage thing. The Evangelical Lutherans, however, are on board. So Pastor Holm's church is a compromise."

Aitkins smiled. "Good for you, my friend. Good for you. I gotta run. Give that beautiful wife-to-be of yours a big kiss, will you?"

"And leave you with an image that will doubtlessly lead to untoward thoughts? I said it before, Daniel: You are a pig. But I love you in spite of your flaws. Go eat some breakfast and then, get yourself straight. I need you back in Ely sober and presentable by December 15th so you can be my best man!"

CHAPTER FORTY-EIGHT

December tenth. *A week to go to retirement. God, I am tired.
And frustrated. And burned out. Other than an occasional drug
dealer stopping in Grand Marais to turn a quick buck, tourists
who don't know that .08 is the limit not just in the Twin Cities
but throughout the state, or young punks from Duluth who
wander up here to burglarize summer cabins—looking for guns
and other valuables to fund their drug habits—it's the same
folks, the same families, over and over and over again.*

Cook County Sheriff Deb Slater paused, sipped warm
cocoa from a battered stainless steel travel mug, and looked out
the driver's side window of the Yukon. The SUV was parked on
the Gunflint Trail, radar on, engine running, the outside
temperature below zero, the vehicle's heater keeping the cabin of
the GMC warm. Slater was waiting to stop folks speeding into
Grand Marais. It was three-thirty in the afternoon. A big yellow
bus carrying children from town would soon be laboring uphill
from the Shore. Slater's eyes closed briefly as she considered the
end of a long, long career.

*Did I make a difference? Sure, I stopped some crimes
and solved some crimes. But did I change any lives over the
decades I wore a badge?* She knew she had. She knew she was
allowing recent events, where an angry tax protester had shot a
juror—the man free, pending sentencing because the crimes he'd
been convicted of were misdemeanors, crimes unlikely to land
him in jail—Sharon Polavina, the foreperson of the jury that
convicted the man for refusing to license and insure his pickup
truck. Ms. Polavina was shot as she walked across the Holiday
convenience store parking lot with a bag of groceries. The
shooter, Barry Larson, having spent his life isolated,
cantankerous, and addicted to the-substance-of-the-month, was a
mess. The rules, any rules, didn't apply to the Larson Clan.
Barry, who'd represented himself during the trial, felt aggrieved

that the jury hadn't listened to him, particularly his main point, that the only entity with legitimacy is the county sheriff and that all other governmental bodies and officials are without authority to impose limits on Freemen.

Larson learned the language of the Sovereign Citizen movement visiting websites and chat rooms promoting the theory that he was not obligated to follow any legal precedent or statute other than admiralty law—the law of the sea—and that, in essence, no rules implemented by government are legitimate exercises of power. To Barry's way of thinking, the jury had been led astray by Ms. Polavina. And so, Barry shot Sharon Polavina three times at point blank range before a young man pumping gas sought to intervene. The Good Samaritan was also shot three times for his effort. Had Barry been a smarter, more efficient criminal, he would have used his dad's forty-five caliber Browning—a relic from his paternal grandfather's service as a Marine during WWII in the Pacific—and done the job completely and thoroughly. Instead, because Barry Larson used a small caliber revolver, both Ms. Polavina and the Good Samaritan pulled through. After Barry unleashed his angry hail of bullets, he calmly placed the empty pistol on the blacktop and walked away. He was arrested fifteen minutes later in The Whitefish Brew Pub, a stone's throw from the Holiday station, contentedly sipping cold beer from a frosted mug. Larson was wholly unapologetic—but cooperative—when two Lake County Deputies walked into the brew house, drew down, cuffed Larson's hands behind his back, and escorted him off his barstool and out of the place.

Barry Larson was in jail, unable to make bail and waiting for a second trial. He hadn't been sentenced on the misdemeanor guilty verdict that sent him off the deep end. Sentencing was being held in abeyance until the attempted murder and assault charges—felonies—were dealt with. The Barry Larson case, Barry being the third generation of his family to spend significant time behind bars, was the tipping point that caused Debra Slater's pessimistic retrospective of her life's work.

Slater recognized that there had been, over the course of her career, great saves, solid efforts on her part in dealing with families disintegrating from the weight of poverty, booze, and anger where she was able to help folks steer clear of perpetual heartache. But there were families like the Larson Clan that just couldn't be "fixed." And while Debra Slater didn't ascribe to poet Steve Kowit's belief that modern man was, in essence, not *Homo sapiens* but *Homo Satanicus*—irretrievably evil and incapable of redemption—Slater found herself at the end of a long, long road: tired of trying to save her fellow man and desperately in need of rest.

The squad radio crackled. Slater's eyes jetted open. "All units, respond to 9112 Dunagee Lake Road. Reporting party says there's a man with a gun threatening . . ."

"Shit. That's Potso Larson's place," Slater said as she turned off the radar, activated lights and siren, and pulled the Yukon from gravel onto asphalt. "What that hell is that crazy old man up to now?"

Dale "Potso" Larson was Barry Larson's father. Dale and his wife Victoria lived in a single-wide mobile home set high above Dunagee Lake, a weed-choked pond tucked away in an isolated corner of Cook County. The Larson trailer, where young Barry grew up learning to duck his father's fists and work boots and to avoid kitchen implements and household objects launched by his mother, was two miles away from the nearest house or cabin and occupied marshy terrain better suited to mosquitoes than people.

"I'm on my way." Deputy Cindy Salo's quick response over the radio was comforting. Slater would have backup when she pulled into the Larson compound to face Potso and his pissed-off, don't-tread-on-me attitude.

256

Slater opened the radio's mic. "Step on it, Salo. Sounds like Potso's going off on Vicky again."

"Rodger. I'm ten minutes behind you."

It took the better part of a half-hour for Deb Slater to negotiate the pockmarked gravel roads leading to the old logging trail that dead-ended at the Larson trailer. It was dark by the time Slater's Yukon pulled into the Larsons' front yard. The headlights of the SUV illuminated the opening in the dense woods. Light reflected off the grills of wrecked cars and pickup trucks strewn about the unkept yard. A decrepit International had been left unattended so long that a maple tree had sprouted through the Scout's floorboards only to emerge through the vehicle's roof. Slater pulled the Yukon between decaying vehicles. Headlights focused on the peeling white paint of the Larson trailer as the sheriff put the GMC in park, opened the driver's door, unstrapped her holster, pulled her M&P .40 semi-auto free of leather, stepped into the cold, and waited for backup. "Salo, where the hell are you?" Slater whispered into her shoulder mic, her voice steady despite the fact that her heart was beating like a kettledrum. "I'm at Potso's."

"I'm still ten out. There was a wreck on the Trail behind you. Scooter Jones hit a tree. Cracked up his F-150. Wasn't drunk this time—just tired. He's not bleeding so I left him in his truck to wait for a tow."

Slater nodded to herself. *Scooter is a handful when he's got a buzz on. Good thing he wasn't drunk. Just got his license back and this would be number four, a felony DUI that could send him to prison. Mamie is fighting ovarian cancer. Last thing she needs is for Scooter to be locked up.*

A scream pierced the night air.

Shit.

"Potso, you no-good-son-of-a-bitch, go ahead and shoot me. Big man, beating up on his hundred-and-thirty pound wife . . ."

Slater recognized Victoria Larson's voice despite the fact the trailer's doors and windows were buttoned up against the cold. The sheriff shivered. She watched her breath ascend and disappear.

"In your dreams you ugly cunt! One thirty? That's your fuckin' left leg, you dumbass. You think you're gonna leave me, take my money, and what, start a new life? With a new man? Ha. What sorry piece of shit would want you, you used-up old whore?"

Slater edged forward. There was no snow on the ground despite the fact it was the second week in December. *Global warming.* The thought came and went as the sheriff concentrated her attention on the soap opera taking place inside the decrepit mobile home.

"That you, Sheriff?" Potso's voice cut through the still, subzero air. "I wouldn't be making any sudden moves if I was you. Might be that I decide to put a couple in this bitch and then turn the gun on you."

"Dale, let's talk this through."

There was no response.

"Dale?"

"I heard ya. It's too late for talkin'. This old woman pushed my buttons one too many times. I've got a mind to end this stupid-ass charade we call a marriage. A bullet for her, a bullet for me. Or, take her out and then take you out. Either way, I'm done for. I know what a third domestic means. It means time in Stillwater alongside that shit-for-brains kid of mine. And that ain't gonna happen."

Slater thought back to similar situations she'd encountered over her lengthy career.

Jack Kobe in the Field Tower in St. Paul. Jacob Ellefson in the little cabin on an island in the middle of Katherine Lake. Both men holding hostages, innocent lives at risk. Well, maybe Victoria isn't so innocent. Maybe she pushed Potso to the brink just to see what would happen. But she's trying to leave the asshole, trying to get away from the violence, and to begin anew. That tells you something about the woman, shows she's capable of redemption.

"Salo, where the hell are you?"

There was no answer to Slater's whispered question. The sheriff was in a bind. Larson's bellicosity was escalating. There wasn't time to wait for backup. Slater studied the trailer. She pulled the layout of the single-wide from memory. *They're likely in the kitchen, by the back door. There's a window in the door. If I can get a bead on Potso through the window, I can take him out. Gotta move before he figures out what I'm up to.*

Deb Slater stepped carefully, avoiding trash, discarded auto parts, beer cans, and dead appliances. She made the rear of the house without detection. Inside, Potso Larson kept up a stream of invectives. The man sounded drunk, likely tippling his favorite beverage—Old Thompson, the cheapest blended whiskey sold at the Grand Marais municipal liquor store—straight from the bottle. Slater pressed her body against the cold skin of the trailer. The sheriff took deep, steadying breaths as she inched toward the back door.

Bang.

Before Debra Slater could assess her chances of taking out Potso Larson, a bullet burst through the trailer wall and tore into the sheriff's left thigh. Slater collapsed. The M&P dropped from Slater's hand. The Sheriff hit the frozen ground and, despite a wave of pain descending upon her, crawled toward the automatic. Before Slater's fingers could touch steel, Potso Larson opened the trailer door, shoved his beleaguered wife onto the ground, stood imperiously over the women, and pointed his .45 in their general direction.

"Don't do it, Potso." Cindy Salo's voice cracked slightly as she emerged from shadow with her Smith and Wesson 9mm aimed at Larson's torso. "You're not fast enough to dodge a bullet. Drop your weapon!" Salo's command lost the tremor that had been present a split-second earlier.

259

Potso Larson looked at Salo. Slowly, nearly imperceptivity, he shifted the barrel of his Browning toward the deputy. "I'm not about to let some two-bit female Barney Fife take me in."

Victoria Larson screamed. "Potso, don't be a fool! You are one stupid, stubborn, sonofabitch but I don't want you to end up dead!"

The old man, his dirty white T-shirt hanging free of the waist of his rumpled blue jeans, his feet bare against winter as he stood on the trailer's back porch, smiled and swung the handgun's barrel toward his wife. "Shut the fuck u . . ."

Bang.

The M&P jumped in Slater's hand. Victoria Larson leapt to her feet. Potso slumped, his legs twitching, his eyes wide and amazed, his back supported by the trailer as he slid into a seated position. The Browning remained in Potso's right hand as his rump came to rest on the treated pine slats of the porch. The hole in Larson's forehead leaked crimson. Blood flowed onto the man's T-shirt, wicking into a large red stain.

"You bitch!" Vicky Larson screamed, kneeling at her husband's side. "You've killed Potso! You stupid, stupid bitch! Now what the hell am I supposed to do?"

Cindy Salo snatched the .45 from the dead man's right hand before Vicky Larson could focus her anger. "She had no choice, ma'am. Your husband gave Sheriff Slater no choice." Salo put a finger to Potso Larson's carotid, looked at Slater, and shook her head.

Victoria Larson's sobs became a thunder of grief. Deb Slater fought against shock as she holstered her weapon, opened her shoulder mic, and called for an ambulance.

CHAPTER FORTY-NINE

"Has the jury reached a verdict?"

Judge Harriet Smythe looked at two rows of seated citizens as she asked the question. The case, criminal charges brought by Assistant Minnesota Attorney General David Posten against Neil Yost and Continental Mining of Minnesota, Incorporated, had taken three weeks to try in Smythe's Hibbing courtroom. The judge was exhausted, tired to the bone after wrangling the state's attorney and four defense lawyers into decorum. There had been two full days of pre-trial motions arguing over witnesses and evidence. Most of the motions in limine had gone the state's way because Posten was a gifted trial lawyer with thirty years' experience. In the end, twelve jurors heard the story of Yost's past, his dishonesty, his callous disregard for the lives of Suzie Lindahl and Antonio Feggetti. *But it's a considerable stretch—from holding someone civilly responsible under a burden of proof that requires probability— to finding that same person <u>and</u> his employer criminally liable under the highest burden of proof our system recognizes: proof beyond a reasonable doubt,* the judge thought as she waited for an answer to her question.

Judge Smythe studied the juror she suspected to be the foreperson, a retired elementary school teacher from Chisholm, Sandi Scott, whose role as leader of the panel was confirmed when Mrs. Scott rose from her seat, verdicts in hand.

"We have, your honor."

"Bailiff, please retrieve the verdict forms."

"Guilty on all counts. I can't believe it!"

Dee Dee Hernesman stood in the cold January air in the courthouse parking lot, flecks of white gently falling on her dark hair. The lawyer hugged Judy Lindahl. Tears flowed freely as Hernesman said the words she hadn't believed were possible when she first discussed the idea of a criminal prosecution to Sheriff Deb Slater.

"Finally," Mark Lindahl said as he stood a few steps away from the weeping women, "finally there's justice for Susie." The man paused to compose himself and wipe away his own tears. "And for Antonio," he added softly.

Dee Dee broke free of Judy's embrace and wrapped her arms around Mark Lindahl. Hernesman nodded at Judy as she hugged Mark. "I told you a Hibbing jury would do the right thing," the lawyer said softly. "I was just a bit off as to which trial would prove my point."

Judy Lindahl smiled. "I never doubted you, Ms. Hernesman. Never. From the moment you walked into our house: your face, your eyes, your openness—all signaled that you were an honest, ethical, hardworking gal. But more importantly, being from Tower, you understand the Range, the way an Iron Range jury would decide a case like this," the woman said before pausing to organize her thoughts. "I just wish we'd been able to take the wrongful death case to trial. Not for the money—the girls are set for life with the settlement even though it's not what we were shooting for—but so a civil jury could have heard about Susie, how troubled she'd been, what a difficult time she'd had, and how, in the last year of her life, she'd started to turn it around. This jury didn't get to hear that story. But God works in mysterious ways. Absent a civil trial, this verdict," Judy concluded, "is about as good as it gets."

Dee Dee Hernesman released Mark Lindahl from her embrace and created space. "Reminds me of a word my pastor used last week in her sermon," the lawyer said quietly as the three of them walked toward the courthouse parking lot. "She said, 'God's love is *indefatigable* and Jesus' compassion for the lost is immeasurable.' I'd say that you both are *indefatigable*. You saw this thing through to the bitter end, and I'm sure Susie knows that you did."

Mark Lindahl opened the driver's door of an aging Ford Taurus, the front fender dented, the bumper held in place by duct tape, and slid onto the cold vinyl seat behind the steering wheel. His wife entered the car on the passenger's side. Dee Dee Hernesman paused next to her Escape. She wanted to add a note of caution to the conversation—likely the last one she would ever have with the Lindahls. She wanted to tell her clients that, yes, the state had proven its case, convinced a jury of Yost's and Continental's criminal culpability, but that years of appeal were likely ahead. Continental, for certain, wouldn't accept the verdict, one standing a century of Minnesota criminal jurisprudence on its head, without stalling and delaying and obfuscating through appeal.

I doubt the verdict as to Continental will stand, Hernesman thought, gauging whether she would disrupt the grieving parents' optimism now that justice had finally made an appearance in the case. *Yost will likely do time. There's enough here to convince the Court of Appeals and the Supreme Court that Yost knew better, ignored the obvious, and sent two young kids to their deaths. But holding a corporation criminally liable for the sins of an employee? That's dicey at best. And even if the verdict against the company passes appellate muster, what then? I don't see Ted Huberty or Roberta Frazier ending up in a cell next to Neil Yost. At best, maybe a fine for Continental and a short prison sentence for Yost. At worst, reversals of both convictions. Can't predict what the appellate gods will do,* Hernesman finally conceded, *so why ruin Mark and Judy's big day with supposition?*

• • •

"You've got to be kidding me! That's wonderful news, David. How can I ever thank you?" Deb Slater sat on a couch in the living room of her Craftsman style cottage on Devil Track Lake, the receiver of a remote telephone wedged against her right ear, as she talked to Assistant Minnesota Attorney General David Posten. Posten had called the former sheriff of Cook County and the former head of the Copper/Nickel Task Force as soon as he exited Judge Smythe's courtroom.

"We set legal precedent, Deb. No longer can large corporations disregard the health and safety of their workers, pay a small civil fine, and wash their hands of responsibility."

Slater mussed her hair, the auburn color of her youth replaced by creeping gray, and smiled. "You still behind the podium, giving your final argument, Dave?" the sheriff teased.

Slater had retired. She'd survived the crazed actions of a drunken "wood tick"—a term locals used to describe reclusive personalities like Potso Larson—spending a full week at St. Luke's Hospital in Duluth once she'd been stabilized at the Cook County Medical Center in Grand Marais, transported by helicopter to Duluth to ensure she didn't bleed out. The thigh wound healed nicely, with only the faintest of red around the bullet hole indicating a minor infection, something she was taking antibiotics for. But Slater had, when she'd regained lucidity in the hospital, borrowed pen and paper from her nurse and, with Annie and Riki sitting in a chair next to her bed, she'd written her resignation. Once the letter was in the mail, Slater made some phones calls, talking with the Cook County Commissioners she knew best, urging them to appoint Cindy Salo as interim sheriff. The majority of the board followed her advice and gave Salo the job. It would be up to Salo to hold onto the position. There was little question in Slater's mind that Ed Neumann would file against Salo when the new sheriff faced her first election, arguing during his campaign—relying upon a hint of personal solipsism that made Deb Slater slightly wary of the man—that he had more experience and was better qualified to be sheriff. *Salo will have to campaign hard. But, if she works at it, stays visible, attends community events, does parades and such,* Slater thought, *she'll win.*

"Congratulations, Dave. Pretty damn good lawyering from a boy who grew up in New London dreaming of being a professional baseball pitcher."

There was a pause on the other end of the line.

"Dave? You still there?"

Posten gathered his thoughts. "I was thinking . . ."

"Yes?"

As Slater and Posten conversed, Duke, Slater's eager black Labrador, the whiskers of his snout displaying longevity, waggled into the room with a tennis ball. The dog sat and waited, ball clamped in mouth, for Deb to pay attention to him.

"Not now, boy."

"Excuse me?"

"Not you, Dave. I was talking to Duke, my retriever. He's waiting for me to toss him a tennis ball. You said you were thinking . . ."

"Ah. Yes. Well, you know there's an All Class Reunion in New London next summer. It's what, our thirty-second? So it's no big deal for the class of '84. But it will be a big deal for the town. By the way, you missed our thirty . . ."

Slater thought back to two summers ago, when Rick had, a month before they were slated to attend her thirty-year high school reunion, taken a turn for the worse. "Rick," was all she managed to say.

Posten hadn't been in contact with Deb during Rick's illness but had known, by speaking to mutual friends, that Rick Slater was on the decline, that Deb had missed the reunion due to her husband's battle with mitochondrial disease. "Deb, I'm so damn sorry. I'd forgotten you weren't there because Rick got sick."

"*Was* sick."

"How's that?"

Deb adjusted the phone. Duke held the ball in his mouth as he waited for Deb to conclude her business. "He'd been sick long before the reunion. That was just the last of it, the beginning of the end."

"Shit. Why the hell did I bring it up? I apologize for dredging up bad times, hard memories."

Slater exhaled. Images of Rick's final days manifested as she sought to maintain her composure. "Not a problem. In fact, it's good to remember. Reminds me of what I had but also reminds me of what I've still got."

"Annie. And the baby. How is Riki, anyway?"

Deb Slater smiled. "Awesome. The awesomest granddaughter God ever created. She is my treasure, my trove. Things come, things go. But love remains. Someone said that once."

"It was good seeing you during the Grand Jury and the trial."

Slater knew what was lurking behind her old friend's words. There was desire and affection, long dormant, finally seeking expression. They'd dated briefly in high school but had gone their separate ways and lived their separate lives. Dave married a law school classmate, fathered three kids—two girls and a boy—and divorced after twenty-five years of solid partnering. The split had come, she'd heard through mutual friends, not due booze or drugs or an affair, but simply due to distance: an emotional void that neither Dave nor his wife Katie could bridge had opened up in their marriage causing them both, amicably and mutually, to throw in the towel. She knew that Dave had always been interested in her but, out of respect for Rick, had never expressed an untoward thought or made an untoward move. *But now that Rick's gone, it seems he might be willing to take a chance.*

"I can't say I like testifying. Never have been too comfortable on the witness stand. But you are good, David, at what you do. You made it easy for me to tell my story to the jury."

"Thanks."

Another pause.

I'm not sure I want him to move this conversation toward the personal.

"About the All Class Reunion . . ."

Slater reached for a tumbler of cool water, put the glass to her lips, and drank needfully. "Yes?"

There was a hitch in the lawyer's voice as he sought courage. "Would you, I mean, this is sort of out of the blue I realize, but would you consider going with me?"

Deb Slater swallowed hard as she pondered the grieving process, the life she'd lived with Rick, the time they'd spent as a couple, as parents, as friends, as lovers. *I don't know if I'm ready to get back on that horse. Life tossed me off, left me bruised, battered, and afraid to put my feet in the stirrups again.* She turned the proposal, one that was innocent enough, over and over in her mind. And then, something Annie had said before the shooting, when they were talking about Annie making the dean's list and how Riki was growing so fast and a myriad of other, every day things, came into focus.

"It's time you started getting on with your life, Mother," Annie had said, the words issued as a directive and not an observation. "You're young, good looking, and nearly free of that god-awful schedule you've kept as a cop. It's time, and I know Dad would agree, that you start thinking of yourself. Riki and I will be fine. Things are going well at school. My coach is making it as easy as possible to stay involved until next season. Thomas is playing nice, paying attention to both Riki and, surprise, surprise, me. Despite the blip in the road a new baby caused, I will be just fine. It's you, Mom that I'm worried about."

Debra Slater had heard her daughter out. But, true to her Icelandic heritage, in taciturn and stubborn fashion, she'd discounted Annie's concern. "I'm OK," Slater had said. "I'm not ready to slow dance with some old geezer bent on seeing my fifty-year-old body in the altogether."

"Mother!" Margaret Ann had shouted into the phone. "Too much information. I'm not suggesting, nor am I interested in you plunging into a torrid affair. I'm merely stating the obvious: You like men. Your man is gone. It's time to see what the world has to offer in that regard. You wait too long and well, that age thing might limit your options. Now, while you're still spry and lively and attractive, you need to dip your foot in the pond and see what the temperature of the water is."

Slater had laughed at her daughter's attempt at metaphor. "I'll think about it," she had said when her giggles calmed and the phone call was near its end. "I'll definitely think about it."

So. Here I am. Thinking about it. Summer is five months' away. The reunion is in the middle of July. Ah hell. If David is interested, why not give him some encouragement? Annie's spot on: Rick wouldn't expect me to sit home and mourn for the rest of my days. He'd tell me, if he was here, sitting next to me, petting Duke's soft, velvety black fur, that I deserve a little enjoyment, a little love in the life I have left to live. Shit, there's no time like the present to walk into that corral, pick out a horse, and get back in the saddle. Shit. It seems the horse has in fact, picked me*!*

"July's a long way off."

David Posten was no fool. He understood that Debra Slater was giving him an opening, a chance to make a connection *before* the all class reunion.

"You're right. It is. You up for a visitor?"

A giddy wave of emotion overcame Debra Slater. "I am," was all she said.

CHAPTER FIFTY

If you could only know my heart
And I could know your touch.
If you could only hear my song
And I could hold your love.

If this story could be written
And the ending came out right.
If this fiction had a purpose
And my yearning had a point.

I'd take you in my arms
Your dark hair all around
I'd keep you in my love
Your voice, the only sound.

If I was free to dance with you
And the music went on all night.
If the singer's voice had power
And my sorrow lost its edge.

I'd take you in my arms
Your dark hair all around
I'd hold you close to me
The band, the only sound.

Gabriella Pierce stood on the wooden stage, her raven hair pulled into a ponytail. Designer jeans showed off the singer's curves. A shimmering silver blouse draped Gabriella's torso as she strummed the last few chords of the song against the laughter and coarse talk and idle discourse filling My Sister's Place in Grand Marais.

Amy Maddox had left the stage, allowing Pierce to debut a new song. Maddox sat on a stool next to Dee Dee Hernesman-Pierce at the bar, the attorney's sterling wedding band obvious despite the dim lighting, the two women facing the stage and joining the packed house in applauding Gabriella's effort. "Well done," Maddox said, patting Dee Dee on the left shoulder, directing her approval not toward Gabriella's performance but toward the ring on Hernesman-Pierce's finger.

The lawyer feigned ignorance. "Whatever do you mean, Ms. Maddox?"

"Mrs. Martin. I'm not on stage so I go by my married name," Amy instructed wryly.

"Then return the favor and call me 'Ms. Hernesman-Pierce,' if you would."

"That's a mouthful. I think I'll stick with Dees."

Hernesman laughed. Gabriella Pierce-Hernesman stepped down from the stage and made her way through the crowd.

"Nicely done," Amy said, embracing her musical partner in a hug.

Gabriella frowned and gently pushed Maddox away. "I stumbled on the bridge," the younger woman said quietly, placing her long right arm around Dee Dee's waist. "It might be better if you play and I sing when I do 'Dark Haired Girl.' Don't want to embarrass the better half . . ."

Dee Dee kissed Gabriella on the lips. The gesture took the singer by surprise.

"What's that for?"

"For a beautiful song, a wonderful partnership, a great life. Pick one."

The women reclaimed their stools. Dee Dee sipped cold beer from a frosted mug. Gabriella and Amy pulled lightly on straws, drawing Sprite and lemon into their mouths as they watched patrons through sideways glances. "So what's your next big challenge, Dees, now that the explosion case is over?" Amy Maddox asked.

The lawyer smiled. "Don't really have anything exciting on the radar. Just more of the same: dog bites, car accidents, a couple of small construction cases that will likely end up in arbitration. I represent Ernst Gassert and Sons. They build high-end lake homes for pack sackers and are always getting sued. Picky rich bitches from Edina and Lakeville, you know. But I can't think of anything coming up that's earth shattering."

Amy Maddox nodded. "I heard that the criminal verdict is being appealed."

Dee Dee returned the nod. "Ya. There's a pretty good chance that at least four justices on the Minnesota Supreme Court will side with the defense and overturn the jury's decision as to Continental." Hernesman-Pierce paused, finished her beer, and placed the empty mug on the varnished pine of the bar. "I doubt they'll touch Yost's conviction. That's pretty solid."

Gabriella frowned. "Do we have to talk law? Can't we talk about something else?"

Amy Maddox sipped Sprite and thought for a moment. "Did they ever find that guy who sabotaged the trucks on the mine site? Cyrus something or other . . ."

"Oliphant. Cyrus Oliphant," the lawyer said, filling in the blank.

"Yes. Oliphant. He sort of disappeared, didn't he?"

Dee Dee nodded. "When Sheriff Slater was removed by the governor for pursuing criminal charges against Continental, the task force unraveled. Couldn't find a suitable replacement for Slater, and, quite frankly, with the permits having been issued and the mine under construction, opponents of copper/nickel mining turned to federal court to stop the project. So the answer to your question is, 'No, they never did find Mr. Oliphant.'"

Gabriella Pierce-Hernesman turned her head to watch an attractive young woman stumbling toward the lavatory. The obviously drunken patron disappeared into the women's restroom and Gabriella's attention returned to the conversation.

"I read in the paper that the Boise Forte Band is supporting the Sierra Club, Friends of the Boundary Waters . . ." Pierce-Hernesman, said, pausing to take a breath before continuing, ". . . and a couple of other 'green' groups seeking an injunction to stop the mine," Gabriella added. "The case is being heard by Judge DeLacotte in federal court in the Twin Cities."

"I thought you wanted to change the topic," Maddox observed through a wide smile.

Gabriella didn't answer.

"DeLacotte's a Ranger," Dee Dee Hernesman-Pierce offered.

"Meaning?" Maddox asked.

"Meaning he's likely to side with Continental despite the fact he was appointed by Bill Clinton," Gabriella interjected, beating her partner to the punch.

Dee Dee nodded. "DeLacotte's a man of principle, but there's a lot of wiggle room for him as to whether or not the permits granted to Continental are supported by research. I think Gabby is right. I can't see an injunction being granted at this stage of the game."

"Time to get back up there and sing," Maddox said, emptying her glass. "Hey, isn't that Sheriff Slater?" Amy asked, pointing to a figure moving toward the three women.

Debra Slater walked methodically across the crowded bar and stood next to Hernesman-Pierce. "How's it goin'?"

Dee Dee smiled. "The dynamic duo here is about to wow us with another set. How's the leg?"

Slater watched Pierce-Hernesman and Maddox climb the stage across the room. "It's taking its sweet time to heal. But I got lucky. The bullet missed the femoral artery. Took out some muscle and chipped the femur but I'll be fine," Slater said evenly, suppressing emotion. "So, how are things?"

Dee Dee Hernesman-Pierce grinned. "Good. Very good."

Slater ordered a gin and tonic. "Sorry I missed the wedding."

"I'll take another," Dee Dee said when the waitress, a young woman with green hair, a nose ring, and eyebrow piercings, brought the ex-sheriff her drink. "I'd say getting shot by a deranged nut is a pretty good excuse for missing my wedding, Sheriff."

The waitress slid a mug full of beer across the polished surface of the bar toward Hernesman-Pierce. Soft strumming began. The high-pitched plunking of Pierce-Hernesman's mandolin joined Maddox's twelve-string Martin to create a rising wall of acoustic sound. Amy Maddox began singing the first verse to "Find the Cost of Freedom." Pierce-Hernesman slid her voice beneath that of her musical partner and the song took off.

"It's Deb. Call me Deb. I'm out of the sheriffing game," Slater said, sipping her drink. "And, yes, I did have a pretty good excuse for missing your big day. But I still would have liked to have been there."

There was a pause in banter as the women listened to the music.

"I have a question about the explosion case," Hernesman-Pierce said thoughtfully. "Don't know if you can answer it, but it's something that's been bugging me ever since you executed the search warrant on Oliphant's cabin."

Deb Slater nodded. "Can't hurt to ask. I'm off the case and, so far as I know, Cyrus Oliphant remains in the wind," the former sheriff said as she drained the gin and tonic. "Ask away."

Dee Dee hesitated, uncertain where to begin. "You remember the inventory from the search?"

Slater smirked. "Not in any detail. That was like, what, a year ago? I'm lucky, with all that's gone on, to remember where I put my car keys."

The lawyer laughed. "I know what you mean. But the inventory from the search. You and the other agents concluded that Oliphant pilfered three sacks of fertilizer from the resort."

Slater nodded. "Now that, I remember. We only found two bags of the stuff in Oliphant's closet."

Hernesman-Pierce gulped beer, wiped her mouth with the sleeve of her blouse, and touched her right hand to her chin as if in deep thought. "The defense in my case, their experts: One of the theories they tossed out, one that never gained traction but caused my clients no end of distress, was that the dead welders brought ANFO to the job site to make their job easier."

"How so?"

Dee Dee watched her partner claim a stool on the stage as Amy Maddox switched from the twelve-string Martin to a six-string Gibson. Hernesman-Pierce returned her attention to the sheriff.

"Johansson and Cutler's experts claimed they found unexploded nitrate prills *consistent* with ordinary fertilizer and *inconsistent* with the ANFO prills stored on the Merritt Pit site. The two types of prills allegedly had different chemical footprints." The lawyer stopped to form her next thought. "But because Cutler allowed Continental to alter the site before our expert could take samples, and because the supposed fertilizer nitrate was destroyed by the defendants' testing, we had no way of knowing if that claim had legs or was pure bullshit."

Deb Slater raised her empty glass toward the waitress. The young woman nodded. "Sounds like bullshit to me," Slater replied.

"Agreed. But their theory," Hernesman-Pierce continued, "was that Feggetti and Lindahl hauled fertilizer onto the site without Gruber knowing it, dumped the shit into the silo, and tried to blow the thing apart to save time."

Slater's eyes grew wide. "Seriously?"

"Seriously."

"Now that," Deb Slater said softly as she accepted a glass of gin and tonic from the waitress and handed the woman a five, "really is bullshit."

"I know. But you can understand why I'm so interested in what happened to the missing bag of fertilizer. Sounds like it wasn't much of a concern to you."

Slater nodded. "Not really. I mean, the explosion that tore that silo apart wasn't something a fifty-pound sack of nitrate could cause. That's pretty clear from the arson investigator's report. Plus, as I recall, Oliphant had an explanation for the missing bag: said he used it on his tomatoes. So we let the issue die. Nothing more to it than that."

"Did you believe him?"

The former sheriff pondered the question before responding. "I did. Cyrus Oliphant is a lot of things. But killing two innocent kids by inadvertently blowing them to bits just to make a point? Not his style."

The music swelled as the folksingers launched into a raucous rendition of "Amy." Gabriella made eyes at Amy Maddox as she belted out the lyrics in a style more akin to Taylor Swift than Pure Prairie League.

"So that's it, that's the big question you wanted to ask?"

"'Fraid so, Sheriff. Now I can let the dead dog lie, as they say."

Slater smiled and, holding her drink up in tribute, pointed to the stage. "Your partner is damn good. So's Maddox. They are having a ton of fun with this crowd."

"So, what do retired sheriffs do to pass the time?" the lawyer asked, changing the subject.

Deb Slater cocked her head. "Read. Travel. Make an effort to get out to the East Coast to watch a few college volleyball games and to see my granddaughter. Maybe take in a high school reunion and see an old friend . . ." The last comment caused Slater's voice to soften.

"Rekindle an old flame, perhaps?"

The sheriff frowned. "Don't know about that. Rick's been gone for less than a year. Still, there is this guy . . ." Deb Slater paused as she considered how deep into supposition and guesswork she should take the conversation, ". . . a high school classmate. Someone I dated before Rick. He wants me to come to an All Class Reunion next summer."

Hernesman-Pierce smiled. "I didn't know Rick, but I can't see why he wouldn't want you to find joy, if that's what you're after."

Slater stared into her drink and shook her head. "Problem is, I'm not sure what the hell I'm supposed to do, how I'm supposed to act, if and when I'm allowed to move on. This widow bullshit isn't something I ever thought I'd have to figure out."

Dee Dee placed her right hand on the sheriff's wrist. "Hey," she said, trying to lighten the mood, "you ever thought of doing PI work? Hoot Holt is getting out of the game, says he's too old to be out on the road, serving papers, knocking on doors. I'm looking for someone to work cases from time to time. The pay is good, seventy-five an hour plus expenses."

Deb Slater lifted her head and looked into Hernesman-Pierce's pewter eyes. "Maybe. Let me think on it."

Dee Dee nodded and raised her beer. Slater did the same with her drink. Mug and tumbler clanked. "Here's to love: elusive, desperate, and unscripted," the lawyer toasted.

Slater smiled. "Maybe. We'll see where this reunion thing goes."

The lawyer grinned. "Think on your classmate's offer, Sheriff Slater, and whether or not you'd like to supplement your retirement with a little sleuthing on the side."

Debra Slater downed the last of the gin and tonic and set her empty glass on the bar. "I will," the former Sheriff of Cook County said, turning her attention to Gabby and Amy as the musicians filled the tavern with another song. "I will."

EPILOGUE

The old man was disappointed. He'd hoped that the federal judge assigned to the case of *Friends of the Boundary Waters Vs. The United States of America, et al.,* would do the right thing. Very simply put, that was to rule in favor of clean water and against the ruination of wilderness. But Judge Evan DeLacotte was nothing if not pragmatic. Though safe in his position as a federal judge by virtue of lifetime appointment, Judge DeLacotte, a graduate of Mesabi East High School and a product of Iron Range culture and heritage—the immigrant pride, the work ethic, and the sense of insularity that binds all Rangers to one another against outsiders—knew the thinking of his family and friends regarding copper/nickel mining. DeLacotte understood that folks born and raised on the Iron Range are perpetually desperate in their quixotic search for an economic grand slam: an industrial development that will, in the face of uncertain taconite prices, reinvigorate the economy of northeastern Minnesota. Far be it for one of their own—who just happens to wear a robe—to stand in the way of progress.

And so, despite the issue being one where DeLacotte could have exercised caution and granted an injunction to slow the permitting process until evidence that an underground copper/nickel mine could operate without catastrophic consequences was assembled, the judge sided with his kindred, not science. There was no proof, so far as the old man knew, of bribes or promises or quid pro quo involved in Judge DeLacotte's decision making. And yet . . .

The eco-terrorist sat in his idling Chevrolet pickup truck on a logging road high above the mine. The Chevy was parked at the edge of a bluff overlooking an earthen berm nearly a mile in length. The dike formed the perimeter of a retention pond designed to store mining waste. The driver and his passenger sat in the truck, silently considering the industrial complex, trying to ascertain what their next move should be. Plastic bags of fertilizer, the nitrate prills soaked in No. 2 diesel, were stacked four bags high in the bed of the pickup. An overwhelming odor of fuel oil permeated the truck's interior. There was only a short interlude available to the man and the woman while the mine went through shift change; one half-hour of down time between shifts. A Roosevelt-Taft parking pass dangled from the Chevrolet's rearview mirror. The man looked at the pass and recalled how easily he'd stolen it from a miner's Ford F-150 in the parking lot of the Portage Bar in Tower.

I'd blow the hell out of the Merritt Pit Mine if it was up and running, the old man mused. Cyrus Oliphant and his companion watched vehicles come and go from the employee parking lot of the Roosevelt-Taft open pit copper/nickel mine. *But Merritt Pit isn't open and security over there is too damn tight. Better to make a statement here, where no one will get hurt.*

Oliphant had been on the lam for the better part of three months. He'd thought that, given Slater and the Feds had executed a search warrant for his cabin, had located two of the three bags of fertilizer he'd stockpiled, and, according to scuttlebutt, that defense experts had found uncharacteristic nitrate prills at the explosion site, the sheriff would come calling for Oliphant with handcuffs. But inexplicably, the criminal investigation had ended and Cyrus Oliphant was never questioned again about the missing sack of fertilizer. *I told the truth,* Oliphant thought. *I used the fertilizer on my tomatoes. Still, why should the Feds believe me? I'm the guy with the history of environmental sabotage, the usual suspect . . .*

Oliphant hadn't waited around for the inevitable. He'd vamoosed, traveling to Seattle where he resurfaced to take part in protests arranged by the Lummi Tribe, a Native American nation opposed to the construction of a coal dock on Puget Sound. The proposed Bellingham pier was designed to transfer high sulfur coal mined on the Crow Reservation in Montana onto ships bound for India and China. Two Native American tribes, one on each side of the global warming debate, were locked in a public relations and court battle over the issue of shipping American coal to Asia. The Lummi opposed the project due to fears that coal dust would destroy Puget Sound. But because the mine slated to supply the coal was located on Crow land, Crow elders fully supported the Bellingham dock. The project, if completed, would provide an annual annuity of several thousand dollars a year for each member of the Crow Nation, and help alleviate poverty on the reservation.

The old man stood with the Lummi. During rallies and marches and demonstrations against the coal dock project, Oliphant met and befriended Martha Talks-the-Truth, a niece of Ojibwe elder Clarence Bighead. Martha had come to Washington State immediately after high school, leaving her parent's modest house on the Boise Forte Reservation to attend college. She'd graduated from Western Washington University with a major in Environmental Studies and a minor in Anthropology. Over coffee and scones at a Bellingham Starbucks, Oliphant and Talks-the-Truth debated environmental issues and strategy and, despite a disparity in age, fell in love.

When the old man suggested that he had unfinished business back in Minnesota, Martha calmly announced that she was going with him. The Ojibwe woman took a leave of absence from her position as the Director of Environmental Policy with the Lummi Tribe to accompany Oliphant back to Minnesota's Iron Range.

"Whatcha thinkin'?" Talks-the-Truth sat next to Oliphant on the dirty bench seat of the battered Chevy pickup, her dark brown eyes staring out the windshield. The woman studied the earthen dike hundreds of feet below them as she sipped steaming coffee from a travel mug. "This truck stop coffee's for shit. Don't you hicks have Starbucks?" Martha asked, not allowing Cyrus to answer her original question before asking another.

The old man turned his haggard, gravity-defeated face toward the woman and answered her second question. "Oh, we do. Just not in Ely."

Martha smiled, exposing a gap between large, pearly, teeth. "Well, maybe we should stick around and open a franchise."

The old man grinned. "To answer your first question, I'm not too sure about taking out the tailings pond."

The woman frowned. "What the hell? I drive two thousand miles, sleep on the ground in a friggin' tent, and take two months' off work without pay all to have *you* decide we're not going to do what *we* agreed to do?"

Oliphant nodded. "That's what I've been thinking . . ."

"Ah. The man's been thinking. Always dangerous when a man thinks too much before he acts."

"Here's the thing. So much time and effort has been put into cleaning up the St. Louis," Oliphant said, referencing the river flowing south from the Roosevelt-Taft Mine toward Lake Superior, "that I'm not sure we should be mucking up decades of hard work to make a point."

"Shit. You've been reading again, haven't you?" Martha quipped, looking intently at Cyrus. "Been studying up on that biography I bought you, *Mr. Environment.*"

Oliphant nodded. "It's not just one man's career, his lifelong struggle to clean up a river. It's Rachel Carson, Sig Olson, Ernest Oberholtzer, Dave Zentner, and a host of others. Their legacies got me to thinking that blowing the dam and sending toxic waste into the St. Louis River—a river that's starting to spawn sturgeon and grow wild rice for the first time in a century—while a pretty solid warning shot, may be killing the patient with the cure."

"Shit."

Cyrus smiled. "I heard that."

"Double shit."

"What say we drive to that hayfield we passed on the way in, unload the ANFO, and make our way back to Bellingham?

Martha watched pickups and SUVs come and go from the Roosevelt-Taft Mine parking lot. "What a waste of time . . ."

"So that's a yes?"

Tells-the-Truth scrunched her face, her flat nose and prominent forehead merging as she considered the question. "Big talker. You get me all riled up, pontificating about the effects of sulfides on *manoomin*, on the possible loss of The People's way of life due to the poisoning of the water, and then you simply decide, without so much as a 'how-do-you-do,' without consulting me, that our plan isn't feasible?"

"That's exactly what I am saying. But you're wrong about one thing . . ."

"How's that?"

"I'm consulting you *now*. You still want to go ahead with it," the old man whispered, his gaze locked on his partner's cocoa eyes, "well then, I'm all in. We'll blow the dike like we planned. But it's just, when all is said and done, I think that'll negate the very point we're trying to make. Freeing that toxic shit and letting it flow into the river is, in hindsight, a terrible way to protest what's happening here. After all, the St. Louis is the mother of the Great Lakes, the largest repository of fresh water in the world. I just think there are better ways to make our point, is all. But if you want to go ahead . . ."

The Ojibwe woman shook her head.

"That's a 'no,' as in, 'no, I don't want to blow the dike and end up in federal prison?'"

"It is."

Cyrus Oliphant put the truck in reverse and backed away from the overlook. Clear of the bluff, Oliphant shifted the Chevy into drive. The old green truck rumbled slowly through clear-cut. After bouncing over rough terrain for more than a mile, Oliphant stopped the pickup in the dormant hayfield. Under cover of descending dusk, the old man and the Indian woman unloaded sack after sack of fertilizer from the truck's bed. When the last fifty-pound bag was stacked on the ground, the old man closed the tailgate. Cyrus Oliphant and Martha Tells-the-Truth climbed into the truck and shut the Chevy's doors. The old man started the pickup, turned on its headlights, shifted into drive, and drove west as Martha Tells-the-Truth sipped disappointing coffee.

THE END

About the Author

Mark Munger is a life-long resident of Northeastern Minnesota. Mark, his wife, René, and one of their four sons live on the banks of the wild and scenic Cloquet River north of Duluth. When not writing fiction, Mark enjoys hunting, fishing, skiing, and working as a District Court Judge.

Other Works by the Author

The Legacy (ISBN 0972005080 and eBook in all formats)

Set against the backdrop of WWII Yugoslavia and present-day Minnesota, this debut novel combines elements of military history, romance, thriller, and mystery. Rated 3 and 1/2 daggers out of 4 by *The Mystery Review Quarterly*.

Ordinary Lives (ISBN 97809792717517 and eBook in all formats)

Creative fiction from one of Northern Minnesota's newest writers, these stories touch upon all elements of the human condition and leave the reader asking for more.

Pigs, a Trial Lawyer's Story (ISBN 097200503x and eBook in all formats)

A story of a young trial attorney, a giant corporation, marital infidelity, moral conflict, and choices made, *Pigs* takes place against the backdrop of Western Minnesota's beautiful Smoky Hills. This tale is being compared by reviewers to Grisham's best.

Suomalaiset: People of the Marsh (ISBN 0972005064 and eBook in all formats)

A dockworker is found hanging from a rope in a city park. How is his death tied to the turbulence of the times? A masterful novel of compelling history and emotion, *Suomalaiset* has been hailed by reviewers as a "must read."

Esther's Race (ISBN 9780972005098 and eBook in all formats)

The story of an African American registered nurse who confronts race, religion, and tragedy in her quest for love, this novel is set against the stark and vivid beauty of Wisconsin's Apostle Islands, the pastoral landscape of Central Iowa, and the steel and glass of Minneapolis. A great read soon to be a favorite of book clubs across America.

Mr. Environment: The Willard Munger Story (ISBN 9780979217524: Trade paperback only)

A detailed and moving biography of Minnesota's leading environmental champion and longest-serving member of the Minnesota House of Representatives, *Mr. Environment* is destined to become a book every Minnesotan has on his or her bookshelf.

Black Water: Stories from the Cloquet River
(ISBN 9780979217548 and eBook in all formats)

Essays about ordinary and extraordinary events in the life of an American family living in the wilds of northeastern Minnesota, these tales first appeared separately in two volumes, *River Stories* and *Doc the Bunny*. Re-edited and compiled into one volume, these are stories to read on the deer stand, at the campsite, or late at night for peace of mind.

Laman's River
(ISBN 9780979217531 and eBook in all formats)

A beautiful newspaper reporter is found bound, gagged, and dead. A Duluth judge conceals secrets that may end her career. A reclusive community of religious zealots seeks to protect its view of the hereafter by unleashing an avenging angel upon the world. Mormons. Murder. Minnesota. Montana. Reprising two of your favorite characters from *The Legacy*, Deb Slater and Herb Whitefeather. Buy it now in print or on all major eBook platforms!

Sukulaiset: The Kindred
(ISBN 9780979217562 and eBook in all formats)

The long-awaited sequel to *Suomalaiset*, this sprawling historical novel portrays the journey of Elin Gustafson from the shores of Lake Superior to the shores of Lake Onega in the Soviet Republic of Karelia during the Great Depression. A tale of love, war, the Holocaust, and human dignity.

Other Books from Cloquet River Press

Back of Beyond: A Memoir from the North Woods (ISBN 9780979217500: Trade paperback only)

The debut effort from Minnesota author Susanne Kobe Schuler, this memoir of building and working at a family-style Minnesota resort during the 1940s is a sure-fire winner. Come, meet the Kobe family, their friends, their relatives, the guests of the resort, and join them for a trip back into a kinder, gentler time set in the deep woods of Northeastern Minnesota.

Visit us at:
www.cloquetriverpress.com
Shop at our online store!

10% of all gross sales of CRP books are donated by CRP to SmileTrain in hopes of helping children born with cleft lips and palates across the world. Learn more about SmileTrain at http://www.smiletrain.org/.

Made in the USA
Charleston, SC
15 September 2016